The Unexpe

Ada Bright has lived all her life in Southern California. She grew up much more fond of reading than sports or socializing, and still tends to ignore all her responsibilities and basic life needs when she's in the middle of a book. She is luckily married to a handsome and funny man who doesn't mind that the laundry never gets put away and she has three amazing children. Ada spent over a decade as a photographer before dedicating herself to writing, though she still believes that life should be documented well and often.

A proud bookworm since childhood, **Cass Grafton** writes the sort of stories she loves to read – heartwarming, character-driven and strong on location. Having moved around extensively and lived in three countries, she finds places inspiring and the setting of her novels often becomes as much a part of the story as her characters. She has an overactive imagination, is prone to crying with happiness as much as she is at sadness, but when it comes to her writing she leans heavily towards the upbeat and insists on a happy ever after.

We love to hear from readers!

You can find us on Facebook or Twitter (@missyadabright & @CassGrafton), or contact us through our blog: Tabby Cow www.tabbycow.com

Also by Ada Bright and Cass Grafton

The Austen Adventures

The Particular Charm of Miss Jane Austen

The Unexpected Past of MISS JANE AUSTEN

ADA BRIGHT & CASS GRAFTON

CANELO US

San Diego, California

CANELO US Canelo US
An imprint of Printers Row Publishing Group
9717 Pacific Heights Blvd, San Diego, CA 92121
www.canelobooksus.com

Printers Row Publishing Group is a division of Readerlink Distribution
Services, LLC. Canelo US is a registered trademark of Readerlink
Distribution Services, LLC.

First published in the United Kingdom in 2019 by Canelo. This edition
originally published in the United Kingdom in 2022 by Canelo.

Published in partnership with Canelo.

Correspondence regarding the content of this book should be sent to Canelo
US, Editorial Department, at the above address. Author inquiries should be
sent to Canelo, Unit 9, 5th Floor, Cargo Works, 1–2 Hatfields, London SE1
9PG, United Kingdom, www.canelo.co.

Publisher: Peter Norton • Associate Publisher: Ana Parker
Art Director: Charles McStravick
Senior Developmental Editor: April Graham
Editor: Julie Chapa
Production Team: Beno Chan, Julie Greene

Library of Congress Control Number: 2023943256

ISBN: 978-1-6672-0653-0

Printed in India

27 26 25 24 23   1 2 3 4 5

We dedicate this book to J.K. Rowling, without whose Harry Potter stories we would never have met

Author Notes

The Baigen family occupied the property in Chawton known as Baigens when Jane Austen lived in the village. At the time, the garden bordered that of the cottage (now Jane Austen's House Museum). For the purposes of this story, a different family inhabits Baigens.

During the writing of this book, we studied numerous texts from respected authorities on Jane Austen's life in Chawton. We also consulted experts at both Jane Austen's House Museum and Chawton House, including Jeremy Knight – a descendent of Jane Austen's brother, Edward – who lived at the property for many years.

As you can imagine, there were occasional differing opinions about the appearance of Chawton village in the early nineteenth century, as well as some of the key properties referred to in this story.

As a result, we have had to make a few authorial choices over which way to go in this respect, but we hope we have managed to tread a plausible path through Chawton in 1813 as we blended fact with fiction.

Chapter 1

Facts are such horrid things. So wrote the teenage Jane Austen when penning her epistolary novel, *Lady Susan*, and it remains as much a truth today as it was then. Jane Austen is still dead, of course. There is no evading this inescapable truth either, here in the twenty-first century. Yet dedicated fan of the author, Rose Wallace, had recently discovered there are some grey areas to what should be hard fact.

For example, the lady stood behind her fastening her authentic early nineteenth-century dress, the final layer in what seemed an inordinate amount of clothing. Perhaps it shouldn't feel so strange. After all, hadn't Rose just been attending the annual *Jane Austen Festival* in Bath along with her best friend, Morgan Taylor, who'd flown in from the USA to finally meet up with her for the first time? And hadn't they, as a result, been dressing up in costume already?

'It is comfortable, yes?'

Rose nodded. 'Yes – yes, thank you.'

The lady walked away to inspect the remaining items spread out on the bed, and Rose drew in a shallow breath. Then, there was the travelling-through-time thing. Not possible. Fact. Only Rose knew this to be more than just a bit grey round the edges. After all, hadn't she just days ago been trapped in an alternate universe all because *someone*

I

had decided to slip through time by a couple of hundred years and then got stuck?

'Rose?' Turning around, Rose took gloves and a reticule from the lady. 'Perchance we should endeavour to seek out the gentleman?'

Aiden! Rose clutched her midriff as her insides lurched. What must he be thinking?

'I'll go and see him.' She opened her bedroom door, then said over her shoulder, 'Jane, I'm worried he won't believe any of this.'

Jane Austen – for yes, it was indeed she – merely raised a brow. 'I remain unperturbed. The gentleman will credit the sense of it when we are arrived at our destination. Any momentary uncertainty will be swept away by fact.'

'Fact?' Rose muttered as she crossed the sitting room of her flat and approached the door to the small room she used as a study. 'He may think the dictionary needs to revise its definition.'

She paused as she raised a hand to tap on the door. What if he wasn't ready, hadn't worked out how to properly don the formal period attire pressed upon him by Jane? What if he'd decided not to go along with this ridiculous scheme? He'd never speak to her again! Rose drew in a short breath. She'd spent three years crushing on Aiden from a distance – Dr Aiden Trevellyan, esteemed archaeologist. Was it really less than an hour since he'd kissed her and turned her world both upside down and into full focus? Until Jane reappeared...

'You will find the application of a hand to the wood efficacious in achieving the requisite sound.'

Rose threw Jane an all-speaking look, but the lady merely smiled and walked over to inspect the array of photo frames on a side table.

'I recall this likeness.' Jane lifted one of the frames and, curious, Rose glanced over. 'It was in your chamber, was it not, at the residence of your mother?'

'That's my dad. It's the only photo I have of him.'

Rose turned away, tried to calm her rapidly beating heart and knocked on the door.

'Come in.'

She stepped into the small room. Aiden had his back to her, his gaze upon the open book on her desk as he studied the instructions on how to fasten a Regency gentleman's cravat.

'Aiden?' Rose's voice sounded hoarse to her ears. 'Are you… are you ready?'

He turned around, and she tried not to stare. How could someone so absolutely gorgeous look even more so? Aiden in full Regency attire had been the stuff of dreams before now; how was she supposed to deal with the reality?

He frowned and looked down at his person. 'Is something the matter? Did I put it on wrong?'

Rose smiled as he met her gaze again. 'Not at all. Are you—' She gestured at the piece of cloth hanging loosely around his neck. 'Can I help at all?'

Aiden walked over, and she willed the habitual colour not to flood her cheeks. It didn't work.

'Can you help me at all? An excellent question. Let's start with why am I stood in your apartment, dressed as I am under the instruction of a woman who professes to be a long-dead author?'

Rose bit her lip. That wasn't exactly what she'd meant.

Running a hand through his hair, Aiden sighed. Then, he took one of her hands in his.

'Rose, less than an hour ago, you and I were… well, let's just say we were in the process of clearing up three years of misunderstanding, and now…' His voice tailed away as he took in her appearance at last. 'You…' He swallowed visibly. 'You look beautiful in costume.'

The heat in Rose's cheeks intensified, and she shook her head. 'I'm not sure Jane would appreciate us calling these costumes.' Rose waved a hand at his outfit. 'Does yours fit okay? Are you… Is it comfortable enough? Here.' She stepped forward, trying not to notice how close they were, and fashioned a knot in the neck cloth as best she could. 'Probably not up to Beau Brummel's standards, but it will have to do for now. I don't know how long we'll…' Her voice faded, but Aiden raised a hand to touch one of her auburn curls where it lay beside her cheek.

'Rose, what is going on?'

'I wish I knew. But you must believe me – and Jane. She is who she says she is. She has a charmed necklace, and it allows her to slip through time.'

'How do you know it's true?'

'Because…' Rose hesitated, then raised her chin and met his gaze firmly. 'Because I do. A few days ago, the necklace was lost and she was trapped here; stuck in the twenty-first century. I was with her when it happened and saw all the consequences. She'd come from 1803, when she lived in Sydney Place, before she became a published author. Everything to do with her disappeared. I saw the evidence with my own eyes; I *lived* it!' Rose shuddered. 'It was a nightmare.' She spoke softly now. 'This is no joke, no illusion. I don't know why she's come for us, but please believe me.'

Rose's eyes pleaded with him, and Aiden held her gaze for a moment. 'Show me at least *this* is real.'

4

'What do you mean?'

His gaze dropped to her mouth, which curved slightly at the edges as Aiden leaned in and placed a firm kiss upon her lips, and Rose threw her arms around his neck and held on to him as they melted into a kiss even more meaningful than their first.

'Ahem.'

With a start, they broke apart. Jane Austen stood in the doorway, frowning. 'Come, we must make haste and return before Cassandra has reason to doubt my purpose. She was not in favour of my mission.'

Aiden and Rose exchanged a look. *What* mission? Then he smiled at her, took her hand again and whispered in her ear. 'I'm in. I've only just found you, Rose. I've no intention of letting go of you so soon.'

Jane tsked. 'We are going to the year thirteen, Dr Trevellyan – 1813 to be precise. Miss Wallace is an unmarried young lady. You must behave according to the social strictures of the time.' Her gaze moved between them. 'I trust you both know what those are?'

Aiden was a historian before he was an archaeologist, and Rose knew he understood exactly what she meant. He nodded, but did not release Rose's hand. 'We understand.'

They followed the lady back into the sitting room, where she flipped open the lid of the small trunk she had brought with her, leaned in and withdrew a cloak.

'Here, Rose, take this. It will be late when we arrive in Chawton; you must not take cold.'

Rose frowned but took the offering nonetheless. 'It's only half-nine. Aren't we going immediately?' She looked down at her attire and then at Aiden in his, only he was frowning too.

'Er… Miss Austen?'

Jane looked over at Aiden. 'Sir?'

'Why did you bring a box full of these particular clothes with you?'

It was Rose who answered. 'Although inanimate objects made in the past can travel forward, for they might still exist today, only those today which had been created by 1813 can travel backwards to that year. If you were in modern clothing, or even Regency costumes made in the twenty-first century, you would arrive…' Her voice faltered.

'You would arrive at my home in naught but the covering in which you were born, sir,' the lady added succinctly.

Aiden said nothing to this, and Rose sighed. After all, what was there to say?

Jane busied herself fastening the clasp on the trunk and then stood to face them both. 'I must presume upon you, Rose. We must make use of your conveyance to return to Hampshire.'

'Why there? Can't we just use the… you know.' Aiden waved a hand. 'To get to – when was it – 1813?'

The lady eyed him keenly for a moment, then cocked her head to one side. 'Young man, you are not unintelligent, for if you were, my friend would not find you interesting. Yet I have found intelligence must always be tempered with common sense, or else the most learned of men oft become fools.'

Aiden smiled faintly. 'Touché.'

'If we were to use the charm here, there too would we be: inside this very house in Bath in 1813, a property inhabited by strangers, not my family. They may be unforgiving of our sudden appearance. Further, it is a carriage

6

ride of more than a day to reach Hampshire. No, we must return to Chawton, whence we shall proceed.'

Rose tried to stay focused. 'But Jane, I can't drive us. I've been drinking.'

'That is regrettable. Sir.' Jane turned to Aiden. 'May we avail ourselves of your assistance?'

Aiden looked from Jane to Rose, then down at his attire. 'You want me to walk to the *Francis* to fetch my car dressed like this?'

It was the first time Rose had seen him rattled by what was happening, and she threw Jane an anxious look.

'There is no cause for alarm, sir.' Jane beckoned to Rose. 'You will be escorting us both.'

'But—'

Rose turned Aiden to face her. 'The *Festival* is in full swing, Aiden. No one will bat an eyelid.'

Jane followed Rose over to the door, then looked back at Aiden. 'Time is of the essence.' She waved a hand at the small trunk. 'If you would be so kind, sir?'

–

The car journey to Chawton took a little under two hours and, for the most part, it passed in silence as each of them seemed wrapped in their own thoughts.

As they left Winchester behind and picked up the A31, however, Rose touched the leather seat on which she sat. She'd never been in Aiden's car before, and she looked over at him in the driver's seat from under her lashes. There was nothing on his face to betray what he was thinking. He looked as he always did: inscrutable, quietly intense and extremely handsome. If it had not been for the heavy silence surrounding them and their unusual clothing, she could imagine it was just a casual drive into the country.

Surreptitiously, Rose's gaze roamed over Aiden's lean frame in the close-fitting coat, then down his long legs to the leather boots encasing them. How was it she was even more attracted to the man than ever? All these years of reining in her runaway thoughts about him hadn't prepared her for this: an entirely different level of fantasy.

'Did you say something?'

Rose started as Aiden turned his head suddenly, then shook her head. 'No, I – er – I just wanted to say thank you for driving us.'

Aiden reached over and covered her hand with his for a moment before he had to change gear again. Goodness knew what he was thinking of her. Rose, for possibly the first time ever, didn't think she wanted to know. Insane would surely be top of the list, simply for believing Jane was whom she said she was.

Rose drew in a shallow breath. They had barely twenty minutes before they reached their destination. What would happen then? Her insides were swirling with anxiety.

Aiden flexed his shoulders, and Rose saw him cast a glance at the rear-view mirror.

'You were saying it's been quite some time since you last saw Rose.'

Jane nodded. 'For myself. For Rose, not so much.'

Rose almost laughed. Then, she sobered. Jane had experienced loss, dreadful uncertainty and upheaval in her life since they had last met in Bath, with her father dying and she, her mother and sister constantly moving from home to home until they found sanctuary at Chawton.

'I am indebted to you, sir, for bearing us to my home so swiftly and with so little inconvenience.'

Rose twisted around to face the lady as best she could. 'Are you happy in Chawton, Jane? We're always told you are, but—'

'There is nothing like hearing it from the highest authority?' Jane smirked. 'Indeed. I am exceedingly attached to our home.' She glanced out of the window. 'We are almost there. I must caution you both, there will be company awaiting our return, notably my brother, who—'

'As I recall, Miss Austen, you had... have several brothers?' Aiden addressed Jane through the rear-view mirror, but Rose could tell Jane continued to look at the back of his head as she merely raised a brow.

Aiden cleared his throat. 'My apologies for the interruption.'

'Curiosity makes one impetuous, does it not?' Jane smiled faintly. 'I speak of my brother, Charles, sir – Captain Charles Austen – the youngest.'

There was a note of pride in Jane's voice, and Rose smiled at her over her shoulder. 'Your own particular brother.'

Jane returned the smile. 'I have not forgotten your seeming a long-standing acquaintance, for all your knowledge of the minutiae of my life.' She returned her attention to the rear of Aiden's head. 'Charles and his family have been passing the summer months in Hampshire.' Jane paused. 'He gave me the charmed necklace, you understand? His involvement in what is afoot is somewhat complex.'

Rose eyed Jane warily, her anxiety increasing at the reminder of their situation. 'Why can't you tell us what this is about?'

Jane waved a hand dismissively. 'Travel is not conducive to the intricacies of conversation, nor is the moment opportune.' She turned back to Aiden. 'Charles will escort you to the great house.'

'Chawton House?' Aiden glanced at Rose. 'I think I'm quite capable of finding it.'

'Even if it were not the dead of night, you cannot arrive as an unannounced stranger on the threshold, sir.'

'But what about Rose?'

Rose felt she had an idea where this was going. 'I'll be staying with Jane at the cottage, I think?'

Jane nodded. 'Most indubitably.' She addressed Aiden's back again. 'We are but four women – now five.' She glanced at Rose and smiled. 'It would be impossible for us to accommodate a single young man, unattached to the family. You will find the arrangements at the great house much to your liking, I do not doubt.'

'Right. Fine.' Aiden shifted in his seat, and Rose cast him an anxious look before turning to stare out of the window. No more words were spoken for the short remainder of the journey, and the car drew to a halt in the small car park in the centre of Chawton just before midnight, for once empty.

Aiden switched off the ignition and released his belt, turning to face Rose. 'Are you okay?'

Rose stared at him, then smiled tremulously. Truth be told, she was more than a little scared now they had arrived. Aside from Jane's mysterious purpose, was Rose willingly going to travel back in time by more than 200 years? And why had Jane brought Aiden along with them? She'd never met him during her recent stay in Bath.

She glanced at Jane in the back seat. 'Will you tell us now what this is all about?'

Jane shook her head. 'All will be revealed in due course. I must beg patience from you both; first we must go back.' With that Jane fiddled with her seat belt until it released, then sat expectantly. Rose looked at Aiden, who returned her stare blankly.

'Aiden, if you don't want to be a part of this, then it's best you leave us here.'

He took her hands in his, ignoring the 'tsk' from the back seat. 'I'll tag along for now.'

Rose smiled. 'Well then, I'm afraid she's waiting for you to open her door.'

Aiden glanced back. 'Oh, of course.' He slid out of the car smoothly, despite his borrowed clothes, opened Jane's door and leaned down to peer through the car just as Rose's hand reached for her own handle. 'You'd best wait there as well.'

Rose sat back in surprise. Had Aiden just winked at her? He couldn't possibly believe this, could he? Perhaps he thought it was a bit of a game, a ruse. She'd better enjoy these last moments with him before he ran screaming from her.

Taking Aiden's hand when he opened her door, Rose was reluctant to let go of it, but Jane's pointed stare reminded them both of her earlier warning. She clearly felt they needed to get into practice.

'If you have kept anything upon you of modern contrivance, it must remain here, for it cannot pass through.' Jane waved a hand in their general direction. 'Join me across the road when you are ready.'

'But where can we put it to keep it safe?' There was no answer from the departing figure, and Rose looked around at the empty car park, surrounded by trees on three sides. How could they conceal anything here and not expect it to be found?

Aiden walked round and opened the boot, removing the small trunk of assorted clothing and lifting the base to reveal the spare wheel area.

'This will have to do.' He put his wallet and phone in the boot, and Rose added her keys and purse too; then he eyed his car keys warily. 'I'll have to take a gamble with these and put them under the wheel arch.'

Rose chewed on her lip, found Aiden watching her and shrugged. 'Last time, time didn't move on. Everything came back to normal, just resumed at the same day and time as we'd left behind. Unless someone is going to jump out of the bushes as soon as we're gone, there probably isn't much risk.'

'Last time,' Aiden repeated quietly as he replaced the trunk and closed the boot, locked the car and crouched down to conceal the keys. 'You mean the last time you travelled through time.'

Colour flew into Rose's cheeks. 'No. Not exactly.' She looked across the street. Jane was watching them, and Rose turned back to face Aiden as he straightened. 'Look, Aiden, I started off convinced she was a madwoman too...'

'Who'd somehow convinced you she was Jane Austen?' He ran a hand through his hair. 'Why is it I feel like I'm being drawn under her spell, too? Why am I almost believing she is who she says, even considering it might be possible to travel back in time with her? Is the fascination with history flowing in my veins tempting me to believe I could do the impossible?'

Rose had no chance to respond to this as her name was hissed from across the street, and before long they stood surveying the Jane Austen House Museum, all shuttered up for the night. There was no one in the street, despite the mild evening, but light still spilled out from the nearby Greyfriar pub, which had only recently closed its doors.

No car lights approached from either direction, and the lady urged them over to stand beside the open gate into the garden of Chawton cottage.

'How did you open that?' Rose stared at Jane. Did she have powers of her own Rose had yet to hear about?

Jane, however, looked unimpressed by her own prowess. 'It has no catch – can you not see? Come; let us make haste.' She extracted a leather pouch and opened it, holding aloft a gold chain bearing a topaz cross, and Aiden frowned, instinctively reaching a hand towards it.

'Wait! Isn't that—?'

'Beware, Dr Trevellyan.' The lady drew back a little. 'The charm has powers of its own.'

'But Jane…' Rose pointed at the relatively short chain, thinking instinctively of Hermione Granger and her time-turner. 'How will there be room for all three of us at once?'

'There is not. An attempt at combining the chains from the other two necklaces with this one was made, but it did not oblige.'

Aiden's brow raised. 'There are *three* of them? I thought—' He stopped as Rose shook her head at him before turning back to Jane.

'But how will it work for all of us?'

'You must not worry so, Rose. One would have to be very foolish not to have made a prior attempt. We merely need to be in contact with each other when I make use of the charm.'

Like side-along apparition, mused Rose. Morgan would be highly entertained by this. Morgan!

'Jane, I need to send a quick text.' She fished in her reticule for her phone and tapped into it, only to find Jane taking it from her as she hit send.

'You must leave it behind, Rose.'

'Yes, yes, of course. I wasn't thinking.' Relieved to have at least sent her friend a message so she wouldn't worry for the present, Rose watched Aiden walk back over to the car to place the phone in the boot. She sighed softly as it was closed and he replaced the keys before turning back to join them as they walked through the gate and followed Jane to a shadowed corner of the garden.

'We are safe here. There is nothing for us to disturb when we arrive.' Jane tucked the pouch away, the necklace held in one hand.

Rose looked around, startled. She'd hardly thought about what the garden might contain back then.

'I must ask you both to step closer.'

Aiden and Rose instinctively stepped towards each other, and Jane rolled her eyes. 'Not to each other, to *me*.'

'Oh!' Rose stood beside Jane as Aiden took up a position on her other side, and the lady urged them a little nearer still.

'You may take hands for this, and you must both rest your other hand on my nearest arm to you. Do not break contact. Once we are connected, I will place the charm about my neck.'

Rose's heart was pounding fiercely as Aiden took her hand firmly in his grip and squeezed it. Clear grey eyes met rich brown ones, and they stared at each other for a moment before each placing a hand on one of Jane's arms. Rose felt a brush of air as Jane raised her hand to place the chain about her neck, and then everything went black.

Chapter 2

'Rose?'

Jane's voice sounded amused.

'Hmm?'

'You may open your eyes.'

She *may*, but could she? Unaware she had even closed them, Rose tried, but for some reason her lids felt heavy, as though they had no interest in lifting. She was still clutching someone – was it Jane's arm, or Aiden's hand? She could barely tell; her senses felt all out of sorts.

'It's fine, honestly, we're okay.' Aiden's whispered words close to her ear were all she needed. Rose's eyes flew open to find him barely inches from her. She looked down, suddenly conscious she was gripping Aiden's hand perhaps a little too strongly, and she released him as she took a step back to look around.

It was darker – the street lamps had all gone, and underfoot was a gravel path instead of the neatly kept lawns she was used to walking on at the museum.

'Wait here. I must establish who has yet to retire. Mama must not know what we are about.' Jane set off towards a door at the back of the house, and Rose glanced at Aiden. He was not looking at the house but beyond her, and she turned around. Her eyes had begun to adjust to the darkness now, aided by a full moon.

'I thought there was a boundary there!' The gardens, which bore little resemblance as far as she could see to the ones surrounding Chawton Cottage in the present day, extended off into the darkness.

'There was, but the grounds were much more extensive in the Austens' day.'

His voice sounded strained, and Rose touched his arm. 'Are you okay?'

Aiden looked down at her, but it was too dark to read the expression in his eyes.

'I wanted to believe you; I didn't want, after all this time, to find out you were delusional, but…'

'I don't blame you. It's impossible, after all.'

Aiden stepped closer. 'There are many things I once thought were impossible.' He touched her cheek, tucked a loose curl behind her ear. The only sounds were an owl hooting somewhere in the treetops and the trickling of water somewhere to their left. Aiden's gaze drifted away from her, straining as he stared left and right as though, if he tried hard enough, he would be able to see through the darkness. His expression was unreadable in the shadowed garden, but she bit her lip. Was this going to make or break them?

'What are you thinking?' Rose whispered.

Aiden said nothing for a moment, but his eyes found hers again and he smiled faintly. 'Best you don't know right now.'

'Rose! Dr Trevellyan! Come, you must make haste.'

They both turned around. Jane was at the corner of the house, beckoning them, and they hurried to meet her.

–

'Good morning, Miss Wallace. I trust you slept well?'

Rose started, pulled from her reverie as she stared out of the window of the dining room at the row of labourers' cottages opposite. How different it looked from the present day, where the Greyfriar pub and Cassandra's Cup tearoom normally stood.

'Good morning, Miss Austen.' Rose tried not to stare at Cassandra Austen as she walked across the room to join her at the window. She knew the lady was forty, and she didn't look it, having a tall, erect posture and handsome features. The contradicting factor was the traditional muslin cap of the older lady she presently wore. Rose had heard so much about her from Jane that she'd long become a living, breathing person to her, but all the same…

Cassandra must have understood some of her feelings, for she smiled reassuringly. 'My sister will be with us directly. It is her duty to prepare the first meal of the day.' She indicated the table. 'Do please be seated. Would you care for a dish of tea or does your preference lean, like my sister's, towards chocolate?'

'Oh! Er, chocolate please.' Rose took a seat, then looked at her wrist – to no avail. How was it she missed things like a watch and her phone so much already? She glanced around the room, then said tentatively, 'What is the time?'

Cassandra was straightening from placing a dish of water on the floor next to an empty cushion.

'Past the hour of nine. Mama will be here directly, and then we may break our fast. Please excuse me; I must fetch more bread.'

As Cassandra left the room, Rose sighed softly. She had barely slept at all, and not just because of the strange taste in her mouth from the powder she had been offered to clean her teeth. Her mind had been full of questions, her heart pounding in her chest over what she'd just done. She'd travelled back in time by 200 years and more! It wasn't possible. Of course it wasn't. Even though she knew Jane had slipped through time to the future, the reality of doing it herself wasn't something Rose had ever contemplated.

Drawing in a shallow breath, Rose looked around the room, noting anything that seemed familiar to how it was represented in the future, but she was distracted by how it felt rather than looked – above all, lived in, as well it should, with the sound of humming coming from somewhere and a large copper kettle singing in unison on the grate.

And what of Jane? She was different too – ten years older than when Rose had last seen her, just days ago! Used to her being in modern dress, albeit rather conservative, it had seemed odd the night before to see her in her natural habitat, dressed according to the day, the same muslin cap as her sister's adorning her chestnut curls.

Last night, it had been a whirlwind, with swift introductions to Cassandra (Mrs Austen having retired already) and Jane's brother, Charles, who had barely been introduced before he swept Aiden from the room.

Agitated, Rose got to her feet again and walked back to the window, staring unseeingly out into the street. How was Aiden feeling this morning? Had he slept at all? What had his time been like at Chawton House? Why had this had to happen *now*?

Rose blew out a frustrated breath. She was twenty-seven years old, and there were so many good things in her life – her cosy flat at No 4 Sydney Place and her challenging but enjoyable job working with James Malcolm at Luxury Lettings of Bath. She'd been having the best week of her life, finally getting to meet Morgan in person after all these years, attending the *Jane Austen Festival* with her, and then Aiden… Rose's insides lurched as she recalled their kisses last night. These things were solid and good and Rose hadn't really had time to process how beautifully folded together everything was in the exact moment when Jane had resurfaced.

Jane Austen… another wonderful part of Rose's life, until she'd met her. Jane had an uncanny ability to turn Rose's orderly life upside down!

'Good morning, Rose.'

Rose spun around. 'Er – good morning, Miss Jane?' There was a question in her voice, and Jane smiled as she crossed the room to check on the large copper kettle.

'You have the right of it, Miss Wallace. Mama will expect formality, and she has yet to comprehend the level of our acquaintance. When she is not present, however, we may speak as we wish.'

Feeling a little easier now Jane was in the room, Rose returned to the table, soon joined by Cassandra and Mrs Austen, who, it seemed, had been forewarned an acquaintance of her daughter's would be arriving late on the previous evening, but not where she had come from.

Rose was a little confused; hadn't Mr and Mrs Austen been told where Jane had gone when she got trapped in the future? She would have to ask Jane later.

'It is not to your liking?'

Cassandra gestured towards the cup of chocolate, and Rose shook her head. 'I am sorry; I am used to it being a little sweeter.'

'Of course.' Cassandra smiled, but Jane tutted and, grabbing the sugar tongs, dropped a piece of something brown and misshapen into the cup.

'Manners, Jane!' Mrs Austen frowned at her daughter and launched into a diatribe Rose could tell had been heard many a time before, if the blank expression on Jane's face was anything to go by as she turned to pick up the toasting fork.

Rose's insides rumbled and she clutched her stomach. No one seemed to have heard, and she warily eyed the piece of dense-looking cake on her plate – pound cake, she had been told – made by Martha Lloyd, the fourth lady resident at the cottage.

'Where is Martha?' She spoke the words without thinking, and Mrs Austen turned to Rose with a frown.

'I beg your pardon?'

Jane threw Rose a warning look as she pushed a piece of toast off the fork onto her plate, and she felt warmth filling her cheeks.

'I – er – forgive me, Mrs Austen. I meant Miss Martha Lloyd. I – I was given to understand by Miss Jane that she lived here with you?'

Mrs Austen studied Rose with an assessing eye for a moment, then raised her chin. 'Martha has gone to stay with her sister for a short while, which makes your visit most fortuitous.'

For the first time, she smiled, and Rose lowered her gaze swiftly to avoid staring. Mrs Austen, it appeared, was lacking a few of her teeth. Eyes on her plate, Rose broke off a piece of the pound cake and sniffed it. Was it plum?

'You do not enquire as to why it is fortuitous, Miss Wallace? Your lack of curiosity is remarkable.'

'Mama!' Cassandra threw Rose a reassuring look. 'Miss Wallace arrived very late last night after a lengthy journey. She is no doubt suffering from an excess of tiredness this morning.'

'Hmph. I do not see it as fitting for young women to be travelling late at night, unescorted.'

'I wasn't – I was not unescorted.' Rose glanced at Jane. What was she to say? Mrs Austen possibly had no idea Jane had been with her; was she allowed to mention Aiden at all?

'Miss Wallace travelled with a friend; he is with Edward at the great house, Mama. You will make his acquaintance later this morning.'

Filled with relief to know she would see Aiden soon, Rose popped some of the cake into her mouth. The consistency was much drier than she was used to, and she cleared her throat after swallowing, then reached for her cup. The brownish lump seemed to have dissolved, and she took a cautious sip, then shuddered.

'I trust you had a servant with you? Travelling unchaperoned with a young man is hardly an improvement on journeying alone.'

'We were chaperoned, Mrs Austen.' Rose put the cup down and patted her lips with her napkin. 'Why is my being here fortuitous, ma'am?'

'Martha oversees all meals but breakfast. Cook has some talents, but an extra pair of hands in the kitchen will be beneficial in her absence. You do bake, Miss Wallace?'

–

The garden in daylight held little familiarity to Rose, other than the service buildings across the courtyard. She glanced at the large open barn (now the museum entrance and gift shop), trying to take it all in, her gaze drifting over the now-working well, past the 'necessary' to what in the present day was a pleasant cottage garden with extensive lawns.

There was little grass and every space seemed allocated to a particular purpose: a fair-sized kitchen garden, a shrubbery walk, an orchard of fruit trees and bushes, laden with fruit ripe for the picking and borders of sweet-smelling flowers, and an extensive herb garden. Wandering about near the orchard were several chickens and, if Rose wasn't mistaken, a couple of pigs!

The bray of a donkey drew her gaze to the farther reaches of the garden, which extended at least three times further along the Winchester road. Turning on her heel, Rose tried to take it all in, then raised her brows in surprise as she took in the cottage itself. It had been so dark the night before, and she had been so disorientated by what had happened, she'd barely paid it any attention, but now she could see the familiar red brick was concealed beneath some sort of whitewash. She looked over towards the road as the loud clatter of hooves and rolling wheels reached her, but there was nothing to see. A tall hedge bordered the garden, with glimpses of a high wooden fence behind, and Rose turned away and ambled along, enjoying the weak sunshine filtering through the trees and mulling over how bizarre it would look if she'd managed to bring her sunglasses with her. She glanced down as she walked.

The petticoat brushing her legs wasn't a new sensation – after all, she and Morgan had been dressed up for the promenade – but wearing stays and the contrivance of fabric, which stood in for underwear, was an entirely new sensation. Her feet felt pinched too, in the shoes lent to her by Cassandra, whose foot size was closer to Rose's than Jane's, but the cut of the leather was entirely more slender than she was used to.

She looked around. Jane and Cassandra had urged her to take some air whilst they dealt with a few household chores and, despite her implication Rose would be required in the bake-house later that morning, Mrs Austen had left them to their own devices and gone to lie on a chaise in the drawing room.

Anticipating Aiden's arrival, Rose hugged her arms to herself as she walked on, making her way past a large water trough and on through the orchard. Far off to the right was a large patch of ground filled with wildflowers, a stile in the wall separating the cottage's garden from a meadow. There was also another herb garden which sent out delicious smells as Rose passed, her hand trailing against the strands of basil and thyme, and she reached out and plucked an apple from an obliging branch, taking a grateful bite.

She looked around guiltily; was this acceptable behaviour? Despite her knowledge of the era, there were still many things she'd never even considered about the etiquette of this time. The apple tasted good, though, and she was starving!

Walking on, she could soon turn around and only see the cottage's roof and chimneys above the trees. She could hear the clip clop of hooves again, and then the wheels of a cart on the dirt road running alongside this part of the garden, and as she neared the back wall, she heard a child's voice singing.

Smiling, Rose leaned on the wall. The house beyond had a large garden, not dissimilar in its make-up, being largely vegetables, fruit canes, a few flower borders and a small cluster of trees. There were several small outbuildings, along with a large shed, which looked like it had been patched together several times over.

'A bit like the Weasleys' Burrow,' Rose mused, her smile widening. It was as she was leaning on the wall, lost in thought, that the shed door opened and a man emerged. He was tall with an unruly head of hair, probably in his fifties, and he shaded his eyes as he scanned the garden.

'Anne. Come along; it is time for your lesson.'

Looking over to where his gaze had fallen, Rose saw a young girl of about eight or nine rise from where she had been sitting beneath a tree near the wall.

'Coming, Papa!' She dusted down her apron, tucked her book under her arm and turned to join the path, taking her father's hand as they met at the corner of the house and skipping along beside him.

'Rose.'

Rose spun around. Aiden was walking towards her, wearing a different coat and waistcoat and a cautious expression on his face; Rose found him completely adorable.

Dropping a quick curtsey, a smile tugged at her lips. 'Dr Trevellyan.'

Aiden's mouth twitched, and he bowed slightly. 'Miss Wallace.'

Rose's smile widened, and she stepped forward but stopped abruptly a few feet from him and whispered, 'How are you? How's the house? Did you sleep?' She drew in a short breath. 'My bed felt really weird; the mattress was sort of lumpy.'

Aiden took a quick look behind him and responded in the same quiet tone: 'Didn't sleep a wink – too busy trying to commit every detail to memory. Can I take notes? You know, write something down to take back with me?'

'If you use ink and paper from this time, it will travel forward. I've seen the proof of it.'

'This is incredible!' He took a step forward and grabbed both her hands. 'Rose, the church – it's the original structure, before the fire.'

Recalling her impromptu lunch with Aiden – was it only two days ago? – in Chawton churchyard brought Rose a pang of homesickness.

'Of course!' Rose smiled at his enthusiasm. 'Your dig to try and locate the original footprint of the church.'

Aiden nodded. 'The building's not in great shape, to be honest.' Then, he smiled widely. 'I saw the outline when we arrived last night and went out as soon as I could this morning and just stared at it. It's obvious why we couldn't find that footprint at the dig – it looks almost the same as the rebuilt church. I want to make detailed sketches.' He paused, a frown on his brow for a moment. 'I don't have a measuring tape but I suppose my feet haven't changed dimension; it will have to do.'

Rose couldn't help but smile. His enthusiasm was infectious. 'I hadn't even considered the church – how exciting. The ladies are bound to have a tape measure.'

'And you?' Aiden sobered, squeezing her hands. 'Any word yet on why Jane wanted you to come here? Not that I'm complaining.'

'No, I've just had the most bitter hot chocolate of my life, and Jane is busy tidying away the breakfast things. Somehow, no matter how much I *knew* they didn't have many servants here, I hadn't imagined the chores the women might have to do as well. Which, by the way, I'm apparently expected to do too.'

'Well, I'm here for you if there's anything I can help with. I don't know how much longer we're going to be here, but I'd love a good hour or two down at the church before we leave.'

Rose smiled. 'Understood, Doctor. Oh, would you be a doctor here? Or will that just encourage people to ask you about their physical ailments?'

'Doesn't bear thinking about. Perhaps we drop it for now. Hey.' He stepped closer. 'Are you okay? You look unsettled all of a sudden.'

Rose shook her head. 'Not especially.' Then, she laughed, and gestured around them with her hand. 'Although there's probably a lot I *should* be unsettled about. It's just my instinct was to reach for my phone and jump on Google to find the answer.'

Aiden held her gaze, smiling faintly. Were they getting closer to each other? Rose could swear there was some leaning going on. His eyes dropped to her mouth, and she closed her eyes in anticipation, only for them to fly open at a loud crash behind them, and they both turned to see Jane bending down to pick up an empty water pail, its contents having trickled away into the border.

'Did you just…?' Rose gestured at the bucket, and Jane shook her head at them both.

'You must heed my warning and exercise more caution.' Jane's voice was firm, but her eyes were sparkling. 'Had I been Mama, you would have found the pail's contents upon your heads.'

They obediently stepped back, and Aiden eyed Jane and her bucket with some amusement. 'I don't think I was ever so well chaperoned even as a child.'

Rose laughed. 'Well, you just take note, Dr – I mean, Mr Trevellyan – I will not have my family's honour brought into question.'

Aiden clipped his boots together. 'Of course, Miss Wallace. I would not dream of it.'

Jane tsked. "'Tis an improvement, but you must comprehend how little I wish to draw undue attention to yourselves.'

Rose exchanged a small smile with Aiden. It was highly amusing to be chastised by a bristling Jane Austen.

'Did my brother not accompany you, sir?' Jane addressed Aiden as they all turned their steps back towards the house.

'I left Captain Austen at the great house. Mr Knight expects a call from you this morning. He seemed keen for your arrival, so I offered to come and fetch you.'

Rose frowned. 'Your brother, Edward, is here too?'

'Yes.' Jane waved a hand in the general direction of Chawton House. 'There are extensive renovations taking place at Godmersham.' She must have seen Aiden's puzzled expression, for she added, 'His Kent estate and main residence.'

Aiden nodded. 'I must admit, I'm a bit vague on the Knight connection.'

'I shall explain as we walk. Let us go directly, for the hour is convenient.' Jane turned to Rose. 'Cassandra has promised to sit with Mama for a time, thus we are at leisure.'

'Is your mother well, Jane? She went to lie down…'

Jane pursed her lips as she led the way back to the house. 'We are familiar with her ailments; they never occur but for her own convenience.'

–

It took over half an hour to dress in the necessary garments for paying a call, and with Aiden paying his respects to Mrs Austen and Jane still upstairs, Rose stood by the door to the street – a door which she was told was in full use, even though it was never used in the present day – whilst fidgeting with the bonnet pressed upon her. It just didn't feel right on top of her piled-up hair.

'Come, Miss Wallace. Permit me to share a contrivance which may assist you.'

Cassandra had come into the room, and she removed the bonnet from Rose's head and replaced it with a fine muslin cap, tucking Rose's unruly curls neatly in.

'There.' She replaced the bonnet, fixing it with a pin, and turned Rose to look in the mirror.

'Thank you.' Rose smiled at Cassandra's reflection. 'Much better.' She turned her head from side to side. 'Jane says you are not coming with us?'

'It is best you have some time with my sister. There is a conversation to be had…' Her voice tailed away, and Rose turned around to face her with a smile.

'Should I be worried?'

To Rose's consternation, Cassandra didn't return the smile, her face becoming wary. 'It is not for me to speak of it. Jane will enlighten you in due course.'

Feeling a return of her earlier trepidation, Rose nodded, and Cassandra opened the door.

'It is a fine day; I will hurry the others to join you.'

Sensing herself dismissed, Rose stepped out into the street outside the cottage, noting the open porch, then stopping short with a gasp as two men on horseback galloped past, dust rising in their wake. The road was much closer than she was used to seeing, with no swathe of grass separating it from the cottage, and she waited for a farmhand to pass with his horse and cart before stepping cautiously down onto the road and crossing over.

Rose walked into the orchard where the car park used to be – where in more than 200 years' time, Aiden's car would be parked – and, skirting the area containing bee hives, strolled under the trees for a while. Her confusion over why Jane had brought her back was intensifying with the length of her avoidance of the subject. It was obvious she didn't find it an easy matter to raise, but what on earth could have arisen for her to take such drastic action and then be reluctant to tell Rose why?

She was pulled from the repetitive circle of her thoughts by a sudden cry, and following the sound, she came to a stile over into a neighbouring field.

Chapter 3

'Ow! Fiendish beast!'

Turning to her left, Rose noticed the young girl she had seen earlier. She appeared to have fallen and was extricating herself from a bed of nettles beside a small stream.

'Oh, let me help you!' Rose clambered over the stile as best her skirts would allow, and the girl looked up, startled, then smiled.

'I am quite well, ma'am. I chased the ball, but found myself unable to cease my pursuit before taking a tumble.' She got to her feet, pushing her blond curls over her shoulder as she rubbed the skin on her arm, exposed by her having only short sleeves to her cotton dress.

'We need some dock leaves.' Rose turned to look around, but the girl shook her head.

'There are none hereabouts. Papa has an elderberry tincture that will suffice.'

'You have been stung before then?'

The girl eyed Rose with curiosity. 'I do not know you. You are not from the village.' She performed an awkward curtsey. 'My name is Anne.'

Unsure of the etiquette, and not sure if she ought to say anything about who she was, Rose returned the curtsey, adding, 'And mine is Rose.'

'Rose – 'tis a pretty name.'

Not wishing to elaborate, Rose looked around, spotting the ball nestled in amongst the nettles. For the first time she was able to appreciate the benefit of wearing leather gloves when it wasn't remotely cold. She stepped forward and leaned in to retrieve it, handing it back to the young girl, who thanked her prettily.

'Anne! What are you doing?'

They both glanced across the field. A tall, slender girl with flowing auburn hair was standing some paces away, frowning from Rose to Anne.

'I took a tumble, Olivia. This lady helped me.'

The frown disappeared, and the older girl smiled. 'How fortuitous you were there to assist, ma'am. Come, Anne. We are to walk to Farringdon.' She held out a hand and, with a quick smile towards Rose, Anne tucked the ball under her arm and skipped across a small wooden bridge to take the hand of the other girl – her sister, perhaps?

Rose turned back, taking the stile with a little more elegance the second time, and walked through the orchard just in time to see Aiden and Jane emerge from the house. She paused on the side of the road, shaking her head in bemusement. It was all so very different. Not just the cottage's appearance, but the proximity to the road as it swept around the corner on its way to Winchester, the duck pond opposite – so much larger than she'd imagined – and the building that housed the future cafe not even in existence.

Rose glanced at Aiden as they joined her and turned their steps towards Chawton House. His expression was inscrutable and she bit her lip. He must be rueing the day he'd ever met Rose, and—

'We are fortuitous in having the use of this land.' Jane waved her hand at the future car park as they walked on. 'We are most fortunate in our home, for we are kept admirably supplied with fruit and vegetables, and eggs, of course, from the chickens, and also have access to the kitchen gardens at the great house.'

'Are the beehives yours as well?' Rose pointed towards the wooden structures nestled beneath one of the trees.

'Indeed; Cass tends them. She makes the most delicious honey. You must sample some when we break our fast on the morrow, Rose.'

Rose's step faltered, and the others slowed to keep pace with her. 'But Jane, won't we have gone home before then?'

'It depends.'

'On what?'

'One moment.' Jane crossed the road and addressed a man busy repairing a wooden gate at one of the cottages – cottages that still stood in the present day – and Rose turned urgently to Aiden.

'You look…' She hesitated as he turned to face her. 'Preoccupied? Was it Mrs Austen?'

Aiden let out a huff of breath; then, he smiled reluctantly. 'She is quite the interrogator. I think I acquitted myself well enough – being a history nerd has its uses – but I was thankful the meeting was short.' He held Rose's gaze for a moment. 'Is it me, or is your friend avoiding telling you why you are here?'

Jane re-joined them then. 'Mr Gold has done much to our cottage to improve it. You may see him later as he is to—'

'Miss Austen.'

Jane glanced at Aiden, a brow raised.

'It depends, I believe you said?'

She sighed, then motioned for them to resume their walk. 'You must have many questions.'

Rose's heart stepped up its pace. At last there might be some answers! But then she and Aiden both spoke together.

'Yes! Why did you bring—?'

'A few, yes. How—?'

Jane glanced at Rose. 'Perhaps if we start with Dr Trevellyan's question? I fear my answer to you will be more complex.'

Unsure if she was relieved or frustrated by the reprieve, Rose nodded. 'Go ahead.'

'Thank you.' Jane looked to Aiden as they continued along the road. 'What is it you would know, sir?'

'I have a myriad of questions, mainly centred around how any of this,' he gestured with his arm at their surroundings, 'can be happening. The necklace you used to bring us here…' His voice tailed away and he met Rose's gaze. 'I've seen it before.'

Jane smirked. 'You *think* you have.'

'No – I'm not mistaking it for the ones alleged to belong to you and your sister, Miss Austen.'

It was Jane's turn to stop walking, and they were obliged to do the same. She turned slowly to face them. 'Might I enquire as to how you feel qualified to make such a statement?'

Aiden raised a brow, and Rose bit her lip, unsure where the conversation was going. 'I thought you had given me leave to ask the questions?'

Jane's taut expression eased as she smiled. 'Touché, sir.'

'I found a topaz cross and gold chain and, if I'm not mistaken, it was closer in age and style to the one you used last night.'

Jane bore his scrutiny steadily. 'How can that be?'

Rose frowned as something teased the edges of her memory, conscious Aiden had sent her a lightning glance again.

'I can't explain why, but I can tell you where. It was in the cathedral, near your...' He hesitated. 'Your er... grave?'

Rose's eyes widened as she recalled her walk with Aiden on the previous evening and his tale of finding a cross and chain at Winchester during some repair work – the walk that had culminated in Jane's sudden appearance.

'How... intriguing.' Jane set off walking once more and they fell into pace beside her. 'I shall satisfy your curiosity as best I can, sir, but though I can tell you how I slip through time, I am not sure any of us comprehends the why of it.'

'Any of us, Jane?' Rose frowned. 'Who else knows?'

'My family.' She glanced at Rose as she led them off the road into a gravel lane to the left. 'You recall, I am certain, the anxiety caused to my parents and sister when last we met. Nothing but the truth would satisfy my mother and father, and the latter's wrath fell in particular upon Charles.' Jane turned to Aiden. 'You are aware my youngest brother is a naval man, Dr Trevellyan?'

'Yes, of course.' Aiden looked from Jane to Rose. 'I still don't know what happened last time you... met?'

Jane all but rolled her eyes, but then she smiled. 'You do not wish your first question satisfied before we venture into another?'

Aiden smiled too. 'It is my turn to say touché, ma'am.' He glanced at Rose. 'Rose can fill me in when we have a moment to talk.'

And when might that be? Rose sighed. Much as she loved Jane, and incredible as their present situation was, she was overwhelmed with a sudden longing for her cosy flat in Bath and the chance to have a private moment with Aiden when they could talk, although perhaps talking wasn't likely to be their first activity… warmth filled Rose's cheeks as she realised two pairs of eyes were fixed on her, Jane's with amusement and Aiden's… well, she was hard put to read the message in his warm, brown gaze, and she turned to Jane.

'Aiden knows all about your brother's gift of the topaz crosses, but he has yet to learn about the special powers bestowed on the third one.'

Jane inclined her head. 'That makes the explanation shorter, if not simpler.'

Rose's gaze wandered as Jane set before Aiden everything she had told her when they had first met: how her brother, Charles, had been in Gibraltar when he purchased the crosses and chains, one of which the seller claimed possessed the power to enable the wearer to slip through time. This power was such that the necklace must pass directly from Charles' hand to Jane's for it to work for her, and it would only ever work for another if she passed it from her own hand personally.

A silence fell on them as she finished her tale, and Rose eyed Aiden warily. She knew how incredulous she'd been when she'd first heard about it, but this time they had all the evidence before them.

Jane shrugged lightly. 'It does not answer for how it came to be in Winchester Cathedral. Sir, what do you make of it?'

Aiden held up his hands in defence. 'Don't look at me for answers, I'm new at messing with the time continuum.'

Jane's eyes sparkled. 'At the risk of repeating myself, touché, sir.' She gestured ahead. 'We should continue.'

Rose frowned. 'But I thought the lane to Chawton House was further on?'

With a smile, Jane shook her head. 'A later alteration. Come, you will see.'

Rose almost took Aiden's hand, but then realised what she was doing and took his arm instead. They both fell into step up the long unfamiliar lane, and the conversation turned to Jane's brother, Edward.

'I trust you found Mr Knight accommodating upon your arrival, Mr Trevellyan?'

'Of course.' Aiden frowned. 'I didn't like to ask your brother about his surname. Are there exceptions to the convention of a lady taking her husband's name on marriage?'

'It would be most singular, upon marriage to another person; when there is marriage with an estate, it is not uncommon.'

'Ah, I see.' Aiden's frown deepened. 'At least I think I do.'

'When Edward was a youth, he was taken under the wing of Thomas Knight, a distant cousin of my father's. He and his wife, Elizabeth, were unable to have children.'

Rose gently squeezed Aiden's arm. 'He was to be heir to their Kent and Hampshire estates.'

'Was?'

Jane paused on the corner, where a carriage ride branched to the right off the lane. 'He is no longer the heir as he has inherited.'

'And part of the agreement was he change his name?'

'Come, let us continue on our way.' Jane turned to lead them along the ride, and soon the church rose before them. 'Upon the death of Elizabeth Knight, in 1812, he was obliged to take the name Knight, and thus is no longer an Austen.'

There was a hint of disapproval in Jane's tone, but before Rose could question her on it, she sensed the loss of Aiden's attention as it was drawn once more to the church, one that hadn't been seen by the human eye since 1874 when most of the original church burned down.

'Aiden?'

He started, then turned to look at her. 'Sorry.'

'You're keen to explore.' It wasn't a question, but she could see the avid interest on his face, and she smiled as her gaze drifted towards Chawton House. It looked beautiful under the morning sun, but like the cottage, the house and its surroundings were so different to how Rose knew them, she almost struggled to get her bearings.

Jane, who had reached the open gateway to the house's grounds, had turned around and was watching them.

'Is aught amiss?'

'Dr – I mean Mr Trevellyan – is curious about the church.' Rose waved a hand, but Aiden had already started towards it.

'Then let us avail ourselves of a fortuitous moment, Rose. Come.' Jane walked back to join her and they followed Aiden into the churchyard where they found him staring at the ground near the front entrance. Assailed by the memory of the day they'd had lunch in this very churchyard – was it really only a couple of days ago? – Rose smiled to herself. Wasn't that when she'd just begun realising Aiden liked her?

'It seems your young man is taking some relish from his circumstances, so much so it supersedes his desire for answers to his questions.'

Rose stirred and looked up. Aiden had just opened the door to go inside. 'I can't blame him. History and archaeology are his life, it's in his blood.'

'Let us give him a moment.'

Leaving Aiden to his speculations, Jane offered her arm to Rose, who hesitated before taking it. It felt so reminiscent of the day when she'd first found out about Jane's exploits, back in the future, and they'd walked arm in arm along the road towards the canal and Bathampton.

They strolled in silence for a short while along a gravel path, eventually coming to a low wall bounding the churchyard. How strange it felt to be here, knowing those all too familiar graves – the ones of Cassandra and Mrs Austen – were not standing in their usual place around the corner.

'Oh!' Rose stared at the land beyond the churchyard. 'This is open fields in the future.' It was cultivated now, including what appeared to be an extensive kitchen garden.

'Edward has plans to move the gardens up beyond the house. They are most inconveniently situated.' Jane waved a hand at the land before them. 'There is talk of all manner of improvements since Mr Middleton vacated earlier this year.'

The sound of voices in the distance drew Rose's attention to her left, and looking over the wall into the fields beyond, she saw a family starting to make its way up the slope towards a bank of trees. They were some distance off, but she was certain the young girl leading the way was her new friend, Anne.

'Aren't those your neighbours?'

Jane followed the direction of Rose's gaze, but then her eyes flew back to meet Rose's.

'Are you okay?' Rose frowned. 'You've gone really pale.'

'I am quite well.' Jane summoned a smile. 'Pay me no mind.' The family was approaching the trees now. 'They have been in the village but these six months. They are particularly fond of walking and are oft seen out together.'

'That's... nice.' Rose watched as the father, who was bringing up the rear, stopped, shading his eyes against the sun as he looked around.

'Nature has given them no inconsiderable share of beauty.'

Rose smiled as she watched them disappear under the edges of the trees. 'I met two of the girls earlier. They were very pretty.'

'It would give me particular pleasure to have an opportunity of improving your acquaintance with them.'

Puzzled, Rose turned back to face Jane. 'Why? We won't be here long...' She paused. 'Will we?'

'I cannot say.'

'But I don't understand—'

'Forgive my evasiveness.' Jane sounded uncharacteristically anxious, and Rose almost held her breath. Was she about to get some answers? 'It was imperative I speak to you alone. Will you forgive my curiosity, dear friend? I would very much like you to tell me about Mr Wallace.'

Rose blinked. 'My father?'

'I understand he is not in your life – has not been for some time? Is my assumption correct?'

Rose eyed Jane warily. What on earth had this got to do with anything? Was Jane stalling again?

'Yes, he passed away when I was very young.' She sighed. 'All I have is that photo of him and me. I don't remember him. I was only two, but I do remember being held, comforted, feeling loved.' Rose glanced at the silent lady beside her. These were things she hadn't thought about in ages. 'You've met my mother, Jane. I don't think for one minute it was her.'

Jane rested a hand briefly on Rose's arm. 'Forgive me for asking, but… do you know what happened?'

Rose shrugged, then leant on the wall, her gaze roaming across the open fields. The family had all disappeared now. 'He used to travel a lot with his work, apparently. There was a boating accident off the coast of Gibraltar.'

'And his family name was Wallace?'

'Yes… My mum seems pretty heartless at times, but she kept his name and hasn't remarried, even after twenty-five years.' Rose turned to Jane. 'Why are you asking me this? I thought you wanted to talk about why you brought me here?'

'That family,' Jane gestured towards the trees, 'bears the name Wallace.'

'Wow!' Rose smiled. 'Do you think they might be distantly related to me?' Then, she frowned. 'It's not an unusual surname, though. Is that why you brought me here – to personally meet people who might be my ancestors?'

Rose wasn't sure how she felt about this. It was incredibly sweet of Jane to think this was urgent enough to bring

41

Rose back in time, but wasn't it also incredibly over-eager? Rose had never considered Jane so sentimental. Perhaps her own father's death had influenced the lady's reasoning.

Jane remained silent, the troubled look on her face intensifying, and Rose hurried to reassure her.

'Look, it's a lovely gesture, bringing me here to meet possible ancestors. And I realise it's not an opportunity people usually get, but—'

'You misunderstand.' Jane held Rose's gaze, then nodded as though she'd come to a decision. 'I do not believe them to be distant relations. I believe Mr Wallace...' Jane hesitated, and Rose's skin began to prickle.

'What is it?' she whispered. 'What do you believe?'

'That the gentleman may be your father.'

Chapter 4

Words of denial rose easily to Rose's lips, but she silenced them, unwilling to embarrass Jane with a swift dismissal of her suggestion. But even so, it was ridiculous.

'I…' Rose hesitated, but Jane's eyes were fixed upon her, her own anxiety plain to see. She genuinely believed this! 'I'm touched you've put so much thought into it.' With a rueful laugh, Rose shook her head. 'I see now why you found it difficult to talk about.'

To her surprise, Jane didn't shrug or brush the matter aside. Instead, she held Rose's gaze, as though willing her to believe.

'Look, Jane, I can't tell you how much it means to me that you've gone to all this trouble.' Rose gestured with her arm. 'Coming all the way to Bath late at night, the trunk of clothes, introducing me to your family… you've put so much thought into it, but—'

'You think me a victim of sentimentality.' Jane raised her chin. 'Your air and countenance betray you. I wish it were so, for would it not be simpler than what I suggest? Come; sit with me and hear me out.'

Bemused, Rose followed Jane over to a nearby stone bench, and she sank onto it beside her friend. Why did everything remind her of when they'd first met? Hadn't they sat like this in Sydney Gardens when Jane first explained about how she had come to be there?

Jane turned in her seat to face Rose. 'Permit me some further explanation. Some years ago, when Charles was in Gibraltar, he befriended a nice Englishman with a young family eager to return to England. That man was a Christopher Wallace.'

'Christopher?' Rose smiled. 'My father was known as Kit, but Christopher was his given name. It's lovely, if he is a relation, that the name goes back so far in the family.' Why had her mind travelled instantly to telling Aiden she'd like to keep the name in *their* family? He loved history; he was bound to appreciate bringing a name from the past into the future, wasn't he? Then, she rolled her eyes at herself. They'd been barely a quarter of an hour into their... understanding, when Jane had appeared to disrupt them. What on earth was she thinking?

'Rose?'

Rose started. 'Sorry. Mind was wandering.'

'Do you not see the connection?' Jane eyed her earnestly. 'Your father disappeared into the sea off the coast of Gibraltar.'

'He died.' Rose spoke firmly. She had to gently knock this bizarre idea out of Jane's head. 'In the twentieth century.'

Jane pursed her lips. 'I comprehend your resistance to the notion, but you understand me well enough to know I am not inclined towards flights of fancy.'

It was true, but before Rose could speak, Jane continued. 'When I was first introduced to the gentleman...' She paused. 'When was it? About six months ago, I think. Yes, Eastertide was upon us.' She fixed her gaze on Rose again. 'I will own to the unusual colour of his hair, paired with the name Wallace, bringing you instantly to mind. I had not forgotten you, of course, but my life had been so disrupted for many years after I last saw you, and then, when we moved here, I finally felt settled and my attention was all upon my writing. I knew, from my stay with you, how important it was for me to fulfil my legacy and write the stories you so loved, Rose.'

Touched by these words, despite her concern over how doggedly Jane was sticking to her belief over this Wallace connection, Rose smiled as Jane picked up her thoughts.

'Like you, my first ponderings were whether these newcomers to the village were, by some strange coincidence, distant ancestors of yours, and I was delighted with the notion. I kept a keener eye out for them, even allowed myself a satisfied smile, thinking I comprehended a secret they did not.'

'That's so sweet. Nothing would please me more than to boast my great-great-great – wait, how many would it be?' She laughed. 'My distant grandparents had been your neighbours!'

Jane's sombre face sobered Rose quickly.

'I liked to imagine I could see some similarity of expression now and again, especially in the daughters, two of whom favour the same colouring as you.'

Involuntarily, Rose's hand rose to her head only to encounter the straw of her bonnet.

'But that is all it was; just a pleasurable supposition, a gentle amusement which I shared with no one.'

'Are you saying you have now shared this thought?' Rose's hand shot to her throat. This was ridiculous!

'I have told no one but Cass.'

'But there's nothing to tell!'

'Do you honestly believe I would have plucked you from your present life, brought you here, on a whim? I overheard Mr Wallace speaking words he could not, *should* not bear familiarity with.'

'Such as?' Rose shook her head. Why was she humouring her?

'He was watching his daughters perusing a book as they shared a garden bench. I declare he spoke quite clearly, though they would not have heard him. '*If only I had a camera, that I could capture such precious memories in a photo*'.' Jane pronounced these words with the air of someone playing a trump card. Rose opened her mouth to retort, but no words came. Then, she shook her head.

'It doesn't prove anything. If I had my phone, I could look up just when the first mentions of cameras and photos were. There are all sorts of odd inventions people were tinkering with way before anything was ever actually built officially. Look at Leonardo and his flying helicopter machine.' She wasn't falling for this. 'There are even words in your own books I never realised were used this early on, like electricity.'

Jane was clearly unimpressed with Rose's logic. 'My supposition does not stand on this slip alone, though I will own to its setting my mind on its current track. Since then, the gentleman has referred to several things he could not possibly know – nothing to raise awareness in general. He is considered an eccentric, and such people are always allowed some liberties, are they not?'

More for Jane's sake than her own, Rose pushed on. 'What other things did he say?'

'Well, for one, he knew my name. There was instant recognition when we were first introduced.'

'But surely it was recognition of your surname? Didn't you say he knows your brother? Even if you hadn't formally met, he must have learned that his neighbours were also Austens?'

'He showed no such reaction when Mama was introduced ahead of me. It seemed to be the mention of my full name, and mine alone. I am convinced he knew I am a writer.'

Rose's spirits lifted. 'But that's true! Oh, Jane, I can't tell you what a thrill it was to realise we had travelled to the very year *Pride and Prejudice* was published.'

'Did you forget I published anonymously?'

'Surely news would travel locally though?' Why was she even arguing the point?

Jane, however, was persistent if nothing else. 'It is not public knowledge outside of our intimate circle. To be certain, it would be unknown to such a casual acquaintance.'

Rose frowned. 'What exactly did he say to convince you?'

Raising her chin, Jane held Rose's gaze firmly. 'He murmured under his breath he wished he had made my acquaintance before his O level examination.'

A strange sensation began to take hold of Rose as her skin prickled. 'No. I mean, you must have misunderstood or misheard him. It could be a Gibraltar thing.'

Jane shrugged. 'That is as may be. I had no idea what an O level was, though the use of the word examination perhaps gave it sufficient clarity.'

'It's like the OWLs? You know, from the *Harry Potter* books you were reading? Exams in various school subjects. He was probably talking about an English Lit paper.' Rose stopped. Was she starting to believe this nonsense?

Jane smiled. 'I regret I was unable to finish them all. I have longed to know the outcome for Mr Potter and his friends.'

Rose grasped at the distraction. 'I can tell you, if you want to hear?'

Jane shook her head. 'I prefer to read it for myself. It will give me something to look forward to next time I slip through to the future.' She got to her feet. 'Come, Rose. We have laboured the point long enough. If you will not take my word on this, then we must endeavour to find a way to prove it one way or the other.'

Rising slowly to her feet, Rose's gaze narrowed as she stared at Jane. 'Why are you persisting with this? You must have misheard him.'

'I did not. And pray, what would you give as his reason for being on such guard? He could have no reason to suspect any of his neighbours would believe someone from the future could exist here. The gentleman is not being as careful as I would advise, were you in his shoes.'

Rose put a hand to her head. 'It can't be true. I mean, how... *why*?'

Jane eyed her sympathetically. 'I believe it more likely to be true than that all of these clues amount to nothing.' The sound of footsteps drew their attention, but Jane continued as Aiden made his way towards them. 'Even so, I cannot be sure without unmasking the man – and thus myself.'

Aiden greeted them with a smile, but then his gaze narrowed as he looked at Rose. 'Is something up?'

Rose had no words.

Jane merely raised a brow. 'A broad question, sir.' She sent Rose a meaningful glance, then inclined her head towards Aiden, and with a reciprocal nod, Rose turned to him. Telling Aiden might be exactly what she needed right now.

'Jane believes her neighbour, a Mr Wallace, is my long-dead father.'

If it were not for her conflicted feelings, Rose would have loved to frame the look on Aiden's face. In the past twenty-four hours, he had navigated the revelation of a secret three-year crush and the discovery that slipping through time was possible with barely a raised brow. This, however, was apparently one step too far.

'Sorry?'

Rose's lips twitched at the unusually high pitch to his normally low-toned voice, but then she sighed. This was no time for humour.

'My father died—' Rose hesitated, glancing at Jane, who turned to Aiden.

'The gentleman was lost at sea when Rose was very young, off the coast of Gibraltar. It was there, a few years ago, that my brother, Charles, met a Mr Christopher Wallace. They became friends, and Charles was instrumental in helping Mr Wallace and his family take up a tenancy on the Chawton estate some six months ago.'

'I see.' Aiden cleared his throat and ran a hand through his hair. 'At least, I think I do. You think there is a connection, and this is the reason you brought Rose here? To ascertain the truth?'

Rose's eyes searched his face. Was he being polite by not rejecting the idea outright? She wanted him to say something simple and brilliant that would put this idea out of both Jane's head and – it was increasingly important – her own.

'Indeed.' Jane gestured towards the lane. 'Come, my brothers are expecting us.'

'Do they know?'

Jane said nothing until they had left the churchyard and turned their steps up the driveway towards the house. 'They are versed in my... activities, but that is all. I have shared my suspicions with no one but my sister.' She started to walk up the drive, then said over her shoulder, 'And now both of you.'

Rose's insides were swirling, her mind full of confusion and questions – so many questions!

'Rose?'

With a start, she turned to Aiden, who offered her his arm, and she took it gratefully. He covered her hand with his, giving it a gentle squeeze, and she drew in a steadying breath. With Aiden beside her, she would find her way through this – whatever it turned out to be.

They had turned their steps to follow Jane, who was some way ahead up the drive now, and they walked in silence for a moment.

Then, he glanced at her. 'Are you okay?'

Rose squeezed his arm. 'I'm fine.' Was she? It was easy to say, but...

'Is it possible, what Jane is suggesting?'

Rose shrugged lightly as they began to walk up the slope to the house. 'I think it's possible this family could be distant relations – and I mean *very* distant. But my actual father?' Rose shook her head. 'How can it be? *Why* would it be? It's sad, but he died. People do. It was an accident, that's all.'

Aiden drew Rose to a halt and turned her to face him, taking her hands in his. 'I hate having to ask but... was he ever found?'

Rose shook her head. 'But neither was anyone else. There were four men on the boat when it went down. It's a lovely idea, I suppose… that he never died, that instead he somehow appeared somewhere else, but…' Rose hesitated. 'I don't want to embarrass Jane or hurt her feelings. She's so obviously convinced about this, but I can't believe it.'

They began to walk again and, at Aiden's pressing, Rose related the whole of her conversation with Jane, then waited for his reaction. Now the words were out, she almost felt purged and some of the tension in her shoulders was easing. In repetition, the odd remarks Mr Wallace had made didn't sound nearly as compelling as when Jane had first mentioned them. Aiden's scholarly mind would soon find a logical explanation and help her explain to Jane how things stood.

Rose looked at him expectantly as they reached the steps into the house, Jane having long disappeared inside. Then she frowned. He was taking a long time to do it.

'You don't agree with me.'

'I'm not sure it's that simple, Rose.'

She drew in a short breath, then nodded. 'Sorry, it's just that I'm starting to feel as though I'm going mad, and you're the least unhinged person I know. Tell me what you're thinking, Aiden; don't spare my feelings. I need your perspective.'

Aiden's face softened, but rather than look at her when he spoke, he looked above her head, across the terraces to the east of Chawton House.

'I am not entirely new to the improbable. There are things I've come across in my research and on various digs that defy explanation. However, the last few hours have taught me I'm but a novice. Perhaps it's this sudden awareness making me more open, or simply my emotional distance from the matter?' He laid a hand against her cheek, his eyes warm and reassuring. 'I can't begin to imagine what you are thinking and feeling, Rose, but we need to accept there may be something in this. If the only person we know who has experience of slipping from one time to another feels this strongly she has recognised another, we might be wise to consider her opinion very seriously.'

'But…' Rose wanted to protest, to say what she knew: her father was dead. But did she really know anything? After all, being in the time period they were was preposterous. Aiden had a point; she'd known he would. She just hadn't expected it to be on the side of the impossible.

Chapter 5

Edward Knight, né Austen, being fully versed in his sister's escapades in toying with time, seemed to find his visitors at least as fascinating as they did him.

Trying not to stare as she was introduced to him, Rose took the seat she was bid beside Jane. Thankful for the interlude, and the distraction from Jane's strange reason for bringing her back in time, Rose looked around the great hall as surreptitiously as she could, trying to take in how the room differed from the present day, noting the stone floor and the heavy curtains hanging by the openings in the oak screen separating the room from the entrance hallway.

'Miss Wallace?'

Turning her attention back to the company, Rose smiled at Edward. 'Forgive me, sir. I was admiring the room.'

Edward straightened in his seat, looking pleased. 'It is a fine one, is it not? Of course, it is nothing to the accommodations at Godmersham, but with my tenant's departure, it was an opportune moment to assess the property and commence improvements whilst some renovations were carried out in Kent.' His expression narrowed as he glanced at Jane. 'We were due to return home after a visit to Henry in town. Fanny,' he frowned at Jane, 'was most put out when I sent her home to Godmersham instead of permitting her the promised excursion.'

'My brother's household has all returned to Kent after passing the summer here in Chawton, and Charles' wife and family accompanied them.' Jane looked from Rose to Aiden. 'We are able to speak openly, for there are but we four here at present; Edward,' she gestured at her brother, 'is well versed in my travels.'

Rose looked over at Edward. Well versed he might be, but his face was disapproving. Jane, on the other hand, looked amused.

'Edward does not consider it fitting behaviour, not least in a sister. He is, nonetheless, intrigued by it all the same. Indeed, when Charles first…' She stopped and looked around. 'Where *is* Charles?'

With a grunt, Edward got to his feet and walked over to the vast hearth where a fire burned merrily. 'He took a tumble on his ride this morning. He has gone to repair the damage to his attire.' Then, he turned to face the three of them, and Rose exchanged a quick glance with Aiden, who sent her a reassuring smile.

'You have made my brother's acquaintance, sir.' He inclined his head towards Aiden, then looked back to Rose. 'He shoulders great responsibility in his profession, with so many lives in his hands, yet it does not take much for him to revert to the foibles of childhood when at his leisure.' He eyed Rose beadily for a moment, and she leaned back in her seat, wondering what he was going to say. 'His foolish gift to Jane is a fine example of his recklessness. Such a secret we must now harbour in our breasts.'

Jane tutted. 'All families have secrets, Edward.'

'Ours is just more fascinating than most, is it not, Sister?'

Rose looked over her shoulder. The young man she had seen only briefly the night before had entered the room. Aged in his thirties, his dark hair cropped fashionably short, Captain Charles Austen was of lean build but his presence was such that he seemed so much larger.

'I trust you rested well after your journey, Miss Wallace.' He bowed formally. 'I assure you, Mr Trevellyan was afforded every comfort we could offer him.'

'And I appreciate your generosity, sir.' Aiden looked to Edward, who smiled.

'We are well supplied with produce from the estate, it is true.'

'Speaking of which, Edward.' Jane got to her feet and joined him by the fire. 'With a visitor in the house, Mama asked if I might petition for some additional supplies.'

'Of course.' Edward waved a hand. 'I shall send word to Parsons; the kitchen garden is at your disposal, as always.' He turned to address Aiden and his brother. 'We are lacking a hostess; otherwise, we would have you all to dinner.'

'You know Cass would be more than happy to oblige, should you think to invite us, Brother.' Jane's expression was amused as she exchanged a look with her younger brother.

'I fear we dine too late to suit Mama's digestion, Jane.'

The conversation fell to discussing comparisons of dining habits, and Rose found her attention drifting and she got to her feet and walked over to one of the tall windows fronting onto the driveway. Her shoes were beginning to rub her heels sore. She'd been able to remove the bonnet, which had been making her head itch, and the gloves, for which she found the weather far too warm. If only she could shed with equal ease the discomfort swirling around inside her or the whirlwind of thoughts spinning in her head.

Should she pay a little more attention to Aiden's approach to all this? He was an intelligent, well-educated man, but although she'd known him for three years, she didn't exactly *know* him, did she? He seemed well-grounded, sensible and, like Jane herself, not given to flights of fancy. Yet how could he even be giving Jane's incredible theory any consideration? It just wasn't possible.

Nor is your being here in the first place. The thought whispered through her mind again, and Rose caught her breath, spinning around to face the room. Jane was at the nearby console table busying herself with preparing some tea now, along with a maid who had entered the room. Edward had returned to his seat, and he and Aiden were deep in conversation about the history of the house. Charles, in the meantime, sat a little apart from them and was studying Rose a little too intently for her comfort, and she stirred under his intense gaze.

'Miss Wallace?' With relief, Rose turned to Jane, who offered her a cup of tea.

'Thank you.'

'Dear Rose.' Jane spoke quietly. 'You really must begin to harden yourself to the idea of being worth looking at.'

Rose summoned a smile as Jane turned away to serve the others, then took a cautious sip of the tea. It didn't taste exactly as she was used to, but it was certainly more palatable than the hot chocolate.

She turned back to look out of the window but had taken only one more sip of her drink when she became aware of someone beside her. Expecting it to be

Aiden, she almost dropped her cup when she realised it was Charles Austen. He wasn't looking at her this time, however, but out through the window.

'There must be much that is alien to you, Miss Wallace.' He glanced over his shoulder, then met Rose's wary gaze. 'My sister speaks very highly of you from her last... escapade. I confess to having been curious these many years.'

'Curious, sir? Over what?'

'Curious as to what sort of female could be even more bold than my sister.'

Rose couldn't help but laugh. 'I do not believe anyone has ever described me in such a way before.'

Charles' brow rose, his eyes sparkling in a manner similar to his sister's. 'How else would you describe someone who, having been thrown out of the life they knew, would stop at nothing to restore it – even under threat of imprisonment?'

Rose's eyes widened. 'Jane – forgive me – Miss Austen has told you all, then. I admit it does sound rather daring when described as such, but much of it was chance. I was also spurred on by necessity. If your sister has told you everything, you will know her writing lives on to inspire millions.'

Her gaze wandering to where Aiden sat opposite Edward, Rose smiled slightly. 'Circumstance can lead us to act out of our natural character, can it not?'

'Most indubitably.'

Charles took a sip of his own tea, but Rose's eyes remained on Aiden. They may only have become close in recent days, but she knew his face almost as well as her own. If she was any judge, he was half listening to Edward and half trying to commit the stonework to memory.

Charles turned to place his now empty cup on the console table. 'Jane is a favourite amongst my siblings, yet even I struggle to imagine the extent of her fame in the future.'

The gentleman's narrowed gaze fastened on Aiden. Why would he be interested in him, other than as a curiosity? She shifted from one foot to the other, but Charles then suggested they join the rest of the party, and Rose fell thankfully into a seat.

'I believe, now we are refreshed, we should turn our attention to the matter in hand: my sister's purpose in bringing you here.' He looked to Rose, then Aiden. 'Has she spoken of it? She was convinced of the necessity, yet Edward and I remain in the dark.'

Edward nodded. 'I agree. I believe we have been sufficiently patient.' His gaze fell on Rose, and she stirred warily. 'What is so important it could not wait 200 years for Miss Wallace to work it out on her own?'

Jane threw him a warning glance, and Edward inclined his head towards Rose.

'Forgive me, madam. With the exception of the rather dramatic occurrence of our sister being lost to us for a while, this is the first time we have had any interaction ourselves with this strange phenomenon.' His gaze remained fixed on Rose. 'At present, I am unsure if my sentiments tend towards aversion or fascination.'

Rose smiled faintly. 'I am not certain how I feel about it either, sir.'

Edward's expression relaxed a little, but Charles laughed, and Rose met Aiden's concerned gaze and forced a smile, wishing he was at her side. Were they expecting *her* to explain their sister's inexplicable action? She had no desire to make Jane look ridiculous in front of her brothers.

Jane placed her cup on a side table. 'I have told you both several times, it is of a delicate nature.'

'The rules of what should and should not be discussed have long become clouded when it comes to your adventures, Sister. I think it best we understand exactly what is afoot.' Charles' tone was pleasant but firm. 'Would you rather I share my own?' He didn't wait for a reply, but turned to look at Rose. 'Miss Wallace shares a family name with my friend, Wallace, who is a tenant here in Chawton.' He turned to his sister. 'Had you not interrogated me on everything I knew about the gentleman, I would be hard pressed to call it nothing more than a small coincidence, for it is a common enough name, is it not? But you sought every possible detail of my acquaintance with Wallace, and I would hazard you believe he and your friend here,' he waved a hand towards Rose, 'are related in some way.'

Edward's face brightened. 'Is this all? But, to what end? It would be a fine coincidence indeed, should the family be revealed so, Jane. But where lies the urgency or obligation to take such drastic action?'

All eyes turned on Rose.

'It is… possible…' She hesitated. 'This man – he may be more closely related than you suspect. I… he…' Rose floundered, and Aiden got to his feet and came to sit beside her, taking her hand in his and ignoring Jane's pointed look before she turned to her brothers.

'I believe Mr Wallace is not a distant relation, but Rose's father, whom she has considered dead since she was a child.'

Edward's eyes widened, and he sputtered, 'Inconceivable!' His gaze flew from Jane's serious face to Rose's anxious expression. 'Is it possible? How? How could it possibly be *possible*!?'

Charles, however, leaned back in his seat and folded his arms across his chest. 'Now that *is* a compelling thought.'

Rose gripped Aiden's hand tighter, willing him not to give in to the strictures of the day and release her, but Jane had turned to Charles.

'How long had Mr Christopher Wallace been in Gibraltar when you made his acquaintance?'

Charles shrugged. 'As I once said, I am not entirely certain, but for some considerable duration. He had acquired a wife and young family. Mrs Wallace was born there, daughter to one of the Commissioner's aides. It was at a gathering in the residence that we were first introduced.'

'Yes, but when was this?'

Charles got to his feet and walked over to where his sister sat. 'Around the time I acquired the topaz crosses – some thirteen years ago? Wallace and I got along famously, and we met several times before I once more set out to sea. He confessed his desire to return to England with his family. I would have given him passage but for our being bound for Ireland, but I was able to put him in touch with an acquaintance whose command was headed for Portsmouth the following month.'

Jane tilted her head to one side as she studied her brother. 'When I asked you about him, you said he had been vague about what brought him to Gibraltar.'

Edward made an impatient gesture. 'Where is all this going, Jane? I do not see—'

'Nor will you, Brother, unless you open your eyes.' Jane shook her head at him and turned back to her younger brother. 'Did you not say he had been shipwrecked in the Straits?'

Charles was staring into the middle distance, and Rose looked from him to Aiden. She felt some sympathy for Edward in all this. Where exactly *were* they going with it? They could debate and dissect what little facts they had all day long, but it wouldn't make it any more likely that Jane's theory would be true.

Aiden sent her a small smile, but then turned his attention back to what Charles Austen was saying, and Rose, comforted simply by knowing he was there, did likewise.

'…and pulled from the sea.' Charles stopped, a faint look of surprise on his face. 'I had forgotten! We did find an odd connection. It seems he was tended back to health by a native woman whom, according to local lore, possessed a talent for healing.' He gestured towards Jane. 'We later discovered her to be the very same woman who, some years later, sold me the charm with the mystical power, Jane, and enabled you to bring your friends here.'

'But did Mr Wallace ever say whence he came, Brother?'

'Yes, I wish to understand this too.' Edward was eyeing his brother keenly. 'Through your introduction, Charles, he is now a tenant of mine. I wish to know more on his background.'

Charles turned back to his sister. 'He came from England, though the name of the vessel I know not. As I said, when I first met Wallace he had been in Gibraltar several years. But,' Charles glanced at Rose thoughtfully, 'I recall now that Wallace owned the loss of his first family.

He gave no indication as to what had happened to them, but there had been a wife and a young daughter.'

Rose's throat felt tight and a tear pricked her eye. It was all just too ridiculous… wasn't it? Everyone's gaze seemed fixed on Charles Austen, who looked around at them then smiled ruefully.

'Hardly proof, I know. The conditions in Gibraltar could be harsh, especially for a child. But it does add to the mystery, does it not?'

A silence descended on them as all eyes turned on Rose. She tried to swallow, but a constriction had risen and instead she coughed. Were they expecting her to say something?

'I— I cannot—' She stopped, attempted to clear her throat, and Aiden placed his other hand over their clasped ones.

'Miss Wallace, what do you recall of your father?'

'Very little. I was only two when he died…' She looked from Jane to Charles. 'He went missing after a boating accident. He was never found.'

'And your family? You have brothers and sisters?'

She shook her head, wishing she did. It would put paid to all this nonsense. 'No. I was – I am – an only child.'

Aiden's thumb stroked the back of her hand methodically, and Rose summoned a smile for him before her gaze was drawn back to the three Austen siblings eyeing her with avid interest. Was it simply the magic of being here, being with this incredible family in these ridiculous circumstances, or was she starting to consider there might be something in Jane's outlandish theory?

Chapter 6

'You will not encounter them.'

Rose glanced at the lady walking by her side as they made their way back through Chawton. Then, she smiled.

'How did you know?'

Jane placed a hand on Rose's arm and drew her to a halt. 'Dear friend, the distraction of your mind may not be visible, but that of your eyes is quite the contrary. Seeking sight of the Wallaces at every turn will serve you little, for they took the path towards Farringdon, some three miles distant, and will likely not return for some time.'

Rose nodded. 'Yes, that was the place the one daughter mentioned earlier.'

They turned to continue their walk back to the cottage, and silence consumed them for a moment as Rose mulled over the fact that – should Jane's supposition prove to be true (not that she was believing it for a moment!) – Anne and her sister would be her half siblings. A momentary ache consumed her. How she had longed for a sister or brother when growing up, fatherless and lonely in their big house, and distanced from a mother who seemed to have no time and even less patience for her.

As they reached the pond across the road from the cottage, Jane drew Rose to a halt again.

'I regret causing you such disquiet, Rose, but I remain steadfast in my purpose.'

'I know you do.'

'What is it you most wish for?'

Rose said nothing for a moment as her gaze roamed over the building before them. *Aiden*, her mind whispered. She wished they had not had to leave him with Jane's brothers. Then, she let out a reluctant laugh.

'A glass of cold water.'

Jane shook her head vehemently. 'You must not—'

'I know.' Rose hurried to reassure her. 'Cholera. Typhoid.' She sighed. 'I just miss being able to quench my thirst so easily.'

'Martha makes the most delicious lemonade. There will be some in the kitchen. Let us refresh ourselves and take some sustenance, and then we can talk further whilst we aid Cass.'

They both watched a donkey cart rumble past, laden with hay, before stepping across the road, avoiding the puddles.

'With what?'

Jane smirked as she led the way through the gate into the garden. 'You will see, and I believe it will provide sufficient distraction for the present.'

-

Jane was not wrong. As the afternoon drew to a close, Rose wiped an arm across her forehead, her desire for a long draught of water prevalent in her mind. It seemed all hands were required to prepare supplies for the winter, and an inordinate amount of canning, pickling and so on had been taking place, with the cook and Mrs Austen in the neighbouring store and Rose in the bake-house with Cassandra.

It had been hard to determine what of many unfeasible things she should focus her mind on. Here she was, out of her own time and comforts, the father whom she knew to be dead possibly living the other side of the garden wall, and Cassandra Austen instructing her in how to salt a pig!

This was, in and of itself, a contradiction, as the lady was one of the most graceful, sweet people Rose had ever met, and though she was performing her present duty with aplomb, it all seemed so very wrong.

'Yes, now add more salt,' Cass instructed in her soft voice.

Rose obediently did so, and then, without having to be told, added another chunk of meat into the cylinder, then glanced to her left and frowned. 'Is that not where the laundry is done?'

'Indeed, but we are not due a great wash imminently.'

Trying to ignore what was hanging from the ceiling behind her, Rose applied herself to the task, conscious of her teacher's eyes on her.

'Somehow, I pictured you doing more sewing than this.'

'You are not mistaken, Miss Wallace. There are plenty of things to put a needle and thread to, but food preparation takes precedence over sitting down to our work.'

'Makes sense,' Rose muttered as she added another scoop of salt to her canister, then eyed Cass again. Would she mind if she asked her something? 'Do you really take on more chores to give Jane time to write? I mean, she is not here and…'

Cass smiled. 'My sister has an obligation to write to our brother, Henry, in London, postponing her visit until tomorrow fortnight. She was due to accompany Edward and some of his daughters before going onward into Kent for some duration.'

Conscious she was the cause of the disruption, Rose threw Cassandra an anxious look. 'I am sorry. It's – this is my fault, all this disruption.' She looked around the room. 'And now you are all obliged to offer me – and Aiden – food and accommodation, and—'

'Miss Wallace.' Cassandra placed a hand on Rose's arm. 'It is impossible to do justice to the hospitality of your attentions towards my sister when we were estranged. I would do anything by return for your comfort, for Jane is everything to me.'

Rose's affection for the Austen sisters increased.

'The sisterly bond between you is beautiful. It is well known amongst her fans, and we owe you thanks. It is obvious she would have found it difficult to find time to write without you.'

Cassandra turned to put her utensils into a large bowl. 'Jane is quite determined. She would have found a way.' She joined Rose at the counter again. 'Never more so than since she returned from her captivity in the future.'

Rose rested her filthy hands on the rim of the counter. Close as they were, Cassandra must surely have read everything Jane had written so far. 'Do you like her stories?'

The lady laughed. 'How could I not? We have all grown up listening to Jane reading aloud from her writing. She is the consummate performer; perhaps you did not know?'

'Do you have a favourite of her novels – the two she has published so far, I mean?'

Cassandra offered a damp cloth to Rose, who took it thankfully. 'Not really; the merits of each will always resonate with me.'

'And what of her present writing? She must be some way into *Mansfield Park* by now?'

With a raised brow, Cassandra lifted the cylinder and placed it on a wooden table.

'It is all but complete.' She glanced at Rose, a smile touching her lips. 'It is quite singular that you know the story before it is written, before I have read it.'

'Does she let you read as she writes, or must you wait until it is finished?'

With a laugh, Cassandra waved a hand at the door. 'Come, let us repair inside and freshen ourselves before dining.'

Rose followed her out onto the gravel pathway leading away from the service buildings, and Cassandra looked over her shoulder.

'We argue now and then when she will not let me skip ahead, or if she is writing too slowly for my pleasure.' She laughed again. 'We have been having some debates about the closing of her present manuscript; I do not like it, but she will not yield. To be fair, I have read the ending before the preceding chapters, so I may not fully appreciate her point.'

Rose laughed too. 'That sounds a bit like my friend, Morgan.'

They had reached the back door into the house now, and Cassandra paused to turn and look at her.

'Indeed? Jane has told me something of her. She sounds like quite the character.'

Cassandra entered the house and, with one last glance back at the bake-house, Rose sighed before following her. How she missed Morgan!

With a rueful smile, Rose hung her apron on the hook in the boot room and walked over to the washstand as Cassandra brought warm water from the kitchen and poured it in. She felt unkempt and uncomfortable. Her stays were digging into her ribs and her feet – well, they were worse than ever in their cramped shoes. Her hair was escaping from its pins – and her hands! How she longed for a shower, or even a bath, and to wash her hair, but it seemed she would have to wait until she was back home.

Rose sighed. With the added complexity of the social gaffes she knew she'd had to cover up in just these twenty-four hours, it was probably a good thing Morgan – and James – were more than 200 years away through a curtain in time.

–

Inspecting her reddened hands as she strolled in the garden after dining early with the ladies, Rose pulled a face. It had taken a lot of scrubbing to rid them of the smell of salted flesh. At least she had achieved a thorough wash in her room with a full bowl of water, some strange-smelling soap and a rather scratchy towel. She'd even managed to eat some of the food: a mutton stew with vegetables from the garden followed by what was known within the family as Mrs Austen's Pudding, but bore quite a similarity to bread and butter pudding. The glass of orange wine pressed upon her by Jane had also helped ease a little of the ever-present tension from her shoulders, although its sweetness had made her shudder.

How she wished Aiden had been there, but he would be dining with the gentlemen and, to be fair, she didn't miss the company of either of the brothers. Edward seemed almost as sceptical of this whole scheme as she was, and Charles unnerved her with his steady gaze and his preference for siding with his sister.

Rose's feet had drawn her, almost against her will, to the low brick wall dividing the Austens' cottage from the house where the Wallace family lived, and she eyed it warily. Could there really be anything in this wild idea of Jane's?

The sound of voices drifted through the early evening air, and Rose stepped behind a young tree planted near the wall as three girls of varying heights entered the garden. Anne led the way, skipping, but Olivia, who had come looking for her sister earlier, was deep in conversation with a slightly taller girl. From their both sharing the same shade of auburn hair, Rose could only assume this was another sister. How many more people were there in this family Jane believed Rose shared?

Fingers of tension gripped her shoulders. The gentleman she'd seen leaving the shed had just pushed open the gate for a lady to walk through, doubtless his wife from the fond look she bestowed on him. He followed her along the path, and Rose's throat tightened as she stared after him.

'I shall join you directly, my dear.' He held the door open for the lady as she disappeared inside after the girls, and then turned to walk along the path leading to the shed. His voice was well modulated and educated, but Rose had no memory of it.

Conscious he was walking in her direction, albeit his gaze was on his feet, Rose looked around anxiously for somewhere better to conceal herself but the tree – really little more than a sapling and completely inadequate as a screen – was the only one at this end of the garden. Before she could take the only possible action of crouching down behind the wall, he looked up.

A small gasp escaped her, and she quickly turned her head to look at the hollyhocks filling the border. Regardless, a movement caught her eye, and she looked back into the neighbouring garden. The gentleman had noticed her, but he merely docked his hat with a smile and disappeared inside his shed.

Turning around in a daze, Rose walked unseeingly back towards the house, her insides doing somersaults and her head spinning.

Either the Wallace genes were incredibly strong and they really were related, or Jane was spot on with her reasoning. Rose may not recall her father or his voice, but that smile she knew. It was identical to the one in the only photo Rose possessed of her father: him cradling her in his arms when she was a mere toddler.

–

The evening seemed torturously drawn out, with the only sounds in the drawing room, when conversation was lacking, being the crackling of the fire, the clink of a spoon in a cup or the turning of a page. Her eyes straining against the candles, which emitted a pungent odour, Rose was thankful to put aside the sewing she had been given to do and followed Jane and Cassandra up the stairs, longing for some privacy.

At the top of the stairs, however, Jane urged Rose to follow Cassandra into the bedroom they shared.

'You do not seem yourself, Rose.'

Rose shook her head as Jane closed the door. She'd been relatively silent since she'd seen Christopher Wallace in his garden.

'You are troubled?'

Rose hugged her arms to herself. 'A little.'

'And the cause?'

Cassandra threw her sister a warning look. 'Do not pester her so, Jane!'

'I do not pester her, Cass. I merely made an observation for which I seek clarification.'

The Austen sisters' bickering would have been entertaining, but for the numbness consuming Rose. She walked across the room, stumbling slightly on an uneven floorboard near the closet, and sank into a nearby chair.

'I have—' She paused. 'I saw him.'

'Whom did you see, Miss Wallace?' Cassandra came over and perched on the edge of her bed opposite, and Jane joined her, her eyes sparkling.

'Mr Wallace.'

Jane rolled her eyes at her sister. 'Of course it was he. Who else could so discompose her?' She looked back over at Rose. 'And the sighting taught you something, did it not?'

Rose looked from Jane to Cassandra before her gaze dropped to her lap. Then, she lifted her hands in a helpless gesture.

'The only photo I have of him is more than twenty-five years old, but the smile… it's uncanny.'

Cassandra's expression softened, but Jane's became even more intently fixed on Rose.

'Your sensibility seems to be opening to the perception of it.'

Rose's resolve crumbled a little further. 'I am…' She sighed. 'I am very curious.'

Jane's smile was smug. 'As I believed you would be.' Then, she leaned forward and grasped Rose's hand, giving it a comforting squeeze. 'I beg you not to distress yourself over this, Rose. If I am mistaken, nothing is lost that was not lost before. And if I am correct… well, let us endeavour to seek out the truth of the matter.'

With a weak smile, Rose stood up, trying to surrender her doubts for the time being. 'I need to try and get some sleep.'

Cassandra bade her good night and walked over to the closet housing a bowl and pitcher, and Jane followed Rose out onto the landing.

'Truly, Rose. Try not to dwell upon it. Once a formal introduction is made, the opening will be formed to find some answers.'

'I know.' Rose's heart quailed at the thought. How did one even begin to address the subject? She would have to ask Aiden and trust in his being with her at the time… She frowned and turned to Jane.

'It is obvious why you brought me here, but why Aiden? You'd never met him.' The frown deepened. 'And how did you come to have men's clothing in that trunk?'

Jane looked evasive for a second, but then she smiled. 'The former, I am not inclined to answer for the present. The latter…' She shrugged. 'The clothes are an assortment left with us by James for mending and alteration.' She tilted her head. 'Do you not feel the benefit of Mr Trevellyan's presence?'

'Yes, of course, but…'

Jane fell into step beside Rose, urging her along the landing.

'Had you been with your friend when I arrived, I may have suggested bringing her instead. She struck me as an intrepid companion, one who would stand by you in all circumstances.'

Fondness for Morgan swept through Rose. 'It is as well she knows nothing of what is happening here. I'm not sure, when I return, if I'll ever tell her; she'd never believe me.'

'She will be so pleased to see you, perchance she will not trouble herself over where you have been.'

'I'm just relieved time is not moving on for her. When I get back, she'll be exactly as I left her, safe with James at her apartment.'

Jane threw Rose a searching look as they reached the bedroom she had been given on the previous night.

'You are mistaken. Time *is* moving on where you came from.'

Rose sank back against the doorframe. 'But why? It didn't move on when you were stuck.'

'Dear Rose.' Jane shook her head at her. 'These are not the same. When I slip through time, everything continues here in my absence, and the same will apply to you – and to Mr Trevellyan and his life.'

'But I don't understand.' Rose's head was starting to spin.

'When I became trapped in your time, we entered a different strand of your life, the one where I had not been part of it, and your original life stalled. You did not move through time. Do you not recall it to be so? Your old life no longer existed, nor did the life strands of the people in it. Yet for myself, here in the past, it was not so. My old life continued to move on.'

'I'd forgotten!' Rose's insides dipped as she turned to Jane in dismay. 'What am I to *do*? I have to go back. Morgan will be panic-struck! I sent her a text but it only said I was with Aiden and would see her the next day. That's now, *today*, and today is over!'

'You wish to go back with all that is unresolved?'

'No. Yes. Oh, I don't know!' Rose felt like stamping her foot. Why was this all so difficult? 'But I have to reassure Morgan.' Her hand shot to her throat as realisation struck. 'Tomorrow is Friday, it's the day of the ball. We were supposed to be at the hairdressers, getting our hair put up. Morgan won't accept my going off on a little jaunt on such an important day!'

Jane didn't seem particularly perturbed by Rose's anxiety. 'You have no need to despair. Once you are restored to your time, she will be pacified; the harm will be thus undone.'

'But Morgan will still be suffering in the meantime. She'll be distraught.' Rose clutched her midriff. This was terrible! What had she done by letting Jane persuade her to come? 'She'll be convinced something awful has happened, go to the police.'

Jane shrugged, repeating, 'All will be well once you are returned to your time.'

'Wait!' A surge of hope spun through Rose. 'Can you take me back to the very moment we left yesterday?'

Jane, however, was shaking her head. 'The charm is not all-powerful, Rose. It has one function and one alone. It cannot move me from one location to another, be it through time or otherwise, and it does not permit me to choose the day of my arrival, merely moves me by year.'

Rose tried to grasp what she was saying. 'So... whatever the day and month it is, that remains the same wherever you go, forward or back? Only the year changes?'

'Indeed.' Jane brightened for a moment, and hope began to rise in Rose's breast again. 'Though if you wish to return to the exact day in September as you left, you have but to tarry here until next year.' She pursed her lips. 'Though I fear it will not be to Mama's liking.' She eyed Rose keenly. 'But I see this will not suffice. So be it. As soon as we have broken our fast on the morrow, we will consider the options.'

–

Rose tossed and turned in her small bed for what felt like hours, though probably was little more than one. The first night, she'd lay awake, her mind spinning, astounded by the strangeness and novelty of her situation. It was as if she'd landed in a dream (notwithstanding the fact she had to use a loo in the garden). She'd gone from being kissed by the man she'd been crushing on for three years to slipping through to the era and home of Jane Austen. Enough to keep anyone awake.

Yet now there was the added complexity of Christopher Wallace, who he was, and the possibility that, even now, the police were in her flat investigating her disappearance. How she longed for the simplicity of her old life!

She rolled over, her eyes straining against the inky darkness towards the wall beside her bed – a wall that, in the future, would display artefacts relating to Jane's sailor brothers.

With a sigh, she flopped over onto her back, kicking off the heavy coverlet. Wearing a full-length cotton nightgown, albeit with short sleeves, just felt like too many clothes to sleep in, never mind the cotton cap on top of her curls.

What time was it? With no clock in the room – not that she would be able to read its face in the darkness – there was no way of telling. Her lids dropped over eyes, scratchy with tiredness. She *had* to get some sleep. Without a clear mind, how on earth would she make any sense of what may happen tomorrow?

Rose's eyes flew open barely seconds later. Had she heard something? The sound came again and she sat up. Something had just hit the outside wall of her room.

With only the fire's glowing embers to guide her, Rose crept over to the window. After a moment's struggle with the iron bar holding the shutter closed, she managed to open it, only to let out a gasp as something hit her window.

Chapter 7

Rose edged closer and peered out, but with nothing but a partially clouded moon by way of lighting, it was impossible to see anything. But it had to be Aiden, didn't it? She lifted the catch and opened the window, longing for the torch on her phone as she leaned out.

'Aiden? Is that you?'

'*By a name; I know not how to tell thee who I am.*'

Rose let out a half sigh, half laugh. Was this really the time for Shakespeare? 'You'd better be who I think you are! Go into the garden.'

Rose grabbed the candle holder from her bedside table, lit the wick in the remains of the fire and shielded the flame as she hurried along the landing. The stairs had to be the noisiest she had ever stepped on, and she winced with every creak, dreading Jane's head appearing around her bedroom door, but all remained quiet.

She entered the dining room, wincing again as the door creaked loudly, and placed the candle holder onto a small dresser before wrestling with the bolts on the front door. Rose stepped outside into the cool night air, then walked along to the gate, into the garden, and had barely passed through it when she was caught up in a solid embrace.

'This feels so good.' Rose rested her head against Aiden's shoulder.

Aiden held her close for a moment. 'I'm sorry I couldn't find a way to come earlier. The brothers Austen keep a tight ship, though I get the impression Captain Austen would've been more helpful had Mr Knight not been there to keep an eye on me.'

Rose laughed softly. 'I always considered the rules of society so romantic in this era. Not any more. It's torture.'

She lifted her head and pulled back a little to look up at him as his arms released their hold on her. Her eyes had adjusted to the darkness now, the moonlight just sufficient for her to be able to make out his features at these close quarters.

His gaze travelled to her head, and Rose whipped the cap off. 'Whoops. Forgot about that!'

Aiden didn't smile, he simply ruffled her curls before taking her hands in his.

'How are you?' He inclined his head towards the dark section of garden, which bordered the Wallaces' residence.

'Stressed! Mainly about Morgan.'

'That wasn't quite what I meant.' He squeezed her hands gently. 'I was talking about what's happening here, not there, which we have no control over.'

Rose sighed, then nodded. 'I don't know how I feel. I go back and forth. One minute, I feel we shouldn't be here, that Jane is just imagining things. The next minute, I'm trying to sort out how I would feel to have half siblings and a stepmother who, to make it all the more incredible, just happens to live next door to Jane Austen.'

'There isn't much precedence on it I'm afraid.'

Rose held on tightly to his hands, her eyes never leaving his face. It gave her a strength and comfort she could never have imagined. 'I saw him.' Aiden's grip tightened. 'And it's an uncanny resemblance.'

'Did you speak to him?'

'Not yet.' Rose didn't want to think about the awkwardness of how it was going to be. 'To complicate things further, Jane reminded me the future or, well… our present, however you want to say it, is moving along without us. Which means Morgan is going to panic if she isn't already.'

'I had begun to wonder.'

'Jane dismisses it, saying all will be well once we are home, but she's not thinking about the distress and worry I'm causing Morgan in the meantime. We don't even know how long we'll be here. I'm supposed to be at my friend, Liz's, engagement party on Sunday too!' Rose bit her lip. 'And what about *your* life? Your work, family…' Her voice tailed away. And who else? She knew so little about Aiden; who was dear to him? 'I wanted to talk to you, to see if you had all the information and measurements you wanted down at the church, because I really think we'd better get back.'

'We'll just have to deal with the consequences when we go home later.' Aiden held her gaze, his thumb stroking the back of her hand. 'You're ready to abandon the mystery?'

'No, yes… It depends on the moment you ask me.' Rose sighed again. 'Now I know how all this works, maybe I can come back after I've reassured Morgan – and we've made sure your car isn't clamped or stolen.'

Aiden shrugged. 'I didn't see any notices. Besides, it's only a car. You don't think Morgan will simply think I've whisked you off your feet?'

'She doesn't even know you… that, er… we've… um.'

'Found each other?'

Rose smiled up at Aiden. 'Exactly.'

He leaned closer. 'Remind me how that happened again.'

There was something incredibly romantic, despite the circumstances, in being held in Aiden's embrace, dressed as he was, and by the time he released her, Rose's mind was blissfully blank. 'I should get back inside before I ruin your reputation.'

Aiden laughed, low and quiet. 'Perish the thought. But actually, I came here for reasons other than attempting to sully your maidenhood. The brothers are going to call on their mother in the morning. If you come up beforehand—'

'I'm not sure if Jane and Cassandra will be busy with chores – or in Jane's case, writing.'

'Even better. If it's just you, we can walk back together. I think we can rely on Captain Austen to keep Mr Knight a few paces back. If you want to, that is.'

'It'll be perfect. Jane said she'll talk to me in the morning about how we can try to sort all this out. I should be able to update you.' Rose tried not to think about her sore feet, which were groaning at her betrayal. She smiled up at him, then shivered, the cool air caressing her bare arms. 'I'd best go in. Thank you for giving me the chance to sleep tonight.'

'At your service.' Aiden clicked his heels together and bowed, and they turned to walk back to the gate, hand in hand.

At the corner of the house, he leant down to kiss her once more, and Rose held on to him, wishing he didn't have to go.

'I'll see you tomorrow.'

Reluctantly, Rose released his hand. Then, she brightened. 'If we go back in the morning, we could spend the whole day together. Well, until the ball.' *After Morgan stops hyperventilating.* Would Rose tell her where she'd been? Perhaps she'd just distract her with the understanding she and Aiden had come to. After all, Rose's crush on Aiden had been a frequent and much obsessed over topic between the two friends.

Aiden's gaze held hers briefly. 'We'll spend much more than a day together, Rose Wallace. I promise you that.'

Rose could feel warmth filling her cheeks, not trusting herself to say anything else and conscious of his eyes on her as she walked back to the door. He raised a hand in farewell as she stepped over the threshold, and was quickly enveloped by the darkness.

Closing the door and replacing the bolts as quietly as she could, Rose turned to face the room. *Please let Mrs Austen be a heavy sleeper*, she prayed fervently, as she picked up her now guttering candle and headed back to bed.

–

Rose felt a little less trepidation on entering the dining room the following morning, knowing more of what to expect from the household ritual of breakfast and therefore able to greet Jane, Cassandra and Mrs Austen with a smile.

'I trust you slept well?' There was twinkle in Jane's eye, and Rose hurriedly took her seat.

'Perfectly well, thank you.'

'Would you care for some toast, Miss Wallace?' Cassandra offered her a plate and Rose took a slice. 'Do you wish for chocolate again, or would you prefer tea?'

'Oh, tea, please.'

Mrs Austen, who was eyeing Rose over the rim of her cup, lowered it, assessing her guest with a keen stare.

'Pray, how long do we have the pleasure of your company, Miss Wallace?'

'Mama!' Cassandra looked uncomfortable, but Mrs Austen was unfazed.

'Beyond our immediate family, my dear Cass, we barely entertain here, beyond Miss Benn's occasional visits. I wish to ascertain we have adequate sufficiency, for our pocket does not.'

'Indeed.' Jane opened a corner cupboard and pulled out a long, metal fork. 'For we are all single women with a propensity for being poor.' She winked at Rose. ''Tis a strong argument in favour of matrimony, is it not?'

Mrs Austen ignored her daughter and turned her attention back to Rose, who placed her own cup on the table and rested her hands in her lap, ready for whatever was coming. 'Will you be passing the winter with us?'

Rose's eyes widened. 'No! At least, not at all, Mrs Austen. I believe I will be leaving—'

'More toast, Rose— I mean, Miss Wallace?' Jane all but tipped a piece of barely browned bread from her toasting fork onto Rose's plate, then turned to her mother. 'With Martha absent, it does not signify we have an extra mouth to feed, Mama.'

'Hmm.' Mrs Austen applied herself to her toast. 'I anticipate word from her shortly on when she will return. Perhaps Miss Wallace will have other friends she can impose upon when she does.' Then, she frowned, grabbing the toasting fork from Jane's grasp. 'What is the meaning of this?'

Jane held her mother's gaze steadily, and Cassandra looked from one to the other.

'It skewers bread and holds it in the flame, turning the bread to toast, hence its name.'

'I comprehend its purpose, Jane, as well you know. *This,*' she tossed the fork onto the table, 'is the old one we discarded. Where is the silver one?'

'Perchance it has gone the way of the missing cream jug and the salver.'

Cassandra shook her head at her sister, then turned to placate their mother, and Jane cast Rose a swift glance, a smile twitching her lips.

Once the ritual of breakfast was over, Rose went up to her room to get ready for the walk up to Chawton House. Her head had felt much clearer when she had woken, partly from having several hours of sleep and partly from having seen Aiden. The moment she was alone, however, everything she'd tried to hold at bay crowded into her head, and she sank onto the bed, the shoes she was resisting wearing clasped in one hand.

How could she possibly satisfy both things concerning her – her friend's distress and this potentially massive thing about Mr Wallace? Besides, she didn't know what Jane's suggestions were going to be; if Rose went back and calmed her friend down, what was she *then* to do? She could hardly turn around and head straight back through time with Jane to resolve whatever this dilemma was here in the past, could she?

Morgan would assume things would go back to normal; they'd go to the ball, finish attending the *Festival* together. Her rental of the holiday apartment only ran until the following Monday morning, after all, and Morgan needed to prepare for her new life in Bath.

Rose bent down and slipped her feet into the shoes, wincing a little. She'd have to bear it – she was unlikely to find a Regency plaster any time soon. She stood up, testing the feel of them, but to her relief, they felt easier, and she picked up the shawl and bonnet leant to her the previous day and opened the door.

Perhaps this was the answer. Morgan was real, her best friend, someone she would never want to hurt, someone she'd hate to cause worry or concern to. She didn't know her father; he'd left her life long before she could ever remember him. Whoever this Christopher Wallace was, he could be nothing more than a distant ancestor. How could that even compare to her friendship with Morgan?

Feeling reconciled, Rose hurried along the landing, down the stairs and into the dining room. Jane must have finished tidying away the breakfast things, for the table was cleared, the fire nicely stoked and there was no one in sight. She was about to turn for the door into the small vestibule when she caught a movement from the corner of her eye and, turning around, she saw a dog curled up on the cushion she'd noticed the day before.

Stepping closer, Rose stared at the dog, then crouched down and whispered, 'Prancer?'

The dog's eyes opened and its head shot up, and she reached out a tentative hand for it to sniff before stroking its head. 'I'm so glad you're okay.'

'He is a playful companion.'

Rose straightened up. Cassandra had come into the room, and she walked over to join her as they both looked down at the dog, who had gone back to sleep.

'I am so glad you found Prancer, Miss Austen – not just for the obvious reason, but also because I felt so bad for his owner in the… well, you know.'

'Indeed.' Cassandra's smile was a little strained. 'Those were difficult times, but though I feared I might never see my sister again, I at least knew where she was.'

Rose followed her over to the window and for a moment they both stared out at the fine September day.

'It is not so for your friend, is it?' Cassandra turned to Rose. 'She has no idea where you have gone.'

'No.' Rose glanced at the clock on the mantel. 'Where is Miss Jane?'

An evasive look crossed Cassandra's features, and she turned away, then said over her shoulder as she left the room, 'Excuse me, Miss Wallace. I am needed in the bakehouse. As for Jane, I believe she walked down to get the post.'

Rose followed slowly in Cassandra's wake. Didn't Jane walk to Alton for that? She would be gone for the best part of an hour. Should she walk up to Chawton House now, and talk to Jane about going back when she returned? Rose paused as she came to the boot room door through which Cassandra had just left, staring down the garden.

In the cold light of a new day, her foolish doubts over this man being her father had receded. How could she give it any credit? A smile reminiscent of her father's from an old photo? The fact this man was called Christopher? It was all conjecture, coincidence, and everyone knew life was full of those.

Despite the thoughts swirling round in her head, Rose enjoyed the walk through Chawton to the great house. Used to living alone and therefore a certain amount of her own company, she was finding the constant companionship of the Austen ladies a little wearing, despite the care Jane was showing her and the kindness emanating from her sister.

Aiden must have been looking out for her. She had barely reached the steps leading up to the front door when he came out to meet her, and her conflicted thoughts faded for a moment. He was wearing yet another coat and waistcoat and looked so at home in them; so much more than she felt in her own borrowed clothes. She was going to miss seeing him dressed like this.

'They will be with us soon. Mr Knight was giving some instructions to his housekeeper and the captain had a letter to write.'

Her hand drifted towards his, but then, realising what she was doing, Rose's arm fell to her side.

Aiden peered over her shoulder. 'Did I miss something? Is Miss Austen at large with her bucket?'

Rose shook her head. 'No. I'm just trying to remember her advice.'

'Did you sleep?'

She nodded. 'I'm not sure when I finally drifted off, but I definitely got a few hours.'

'I'm glad you managed to escape alone this morning.'

'Cassandra seemed to have a morning's baking in mind. Thankfully, they haven't yet asked me to try my hand.'

'It's not your forté, then?' He grinned. 'Nor mine! Though I can cook – I make a mean chilli con carne if you ever want one.'

Rose laughed. 'I'll take you up on it once we're… home.' She sobered. 'Jane took herself off to get the post this morning, so I've yet to hear what her ideas are on getting us back today.'

'I'm not sorry. I really did want some time alone with you.'

'Good morning, Miss Wallace.'

They both started and took an instinctive step away from each other as Charles Austen strode down the steps and performed a smart bow.

'Good morning, Captain Austen.' Rose did her best to curtsey, feeling horribly self-conscious.

'It is a fine morning for a stroll, is it not?' He waved a hand at the autumnal sunshine bathing the grounds in soft golden light. The watery blue sky sported barely a wisp of cloud, and the only sound was birdsong from the distant treetops.

Rose sighed. It was all so tranquil. How could she be harbouring such turmoil inside?

'Miss Wallace?'

'Forgive me, sir. My mind is somewhat distracted.'

Charles Austen eyed Rose with sympathy. 'Of course.' He glanced at Aiden, whose gaze remained fixed on Rose. 'Why do you not set off? I will seek my brother and we will follow on directly.' He waved a hand at them and turned and took the steps back into the house two at a time.

They did as they were bid, with Aiden offering Rose his arm, and she took it thankfully.

'Any further revelations this morning?'

'Not really, but I'm completely at odds with myself. My head keeps telling me the facts: Morgan is what matters. She's real, she's my friend. I must go back to reassure her I'm not dead or worse.'

'And?'

'I can't rid myself of the *what if* in all of this. If we weren't here…' Rose's voice tailed off as they passed through the gate and St Nicholas' Church loomed to their left. 'The fact is – and it is *fact* – we *are* here. We are living the impossible, so how can I say anything is no longer a possibility?'

They continued in silence for a few paces, and then Aiden glanced over his shoulder.

'The gentlemen are behind us but some paces away. They will hear nothing of what we say.'

Rose drew in a long breath of the still-cool morning air as they reached the road and turned their steps to the right.

'So, continue. It might help to talk about it, and I know there isn't much chance at the cottage, with Mrs Austen not knowing what's going on.'

With relief, Rose took Aiden at his word, spilling out all the confusion that had filled her mind since seeing Christopher Wallace on the previous evening. He said nothing, but let her keep talking until she ran out of words.

Then, he stopped walking and turned her to face him. He cast a quick glance back towards the men, before taking Rose's hand.

'They will have to bear with me, I'm afraid. I find it incredibly hard not to hold your hand.' Rose smiled, despite her agitation. 'You're waffling. I'm not surprised, your head must be all over the place, but let's examine what we have.'

Rose glanced back at the approaching men. 'Can we walk on? I don't want them to catch up.'

'Of course.' Aiden placed Rose's hand back on his arm and they resumed their walk. 'Go on.'

'Morgan and I are very close. But this is the first time we've met and I can't just abandon her. Jane needs to get us back.'

'And where is Miss Austen now, Rose?'

Rose stared along the road. 'Alton?' But was she? Cassandra had seemed evasive, and Jane had had an air of mischief about her at breakfast.

They were not far from the patch of land belonging to the cottage, the land where, in the future, Aiden's car waited for them. Then, Rose's heart leapt into her throat, and she gripped Aiden's arm. Coming towards them, albeit on the opposite side of the road, were Christopher Wallace and his wife.

Rose turned frantically to Aiden. 'Help me. What do I do?'

'Stay calm. We just incline our heads – we aren't acquainted, we don't need to speak.'

They began to walk again, but before they had gone two paces, a voice came from behind them.

'Ah, Wallace, well met!'

Glancing over her shoulder, Rose saw Charles Austen, with his brother in tow, striding across the dirt road to reach the other side just before a coach and horses rumbled past. The ensuing dust and noise was sufficient distraction for a moment, and Rose blinked, trying to clear her eyes. Then, to her dismay, Charles turned and beckoned to them both.

'Come, it is time you made some new acquaintances.'

Rose froze. 'I can't. Aiden, I need to…'

But it was too late to back down. The two parties of people were already moving towards each other to become one.

'Mr Wallace, Mrs Wallace, permit me to introduce some of our friends to your acquaintance; they are come from Bath to make some stay with my sister, Jane.'

Acknowledgements were exchanged and Mr Wallace addressed Aiden. 'And how has your visit to Hampshire been thus far, sir?'

Rose tried not to blatantly stare at him as Aiden exchanged a glance with her, then cleared his throat.

'Quite enlightening, Mr Wallace. This is not a place I have had the pleasure of visiting before.'

The man smiled, and Rose tried not to see a likeness, but then something caught her eye and her gaze was drawn to the orchard where Cassandra's bee hives nestled. She blinked twice, very deliberately. Was she hallucinating now?

From behind a tree had stepped a rather disgruntled-looking Jane Austen, along with a young woman who was fidgeting with her clothing, a young woman who was achingly familiar.

Chapter 8

Rose's mind went blank for a second, then began to spin. She was aware of voices around her, of Charles and Edward speaking to the Wallaces, of the latter moving away down the road, but though she heard voices around her, she couldn't distinguish any words. Morgan was *here*?

Her heart thumping in her chest, Rose turned frantically towards the three remaining men. 'Excuse me. I'm so sorry, I must… go.'

Leaving Aiden to cover for her, Rose walked as fast as she could in her long skirts towards the newest resident of 1813, only to find Jane, in just as much of a hurry, coming towards her along the road.

'Before you speak a word, Rose, this was not my intention! Your colonist—'

Morgan was looking back towards the tree from round which she had emerged, and Rose gasped, a hand flying to her mouth as she walked. James Malcolm, her straight-as-a-die, fully grounded boss, half dressed and dishevelled, was here too!

'Oh my God, Jane! What did you *do*?' Before Jane could answer, Rose had hurried past her towards her friends, who seemed now to be in urgent discussion.

Jane, almost as tall as Rose and with a similar stride, kept pace with her. 'I did not expect to come across them. Yet there they were, standing in the car park, not far from where they are now. It seemed the perfect opportunity to speak with your friend, assuage any concerns she may have had – to ensure you had the time you needed to resolve the situation with your... with Mr Wallace. After the past four and twenty hours, I feared your intent was to use Miss Taylor's potential distress as a way out of your current dilemma, and I believed—'

'We'll discuss my issues later.' Rose threw Jane an exasperated look as they reached the orchard. 'Right now, would you care to tell me how your attempt to reassure my friend turned into *this*?'

Jane stayed Rose with her hand. 'I will, but I believe you must first address your friends' needs.' She inclined her head towards Morgan, who stood beside James. Looks of utter confusion were on their faces.

Rose sped across the grass, her emotions almost rivalling those from her first ever meeting with Morgan. Had that really only been a week ago?

Morgan held up her trailing skirts, her face transforming from bemused to delighted as she skipped towards her, almost falling in the process. 'Where have you *been*? We tracked your phone to Chawton but... are you all right?'

Rose hugged her tightly, her throat so taut she could barely speak. 'I'm fine.' She tried to smile as they released each other. 'Oh Morgan...' At a loss, she stepped back, and looked over at James.

He potentially would look very handsome in Regency garb, but for some reason, he wasn't fully dressed, sporting some breeches and a coat, which he was attempting to hold closed across his bare chest. His feet were likewise unshod.

Torn between concern and amusement, Rose raised her eyes to his as she began to accept what she saw.

James looked less satisfied. 'Okay, this is pretty impressive. How did you pull this off? Where are my shoes?' He touched the breeches gingerly. 'And my suit? I just had it cleaned—'

This was going to take some explaining! Rose turned to Jane as she joined them, her look uncompromising.

'I came out of the museum and there they were.' Jane shrugged lightly. 'There seemed some fascination with Mr Trevellyan's conveyance. It seemed the most fortunate circumstance, thus I hurried over to pass on whatever reassurance I could to your friend.' She glared at James. 'The gentleman would give me no audience, but your friend...'

'Hey, where are my keys? I was just holding them.' James bent down to look at the ground.

Rose glanced at Morgan, but her attention had drifted as she looked around. A split second later, Morgan swung around and pointed at Jane. 'You *are* Jane Austen!' She paused, frowning. 'You look older than Crazy Jenny, though!'

Jane rolled her eyes, but Rose grabbed Morgan's hand, her voice low as she glanced around. 'Yes, she is. And you've just arrived in Chawton in 1813.'

Conscious James was looking from Rose to Jane to Morgan in disbelief, Rose turned back to her friend.

'Trust me, Morgan. And you really have to pretend to be a normal English lady from the early nineteenth century.'

Morgan looked taken aback. 'But I don't know how to *do* that. How long have you known... you *have* known, haven't you? That's why you've been so weird about Crazy

Jenny.' Morgan looked to Jane apologetically, but then her eyes, already large, went round as saucers. 'Is that *Aiden*?'

Rose glanced over her shoulder and sighed. Aiden, Edward and Charles were making their way across the field towards them. She took Morgan's hands in her own. 'Listen, there is so much I have to tell you, but I need you to be patient. Please? Just smile and nod?'

Morgan opened her mouth to speak then closed it, and Rose whispered, 'Thank you.'

She turned to James. Years of working with him had convinced her that he, not her exuberant American friend, was going to be the tough one to get through this initial set of introductions.

'James.' She spoke firmly. 'I know you think this is all some sort of trick. Can you please just go with it until we can sit down and talk?'

'Did you do this?' James gestured down at his appearance. 'Is this because I refused to get dressed up for the ball? How did you—?'

Rose put a finger to her lips and thankfully, James stopped, then noticed the approaching men.

'Oh good, more characters.' James frowned as the men neared them, then tugged at his coat and leaned down towards Rose. 'Is this one of those Jane Austen Murder Mystery Adventures?' He looked up. 'Aiden... mate! How the hell did they talk you into this?'

They instinctively shook hands, even as Aiden raised a brow at Rose, as if to say, *How did this happen?*

Rose lifted her hands, and Aiden eyed James' attire before putting a hand on his shoulder. 'We need to talk, pal.'

Morgan looked between them and muttered to Rose, 'So should *we*.'

'What the devil is going on, Jane?' Edward Knight eyed the newcomers with distrust as he joined them, and Rose glanced over at Charles, who was at his side, but he was merely observing, a faint smile on his lips.

'Miss Taylor, Mr…' Jane looked at James, who stared blankly back. She tsked, and turned to Rose.

'Malcolm.'

'Thank you.' Jane resumed her introductions. 'Miss Taylor, Mr Malcolm, permit me to introduce two of my brothers to your acquaintance: Mr Edward Knight of Godmersham and Captain Charles Austen.'

Both brothers instinctively bowed, and Rose stared meaningfully at Morgan, who blinked, then roused herself, dropping an attempt at a curtsey.

James, however, looked from the gentlemen to Rose. 'Er, not sure if I'm playing the game, yet.'

Rose drew in a short breath. 'Jane?'

Jane waved an arm at Morgan and James. 'Miss Taylor would not accept my assurances you were well, insisted on seeing you, became very distressed. Reluctantly, I conceded. The gentleman,' she threw James a look, 'was harder to persuade. I do not think he believed me. He refused to change his clothes, merely attempted to humour me in donning these two items,' she gestured at James in his breeches and coat, 'over his own clothes. Miss Taylor was more obliging in both donning the attire and taking my hand as instructed, but as I dropped the chain about my neck, Mr Malcolm grabbed her arm. I had no idea it would work without intention!'

Edward looked astounded. 'Well, take them back, then!'

'I intend to!'

'Wait!' Rose and Morgan said at once, and Rose looked apologetically at the brothers. 'Please, can we just have a moment? I need to explain some things to my friend.'

Edward threw his sister a mocking glance. 'Yes, of course, because the more people who know about this, the better.'

Jane pinched his arm. 'Perhaps you should pay your call upon Mama, Edward? Charles? Let us give Miss Wallace some time to talk to her friends and it will surely set things to rights. Perchance the incident will prove serendipitous.'

Charles laughed. 'Indeed! How splendid is hindsight!'

Jane raised her chin. 'I am known for my keen intuition; it is often on the mark.'

She took Charles' arm and Edward, after eyeing the newcomers warily, fell into step behind them as they crossed the field towards the road. 'We shall have to up sticks and relocate the ever-increasing party to Kent if you insist on bringing the entire future nation of England back with you.'

'Rose, seriously, I need to know what's going on.' James stayed Rose with his hand on her arm as she began to lead them across the field.

Turning back, she summoned a smile. 'I know, James.' She looked at Morgan, who seemed torn between excitement and curiosity. 'Please, let's just get somewhere a bit more...' She gestured at his state of dress. 'Suitable.'

Nothing more was said as Rose and Aiden led Morgan and James across the road, a precarious enough challenge, with the conditions underfoot, but even more so for her boss in his bare feet. She ushered them through the gate into the garden of the cottage, Morgan's eyes roaming from left to right.

'It's so different to when we were here a few days ago!'

Rose smiled. 'I know. Come on.'

She led them down a gravel path until they were out of sight of the house. It wouldn't do for the Austens' few servants to see them. The walk, however, led Rose no closer to understanding what on earth she was going to say to her friend and boss to explain how they came to be where they were.

They came to a part of the orchard where there was a bench, and Morgan, whose dress was far too long for her and caused her to stumble frequently, dropped onto it with a relieved look on her face. Rose felt too agitated over how to explain the situation to sit still, and remained stood beside Aiden.

'Are my keys over here? Bloody hell, they nicked my mobile too? My wallet had better still be where I left it in the car! I really don't have the time for this. How did you get my socks off?' James gestured at his now filthy feet.

'There's a water butt by the shed.' Rose gestured back down the garden, and James just stared at her blankly.

'Just tell me what this is, so I can get my things back and go home and take a shower.'

'Look James, I can explain—'

'Rose,' Morgan hissed. 'Don't look now, but there's an old servant over there, watching us!'

Rose looked around. Morgan was pointing over towards a vegetable patch on the opposite side of the garden, and she spun back to face her friend.

'Shh… That's not a servant. It's Mrs Austen!'

Morgan's eyes widened. 'Why is she dressed like that?'

'Cassandra says she loves to garden; tends to wear overalls when she does. It's a bit eccentric, but…' Rose glanced anxiously over to where the lady had been digging up potatoes, but thankfully, the manservant, William, had hailed her – no doubt to tell her she had callers – and she was already entering the back of the house. 'Please, James. Sit.' Rose gestured at the place beside Morgan, but James didn't move until her friend grabbed his arm and pulled him down next to her.

'We need some answers, Rose. This is…' He gestured around them. 'Beyond weird.'

'I know.' Rose drew in a shallow breath. How on earth could she begin? She reached out her hand to Aiden, who grasped it, and Morgan's mouth dropped open.

Rose smiled faintly. 'Later. I'm sure you have a shed-load of questions, but there's a lot I need to tell you both too. I think if I go first, I may answer some of them?'

Morgan nodded expectantly, and James looked from Rose to Aiden, then sighed. 'Go for it.'

'Something happened to me last week, something neither of you has any knowledge of. Morgan knew I had some suspicions about my upstairs neighbour at home. You've seen with the evidence of your own eyes now, she really *is* Jane Austen.'

'But—'

'Please, James. Let me finish?'

He held Rose's gaze for a moment, then Morgan took his hand and he nodded.

'She had slipped through time to the present. It seems she makes a bit of a habit of it. You'll have seen how, by now.'

'The necklace? It's like ours!' Morgan beamed, and Rose could feel some of the tension in her shoulders easing. How much better did she feel now Morgan was here?

'Yes, similar. None of us ever knew there were three; it's how Jane slips through time. Her brother – the naval captain you've just met – was told of its magical properties when he bought it for Jane.'

James looked sceptical, and Rose shook her head at him. 'You know it works. You know I'm telling the truth.'

'Come on, mate.' Aiden gestured at James' appearance. 'Can you think of a better explanation for how you're here and your underwear isn't?'

Rose covered her amusement with a cough, but Morgan burst out laughing, and Rose watched James as he considered all he had just experienced. Finally, he nodded reluctantly.

'Well then, you remember when I left you both, outside the Pavilion on Sunday after the dance class?'

They both nodded in unison, and Aiden gave Rose's hand a reassuring squeeze, which she returned.

'Something happened after I ran after Jane, or Jenny as we then thought of her.'

It took Rose the better part of an hour to tell them how she'd become trapped in an alternate reality, lost to her friends as she knew them. They had so many questions for her, and even Aiden, who'd not heard about it in detail, was eager to learn more. By the time she'd explained how a different Morgan, herself and Jane had managed to turn things around, her throat was dry, but she felt reasonably confident Morgan believed her, though James looked to be in an even deeper state of shock.

She didn't want to say anything about her walk with Aiden, the one where they'd realised they both had feelings for each other, so she glossed over it, leading into Jane's rcappearance and their journey back through time.

Rose had been pacing to and fro as she talked, pausing only to answer a question here and there, but now she returned to her place by Aiden's side and faced her friends. 'I don't know if you'll ever forgive me for not telling you, when everything went back to normal. My only defence is that I honestly couldn't imagine you'd believe me. But I have to admit,' her voice broke and Aiden put his arm around her briefly, 'it's so wonderful to see your faces and to have you know the truth.'

Morgan stood up, tripped on her hem and almost fell, laughing, into Rose's arms as she hugged her. 'I'm terribly sad that you went through that relatively alone, but glad that fate is determined our friendship is meant to be.'

'You're not upset?' Rose was holding back tears of relief.

'I am!' Morgan stepped back. 'But not *at* you. After all, I did get to be part of the adventure, just not *me* me. Hey, how was my hair?'

Rose gave a watery laugh. 'Your hair was a bit different – you wore it up, mostly, but you also wore fake glasses so people would take you more seriously.'

Morgan tilted her head to one side. 'Were they cute?'

Rose sniffed away the threat of tears, feeling lighter than she had in days, but still conscious she'd said nothing to Morgan about why Jane had brought her back. 'Yes, you pillock!'

With a grin, Morgan resumed her seat beside James and patted his knee. 'I might try that.' She turned to him. 'Will you still love me in glasses?'

James looked from her to Rose, then to Aiden. 'You're all treating this as some sort of joke. This is… this is…'

Aiden shrugged. 'Incredible?'

'Yes, no… I don't know. I mean, it's not even possible, *any* of it.' He eyed Rose warily. 'We've put our faith in a magical necklace that apparently didn't come with an instruction book. Just how reliable is it?'

With a laugh, Aiden gestured at James' attire. 'I don't think you really put your faith in it, did you?'

With a rueful smile, James looked down at his clothing. 'I didn't believe for a minute Morgan was going anywhere, despite what the mad… I mean, Jane Austen, said. I threw these on over my clothes just to pacify her.'

'It's a seriously good thing you did.' Morgan smirked.

'But we need to go back. She can just take us back, right?' James looked from Rose to Aiden.

'Why don't we ask her?'

Aiden gestured down the path. Coming towards them was Jane, a long coat over her arm, followed by Cassandra, her face alive with curiosity and a pair of boots in her hand.

As they all set off back along the path towards the ladies, Rose cast an anxious glance back towards the other end of the garden.

Chapter 9

It didn't take long for the introductions to take place between Cassandra and the two new arrivals, and despite the situation Rose couldn't help but be amused by the avid interest on both hers and Morgan's faces as they realised who each other was.

Both the Austen ladies seemed keen for James to cover himself up, and urged him to don the boots and greatcoat (the former borrowed from William, the latter left behind by Jane's brother, Henry, on his last visit from London), and he had barely done so when Rose saw Edward Knight coming towards them.

He eyed James keenly. 'An improvement, but we shall have to do better. You had best come with me, sir.'

James' startled gaze flew to Rose. 'But I have to get back! I can't stay here!'

'Pray, do not take on so, Mr Malcolm.' Jane came to stand before him. 'I shall do as you wish, and return you both to your home directly, but we cannot repeat the recklessness of our recent adventure, for our arrival was almost witnessed. We must wait until darkness falls.'

Edward grunted. 'You would do well to not repeat your foolish adventure at all.'

Jane turned away, but not before she had exchanged a small smile with Rose.

'One should not travel such a distance on an empty stomach either.' Edward's gaze roamed over the gathered party; then, he sighed. 'The cottage cannot accommodate such numbers. You had best dine at the great house before you leave.'

'Thank you.' Rose spoke a little more loudly than usual in an attempt to cover Morgan's 'Oooo!' and her friend caught herself, curtsied out of turn and muttered her thanks.

'I will collect Charles and meet you at the gate, sir. Mr Trevellyan?' Edward turned to Aiden. 'You will accompany your friend.'

It wasn't so much a question as an instruction, and Aiden bowed. 'As you wish, sir.'

Morgan's eyes were darting from Edward to James to Aiden and then back again as she took everything in, and Rose touched her arm.

'This is awesome!' Morgan's excitement was almost tangible as she turned to Rose. 'We're going to dine in that big house we did the tour of last week!'

'I will see you later.' Aiden's voice in her ear had Rose spinning around to look at him. He smiled reassuringly. 'It will be okay. Jane will get them home. Make the most of your afternoon with Morgan.'

Morgan was looking between them with renewed fascination, and he smiled at her before turning to join Edward as he made his way back down the garden.

James hesitated before following them, and Rose thought for a moment he was going to protest again, and insist on being taken home immediately. To her surprise, however, he turned to Jane.

'I'd like to apologise to you for my attitude earlier. I didn't believe what you were saying or even *in* you.'

103

He glanced at Rose, then bowed awkwardly to Jane. 'I hope you'll excuse me; the circumstances were rather… demanding.'

Jane studied him in silence for a moment, and Rose held her breath. ''Tis quite forgotten, sir, and you do yourself a disservice. Your concern for your friends is admirable. Rashness is much in the common way when one's loved ones are under a perceived threat.' She cast a look at Morgan, who was wrinkling her nose and frowning, then turned back to him with a sigh. 'Such disruption was never my intention. The best of deeds can go awry, can they not?' She smiled. 'Come, Mr Malcolm. I find I can forgive your impertinence if you can forgive my impetuousness.'

Rose bit her lip. She could tell James was trying to be certain he knew exactly what the lady stood before him was saying, but then he smiled too, performed a much neater bow and turned to Morgan.

'I hope to be in a better state when I see you later.' He dropped a kiss on her cheek and, ignoring Jane's tsk, raised a hand to Rose before turning to follow the others.

Watching him go, Rose could feel agitation seeping into her shoulders again. Morgan didn't seem to have picked up on Aiden's words, implying only James and Morgan would be leaving. Should they just go back and be done with it? But what if… She felt restless and out of sorts again. How was she to even unravel *any* of this mess?

'What's that smell?' Morgan was pulling a face.

'Partly it's the manure on the fields, only it's a bit more pungent than we're used to.' Rose lowered her voice. 'Wait until you smell some of the food.'

'What's the other part?'

Cassandra, who had remained silent for some time, smiled kindly at Morgan. 'It is best you do not comprehend the source, Miss Taylor. There is much to adjust to.'

'Luckily, I'm not here for long, no offence.' Morgan winked at Rose.

Rose tried to smile as the tension in her shoulders increased. Despite being thankful she'd had the chance to tell Morgan and James about what had happened to her the previous week, and grateful as she was for their seeming to accept the validity of where they were and how they'd got there, there was so much more to tell.

'I think we may need to make some adjustments to Miss Taylor's gown before this evening, Cass.' Jane gestured towards Morgan's hem, which she was currently standing on.

'I will see if we can find a better-fitting garment for her.' Cassandra gave them an all-embracing smile and turned to head back to the house.

Rose stood quietly between Jane and Morgan, watching her go. The weather was perfect, the sky the watery blue so typical of autumn, a gentle breeze weaving through the leaves hanging perilously on to the branches of the nearby trees.

Then, Morgan slapped Rose's arm.

'Ow!'

Morgan was grinning from ear to ear, looking much more herself. 'You and *Aiden!* Tell me. Now.'

'Oh, that.' Rose glanced at Jane, who raised a brow.

'I do not believe I have been told this particular story either.'

Warmth filled Rose's cheeks under Morgan's determined gaze and Jane's curious one. 'I don't know how to start. And I'm not going to kiss and tell!'

'Which means you've definitely been kissing.' Morgan and Jane exchanged a knowing look.

'Indeed. I confess I have been a witness.'

Morgan laughed delightedly and clapped her hands together, then met Rose's gaze and laughed again. 'There I go again! So? Forget the kiss, tell us all.'

Rose gestured vaguely down the path Aiden had recently trod. 'There's not a lot to say, really. After you left us outside your apartment, he walked me home and we…' Rose looked from Morgan to Jane, then shrugged. 'We found out we had a mutual…'

'Admiration?' suggested Jane.

'You *both* fancy each other! I *told* you!' Morgan punched a fist in the air, then, at Jane's look, dropped her arm to her side. 'Sorry. Getting a bit carried away.'

Rose sank onto the bench Morgan and James had recently vacated. 'I couldn't quite believe it. In fact, we'd barely had a moment to accept it when…' Her gaze fell on Jane, who grimaced apologetically.

'Forgive me; I had no notion of your attachment being so recently formed.'

Rose shook her head. 'I know.' Then she looked at Morgan. 'It's incredible and wonderful and at the same time like a dream I can't wake up from. Like so many things recently.' She looked at Jane, then raised her hands in a helpless gesture. 'How did this become my life? Two weeks ago, I didn't think Aiden knew my name, I was worried Morgan and mine's friendship might not work in person, and I spent most of my free time daydreaming over what life would be like living inside the pages of a Jane Austen novel.' Rose waved a hand, embracing her surroundings and the two young women before her. 'Now, I'm having a hard time not thinking of what Aiden and I could name our children, my best friend is flat hunting in my home town, and my favourite author cares so much about me, she kidnapped two people I love and brought them to the past.'

Jane made a small sound. 'It was never my intention, Rose.' She glanced at Morgan, then smiled. 'But nonetheless, I am pleased for you it has happened.'

'Aww, you know what she means.' Morgan put her arm around Jane's shoulders and hugged her, prompting an expression on Jane's face Rose wished she could capture on her phone.

Then, Rose frowned. 'Wait. How did this happen anyway? Morgan, what on earth were you and James doing in the car park in Chawton? You should both be in Bath!'

'Your phone was in the trunk. I told you, I tracked it. I was so worried about you! Then, we got to the car, and James knew it was Aiden's and I thought he'd murdered you and we'd find your body in there!'

Jane's brows rose and she exchanged a look with Rose, who shook her head at Morgan. 'You watch too much CSI.'

Morgan grinned. 'I was so relieved when the trunk only held… well, a *trunk*!'

'And you, Jane?' Rose turned to the lady, who looked a little sheepish. 'What made you travel to the future again?'

'I had… an engagement I was obliged to attend.'

Rose frowned. 'What sort of engagement?'

'She came over from the museum.' Morgan beamed at Jane. 'I was so relieved to see her.'

Jane stepped away. 'I must leave you. If we are all to dine with Edward, we need to hem whatever skirt Cass has found.' She turned away, then said over her shoulder,

'Rose, if you could bring Miss Taylor to my bedroom? We had best conceal our practice from Mama.'

She hurried down the path, and Rose sighed. What had Jane been up to?

'Hey.' Morgan came to sit beside her, bundling her skirts into her lap. 'You okay?'

Rose nodded. 'Yes, I'm fine.' She summoned a smile, trying to push away the anxiety crowding in upon her. Time was ticking away, and so was the day. If Jane was intending to take James and Morgan back, she'd better make the most of the time, especially if she might go with them.

'Come on.' Rose got to her feet. 'We need to make you presentable if we're to dine at the great house.'

–

Rose smiled as she perched on a chair in Jane's room. Morgan had such joy for life, she was already embracing her sudden appearance in 1813, questioning both Jane and Cassandra on etiquette, and constantly having to be told to remain still on the low stool she stood on so the latter could shorten the hem on the charming dress they had loaned her.

Jane, on the other hand, seemed to be avoiding Rose's eye, but she was determined to satisfy her curiosity.

'Why did you use the charm today, Jane?'

There was no response, and Cassandra nudged her sister. 'You had best speak of it. To be certain, in the circumstances, does Miss Wallace not have a right to comprehend your purpose?' She raised her kind eyes to Rose and smiled. 'I only wish *I* understood!'

Jane handed her sister another pin, then let out a huff of breath. 'As you wish.' She laid the remaining pins she held on the mantelpiece, rummaged in the sewing box and extracted a sharp, thin tool and walked over to where Rose sat.

'Raise your feet.'

Rose blinked. 'I beg your pardon?'

'Please be so kind as to do as I ask.'

Bewildered, Rose lifted her feet off the wooden floor, and Jane bent down and inserted the tool into a crack between two boards. With a swift flick of her hand, the board lifted to reveal the cavity below, and Jane straightened and stood back.

'There.'

Rose stared into the empty space. 'Where?'

Morgan twisted around on her pedestal. 'What's up?'

'Miss Taylor?' Cassandra gently turned Morgan back to face her.

'Oh! Sorry!' Morgan laughed. 'I have my back to you, Rose. You'll have to give me a running commentary.'

Eyeing Jane in confusion, Rose shrugged. 'You went forward in time to…' She stopped. Absolutely nothing came to mind.

Walking over to the bed, Jane reached under her pillow and extracted the pouch in which she kept the charmed necklace.

'You recall, do you not, the effect of the charm on the safe in Sydney Place, Rose?'

Rose cast her mind back to the previous week with little difficulty. 'Yes, of course. When the necklace was inside the safe, it created some sort of… portal through time.'

'Wow!' Morgan twisted round again, then turned back. 'Sorry, Ca— Miss Austen.'

'And thus you recall my use of it?'

Where was Jane going with this? 'You used it.' She glanced over at Cassandra, but she was busy threading a needle, the thread held between her teeth. 'You used it to exchange letters with your sister.'

'Indeed. And for what else do you recall?'

With a frown, Rose tried to focus on when she'd first met Jane in Bath and what she had told her. 'Only you could open the safe if the charm was inside?'

'This is also true. But that is not my meaning.'

'Must you tease so, Jane?' Cassandra's exasperation with her sister was evident, and Morgan glanced over her shoulder at Rose and winked. 'Can you not speak plainly and enlighten your friend?'

Jane made a small sound. Rose wasn't sure it hadn't been a suppressed snort, and she tried not to smile as Jane turned to face her. 'Do you recall how I was able to support myself in the future?'

'Oh! Yes. You brought things with you from the past and sold them in the future, where they had a much higher value, at the antiques centre in Bath.' Rose looked at Cassandra, who nodded encouragingly. 'And sometimes, your sister placed things in the safe for the same purpose.'

With a smile, Jane nodded. 'It was a most satisfactory arrangement. As you know, I could not send things back to the past unless they had existed back then. Thus, Cass was also obliged to keep me supplied with paper and ink, that our correspondence could continue uninterrupted.'

'You know, you're probably causing all sorts of problems for people who try to date antiques... imagine having a two-hundred-year-old thingamabobber that's had a free ride through time.' Cassandra had urged Morgan to turn around on her perch, and she faced them now, her features alive with interest. 'Imagine the scandal!'

Jane raised a brow at Morgan, but continued. 'Since we are now in Chawton, I needed to find a similar... contrivance, a substitute for the safe.'

'So you can retrieve things to sell in the future when you stay for a while, like a toasting fork?'

Jane got to her feet, gesturing towards the hole in the floor. 'It was a simple but effective solution.'

Rose frowned. 'Was? And how does this explain *today*? What engagement did you have?'

'Maybe she was meeting with a secret lover,' piped up Morgan with a grin, but she sobered under Jane's quelling look, then shrugged. 'Well, I thought it was funny, anyway.'

Jane walked over to stare out of the window for a moment and said nothing. Then, she turned to face the room, leaning against the sill.

'I was discovered.'

'No!' Rose stared at Jane in disbelief. 'They knew who you *were*?'

Jane tutted. 'Do not be foolish, Rose. Why on earth would they suppose me to be... me?'

Morgan was looking from Rose to Jane. 'So what *do* you mean?'

Walking over, Jane picked up the scissors and offered them to her sister as she finished her sewing. 'I was about to lift the floorboard,' she gestured to the hole, 'in my bedroom when one of the... what is they call them? Volunteers walked in. I had to improvise, profess to a fascination with the flooring and the display cabinet in one the other bedrooms housing the items that had been discovered under the boards over time.'

Rose frowned again. 'But I still don't see how...'

'I was dressed much as I am today.' Jane waved a hand at her authentic clothing. 'They took me for a devoted follower... of myself.' With a laugh, Jane turned her now sparkling eyes on Rose. 'It was most amusing. They were inordinately impressed with my knowledge of both my home and Jane Austen.'

Cassandra turned Morgan about. 'It is comfortable, yes?' She held out a hand and Morgan stepped down from the stool.

'Awesome!' She did a twirl, the skirt skimming the floor but barely touching it. 'How do I look?'

'It becomes you very well, Miss Taylor.' Jane smiled, then turned to look at Rose. 'The lady who had come across me insisted on taking me to meet another lady, whom she explained was responsible for the volunteers. Hence my engagement earlier today.'

Rose was struggling to understand, but then realisation dawned and she started to shake her head in denial. 'You can't be... you're a *guide* at the museum?'

Jane beamed. 'Is it not both singular and invigorating? Did I not profess an interest in gaining an occupation when I believed myself stranded in the future? Now I have attended...' She hesitated. 'I forget the term...'

'An interview?' Rose spoke faintly. This was getting more ridiculous by the hour!

'Indeed. And now I am engaged and obliged to attend...' She reached down into the hole, which Rose had thought was empty, and withdrew a folded piece of parchment. 'Here it is. I wrote it down, lest I forgot. Twice a week for just a few hours.' She looked up. 'Is it not diverting?'

Rose got to her feet, a hand to her head. 'Oh yes. More than I can possibly say. I think... Morgan.' She turned to her friend, but Cassandra had now helped her into a spencer and was already busy adjusting the sleeve length. 'Do you mind if I wait in the garden for you?'

Morgan looked up and grinned. 'Not at all. I've got so many questions, I could stand here all day!'

Jane was busy replacing the floorboard, and Rose smiled faintly at her friend and hurried from the room.

Chapter 10

Rose headed back to the garden, trying not to think about Jane's latest escapade and the implications of what she was doing. There would be so much more to come: more explanations, more incredulous looks and reactions from her friends, and ultimately, decisions. Ambling along the path towards the orchard, her attempt to empty her mind was interrupted by a call.

'Miss Wallace!'

Turning around, she saw the cook beckoning her. 'Not the baking', she whispered to herself as she walked to meet her. 'Please, not the baking.'

Five minutes later, a relieved Rose was entering the kitchen garden, a basket on her arm and a pair of strange-looking iron clippers in her hand, with instructions to pick some beans and peas. Mrs Austen, it seemed, was not impressed with more visitors and felt Rose needed to earn her keep.

Bending to her task, Rose's mind bent likewise to the matter in hand. Was there really any reason not to return to her own time with her friends? And would Aiden come with her? She straightened, stretching her back, conscious of the stays digging into her ribcage. She certainly wouldn't miss the clothing! But Aiden… surely he'd come back? Much as he was fascinated by being able to walk inside some of the history he so loved, he had a job like all of them, a life to get back to. And what about them – did *they* have a future to get back to? It certainly felt like it.

Rose turned her attention back to the bean canes, and soon had enough in her basket to move along to where the peas were growing. They would be the last of the season, she supposed. It was hard to imagine being back in the busyness of Bath while amongst such a peaceful, rural scene – despite the country aromas.

Smiling, Rose walked back towards the path to the house, but then she paused. What about the unresolved matter of who Christopher Wallace really was? She bit her lip, the habitual swirling of her insides increasing as the conundrum returned to the forefront of her mind. What a fool she must have looked earlier. What must they think of her? Her distraction would have seemed rude, whatever century she was in.

She glanced over her shoulder towards the low wall at the far end of the garden separating the cottage from the Wallaces' house. What if Jane wasn't imagining or mishearing things? What if... Rose blew out a frustrated breath. It was all too complicated *and* too ridiculous!

She picked up the basket. Cook would be chasing her if she didn't hurry, but before she took more than a step, a faint sound reached her ears, of humming from the neighbouring garden. There was something vaguely familiar about the tune. Then, she smiled. Anne Wallace must be in her place beneath the tree where she'd first seen her.

Turning her steps towards the house, she hurried on, intent on her errand, but as she approached the door to the kitchen, she saw a slender figure with auburn hair open the small gate in the hedging, holding something in her arms: Prancer!

Rose walked to meet her, though the girl was having such a job holding onto the wriggling dog, she had yet to look up and see her.

'Be done, Link! You are home now.' She straightened up, having released her charge, who shot down the garden without a backward glance at his saviour. 'Oh! Forgive me!' She dropped a quick curtsey, colour filling her cheeks.

Rose reciprocated, her interest quickening. 'Thank you for bringing him home. Does he wander often?' For a second, Rose recalled Prancer's elderly owner's relief at no longer having to chase after him.

The girl – Olivia, Rose recalled – nodded, standing awkwardly by the gate. She looked about fourteen, but it was hard to tell, and she seemed incredibly shy. They had not been formally introduced. Was it inappropriate to even speak to her?

Then, Rose noticed the book tucked under her arm and, unable to help herself, pointed at it.

'What are you reading?'

Olivia's grey eyes widened, and she quickly hid it behind her back, the colour in her cheeks spreading down her neck, and Rose felt terrible.

'Forgive me? I do not mean to pry. I am a great reader, that is all, and curious.'

Olivia brought her arm around and held the book out to Rose, but didn't move from her position by the gate, and sensing the girl's reticence, Rose smiled warmly and stepped forward to take it.

Rose studied the title for a moment, then raised impressed eyes to Olivia. 'You read in French?' She looked at the spine again. 'This is *The Swiss Family Robinson*, is it not? I read this years ago and loved it!'

'But… it is published but a twelve month.' Olivia frowned. 'And the French version only this year. Did you read it in its original, in German?' She stopped, looking culpable. 'Forgive me, I do not mean to be impertinent.'

Realising her gaffe, Rose felt the easy colour filling her cheeks. Stupid mistake!

'You are quite correct. I am confusing it with another.' Rose handed the book back. 'Why did you wish to conceal it?'

Looking all the more uncomfortable, Olivia Wallace took a step backwards as if she would leave. 'I have been in the meadow down yonder. I like to go there to read.' She sighed. 'My mother does not entirely approve, but Papa says we must improve our minds by extensive reading as best we can. He is an avid reader and we are fortunate to have a large library at home.'

Trying not to think about the similarities between this man and herself, Rose summoned another smile. 'I mean no disrespect to your mother, but I think your father has the right of it in this particular matter.'

Silence descended on them both and, conscious she probably shouldn't even have indulged in this much conversation when unacquainted, Rose wasn't surprised when the girl took her leave.

'I must go, my sisters…'

'I think I just heard one of them – Anne, would it be?' Rose waved a hand towards the back of the garden. 'She was humming.'

Olivia stepped back through the gate, then turned to face Rose again. 'Indeed. She sings and hums the whole day long, even when she is reading. Excuse me, ma'am. I must away home or I shall be missed.'

With that, she was gone, and Rose turned back to the kitchen. That was two members of the family she had spoken to and both seemed charming. Was she drawn to them for this reason, or was it the chance – the ridiculous, outrageous chance – they were somehow related to her?

The afternoon passed relatively smoothly, and before long it was time to dress for the approaching dinner at Chawton House. Rose did her best to assist Morgan, but in the end, Cassandra took over otherwise, as Jane pointed out, the others would be eating dessert before they arrived.

Waiting for the ladies to join her, Rose wandered around the ground floor of the cottage, her eyes devouring every detail in the drawing and dining rooms, hoping against hope she would be able to commit things to memory so that next time she visited the museum, she could recall the differences. Would Jane be prepared to show her one of her manuscripts? Rose was gently running a hand over Jane's small writing table when she heard the clatter of footsteps on the stairs and Morgan burst into the room.

'Rose, I get to wear a bonnet! An actual *bonnet*, just like yours.'

Rose laughed, eyeing her friend in amusement. She was waving two bonnets in the air.

'Which should I wear? What I wouldn't give to show the ladies at the *Festival*!'

'This one.' Rose pointed to the smarter of the two. 'The evenings are cool. Did they sort the sleeves out on the spencer?'

'Yes! They're so kind.'

Rose glanced at her wrist, then sighed. 'I can't get used to not wearing a watch. Are we late?'

Morgan shook her head, dropping the excess bonnet onto a nearby chair. 'Can you do my ribbons?' She popped the other one on her head and Rose obliged. 'Jane and Cassandra are just getting ready themselves. They said they'd be with us… directly.' Morgan frowned but Rose laughed.

'Which means *not* directly, but at some time convenient to them. Reminds me of an old neighbour I had in Bathampton, who was forever saying she'd do something "just now". As a child, I found it so frustrating, hopping from foot to foot waiting on her.'

Morgan grinned, then walked over to the mirror above the mantelpiece to admire her appearance.

'Come on, let's go outside and wait.' Rose turned for the door and Morgan followed in her wake, and they strolled around the part of the garden nearest to the road, amusing themselves with comparing their memories of how it differed from when they'd visited the museum earlier in the week.

Rose was almost unaware of how much more bearable she was finding her situation now Morgan was with her. She looked around, delighting in the scene, thankful for having been given this unique chance to experience it, then turned to the nearby border of herbs, bending down to inhale them.

Morgan, however, tapped her on the shoulder.

'Rose!'

'What?' She straightened up, a heady mix of basil, rosemary and sage in her nostrils.

Morgan was frowning.

'*What?*'

'I've just realised, you never said why you're here. Why did Jane bring you back? Your story earlier ended with her turning up. Did you just feel like having a look?' Morgan gestured around her. 'I can see why you would. I mean, it's right up your street, and Aiden's, but—'

Her contentment fading almost as quickly as it had come, Rose stared at her friend. Would she be able to take in even more absurdity in the space of so many hours? It wasn't that she didn't have faith in Morgan, or her smartness, but all of this defied intelligent thought on another level.

'No, not at all!'

'But why, then? Why did she want you to come? Did she just want you to experience her world as she'd experienced ours?'

Rose shook her head, her mind struggling with how to start the conversation. 'I wouldn't have done that, left on a whim without—'

'Then, what did—'

Rose put a finger to her lips and shook her head again. 'Shh!'

The sound of voices had drifted over the high hedging, and Rose swallowed quickly. However much she might question Jane's hearing, her own was not at fault: the Wallace family were out for an early evening stroll, out of sight at present behind the screening. Almost against her will, she edged closer to the wooden gate, but keeping well back so she wouldn't be seen, conscious of Morgan keeping close to her side.

'What is it?' she hissed.

'I think it's the neighbours.' Rose waved a hand vaguely.

'Oh.'

Rose's heart clenched in her chest as she saw the head and shoulders of Mr Wallace pass by the gate, which was lower than the surrounding hedging, his wife's bonnet bobbing at his side; they were clearly deep in conversation.

'So,' whispered Morgan. 'Are we hiding from them, or spying on them? And why?'

'Shhh!' Rose tugged on Morgan's arm, who was on tiptoe, trying to see over the gate from where they stood some paces back.

Two more bonnets passed by, one slightly higher than the other: the two elder girls. Rose waited, knowing there would be one more, after which she could procrastinate no longer. All of a sudden, however, she paled, a hand shooting to her throat.

'What is it?' Morgan turned Rose around to face her. 'You look strange!'

'I…' Rose strained, listening.

Anne wasn't visible at all as she passed the gate some paces behind the others, but her breathy, high-pitched voice, humming and singing floated through the still evening air towards them, and Rose clutched Morgan's arm.

'No.' She shook her head, her insides swirling anew. 'No; it's not possible.'

Morgan laughed. 'Rose, I'm currently wearing no recognisable underwear and what feels like a brace around my chest. I think there's a good chance I'll be open to *anything* you have to tell me. Rose?' She detached Rose's grip from her arm and turned her around. 'Look at me. What is it?' She frowned. 'You look like you've seen a ghost!'

Closing her eyes briefly, Rose drew in a steadying breath before opening them to meet her friend's concerned gaze.

'Did you hear it?'

'What?'

'That song.'

'What song?'

'The song Anne was singing bits of.'

Morgan frowned. 'Who's Anne?'

Rose put a hand to her head, almost knocking her bonnet sideways. This couldn't be happening.

'Rose?'

'She's the youngest of the neighbours' children.' Rose started shaking her head from side to side. 'No, this just is *not* possible.'

Morgan took her arm, urging her across the garden to a nearby bench, and Rose stumbled alongside her. Without her friend, she didn't think she could have moved, because her legs weren't going anywhere of their own volition.

'Sit.'

Rose sank onto the bench, and Morgan sat beside her. 'So I'm guessing the most pertinent question here is, what song was it?'

Rose gestured helplessly with a hand. 'Did you ever see *Shallow Hal*?' She turned to look at Morgan, who looked mystified.

'Uh, no, I don't think so.'

'No – why would you? I was only about eight when it came out. You'd still have been in nappies.'

Morgan laughed. 'Hey, I wasn't in diapers when I was five!'

'It had Jack Black and Gwyneth Paltrow in it?'

'Maybe?' Morgan looked thoughtful. 'I think I may have skimmed through it on *Starz* once?' She eyed Rose warily. 'You're asking a lot of disconnected questions, Rose. Are you sure you're okay?'

Rose pulled a face. 'Not really.' She turned in her seat to fully face Morgan. 'Look, there's a song in the film soundtrack called "Love Grows Where My Rosemary Goes".'

Morgan looked expectantly at Rose, clearly waiting for the punchline. 'Well, it's cool that the song is so old.'

'It's *not*! That's what I'm trying to tell you. *That* song is not from *this* time.'

'Ha!' Morgan grinned. 'Maybe Jane took this girl to the present on one of her jaunts!'

Rose faltered for a moment. Could that be possible? Then, she gave herself a mental shake. No, surely not! She gestured towards the hedging to their right.

'And Anne was humming the tune, singing the chorus. Every word.'

'Ooh.' Morgan's eyes grew round. 'So... you think...' She paused, frowning. 'I'm sorry, I don't understand why that's important.'

Rose covered her face with her hands. 'It's why Jane brought me here.'

'What? Because of a song with your name in it?'

There was no easy way to say this. 'She thinks I'm related to the Wallace family – that's their name, the neighbours.'

Morgan's brows rose; then she smiled widely. 'That's so cool! Wow, what I wouldn't give to be able to meet some of my ancestors!'

'Not ancestors. At least, not Mr Wallace.' Rose's voice almost broke on saying his name, and Morgan eyed her with increasing concern. 'Morgan, Jane thinks…' It was so hard to say! 'She thinks he's my father.'

'Who?'

'Christopher Wallace.'

Morgan frowned. 'Jane Austen thinks Notorious B.I.G. is your father?'

'What?' For a long, confusing moment they stared at each other, then Rose shook her head. 'No! The neighbour's name is Christopher Wallace. And so was my father's.'

'That doesn't make any more sense than what I said. He died. Years ago. As did Biggie Smalls since we're on the subject.' Morgan looked torn between disbelief and amusement. 'She's really crazy, then. D'you think her brains have been addled by all the time hopping? Can't be good for you, can it? And she really thinks this Wallace man is your dad?'

'Yes.'

Morgan's gaze raked Rose's. Then, she sobered. 'And so do you.'

'I didn't! Not until… I mean, I think I can explain everything else. Coincidence, mainly… and he could've been mumbling; he could just be a genius inventor, only now…'

Morgan stared blankly at her, and Rose couldn't blame her. She knew, however, the time had come to tell her friend everything Jane believed. It was a surprisingly short explanation, mainly because Morgan looked too surprised to interject or ask questions.

'But—' Morgan sank back against the bench. 'Wow. I mean, if it's true… which it can't be, can it?'

'You're where I was about twenty-four hours ago.'

Then, Morgan frowned. 'But how does this girl singing a song from years ago tie in?'

'My mum told me my dad loved the song.' Rose could feel her throat tightening, and she grasped Morgan's hands. 'He—' She drew in a shaking breath. 'I was told he chose my name from it.'

Morgan gave her hands a gentle squeeze. 'Then there's the proof there's nothing in this, Rose! If he named you, that was twenty-seven years ago.'

Rose was shaking her head, and Morgan frowned. 'What?'

'It was an old song. A one-hit wonder by a group called Edison Lighthouse.'

'Never heard of them!'

Despite her rising emotion, Rose let out a watery laugh. 'No, I'm sure you haven't. But once I knew where my name came from, many years ago, I looked it up. The song is from 1970.'

Morgan's eyes widened, but then she saw the direction of Rose's gaze. Someone was coming out of the door.

'Come, Miss Taylor. You will be in need of this later.' Cassandra was holding out the spencer.

Morgan smiled politely, then turned back to Rose. 'Are we still going?' she asked quietly.

Rose hesitated, then nodded. 'Yes, yes, let's go.' She smiled tremulously at her friend. 'With you there, I'll be fine. Besides, it will have to be our substitute for the *Festival* ball we're missing out on tonight.'

With a final squeeze of Rose's hand, Morgan got up and walked over to meet Cassandra as her sister and mother came out of the house. Mrs Austen turned straight for the gate, but Jane's gaze travelled from Morgan to

Rose, and she frowned, hurrying over to where the latter remained, motionless.

'Come, we must make haste, Miss Wallace.' She spoke loudly, but once her mother had disappeared from view, she took Rose's arm. 'Rose? Has aught untoward arisen?'

Rose got unsteadily to her feet. 'I will tell you as we walk.' She gestured weakly after the others, who were already turning for the gate, Morgan's concerned gaze still upon her.

The feeling was slowly returning to Rose's legs. Her mind, however, was in deeper turmoil than ever. The thought of sitting through a formal dinner in company was the last thing she needed right now!

Chapter 11

Rose had dreamed of the delights of dining in a stately home ever since she'd fallen in love with Jane Austen's novels as a teenager. Dining at Chawton House, which had only been open to the public in more recent years, had been beyond her wildest imaginings.

As the various dishes were placed upon the table in the elegant wood-panelled dining room, however, she suppressed a heavy sigh. Now she was actually a guest of Edward Knight, it was not exactly living up to the fantasy.

Putting aside the tumult of emotion in her breast and the confusion in her mind, Rose could tell, for example, that their host was struggling with his assorted guests. The added complication of having Mrs Austen in attendance – eschewing her usual preference for dining early – only made things worse. Although she'd found out about Jane's escapades when they had lived in Bath, she had no idea her youngest daughter had been up to no good again, nor that almost half the people at the table didn't normally reside in the present century!

Having to play act was clearly proving as much a challenge for Edward as it was for his four misplaced guests, the strain showing plainly on his face.

'Yes, thank you, Mama.' He turned to address Mrs Austen, seated to his right. 'The delay is unfortunate but as soon as…' His gaze flicked briefly over his unexpected visitors. '…we are able, the journey to town will be reinstated, and the proposed visit to Wedgwoods can then take place.'

Mrs Austen frowned. 'I am at a loss to comprehend this disruption. Fanny was most displeased at being sent onwards into Kent instead of the promised visit to your brother, Henry.' She fastened her beady eyes on Edward. 'You planned to order a new service by summer, yet autumn is upon us, and still we dine upon the old.'

Cassandra sent her brother a warm look. 'I like this design very well, Edward. It is no hardship to enjoy another meal on it.'

Rose took a sip of her wine. Edward had proudly proclaimed it to be French, hard to come by during such turbulent times, and she savoured the coolness as it trickled down her throat. Her gaze drifted around the table as the Austens carried the conversation between them.

Aiden seemed the most at home, chatting quietly with Charles. James, now more formally dressed, on the other hand, was eyeing the courses presented to him with some trepidation. Morgan, meanwhile, after getting the third degree from Mrs Austen about her unusual name, her family's connections and their standing in the world, was sitting bolt upright in her chair, clearly afraid of making another faux pas.

Rose eyed her friend sympathetically. Yes, they had attended an event on etiquette earlier that week at the *Festival*, but neither of them had taken it seriously, nor had they expected having to put it into practice.

Having moved her own chair out to sit down, then refusing the soup (a definite no-no), which earned her a stern look from the lady, Morgan was now watching everyone's every move and copying them rather than following her own lead – from which silverware to use to which dishes she was permitted to choose from and when to take a drink from her glass.

Rose caught her eye and mouthed, 'Relax.'

Morgan smiled, then nodded.

'Miss Taylor.' Mrs Austen, however, had come back for more from the latest acquaintance of her daughter to arrive on her doorstep. 'Pray, tell me. Whence do you hail? Your accent is unusual, and to be certain, not of local origin.'

'Am—' Morgan stopped, throwing Rose a frantic look. 'I, er…'

'Shall we just say, Mama,' Charles sent an almost imperceptible wink in Rose's direction, 'Miss Taylor arrived here by way of Gibraltar.'

Jane choked on her drink, and Charles leaned over and patted her gently on the back. 'There, there, dear sister.'

Rose smiled at the lady. 'My friend is from a northern country, ma'am, much distant from Hampshire.'

Mrs Austen raised a brow. 'Indeed? Yet I believe you have come from Bath, Miss Wallace. How is it so you and Miss Taylor are intimately acquainted?'

It was Rose's turn to hesitate, conscious everyone was now listening to the conversation.

'They met through a mutual acquaintance, Mama.' Jane spoke firmly. 'I believe Miss Taylor was in Bath for a season, were you not?' She turned to Morgan, who nodded quickly.

'Yes! I mean, indeed. I was. Just for a season, looking for love… or marriage I mean or, well, you know.'

'We have maintained a regular correspondence since we were first… introduced, ma'am.' Rose smiled at Mrs

Austen, whose gaze roamed from her to Morgan and back again. If she only knew!

Thankfully, there was a diversion as the many dishes were cleared and the second course was served, including an array of desserts amongst the further savouries.

'Would you care for one of the ices, Miss Wallace?'

Rose looked up, then smiled at Edward down the table. 'Yes, thank you!' Any chance to take in something cold would be welcome.

A servant placed the delicacy before her, but Morgan was frowning.

'I didn't know you had ice cream back then!'

It was Mrs Austen's turn to frown. 'Back *when*, pray?'

'It will be the last until the winter.' Edward turned to his mother. 'May I tempt you with a little more wine, Mama?'

Morgan threw Rose an expressive glance and picked up her spoon.

'You are fortunate in your cook, Edward.' Mrs Austen had turned her attention to her son. 'We are thankful for Martha; she is our only constant.'

'She would not be so, if you did not persist in sending our cooks onwards, Mama.' Jane sipped her wine. 'This is excellent, Edward. French, is it not?'

'Indeed.' Edward raised his glass to inspect the colour.

'You are also fortunate in having no need for thrift, my dear.' Mrs Austen's voice was admonishing as her beady eyes took in the lavishly appointed table and its generous contents, then roamed over the strangers in her midst.

'Let us be above vulgar economy, Mama.' Jane sent the ghost of a wink in Rose's direction. 'Let us drink French wine and eat ice whilst we may.'

'Why did you send the last cook on her way?' Charles was leaning back in his chair, nursing his glass in both hands, his eyes on his mother.

Mrs Austen pursed her lips. 'She was derelict in her duties.'

Jane turned to her brother. 'Mama professes she had many qualities, but sobriety was not one of them.'

Morgan's eyes widened, and she hissed at Rose, 'They never talked like this in *Pride and Prejudice*.'

About to take a mouthful of her dessert, Mrs Austen lowered her spoon, a look of surprise on her face.

'You are familiar with that novel, Miss Taylor?'

With a swift glance towards Jane, Morgan turned back to the lady. 'Er, yes.'

'Miss Wallace and Miss Taylor are both aware of my efforts, Mama. There is no need for discretion.'

'On the contrary, Jane, there is oft a need for discretion when it is sadly lacking.' Mrs Austen turned an admonishing eye on her youngest daughter before turning back to Morgan. Her features, however, had lost their assessing look, and she smiled. 'And pray, what did you think of it?'

'Oh, I loved it!'

Rose held her breath as Morgan's eyes widened at the lady's lack of teeth before she dropped her gaze and applied herself to her dessert.

'I will own to preferring it to the first.' Mrs Austen turned to James. 'And you, sir? Have you read my daughter's works?'

James looked guilty as he shook his head. 'Not yet.'

'To be certain, it has only been in circulation these seven months or so, Mama, and gentlemen oft have less time for leisure.' Cassandra spoke soothingly, then turned the conversation to Edward's family, and as he had so many children, the topic kept Mrs Austen engaged until it came time to separate.

With a glance at the ornate clock on the mantelpiece, however, the lady declared she would return to the cottage, accepting Edward's offer to accompany her, and soon they had set off down the driveway. The others tarried a while, relaxing now they were freer to talk, until Cassandra suggested the ladies withdraw. They were soon joined by the remaining gentlemen, who had no desire to separate when there was still much to discuss.

Accepting a glass of wine from Charles, Rose sank onto a chaise, moving her shoulders restlessly in an attempt to ease the tension, thankful when Aiden came and sat beside her.

'You looked distracted during dinner.'

Rose summoned a smile.

'I need to talk to you about something that happened earlier, but—'

'Well, that was somewhat onerous.' Edward strode into the room as the door closed behind a departing servant.

'It was the most amazing dinner I've ever had in my life! I'm sorry I didn't eat the food.' Morgan beamed at him. 'I know it's a once in a lifetime chance to have an authentic meal here, with you all, but I was so afraid of doing something wrong. Oh my gosh, it feels good to talk. It was really hard not to talk much.'

Conscious that Edward, from his expression, wasn't quite up for some unfiltered Morgan, Rose bit her lip, but Charles was laughing as he handed his brother a glass. 'You had little choice, with Mama grilling you in such a way. She has found your accent unusual, to be certain, but seems quite reconciled to your being from somewhere quite northwards.'

'It's not just the accent.' Morgan grimaced. 'I have a tendency to get carried away and tell people all the wrong things I shouldn't tell them. In general, I avoid secrets because it's impossible for me to keep them.'

'That is… unfortunate.' Edward threw his sister a significant look.

'Oh, not this!' Morgan was keen to reassure him. 'I can keep serious secrets.'

Jane shrugged lightly. 'It is of little consequence; who would believe you if you told them?'

'So true.' Morgan glanced at James, who walked over to sit beside her. 'Speaking of, when were you thinking of disapparating us?'

'Dis-what?' Charles bit back on a laugh, his gaze going from Morgan to his sister.

'It's a reference to something from a popular book in my time.'

Rose looked at Jane, but her gaze had drifted to the window, then back to the newest arrivals.

'There will be sufficient darkness to take you within the hour.'

Relief filled James' face, and he put a hand on Morgan's back, then withdrew it quickly. 'Sorry, sorry. Just glad to know I won't lose any business over this… *business*. With Roger gone…' He glanced at Rose. 'I need you on hand or I'll be down to the part-timer and the temps.'

Jane and Cassandra exchanged slightly puzzled looks; Edward frowned, and even Charles looked as if he was struggling, and despite her turmoil, Rose wanted to laugh.

'Er, James, I am not sure that translated very well into Regency English.'

It was James' turn to frown. 'Oh!' His expression cleared, and he turned to Jane. 'Sorry. Not something for you to worry about. Rose, you can stay on holiday until Monday, of course. So long as I get back tonight.' He glanced at Morgan, a faint smile on his lips. 'Mr Darcy will be getting frantic as it is.' Then, his smile faded. 'My keys had better still be there!'

Morgan's eyes grew round, and a hand flew to her mouth. 'Oh no! I'd forgotten about him!'

'Her,' James added instinctively, but Rose had seen the continued confusion in those around them.

'There is no need to be alarmed.' She addressed Edward, as he seemed to be struggling the most. 'It is not a fictitious character somehow transported from the pages of a book, just the name given to a kitten Mor— Miss Taylor found.'

Charles laughed and drained his glass, and even Edward smiled at this, though Rose suspected it was more from relief at the mundane explanation than anything else.

'There, Edward.' Charles waved a hand towards where Aiden and Rose sat. 'You are down to two unexpected guests instead of four.'

James, however, was frowning as he looked over to where Rose and Aiden sat. 'Wait, aren't you two coming?'

'I suppose that depends on Rose's plans.' Aiden glanced at her. 'I don't foresee any problem with my losing another day or two in the present. I'm freelance, and not known for checking my phone.' He smiled ruefully at the blank faces around him. 'It means I am not answerable to anyone in my profession and they are used to a delay when trying to communicate with me.' He took Rose's hand, and no one raised a single brow this time. 'If Rose wants to stay a little longer, I'd be more than happy to soak up a bit more of the history.'

Charles walked over to the console table and picked up the wine decanter, topping up his own glass before walking over to them and doing the same. 'As the mystery of the neighbour has yet to be solved, I suspect you will remain a while?'

'What neighbour?' James held up his glass as Charles offered to refill it, then looked at Morgan, who raised her brows.

'Does everyone else know about the, umm…'

Rose glanced guiltily at her boss. 'Everyone but James. Sorry,' she added, as his gaze flew to hers.

James held up a hand. 'Keep all the secrets you want. I don't want to know anything else. I didn't want to know *this* to be honest.' He gestured around the gathered company, and Morgan sent him an exasperated look. 'Not that it isn't *lovely* to meet you all, of course.'

'Is it a possibility to maybe *tell* him, because I've come to a decision that doesn't make a lot of sense unless that is known.'

Rose stared at Morgan, unsure of her meaning. 'What are you saying?'

'I'd like to stay as well. This is a big deal for you, and I've been absent for a lot of big things in your life this last week. I'd like to be here for this one.'

James leaned forward. 'What?'

Morgan looked like she might reach out for his hand but thought better of it. 'Just another day or two. You can take care of Mr Darcy and maybe tell my mom—'

'I can't let you!' Rose protested. 'It might not be anything at all.'

'You do not truly believe that, Rose.' Jane got to her feet. 'When we were walking here and you told me of your most recent discovery, you were speaking as if it were fact – were you not aware?'

'What recent discovery?' Charles looked to Cassandra, who shrugged, then over at Jane.

'Morgan, you must go home. I would've gone with you happily, but...' Rose's voice tailed away. Until the impossible had turned into the highly likely.

'No, I have it all worked out.' Morgan got up and paced in front of the fireplace. 'I'm going to have James text my mom and tell her we went off to a three-day, full cosplay, live-in-Regency-times thing where we can't have technology. It's basically the truth and should give you a few days to find out what you need to find out.'

James pressed his fingers to the bridge of his nose. 'I don't want to know, I don't want to know,' he intoned, then sighed heavily. 'Fine, I need to know, please. What the devil is so important?'

Chapter 12

Considering James had one of the most rigid, unimaginative minds Rose had ever encountered, he took the revelation of Jane's purpose in bringing her back in time fairly well, in that he said nothing until everyone had chipped in their own particular theory.

When silence prevailed, he got to his feet and paced over to one of the windows, a hand to his head, then turned to face the others.

'So, is the principal theory Rose's... this *man*,' he gestured vaguely with his hand, 'was born of this time, managed to travel forward at some point, father a child and then, a few years later, decided to return to his past? Or do you think he is from our time,' again he gestured, this time towards Morgan, Rose and Aiden, 'and somehow travelled here – to the past – and was trapped?'

Jane smirked. 'It is not unheard of, sir, for such a mishap to occur.'

Rose's brow wrinkled. 'I'd not actually considered the first option.' She looked over at Jane, who shook her head. 'If he was raised here, I would be very surprised.'

James grunted. 'I'm stunned anything can surprise you any more, Rose, with all this going on. So.' He turned to face Jane. 'It's the assumption this Mr Wallace disappeared from the present and has lived here for these twenty-five years?'

Charles swirled the wine in his glass. 'When I met him in Gibraltar, he was already married with four young children.'

'Four?' Rose looked from Charles to Jane in surprise.

'Had I not mentioned the eldest?' Jane smiled. 'A small lapse. There is also a son away at university.' She looked at her brother. 'Do continue, Charles.'

'Excepting a few eccentricities and a strong desire to move back to the mainland, he was much the same as any man of my acquaintance. Since that time, we have maintained a steady correspondence and six months ago, he came here to live.'

'How many years ago exactly was that? That you met him?'

'About thirteen?'

James looked back at Rose. 'What do you plan to do? Introduce yourself, Rose?' James' voice softened, as did his expression, and he walked over to where she sat. 'He's not going to want to return, to become your missing father.'

'I know!' Rose's head was spinning. This constant talking about the situation was vying with the sensible part of her brain. 'He has a life here – a wife, children.'

'He has a wife and a child in our time as well,' James reminded her gently.

Rose raised her chin. 'Both of whom can support themselves. That is not the case, should he leave his family here to fend for themselves.' Rose got to her feet, and Aiden did likewise. 'James, I can't leave yet. I have to at least find out the truth, and for that I need a bit more time.'

Her boss held her gaze for a moment. 'I can't quite believe we're even having this conversation. I feel bad for leaving you here.'

'I have the support of all these lovely people.' Rose looked around the room – most of those gathered had been strangers to her until two days ago, but she was convinced she was right.

'Well then.' James leaned forward and kissed her cheek. 'I'll see you soon.'

'Yes, good luck this weekend.'

He smiled faintly.

'Sir?' James looked over at Jane. 'Darkness has fallen; now would be opportune if we are to see you on your way.'

'In that case,' James grasped Morgan's hand and looked down at her, 'I guess it's time for me to get going.'

Morgan's infallible cheer disappeared for a moment before she rallied and smiled at him. 'Good luck with the transitions this weekend. Don't be fooled by any females who get locked out of their properties. They're probably just flirting with you.'

James smiled. 'If someone gets locked out they can climb through a window. I'll be taking care of Mr Darcy.'

Rose bit her lip. Morgan's smile was tremulous and the enormity of what her friend was proposing struck her forcibly. She seemed to have no sense of the precariousness of slipping through time, but then she'd not lived through what Rose had the previous week.

She glanced at Aiden, who seemed to sense her disquiet and nodded, and she stepped forward to her friend's side.

'Morgan, you need to go back.' She looked from her to her boss, two of her closest friends, and crossed her fingers that they wouldn't question why she had just become insistent. Jane might hopscotch around history with aplomb, but Rose knew better than most that things could go wrong. It didn't matter how unlikely; Rose wouldn't be the cause of James and Morgan's separation from the life they knew and each other.

Her insides swirled for a moment at the realisation she herself could fall victim to the same jeopardy, but she ignored it. Morgan was clearly gathering herself for an argument.

Rose took her hand. 'Your family is not going to be satisfied by one text, and just how well do you think James will fare against the full wrath of the Taylor family?'

She focused on Morgan, trying to send her firm vibes that she would not be swayed, but she thought she saw gratefulness in James' face. 'Besides, I need you to get a message to my friend, Liz, in case I'm not back by Sunday.'

'I can't leave you here!'

'Yes, you can.' Rose smiled. 'Are you saying you want to use a toothbrush made from animal bone, eat animal fat and have no shower at your disposal?'

For a moment, amusement returned to Morgan's face. 'Good point. Not sure I can handle this going commando thing much longer either!' Then, she sighed. 'But I'm your friend. I don't want to leave you alone in the middle—'

Rose clasped her hands together. 'You are my *best* friend, but you're not leaving me alone.'

Morgan looked at Aiden, then over at where Jane and Cassandra stood side by side. She smiled a little, but still looked about as miserable as Rose had ever seen her.

Jane cleared her throat. 'There is something I can do for you, and it may lessen the pain of separation by a very frequent and most unreserved correspondence.' She touched her sister lightly on the arm. 'We told you, did we not, that Cass and I devised a way of communicating through time? There is no reason why you and Rose should not do the same.'

'Could we?' Morgan's eyes lit up in an instant, and she clapped her hands together. 'That would make me feel *so* much better.'

Rose stared at Jane, then realised her intent. 'The space under the floorboard in your room.'

James huffed out a breath. 'I don't want to know. I really don't want to know.'

Jane merely rolled her eyes at him and turned to Edward. 'If you would not miss a page or two of parchment, some ink and a pen?'

Edward looked like he just wanted to be done with whole matter. His gaze roamed across his unusual visitors, and he nodded slowly.

'Of course. Be my guest.'

–

Despite his blatant discomfort at being more than 200 years removed from his normal life, Rose had been unsettled to see James leave. His parting shot of 'You'd best be in early on Monday. There will be a lot of fallout from the last week,' hadn't helped, as her mind had fled back to her own life in Bath: her home; her friends; her job.

Morgan had looked as sad as Rose felt as she'd released her from a fierce hug, tucked the slip of parchment bearing Liz's number up her sleeve and followed Jane and James from the room. Rose was relieved the remaining occupants left her alone to compose herself.

She had drawn in a few shaky breaths and wiped her eyes, before a hand touched her gently on the arm, and she turned to meet Cassandra's concerned gaze.

'Do not be sad, Miss Wallace. 'Tis surely but a parting of short duration.'

Rose's throat was tight, but she summoned a watery smile, grateful for the lady's understanding. She glanced over to where Charles and Edward stood in conversation with Aiden, then looked back at Cassandra.

'This is so strange and incredible all at the same time. I do not know if I am coming or going. Simply being here in 1813 is weird enough; seeing Morgan and James today was almost unfathomable. If it wasn't for what happened this last week, I would assume I am going mad or it was all some weird dream. I appreciate your sister's reason for bringing me here, but I still cannot decide what to think about it.'

'I think you do know, Rose.'

She turned around. Aiden had come to stand beside her, and he smiled at Cassandra before turning to Rose.

'So what are you going to do next?'

Rose stared at him. What should she do? What *could* she do? Would the Wallace family consider themselves acquainted with her now? She'd not even given them the courtesy of a good morning when Charles had introduced them earlier, distracted as she was by seeing Morgan.

'Miss Wallace, would you care to join us for a moment?'

All three of them turned to look over to where Edward Knight stood before the fireplace. Charles had returned to the console table with his empty wine glass again, but Cassandra held out a hand to her and Rose took it and walked with them to join Edward.

'Charles has made a suggestion that I feel we ought to consider in the meantime.'

Re-joining them, Charles raised his glass in a salute. 'Then make the invitation, Brother.'

Edward bowed in Rose's direction. 'I feel it incumbent upon me to offer you—' He hesitated, then raised his chin. 'I fear we trespass too much upon Mama's hospitality. It would be better for all if you were to adjourn to the great house for the remainder of your sojourn in these parts.'

'Oh!' Rose looked to Cassandra for guidance, but she was smiling encouragingly.

'I do think it best, Miss Wallace. Martha is due to return on the morrow, and we need no added complexity. Do not be concerned, for Jane shall wish to accompany you.' She waved an elegant hand. 'There are ample accommodations here for you all.'

Releasing a relieved breath, Rose turned back to Edward. 'I thank you, sir, for your consideration. If you think it best, then I would be happy to stay.'

Rose tried to keep the conflict from her features, but her head was trying to grapple with the fact she was now going to be *staying* in Chawton House. Morgan would have been made up! She knew it would remove her chances of observing the Wallace family from the end of the garden but, considering the brothers were already acquainted with them, she may get *more* opportunities to actually interact with her fa— Rose stopped herself. She couldn't think it, not yet.

'Then we look forward to receiving you after you have broken your fast on the morrow.' Edward turned to accept a glass of brandy from his brother, who then offered the same to Aiden, and Rose, feeling herself dismissed, turned around in search of Morgan, only to recall she was no longer with them.

She bit her lip, then followed Cassandra over to where the paraphernalia for making tea had recently been laid. Had Jane left already? Had James and Morgan travelled back as easily as they had come? Was James' car still safe, their modern-day belongings secure?

'Come, Miss Wallace. Take some tea and my sister will return directly with the necessary assurances.'

Rose took the offered cup with a grateful smile and sipped, her gaze drifting, as it so often did, in Aiden's direction. He was deep in conversation with Charles, but Rose frowned. Though they were clearly engaged on whatever topic they spoke of, she felt somehow she was the subject, and when Aiden looked up and caught her eye, he excused himself and came over.

'Captain Austen has suggested Edward host a picnic for some of the principal families in the village, and can include the Wallaces. After church on Sunday.'

The tension Rose had carried with her since her arrival in Chawton resurfaced rapidly, gripping her shoulders, and she placed her cup unsteadily on a nearby side table. 'I'll be so nervous, it will take everything I have to speak to them. What do I say?'

Aiden eyed her with sympathy. 'You'll know when the time comes.'

'But it isn't absolutely certain, is it? I mean, this song… I know it's impossible for anyone in 1813 to know the tune and the words to it. But I must have misheard, mustn't I? I may have thought it, but it probably was just a bit similar…' Her voice tailed off. Aiden wasn't rushing to agree with her.

'Rose.' His face was serious. 'Why are you finding it so hard to accept, when you say you just spent some days trapped in an alternate reality with Jane Austen and you're now here, in 1813? That's two impossible things in the space of a week. How many more do you need before you start realising this has as much likelihood of being real as anything else?'

'Perchance you fear it has *no* truth,' added Cassandra wisely.

Rose looked from one to the other, the swirling of her insides taking up their familiar dance as she realised they had an all too valid point. Hadn't she just lived two weeks in the space of one, both beyond explanation? The most important thing she'd learned had been she had to step up, not be so reticent. Did Aiden know just how much that lesson had to do with him?

Rose lifted her shoulders in a light shrug. 'Right. Okay. I'm ready. I don't want to give you false expectations, though. I'm still not going to get up and do karaoke.' She drew in a short breath. 'But maybe now I'll sing along from my seat.'

'Well that's a birthday present wasted!' Aiden winked. Then, he took her hand. 'I know you can do this, Rose.'

–

Despite Cassandra's reassurances, Jane had not returned by the time she and Rose made their way back to the cottage and, not feeling up to putting on a front for Mrs Austen, Rose excused herself and went upstairs. The temptation to slip into Jane and Cassandra's bedroom and check the loose floorboard for news from Morgan was severe, but then Rose realised, without Jane and the charm, the portal wouldn't work.

She tried to sleep, tossing and turning, her mind swinging this way and that, only falling into a slumber

as the first fingers of dawn tapped gently on the shut-
ters. When she finally awoke, Rose raised heavy lids,
then flopped over onto her back. Seriously, 1813 was not
conducive to a good night's sleep!

-

Jenny, the maid, brought water for washing, and Rose
prepared wearily for the day, tying her hair back with a
piece of ribbon and trying not to dwell on what she might
possibly say to Mr Wallace when she saw him at the picnic
on the following day.

Keen for Jane's account of her friends' safe return, she
hurried from the room and along the landing, pausing at
the top of the stairs with a frown. Unless she was much
mistaken, there was a quite heated exchange going on
behind the closed door of the bedroom shared by Jane
and Cassandra. She held her breath, trying to decipher the
words, but suddenly there was silence. Had they become
aware of her presence?

With an anxious glance at the still closed door, Rose
fled down the stairs as decorously as she could, to find
Mrs Austen already at the dining table and complaining
loudly about the breakfast things not being prepared and
demanding in a strident voice to know where the new
condiment set – a gift from Edward – had gone.

After greeting her, Rose crouched down to pat Prancer
in his basket, and the sound of footsteps on the stairs soon
heralded the arrival of Jane and Cassandra, who hurried
away to the kitchen. The former returned soon after with
bread for the toasting fork, and Cassandra followed her in
with a tray of cutlery.

As Cassandra unlocked the tea caddy and prepared to
make the beverage, Rose eyed Jane warily. She didn't

look herself this morning, and for a second, she panicked something had happened to James or Morgan. There was nothing to be done about it whilst they ate, however, but once Mrs Austen had left the room and Jane began clearing the table, Rose got to her feet and carried some plates as they headed for the kitchen.

'Jane? Is something wrong? Did they get home okay?'

Sending her a significant look, Rose held her tongue as they entered the kitchen, where the cook was busy with her mixing bowls. Once in the drawing room, however, Jane closed the door.

'They are safely restored to the present day.'

'Then what is wrong?'

Cassandra slipped through the doorway from the vestibule, closing it behind her. 'Tell her, Jane.'

Chapter 13

Jane blew out a huff of breath. ''Tis naught of consequence.'

'It *is*!' Cassandra threw her sister an exasperated look, then turned to Rose, speaking quietly. 'Your friends are perfectly well and back where they should be, but there were some difficulties with Jane's return last night.'

Rose's heart sank. 'Oh no! What sort of difficulties?'

'Cass makes too much of it.' Jane waved a frustrated hand.

'I do *not*! You forget all I suffered when you were trapped in the future!'

'Dear Cass, that is beyond us now.' Jane took her sister's hands. 'I promised I would be more careful in future.'

'This is all very well when you are the master of your own destiny, but not when you put your life in the hands of a…' She gestured with her hand. 'A recalcitrant *charm*!'

'My life was not at risk!'

'Wait!' Rose interrupted the argument, and both ladies turned to look at her. 'Please, just tell me. What happened?'

Jane's face assumed a stubborn look, and Rose tried not to be amused, for Cassandra's concern was blatant.

'My alarm was valid, for my sister did not return promptly last night. Indeed, she did not reappear for some hours.'

Jane did not seem to share her sister's concern. 'The museum was closed.' She frowned. 'Did you have something else you needed to do in the future?'

Cassandra threw Jane another exasperated look. 'When she tried to return, it sent her to a different year than was her intention.'

Rose stared at Jane. 'Where did you go?'

Jane walked to the door and grasped the handle. 'I have no idea. It was the middle of the night, but the museum did not yet have that purpose. From its appearance, it was merely three labourers' cottages.' She glared at Cassandra. 'But I returned, did I not?'

If Rose wasn't mistaken, Cassandra had released a lady-like snort. 'Indeed. By way of the pond!'

Jane opened the door, and winked at Rose. 'Then is it not fortunate I had little admiration for my shoes?'

She left the room, and Cassandra turned her expressive gaze on Rose. 'I fear for her at times, Miss Wallace. She had a propensity for being headstrong in her youth, but since her... well, since she was lost to us, she seemed reconciled to being here. She became focused on her writing. But of late, a recklessness has come upon her.'

Knowing full well Jane had just four years left to live, Rose bit her lip. It seemed she hadn't told her family that and they were completely in the dark as to how little time Jane had left in this world.

-

Having so few clothes and accessories to her name, it took very little time for Rose to prepare for the removal to the great house. Jane was seeing to her own packing, promising to bring further garments of Cassandra's to share with her, and Rose made her way along the landing, surprised by the sadness she felt at her time staying in the cottage coming to an end.

Jane's door opened and she peered out. Spotting Rose, she stepped forward and offered her a folded piece of paper. 'Did I not say the portal would suffice?'

Rose took it gingerly, as if it might disappear into thin air if she were too rough with it, then clutched the letter to her chest as she went downstairs. Would the impending change of residence mean this tentative connection to her friend, to her old life, would cease almost as soon as it had started?

She walked quickly out of the house into the garden, emotion gripping her throat even as she unfolded the paper, only to find herself smiling. Morgan had clearly had some trouble with the quill and ink. There were several blots in the margin and the handwriting was stilted. There was also a column at the bottom where she had been practising and another hand which Rose recognised as James'. With a lighter heart, she read:

> *Rose! We're home. There was no sign of James' suit, but everything else (including his phone and keys, thank goodness!) was turned in to C's Cup. Jane warned me that I should keep anything I say timeless if you know what I mean so I'm not sure how to say this: First thing I did when I got back to my handheld everything device (I followed instruction and left everything modern in James' trunk unlike some people…) was to search the information getter for the history of that song. As far as I can tell, it's just exactly what you already know. So I hope you can clarify if you*

heard what you thought you heard because that might be important!

Mr Darcy gave us a good scolding when we got back, but did nothing undignified while he was alone. He won't get off of James now, though, and wants to be cuddled every second. I am very offended that he loves James more than me, but I have my ways. Imagine a winky face here. I'm going to get him some treats from ~~Waitrose~~ the market. I don't mean to brag, but I can't tell you how glorious it is to know how easy it is to get to the market here and now, if you know what I mean.

I am, of course, dying to hear how things are going there, but I don't know how often I can get to Chawton from Bath, let alone be in Jane's room long enough to lift the floorboard, so don't stress. You should start writing though because it takes an insane amount of time to write with this stupid quill.

Aiden's carriage was fine. James tucked the keys a bit further back, no one will know they're there. He's working, as I'm sure is not a surprise to you. He gave me a spare key you keep in your desk so I can go by your place to make sure the mail isn't piling up and water your plants. You still have a landline too, right? So if someone calls looking for you, I'll make sure that's all taken care of. I don't have to redact that because calling means something different there but it's all okay, right? This is sort of fun, like being a secret agent. But not fun because I want to know what's happening with you. Also

we should make a plan for how you can contact us
when you're ready to be picked up. Much love, M

There was as a short addition in James' handwriting:

Hi R, testing the quill and can confirm it does
work and M is just being impatient. That was a
brand new suit, Rose, and I am not...

It looked like the pen had been whipped from James' hand if the streak of ink was anything to go by, and Rose stared at the words, a smile on her face and tears, ridiculously, in her eyes. She sniffed and carefully folded the parchment, then stood up and hurried back into the house in search of a quill and ink, keen to respond and ask Jane to hide the message in the portal before they left for Chawton House.

The disquiet tumbling through her mind over Christopher Wallace and his origins was currently in combat with her anxiety over Jane's experiencing some problems with the use of the charm. She hadn't dared to tell Morgan about what had happened, and Rose eyed the charm warily, nestled in its place under the floorboard, as Jane placed her letter with it. Was she right not to trust it?

'Is aught amiss?' Jane rose from fixing the board back in place.

'No, nothing.' Summoning a smile, Rose turned for the door. Speculation was pointless, and she had a more pressing matter to focus on for now. 'I'll wait in the garden for you.'

Rose ventured outside again, ambling along, her eye caught by the Austen ladies' donkey, eating grass in the far orchard. She was keen to join the men at the great house. Being with Aiden was a balm to her worry and she wanted to relay to him that the messaging system had worked. But also, it was far easier to be themselves around Edward and Charles, for although the former was clearly not overjoyed by the outcome of his sister's deeds, they at least both knew who their visitors were and where they were from, so the strain of pretence was much less.

A faint sound reached her, and almost against her volition, Rose's gaze was drawn towards the low wall bounding the Wallace family's garden. Should she take this one last opportunity? Any other sighting of them would be purely chance and most likely in varied company.

Her curiosity overruling her sense, she stepped onto the grassy verge and crept towards the boundary. There was someone in the garden. Was it Mr Wallace? Rose hadn't realised how much she wished it was until she felt disappointment wash over her. It was Olivia, a basket on her arm, and as Rose watched, she bent to cut some herbs before dropping them into it.

Rose turned to ostensibly inspect the leaves of the sapling near the wall for a moment, then froze. There it was again, the familiar tune drifting to her on the breeze in snatches as Olivia went about her errand.

Edging towards the wall again, and feeling all the stupidity of what she was doing, Rose peered cautiously over. The girl had moved closer to the end of the garden, and suddenly she looked up.

'Oh, good morning.' A rush of pink filled her cheeks and she bobbed a curtsey, and Rose did the same.

'Sorry. I mean, forgive me. I did not mean to startle you. I was…' Rose drew in a calming breath, though her heart was beating rapidly and her skin was tingling. 'I was enjoying your singing.'

Olivia's eyes widened, but she said nothing, moving from foot to foot, and Rose wondered if she should just leave. She wasn't sure Mr and Mrs Wallace, having already been at the receiving end of Rose's bad manners the previous day, would want their daughter to be talking to her.

'Good morning, Miss Olivia.'

Rose started. Jane had come to stand beside her.

The girl repeated her curtsey. 'Good morning, Miss Austen.'

'I believe my friend is curious as to where you learned your pretty tune. It is not one I am familiar with?'

Olivia's features brightened. 'You are not the first to speak so. We have yet to meet anyone who is.'

The tingling of Rose's skin intensified and she held her breath, her gaze fixed on the young girl before them. She was thankful for Jane's presence, for she didn't think she could have summoned a coherent word.

Jane smiled kindly at Olivia. 'How intriguing. Pray, how came you to learn it?'

To both Jane and Rose's surprise, a head suddenly popped up from behind a bank of ferns to their left. Anne!

'I know the answer to this!'

She hurried around the nearby border and approached the wall, a wide smile on her face. 'Papa taught us!' She turned to look at her sister. 'Did he not, Olivia?'

Olivia seemed less wary now Anne had joined her, and stepped a little closer. 'He sang it to us when we were small. We all know it.' She waved a hand towards the house. 'Papa says he loves the name Rosemary, though 'tis a most unusual one.'

''Tis but a herb, though a pleasant one.' Anne beamed at them over the wall, and Rose could not help but smile at her enthusiasm. 'We used to tease Papa, did we not, about the words?' She looked up at her sister, who smiled.

'Indeed.' She looked from Jane to Rose. 'We felt it should not be "Love Grows Where My Rosemary Goes", but the reverse! Rosemary *grows*, do you see?' Olivia looked expectantly from Rose to Jane this time. 'But Papa was adamant he had the right of it.'

Jane cast a quick glance at Rose and seemed to realise she was struggling. She turned to both girls, smiled once again and took Rose firmly by the arm. 'You do it much justice, for you both sing it so sweetly. We must bid you good day.'

Tugging Rose into a curtsey as both girls bobbed in response, Jane turned her around and led her away. Stumbling a little on legs too weak to support her, Rose clutched her midriff, which was churning wildly. There was no denying it now: her father, by whatever fair or foul means, was alive and living in the early nineteenth century!

Chapter 14

Jane had given her a few minutes to compose herself before suggesting they begin the walk up to the great house, and Rose had drawn in a steadying breath, her arms wrapped around her middle, before following Jane out of the gate into the road.

Rose had very few memories of her father, and those she had, she suspected had been created by her imagination around the only photo she had to remember him by. She had been so young when he had died – disappeared, apparently – that whatever sense of loss she may have experienced was just a distant memory.

She was conscious of Jane eyeing her discreetly as they walked, and Rose lifted a hand before it dropped helplessly to her side. 'I don't know why I'm feeling so disturbed. You did tell me. The evidence has been growing for the past few days.'

She glanced at the lady walking by her side, but Jane merely squeezed her arm gently and said nothing.

With a sigh, Rose threw a final glance towards the lane leading to the Wallace house before turning resolutely away. She needed to talk to Aiden. He was the only thing she had to cling onto from her old life, the only tangible, logical presence in all of this insanity.

It did not take long for Rose to settle into the elegant chamber she was shown to by Edward's housekeeper, and she was thankful to discover a connecting door to Jane's almost identical room.

They returned downstairs, and Rose was almost desperate for some sight of Aiden. Jane seemed to sense her urgency, and on speaking to Charles determined he was out walking in the grounds.

'Go, Rose. Take some air. I will remain with my brothers, that you may have some time to talk.'

With a grateful smile, Rose almost flew out of the door and down the steps onto the gravel sweep. Her gaze roamed down the driveway towards the church, then over the surrounding fields. There was no sign of Aiden here, so she turned her steps up towards the back of the house and the grassy walk leading to where she knew in the future there would be a rose garden.

It did not take her long to see him, and she smiled faintly, despite her general disquiet. He was in conversation with one of the gardeners and seemed to be asking about the glasshouses.

Once he saw Rose, however, he excused himself and came to meet her, and before he could speak, she blurted out what had just happened. He led her to a bench, shielded by close hedging on three sides, and dropped into the seat beside her.

'No matter how much the possibility has been mooted between us all, confirming it was always going to be a shock.'

Aiden's voice was sympathetic, but also logical, and Rose's agitation calmed.

'Rose?'

She let out a huff of breath, then summoned a smile. 'You're right. Part of my turmoil is that I don't know how to feel. Clearly, this man is my father and yet…'

'We have faced some unbelievable facts these past few days, but you're doing brilliantly in a challenging situation.'

Rose smiled ruefully. 'I wish I felt I was!'

'Tell me what you're thinking. It may help to share it.'

'I'm starting to realise I, privately, defined myself as a girl without a father. I was barely two when he… left. As a child, he held the same place as a favourite fictional character. As I grew up, I saw friends with their fathers and felt some sense of how there was something I'd never had, you know, the way as a teenager, you miss the kisses you haven't even shared yet?'

Aiden smiled faintly and took her hand, but Rose felt shallow and full of guilt. 'Then, as an adult, I didn't dwell on him any more than I did a distant ancestor. And now…'

Aiden squeezed her hand. 'Go on.'

'I see the daughters he's been able to raise, and I envy them. I've lived my whole life without needing him, but now it's as if I suddenly have a huge hole in my heart.' Rose stopped. Her throat was tight and she wiped away the sudden wetness on her lashes. 'How can it be so different, so fast? This man is no one to me, and I'm nothing to him, and yet it feels as if my world will end if he doesn't want to know me.'

Aiden turned in his seat to face her. 'None of us can predict how he will react. His response will be what it is. All you can do is make a choice over whether to reveal who you are, and whatever decision you come to, you need to be able to live with yourself afterwards.'

Had she really been expecting platitudes and empty assurances? 'Usually your straightforward way of talking reassures me.'

'Usually?'

Rose nodded. 'You don't understand how far I've come just in the last week. I'm normally paralysingly shy.'

'You keep saying that.' Aiden leaned towards her, speaking softly. 'But how can an alternate reality survivor, a history-saving time traveller, ever be considered paralysingly shy?'

Regardless of whether anyone saw them, Aiden swept her into his embrace, and she melted against him, losing herself in the moment, until the persistent call of a passing rook penetrated her mind.

Pulling back, she straightened up and looked around frantically. 'Oh my God, Aiden, what if someone outside the Austen family saw us kissing? Mr Wallace would have to reject my acquaintance for the moral good of his daughters!'

Aiden dropped a kiss on her nose, then tucked a loose curl behind her ear. 'You forget he wasn't raised in this society.'

'No, but he's been here a long time, and he's raising his children here.' Rose folded her hands primly in her lap. 'I have the morals of a Regency hussy.'

Aiden laughed, turning to face the open grounds before them. 'Well then, we must control ourselves a little longer.'

'One point in favour of going home, isn't it?'

A strange look filtered across Aiden's features. Then, he said quietly, 'Is there another option?'

Rose blinked; she'd never even considered staying here. Where had that come from? She shook her head, embarrassed. 'Of course not.'

'Well then.' Aiden got to his feet and offered her his arm. 'Let's join the others and find out the plans for this picnic tomorrow.'

–

As the day progressed, the occupants of Chawton House separated to attend to various interests. Edward professed a need to meet with his steward, who was not based on the estate generally, and disappeared in the direction of the estate offices. Charles suggested accompanying Aiden on a ride around the neighbouring villages, which offered a wealth of historical sites of interest, and Rose had urged him to go, but as they strode towards the stables, Jane begged Rose to excuse her too.

Left to her own devices and company, Rose paced restlessly around the oak-panelled room on the first floor, frequently pausing in the alcove where the window looked down the driveway. Her insides would not stop churning or her mind spinning. She had to do this; she had to be brave about it, but how on earth would she make a beginning at the picnic? There had better be wine on offer!

If only Morgan were at the end of a phone, a text or a video call. She was only in Bath, but hundreds of years away in time, and Rose had never felt so bereft, so in need of her reassuring company, not even during her foray into the alternate reality.

'Jane, would it be possible to… oh, sorry!'

Rose had hurried into the neighbouring room, where Jane had taken herself, and she was now hurriedly pulling her slope over the page she was writing on.

'Is it *Mansfield Park*?'

Jane hesitated, then smiled. 'You know my habits. It is instinctive for me to conceal my purpose. I forget who I am with. How may I assist you?'

'Would it be too much to ask to send another note to Morgan? I know I only just wrote, but...'

'You are used to easy communication, yes?' Jane's tone was understanding, and she gestured towards the bureau against the far wall. 'Edward has ample resources at his disposal. Take what you wish. May I leave you to your own devices for a time? These edits are long overdue, but I shall endeavour to call at the cottage at the soonest opportunity.'

'Yes, of course.'

It took Rose over an hour to pen the relatively short note to Morgan, updating her on the morning's revelation, and several ruined sheets of precious parchment. She began to understand her friend's difficulty in mastering the use of a quill and ink. Had the consumables not been Edward's she would have been riddled with guilt at the wastage. Should she wait for whenever Jane was ready? Rose peered out of the window; she was growing impatient with her own company. She would walk down now, get some air and walk off some of her agitation. She tucked the carefully blotted letter into her reticule, grabbed her bonnet and shawl and hurried out of the house and down the drive.

How long would Aiden be gone? She had no idea how far Charles would decide to roam. Rose's spirits lifted as she walked towards the lane into the village. Charles may rue having made the suggestion. He had no concept of how deeply Aiden could lose himself in history when given the chance.

As Rose neared the cottage, however, she hesitated. Wasn't Martha Lloyd due to return today? Hadn't they moved to Chawton House to avoid further awkward questions? She bit her lip, her hand going to her reticule. She really needed to know she'd sent her letter on its way through time, even if Morgan didn't get over to Chawton again for a day or so to retrieve it.

'Good afternoon, Miss Wallace.'

Cassandra was walking along the road towards her, and they met on the corner by the pond.

'Good afternoon, Miss Austen.'

'I have been for the post.' Cassandra raised her hand, which contained a couple of letters. 'Perhaps you would be so kind as to pass this to my sister?' She handed one over. 'It is from our brother, Edward's, eldest. She and Jane are regular correspondents.'

Rose was well aware of the closeness of Jane and Fanny Knight and smiled as she took the letter. That she should be holding such a piece of history!

She opened her reticule to place it inside and was reminded of her purpose. 'May I trouble you to put this in the usual place, Miss Austen? Your sister was busy with her writing, but says she will call to do what she must later.'

She held out the letter addressed to Morgan, and Cassandra took it. 'Your friendship with Miss Taylor reminds me of my bond with my sister. Corresponding with her is all that keeps me sane when she travels.'

Rose smiled. Cassandra was the sweetest person. It wasn't the time to point out she'd been used to being

162

eight hours away from Morgan's time, not more than 200 years. She could understand, after all, why she and Jane had missed each other so much when Jane became trapped in the future. How sad was it to consider the many years Cassandra would live on in Chawton without her sister's companionship?

'You are well?' Cassandra was peering at Rose in concern, and she summoned a smile.

'Yes. Forgive me. My mind was wandering.'

They parted company, and Rose watched the lady enter the house before turning on her heel to retrace her steps. The gratification of a swift response from Morgan was beyond both their reaches, but at least this was something.

She had no idea how long Jane would be engrossed in her writing, and the thought of roaming restlessly around the great house with no one to distract her wayward thoughts wasn't appealing. Looking around, Rose noticed the stile she had climbed over the other day, when she had found Anne Wallace in the nettles.

She hurried across the road and was soon in the field beyond, relishing the autumnal sunshine, its gentle warmth caressing her arms, wishing she could shed her bonnet and gloves and free her hair from its restraints. There were sheep grazing nearby and the tips of the leaves on the distant trees were turning to burnished gold.

Trying not to use her usual stride, she made her way along the field, but had barely gone a few paces when she became aware of someone coming towards her.

It was Christopher Wallace.

Rose's heart felt as though it had leapt up into her throat before sliding back into position, and she almost gasped at the effect.

Calm, keep calm. Breathe, she intoned, trying to take her own advice as he neared her. His gaze was on the ground, and he didn't seem to have detected her presence, and Rose cast around frantically for some way of concealing herself, but it was a vast open field aside from the grazing sheep, and she didn't think they'd oblige if she tried to hide behind one of them!

'Oh! Forgive me!' Mr Wallace had looked up and seen her, and he raised his hat, his gaze narrowing. 'Were we not introduced recently?'

Rose opened her mouth, but no words came and, conscious of warmth filling her cheeks, she nodded. This was her father, that was his voice. Had he read stories to her at bedtime? How was it she couldn't remember it?

'I do not recall a name?'

With a start, Rose's gaze flew to his. *Come on, Rose. At least show better manners than you did yesterday!* Pulling herself together, she tried to smile. 'I hope you will forgive me. We were being introduced by Captain Austen when… something startled me. I left rather precipitously.'

'Then permit me to do the honours.' He bowed formally. 'Christopher Wallace, at your service, ma'am.' He smiled and Rose's insides did a strange dance. That smile; the smile in the photo in her flat…

'I, I…' She tried to clear the restriction in her throat. 'We share a name. It is a coincidence, is it not? My name is also Wallace. Miss Wallace.' Something stopped her from giving her first name. Was it done for women, when introducing oneself to a gentleman? For the life of her, her mind was blank and she couldn't remember!

He looked surprised, then smiled. 'Coincidence indeed. Well, I shall not keep you from your rambles, Miss Wallace. Good day to you.'

He raised his hat once more and set off along the path towards the stile, and Rose stayed motionless for a moment, her mind racing. What should she do? What could she say? Should she not seize the moment? Was she a history-saving time traveller as Aiden had said or not?

'Wait!'

Christopher Wallace's steps slowed, and he turned around.

'Please wait.' Rose hurried to catch up with him, her heart pounding in her chest. Was she really going to do this?

She fetched up in front of him, conscious of the wary look in his eyes.

'There is something I wish to say to you.'

He inclined his head. 'As you wish, ma'am.'

'I… I know who you are.'

His gaze snapped to hers, the wariness increasing. 'I would be surprised if you did not. Were we not just introduced?'

There was no going back now. Rose raised her chin, straightened her shoulders and tried to ignore the swirling of her insides. 'Yes, but not properly. I know where you came from, about your past. You—' She hesitated, swallowing hard this time as he took a step back from her. Would he believe her? Suddenly, she unfastened her bonnet and pulled it from her head, revealing the auburn curls so similar in shade to Christopher Wallace's own hair. 'You will think me mad for saying this, but I have to. I believe you are my father.'

Chapter 15

To Rose's surprise, Christopher Wallace laughed. 'Forgive me, madam. I think you mistake me for someone else.'

'Do you? Do you really?'

He shook his head, waving a hand dismissively, but then his gaze fell on her hair, the pinkened cheeks, took in the grey eyes, so like his, so like Olivia's, and he faltered. 'You cannot be my...' He shook his head. 'She... I lost her, many years ago. She cannot be here.'

'But you do own to having had another child? An older child?'

'How do you know this?' He looked unsettled, tossing his hat to the ground and running a hand through his auburn curls. 'Have you been speaking to my wife?'

Rose shook her head, and he began pacing, gesturing with his arm. 'Perchance we are related in some way, but I know not how. We share a common name, a less common shade of colouring, but this is merely conjecture.'

Rose released a huff of breath. For some reason, she felt on surer ground, despite his denial. Having come from where he had, surely he realised the incredulous could become credible?

'You have slipped up. Did you not recognise Jane Austen for who she was?'

He turned on his heel. 'I know not of what you speak.'

'Yes, you do. She told me.'

'Miss Austen would do well to mind her own business. So she tells tales. That is where you are getting your information.' He stared keenly at Rose. 'It is many a year since I faced such interrogation. I had not supposed they would enlist women for such duties.'

Rose almost rolled her eyes. Should she mention the song? She certainly wasn't about to start singing it!

Christopher Wallace retrieved his hat and brushed it clean. 'I will take my leave of you, madam. Good day.'

He turned away again and began walking towards the stile, and Rose drew in a deep breath, raising her voice.

'You came to the past twenty-five years ago. I know not how. You left behind a wife and a daughter. You lived in a large house in Bathampton.'

He stopped but did not turn around. 'You cannot know this.'

'But I *do*. I am that child!'

He spun around. 'Do not torment me so! What you speak of is impossible!'

'As is your being here... Kit.'

His eyes widened at the use of Christopher's Wallace's nickname. His mouth opened, then closed again. He had gone terribly pale, and Rose took a step towards him. Perhaps she had given him too big a shock, but it was too late to stop now.

'You disappeared after a boating accident off the coast of Gibraltar in 1995. No body was ever found. Now I know why.'

He had paled even further, but no words came, and Rose took another step towards him, pleading with her eyes. 'You are my father, the father I lost when I was two years old. I have a photo of you; you are holding me and smiling. It is at the seaside somewhere and you are wearing a T-shirt with Duran Duran on it.'

He stared at her, then walked away a few paces, and Rose's heart sank. He didn't want to know her. She was part of a past he no longer wished to own. A tight band was gripping her chest and she could barely breathe. Her eyes ached with the effort to hold back tears.

Then, he swung around and strode back across the grassy path, stopping in front of her, his frantic gaze taking in her features. Rose held her breath as he reached out to touch one of her auburn curls. Then, he let out a guttural sound, as though a sob had been wrenched from him.

'Rose,' he whispered. 'My little Rosie.' His voice cracked as he swept Rose into his arms and hugged her so fiercely she felt she might break, but she didn't care as the tears finally flowed.

Recalcitrant though time had been in recent days, Rose was conscious of its stillness, of its weight around her – around them both – as they stood enfolded in each other's arms for the first time in twenty-five years.

Slowly, however, the outside world began to intrude: the sound of birds calling as they circled over the treetops, the bleat of the nearby sheep and the slow rumble of distant wheels on the road beyond the orchard.

Releasing each other, Rose and her father stepped back, both of them finally allowing themselves the indulgence of staring. Christopher Wallace was a good-looking man, tall and broad-shouldered, with a shock of auburn hair and the same grey eyes as Rose. Eyes which were now narrowing as he took in the figure before him.

'How can this be?' He ran a hand through his already unruly hair. 'This has to be a dream, or worse – a hallucination.'

Rose shook her head tearfully. 'You have no idea how many times I've thought the same in recent days, for several reasons.' She sniffed, then wiped her eyes with the back of her hand. 'It *is* real. I... well, for my part, I'm here because of Jane Austen. She... we...' Rose waved a hand, as if it could possibly encompass all that had happened since she first met Jane. 'We are friends. Something about you alerted her to the possibility of you not being from this time, so she came to fetch me, from the future.'

Confident this would confirm things, Rose looked expectantly at her father, but his face fell.

'Definitely a dream, then, and not a very coherent one at that.'

Rose took both his hands, smiling despite the disappointment in his face. How strange was it, despite his long residence in the past, that she had more experience of the shifts of time than he?

'I am *real* and so are you. We are flesh and blood. I have travelled through more than 200 years, I cannot have come this far only to have you dismiss me as a figment of your imagination!'

She could tell from his earnest gaze upon hers, the tightening of his grip upon her hands, that he wished to believe her.

'Dream or not, Rosie, I shall not turn away from you.' He looked around, his gaze moving from the grazing sheep to a small dung heap nearby. Then, he wrinkled his nose and turned to look down at her. 'I'm not dreaming that smell, am I?'

Rose shook her head. 'No, sir.'

He winced. 'You have no need for formality with me, child. I cannot believe it, but I must. If such a strange alteration has taken place in my own life, why should it not be so for others?'

'And…' Rose bit her lip. 'Are you happy?'

Smiling now, Christopher Wallace squeezed her hands before releasing them.

'I am indeed, though your presence makes my life complete.' He frowned as he brushed his hat and returned it to his head. 'Though it could be quite… uncomfortable to explain, if you truly are here – obviously you are, even though you cannot be…'

'You must accept it.'

Grey eyes held grey for a moment; then, he nodded. 'I do so with a pleasure beyond my own comprehension. There is much we need to discuss, much I must explain, both to you and to…' He paled. 'Oh lord, how complicated is this?'

Rose felt a little awkward. After all, his family were unlikely to know anything of his previous life.

'I don't wish to cause you any difficulty. If you think there is a better way, other than owning who I am…' Her voice faded. It was the last thing she wanted, but she was the interloper here, was she not?

Christopher, however, shook his head. 'Not at all.' Then he grinned, and Rose could not help but smile. 'Besides, what is life without a little absurdity? A little challenge?' He sobered. 'Talking of which, how… uh… how is your mother? Please tell me she is not with you!'

'No!' Rose pursed her lips. What else was there to say? 'She is, well, the same?'

His lips twitched. 'So, how long are you visiting your friend, Miss Austen?' He lifted his hands, acknowledging the ridiculousness of his question. 'How long do I have you for?'

The reminder of the tenuousness of her situation returned to Rose in full measure. 'I do not know. I came not knowing Jane's purpose. I have passed three days here, with each one growing more and more certain you were my father.'

'I am curious, what convinced you?'

'The song. The one you taught your daughters.'

Culpability filled his face. 'Your sisters…'

Rose nodded, and he shook his head 'You must have had quite a few days of it.'

'And you must have had quite the years of it.' Rose eyed him warily, unsure how he would feel about explaining why he had never returned to the present, why he had abandoned his wife and child.

'I am adjusted. I have passed nigh on as many years here as I did in my earlier life.'

'Did you…?' Rose was conscious of heat filling her cheeks as emotion grew in her breast. 'Did you never think of returning?'

A silence embraced them both, and she raised cautious eyes to his only to be surprised by the look of shock on his face.

'Never *think*?' Christopher Wallace resumed his earlier pacing. 'What sort of man do you believe me to be, Rosie?' He turned on his heel and faced her. 'You believe I had a *choice*? That I chose to stay hundreds of years away from you? You were my life!'

'Sorry!' Rose hurried forward and took his hand. 'I assumed you were able to pass through time in both directions, as Jane has!'

He drew in a long breath. 'I never had such an option. To this day, I know not exactly how I came to be here.'

Rose stared at him, at first in disbelief, then with great sadness at all he had endured. What must it have been like to be trapped here, with no way of returning?

'I am so sorry. I can't begin to imagine what it was like.'

'Dearest Rosie.' Christopher Wallace's eyes were wet as he raised a hand and touched her cheek lightly. 'If you only knew the anguish I felt when I lost you... when I had no way of getting back to you.' His hand dropped to his side. 'We have so much to discuss; how can we—'

'Christopher! What are you about? We have been waiting on you this half hour!'

Spinning around, her father docked his hat. 'Forgive me, my dear.'

Rose peered around him. Mrs Wallace was in the orchard by the stile, and her smile faded as she realised someone was with her husband. The last thing Rose wanted was to cause anyone distress, and she knew it was time to leave.

'Coming, my dear!' He turned back to Rose and bowed formally. 'Until we meet again.' He raised serious eyes to hers. 'Which I trust will be timely.'

'Mr Knight is sending out invitations to a picnic on the morrow.' Rose spoke hurriedly, quietly, conscious of the frown on Mrs Wallace's features. 'Please say you will come?'

He bowed again. 'You may depend upon it, ma'am.' He winked at Rose, then turned on his heel and strode towards the stile. Mrs Wallace had likewise turned away and was making her way back across the orchard, and he looked over his shoulder.

Rose laughed. 'You will fall if you do not take care!'

'It would be a pleasant trip, would it not?' With a grin, Christopher Wallace scaled the stile with ease and waved a hand as he disappeared under the trees.

Emotionally spent yet elated, Rose waited a few moments before following her father over the stile and through the orchard. As she returned to the road, she could just see their backs as they entered the gate to their house.

What on earth should she do now? She needed time to gather her thoughts, time to think, time to absorb the enormity of what had just happened! She hesitated on the side of the road, oblivious to a passing cart and some children playing near the pond.

'Miss Wallace?'

With a start, Rose looked to her left. Cassandra had joined her, an empty basket on her arm, and was eyeing her with some concern.

'Miss Austen!' An idea suddenly came to Rose. 'Please may I borrow a quill and some ink? I must write a further note to Morgan, Miss Taylor.'

'Of course.'

'Shall I wait in the garden?'

'There is no need. My visits are complete, and Mama and Martha have gone to call upon Miss Benn.' Cassandra gestured along the lane ahead. 'They will be some time.'

Following Cassandra across the road, Rose sighed. Goodness only knew what Jane's sister must think of her, with her distracted air and no doubt pale as a ghost! But what could she possibly say? No words could match what had occurred just moments before.

Now the idea had taken hold, Rose was desperate to tell someone, though, and who better than Morgan?

Thankful for Jane making it possible for them to communicate, however awkwardly, Rose's long legs wanted dearly to rush ahead, but she forced herself to keep pace with Cassandra as they reached the gate into the garden.

A few minutes later, Cassandra ushered Rose into a seat beside the small table by the window in the dining room.

'I cannot sit here!' Rose stared up at Cassandra, but she merely frowned.

'Why ever not? My sister finds it more than conducive for composition.'

Precisely! Rose chewed her lip as Cassandra fetched paper, ink and a quill and then left the room, and she gently touched the wood of the table, smoothing it in reverence, before dipping the quill into the ink. Then, she frowned. Where were the words? How could she possibly explain what had just happened? Knowing how arduous writing in this old-fashioned method was, this was no time for a long explanation; brevity would have to suffice.

> *Met him alone, by chance, on a path across the fields. Told him who I was! He's my father, Morgan, he really is! There's to be a picnic tomorrow and he's coming. More when I can! R*

–

Jane was as good as her word, and was soon able to return to Chawton House, confirming she had placed Rose's letter and the additional note under the floorboard. It was now only a matter of time before Morgan managed to get back to Hampshire from Bath.

Trying to ignore her frustration over the delay – talking to Morgan was essential to her peace of mind – Rose stood at the window, watching for any sign of Aiden. He and Charles had been gone for the entire day, and Edward was growing impatient for their return.

'This truly is too much, Jane.'

Rose turned around. Edward was pacing to and fro in front of the fireplace, and Jane was eyeing him with amusement from across the room. She cast Rose a fleeting glance. Had she winked at her? Biting her lip, Rose looked over as the door opened, but to her disappointment, it was merely a servant come to clear the tea things.

'How typical of Charles, to absent himself when there is so much to do. Was not this,' Edward waved his arm in irritation, 'whole picnic notion one he raised?'

Cassandra, who had joined them in staying at the great house now Martha Lloyd had returned to keep Mrs Austen company, hurried to his side. 'There is little for you to trouble yourself with, Brother. It is not as though we are travelling; we are hosting it here. The servants are well versed in what to prepare, and all our guests will happily contribute a dish, as is tradition.' She smiled around the room. 'I have liaised with Cook and all is in hand. We simply needed to extend the invitation and that is done.'

Edward grunted and dropped into a nearby chair. 'And pray, Sister, who might our guests be, other than the Wallace family?'

'Dear Edward.' Cassandra spoke soothingly. 'We have asked Miss Benn, the Prowtings, Captain and Mrs Clement.' She paused as Jane faked a yawn. 'And Mr Papillon and his sister. That should be sufficient, should it not, with Mama and Martha joining us? Oh, and I understand the Hintons to be away.'

'Which saves us the trouble of excluding them.' Jane smirked at Edward, and when he threw her a warning look, she lifted a brow. 'They are hardly the best company, Edward. Mr Hall passed an intolerable evening at their home in the winter. There was a monstrous deal of stupid quizzing and common-place nonsense talked but scarcely any wit.'

Rose turned back to look out of the window. So many people. But then, she supposed it would be so much easier to speak to her father under the cover of others. Something caught her eye, and she peered down the drive. Two men on horseback were cantering towards the stables, and her heart leapt. Aiden was back.

Chapter 16

Sunday dawned fair, and Rose breathed a sigh of relief as she followed the rest of the Austen family down the drive for the morning service. Filled with trepidation at coming face to face with the Wallace family, she was relieved to find they were not in attendance, and when she whispered to Jane, who sat beside her, she confirmed they often attended evensong instead.

Her relief was tempered by her desperate need to lay eyes on her father again, but Rose tried hard to put her thoughts aside. He would come to the picnic, wouldn't he? He had said he would, and she had faith in him.

She cast Aiden a discreet glance as they began the first hymn, then tried to conceal her smile. Though he was mouthing the words, she was pretty certain his concentration was on the roof trusses. She followed his gaze, then looked around the interior more carefully. It was a little run-down and in need of some love. Rose returned her attention to her hymn book. She could almost be describing herself before Aiden…

She peeped at him under her lashes. He had been eager to hear about her encounter with her father the previous evening, but having already told Jane about it, Rose did not wish it to be openly discussed over the dinner table. As such, he had come to sit beside her after the gentlemen had re-joined the ladies, with Jane taking to the pianoforte at Edward's request, and the two brothers holding a quiet discourse as she entertained them.

Aiden's admiration for Rose's attempt to seize the moment had been heart-warming, and he had allowed her to talk herself dry before even hinting at how much pleasure his own day had brought him.

As they settled back into their pews for the sermon, she cast him another glance from under the rim of her bonnet. Everything she had learned since their strange journey to the past only attracted her more; she only hoped he felt the same.

–

Once the service was over and the requisite interactions with the congregation had taken place, the Chawton House party took their leave, attended now by both Mrs Austen and Martha Lloyd, who seemed like a very steady, pleasant-natured woman. They returned to the house, which was already full of bustle as the servants gathered the necessary items for the picnic on the sunny terraces adjacent to the house: cushions, blankets, serving trays and all the assorted accompaniments for dining al fresco in style.

Rose's only knowledge of such things came from her reading of Jane Austen's *Emma* and its infamous picnic on Box Hill. On that occasion, everyone had travelled by carriage and the servants had had to carry everything some distance to their chosen spot.

Jane had disappeared for a while, and Rose didn't want to know where, fearing she had taken it into her head to slip through time again. She had sufficient distraction in the meantime, though, as Mrs Austen had engaged her in conversation with Martha Lloyd. Trying her best to concentrate so as not to slip up, Rose looked up in relief as Jane returned to the room.

'Miss Wallace, would you be so kind as to come?' Jane held the door open, and Rose excused herself and hurried over.

'What is wrong?' Had her father decided against coming? Her insides were twisting in anticipation of disappointment, but Jane shook her head and opened her reticule.

'I did not err in my assumption your friend would communicate at the earliest opportunity.'

Taking the letters from Jane, Rose smiled gratefully, then hurried up the stairs to her room, collapsing onto the bed and then starting to laugh. There was not one response from Morgan, but several. The first was clearly written before Morgan had read Rose's second short note:

> *I got a train and a cab to Hampshire, and I spent the morning at the cottage today, wondering where exactly you were at that same moment. Do you remember how we used to call our friend Crazy Jenny? Well, trust me, I am definitely dubbed Crazy Californian by the docents here. I got caught kneeling on the floor in Jane's room looking for the loose board, told them I was praying for her. Not that praying is crazy, but considering the situation, it looked a tad excessive. I've found a place to stay closer to where you are – I need to be here for when you need me. Found a really nice lady, runs a bed and breakfast just a twenty-minute walk away from the cottage. I'm in the Tower Room, I couldn't resist a room with a name*

like that! The proprietor will cook me anything I need for breakfast. Result! P.S. I'm making lists of places to look at to rent in Bath and James is going to take me somewhere a little less densely populated to learn how to drive a modern carriage in this country. Wish both of us luck and tell me what's going on. No pressure, but I'm desperate and you know how I get when I'm desperate. P.P.S It's taken me three hours to write with this system. Not really. But sort of.

Rose smiled; she did indeed know how Morgan got when she was impatient. Rose would describe it politely as mercilessly repetitive. The next letter was almost unreadable it was so smeared:

Tell me EVERYTHING!! I can't believe it but I knew it. Can't write with this stupid quill while I'm crying. Love!!

There was an even tinier piece of parchment next:

And I'm so proud of you! Way to seize the moment! Oh, I'm so happy!

Rose moved on to the last one, which was a variation on the same: Morgan expressing extreme happiness and extreme curiosity, all the while saying she understood if Rose needed time before she could write again. Knowing her as Rose did, that meant Rose should risk everything but bodily harm to update her friend immediately.

As the hour for the arrival of the picnic guests approached, Rose returned to her room. Both Jane and Cassandra had proposed they change into something more suitable for company, and with the help of one of Edward's maids, she was soon wearing yet another modified gown of Cassandra's, her hair suitably dressed and a shawl and some shoes bestowed upon her.

Staring at her reflection, Rose could feel her anxiety returning. Would her father really turn up? Had he told his wife about her? What, if anything, did she already know about his past? Did she know the truth? Rose tried to observe herself in the mirror as if she didn't know who she was. Did she look suitably elegant, a daughter to be proud of? Her father already had three daughters – and hadn't there been mention of a son, too?

With a sigh, she turned away, clutching her shawl as her insides began their familiar dance. Why was it she felt more nervous of the pending meeting with her father's family than she had when she'd bumped into him yesterday?

'Come, Rose; it is time.'

Jane's head had appeared around the door, and she came into the room and walked over to where Rose stood.

'You will mangle it beyond all recognition if you do not take care.' She removed the silk shawl from Rose's taut grasp and walked around to drape it over her arms. 'There, that is better. Come.'

She looped her arm through Rose's and they left the room, making their way downstairs and out into the weak sunshine. An open carriage could be seen slowing down on the main road, and there were people approaching the gate near the church who were also on their way to join them.

Jane tugged on Rose's arm, and she turned away.

There were several servants ferrying all sorts of items to the level terrace where a serving table had already been set up, along with a white canopy of some sort.

'Here, take this.' Jane stopped to pick up some cushions where they had been piled ready for the guests and thrust two of them at Rose. 'We shall be able to secure the most favourable situation.'

Rose hugged the cushions to her chest as they walked over. 'The weather could not be more perfect. Do you think it will hold?'

Jane glanced up at the sky. 'I never make suppositions of the sort; I find it provokes the weather to defy expectation.'

When they reached the area set up for the picnic, Rose followed Jane's directions on where to place the cushions, then turned to observe the scene. An array of serving trays containing food were spread on the white cloth over the table, with two servants busying themselves with an urn of hot water and a large bowl of dark liquid with small cups hanging from it.

'It is rum punch. I would recommend the fresh lemonade over it.' Jane inclined her head towards a large glass pitcher of pale liquid.

Trying to ignore her growing nerves, Rose looked around. No one else from the house had joined them yet, and she felt conspicuous and on her guard at the same time.

'Will they be prompt, Jane? The Wallaces, I mean. What is the normal etiquette? At home, people tend to be fashionably late.'

'It would be considered rude to be intentionally late, but one does not hold someone to the second.' Jane looked down the path. 'But you need not fear it so.'

Sure enough, a group of people had gathered on the gravel sweep at the side of the house, and Rose's gaze raked the faces for her father's family or Aiden, but they weren't amongst them yet.

Before the party began the walk up to where the picnic was laid out, however, Cassandra came out of a gate in the wall around the courtyard and hurried over.

She was smiling as she reached them, a basket on her arm filled with various linen inners, each containing a different item.

'For the girls. We shall make some lavender bags. I believe the middle child is very shy; it helps to have one's hands busy in such cases.'

'A wise notion.' Jane glanced at Rose, then swiped gently at her hand, which was once more twisting the end of her silk shawl. 'Rose is nervous; perchance she should join you.'

Rose opened her mouth, then closed it, trying to smooth the creases she had unwittingly made in the shawl. 'I am.'

Cassandra reached out with her free hand and patted Rose's arm. 'From what my sister tells me, the hardest part is over, is it not? You must anticipate the time you have with this father you had thought to have lost.'

Rose endeavoured to ignore the dip of her heart at the mention of time and loss. 'I know, I know, but what do I… I mean, how do I…?' She put a hand to her head, looking from Cassandra to Jane. 'I just cannot think…'

'I believe when Cass said anticipate, that was not quite her meaning.' Jane shrugged at Cassandra's look. 'You are totally indisposed for employment and worrying so will only drive you to madness. Come, I will regale you with some tales of our illustrious guests.'

–

Before long, people had begun to walk over to the upper terrace, where several servants had taken up their positions, relieving the guests of the baskets containing their offerings and ferrying the wares to the end of the table left clear for them.

Jane had been amusing Rose with opinions on some of the local families as they neared where the rest of the family were greeting the new arrivals.

'Be warned,' Jane whispered. 'Mr Papillon, bless him, blunders on the border of a repartee for half an hour together without once striking it out. And as for Captain Clement – Charles would have it he is a brave man. He was at Trafalgar, you know, but do not permit yourself to become ensnared in a conversation with him.' She sighed exaggeratedly as they fetched up by the company and waited for Edward to do the necessary introductions, then added, 'I fear we are in great danger of suffering from intellectual solitude.'

Trying not to laugh out loud at Jane's outrageous commentary, Rose greeted those she had met at church and delivered the best curtsey she could summon when introductions to the others were made. The vicar, for all Jane's teasing, seemed a pleasant enough man, and his sister had a kind smile. Miss Benn was very sweet and couldn't help but remind Rose of poor Miss Bates in *Emma*. The Prowtings and their married daughter, along with the much maligned Captain Clement, paid Rose little mind, and she was freely able to turn her attention to the last of the party to arrive: the Wallace family.

Looking around frantically for Aiden, Rose was grateful when he materialised at her side as the Austen family made the remaining introductions. The girls all performed neat curtsies, but Rose couldn't help but scan each of their features, seeking a resemblance. Both Mary and Olivia shared her own colouring, their curls unadorned by bonnets, but Anne favoured her mother, with blond hair and blue eyes.

Then, Rose looked at her father. He was smiling widely, and as Cassandra led the three girls over to the rugs spread across the grass, he stepped forward, his wife on his arm. Vaguely aware of Jane urging her brothers and Aiden away, Rose could feel the easy warmth filling her cheeks as he spoke, and she tried to focus on his words, wary of looking at Mrs Wallace. What did she know?

To Rose's surprise, however, the lady stepped forward eagerly and took one of Rose's hands in both her own, pressing it firmly as she held her gaze expressively.

'It is a great pleasure to meet you again, Miss Wallace.'

Rose's eyes widened as her heart swelled in her breast. 'I—' She tried to clear her throat. 'And I you, ma'am.' Her voice was strained with emotion, and the lady patted her hand before releasing it.

'There, there, my dear. We shall enjoy some conversation in due course.' She turned to her husband. 'Come, Mr Wallace, we must do our duty and socialise for a time, and then you may speak to your… to Miss Wallace at your leisure.'

Rose watched them walk over to exchange pleasantries with Mr Papillon and his sister, her delight tempered by doubt. Her father must have admitted to her being his daughter, which was heart-warming, but what else did the lady know or understand? It would be good if she could know this before they spoke again!

The weather continued to hold as the afternoon progressed. It was a little chilly, but the sun remained valiant against the constant charge of white clouds across the sky. The company seemed well settled on their rugs and cushions, happily indulging in the fine fare on offer.

Rose had been seated with Jane, who seemed to have appointed herself her own particular guardian, and as she set off to secure them some more lemonade, Rose allowed her gaze to drift over the gathered company.

Mary Wallace was in conversation with the unmarried Prowting daughter – was it Catherine? – sharing a moment of merriment, and Rose smiled as she looked over to where Cassandra continued in company with Olivia and Anne. The former had her head down, busy fastening a lavender bag, but Anne was chatting energetically to the lady. Rose could only assume, from the lack of awareness when they greeted her earlier, that they knew nothing of her close association with them.

Mr Papillon's sister, Elizabeth, was strolling with Miss Benn, her parasol bobbing in the light breeze, and Edward was talking earnestly to Captain and Mrs Clement, gesturing up towards the land behind the house, no doubt outlining his vision for his new gardens. The rest of the gentlemen, Aiden included, had walked down onto the expanse of grass where a target had been set up for archery.

Naturally, Rose's eyes were drawn more often than not to her father but, not wishing to attract attention with her interest, she tried not to stare. He often met her gaze with his own, however, and would incline his head and smile. Their time to talk would come, Rose was certain.

Her gaze drifted almost as often towards Aiden. He looked more self-assured and confident than anywhere she'd ever seen him. Even when enthusing about his favourite subject, she couldn't recall seeing him more in his element. Aiden's attention seemed drawn to Christopher Wallace too, and Rose bit her lip. What should she tell her father about him? What *could* she tell him? They were hardly in a relationship yet.

With difficulty, Rose dragged her gaze away from him, her eyes scanning the charming scene. Never had a period film captured the perfection of this day. From the gentle weather and the epic, untouched scenery, to the feelings coursing through her veins, this was a day she would never forget.

'Another slice of my walnut cake, dear Miss Wallace?'

Looking up with a start, Rose realised Mrs Wallace had walked over to where she sat and was leaning down, offering a laden plate to her.

The kindness of her look, the gesture, was sufficient to encourage Rose to take a slice, even though she was no longer hungry.

'Thank you, you are too kind.'

'Not at all, my dear.' She straightened. 'Mr Wallace! Would you be so good as to join us?'

Mr Wallace looked up, then leapt to his feet, excusing himself from the reverend and hurrying over.

'Would you care to show Miss Wallace the horse Mr Knight has offered to sell to us? I believe he said it was in the far-most stable?'

'Most indubitably.' Christopher Wallace held out his hand and Rose grasped it, rising easily to stand beside him.

'There, my dears.' Mrs Wallace beamed at them both. 'I shall see you both directly.'

Rose wished she could tell the lady how much she appreciated her kind gesture, but she tried to look grateful, then took her father's proffered arm as they walked back towards the front of the house.

With Charles and Aiden halting their target practice to watch them, Cassandra eyeing them from the rug beside the girls and Jane nodding happily from her position by the jug of lemonade, Rose was once again thankful there were a few others there, at least, who had no idea what was going on!

Chapter 17

Rose and her father walked in silence until they had reached the gravel sweep running along the side of the house, but it was both companionable and full of anticipation, not fraught with the tensions that had gripped Rose in recent days.

As they rounded the house, Christopher looked down at his daughter and smiled. 'Do you ride?'

Rose laughed. 'A little; there haven't been many opportunities in Bath.'

He raised a brow. 'You still live in the area?'

'Yes, I love it. I have a dear little flat in Sydney Place.' For a moment, a pang of homesickness swept through Rose, but she brushed it aside. 'Why did you ask if I ride?' Was he thinking of suggesting they go for one now? She didn't think a week's pony trekking in Devon was going to suffice for the demands of galloping across the fields without a hard hat!

He drew them to a halt. 'Much as I appreciate my wife's intervention, the stables do not hold much appeal in such fine weather. Shall we walk down to the church?' He gestured towards the stone building, not hidden behind trees as it was in the future.

'Yes, of course.' Rose fell into step beside him. 'You told your wife about me.'

'I did.' Christopher glanced at Rose. 'That you are the daughter I long thought dead. I have never hidden you from her. She knew I had been wed, for I shared the intelligence with her soon after we met. The year of your birth remains a secret, however.'

Rose chewed on her lip. 'I'm glad I know what she understands. I was worried I might end up in private conversation with her and would put my foot in it.'

A laugh rumbled through the man beside her, and Rose raised a curious face to his. 'You cannot comprehend how singular it is, after all these years, to hear modern phrasing such as putting one's foot in something!'

With a rueful laugh, Rose nodded. 'You're right, I can't imagine.'

'You do not mind – that I told her?'

'Not at all. It makes things easier if the facts are simplified.'

They had reached the church now, and Christopher stood aside so that Rose could precede him into the grounds.

'She is a very understanding woman. Her generous heart, her compassion, were what drew me to her from the beginning.'

Rose didn't like to comment on how those were two things her own mother seemed to lack. She doubted her father would have forgotten.

'She seems exceedingly lovely in every way.' Rose stared at their feet, moving in unison along the path through the graveyard. 'So, she doesn't know the year of *your* birth either?'

Christopher was silent for a moment. Then, he waved a hand towards a bench facing out over the fields where

Rose had seem the family walking the other day. 'Come, let us sit for a while.'

Rose settled beside him, her heart swelling as he took one of her hands in his. His face, however, was uneasy.

'What is it?'

Christopher turned in his seat, his grey eyes softening. 'Long have I dreamed of being able to talk of this to you, and long have I thought it impossible.'

Rose smiled. 'Then let us take advantage of our present circumstances. Tell me what disturbs you so? Does she know the truth of where you came from?'

He removed his hat, placing it on the seat beside him. 'No, she does not. Believe me, the guilt has haunted me long enough – a lie by omission is still a lie, is it not? And Louisa does not deserve dishonesty.' He ran a hand through his hair, then looked back at Rose. 'But there are times when the first two decades of my life seem so unreal. I have made every effort to make up for keeping my secret through my love and dedication to her and to our children.' He shrugged lightly, though Rose didn't think he felt it lightly at all. 'And, as I could neither explain nor alter my circumstances, I decided it would have to suffice.'

'And have you never slipped up?' Recalling his teaching his children the song about Rosemary, Rose realised he could never have expected to be called out on anything if he did. After all, if not for Jane Austen and her slipping through time, who else would understand his meaning?

Christopher let out a small laugh. 'I am considered quite the eccentric, my dear. It has covered all manner of mishaps over the years.'

Rose squeezed his hand. 'I can't imagine all you have been through. I thought I had experienced something quite incredible this past week, but at least my torment had an end to it – and a fairly rapid one at that.'

He peered at her intently. 'I am displeased to hear of your torment. Is the matter truly resolved?'

As best she could, Rose quickly told him about Jane's becoming trapped in the twenty-first century, its repercussions and how they had managed to resolve things. When she had finished, he stared at her in silence for a moment. Then, he smiled.

'You are quite the resourceful young woman, my dear. I am proud of you.' He frowned. 'When you first mentioned Miss Austen as being your friend, I began to doubt if this was her time of origin, despite knowing of her authorial achievements.'

'Then now you understand. It is through the use of her charmed necklace that I am here.'

'And you say Captain Austen bestowed it upon her? Does he… Is he aware of who I am now?'

'Yes. He explained how he met you in Gibraltar, of course. But do you really not know how you came back here?'

'I cannot say. To be certain, I possessed no physical charm I am aware of that raised me from the ocean almost 200 years distant. And you can perhaps appreciate that, in this time, my avenues for seeking answers were limited, not least given my lack of means and acquaintance.'

'No Google,' murmured Rose under her breath. She wasn't sure how she'd survive without her go-to resource.

Her father frowned, and she shook her head. 'Nothing. Something invented after you… left. So, what *do* you remember?'

His gaze drifted over the low stone wall bounding the churchyard, though Rose suspected he saw nothing of the view. 'I went on a business trip. Four of us decided to take a boat out. We were warned not to by the locals; they said there was a storm coming. It was a beautiful day – cloudless. We just laughed at them.' He sighed. 'Such arrogance. We were out on the water some hours later, not far from the shoreline, just fishing, laughing, relishing the heat of the day when the waves began to boil and swirl, like some sort of vast cauldron. Someone was in the water and I remember diving in, swimming towards them.' He shuddered and Rose held even tighter onto his hand, her heart breaking for his past fear and anguish. 'It went black. There was nothing. When I opened my eyes again, I was in another world.'

'You fell into the sea in 1995 and emerged in...'

'1788 – not that I realised it immediately.'

'That's incredible!' Although Rose had known of his disappearance and reappearance, it was incredible to hear it spoken of so matter-of-factly.

'It is, and yet, it is the entirety of my experience.'

'What happened? How were you rescued?'

Christopher's gaze returned to the distance. 'I was washed up on the shoreline, drifting in and out of consciousness. Apparently, a ship had foundered on the rocks; there were bodies being washed up beside me. When I fully awoke, I was being tended by a native woman in her hut – Drusilla was the name she gave. She was held in some reverence by the locals, and a little in awe, for some said she possessed an unnatural power for healing.'

He fell silent, and Rose suspected he was lost in memories. After all, he had not been able to speak of any of this in twenty-five years.

Stirring in his seat, Christopher turned to look at Rose again. 'I spent a long time thinking madness had taken me. Surely I would awaken in a hospital bed with a crazy dream to tell? But there was no waking from my nightmare.'

He lowered his head and Rose scooted closer to him on the bench, holding tightly to his hand.

'Do not speak of it, if it upsets you.'

'I am not accustomed to speaking of it, but there is no harm in doing so to you. You have as much right as anyone to hear why I was unable to return and be the father I should have been.'

Rose squeezed his hand. 'Although I was young when you left, I never doubted you loved me.'

Tears filled Christopher's eyes, and he raised a hand to touch her cheek. 'My sweet Rosie. You were such a darling child, the light of my life.' He ducked his head, then dashed his arm across his eyes before raising it again. 'The more time passed, the more desperate I became to get back home. To you, to my version of reality. But how could I, when I had no notion of how I came to be there? I was a stranger in the strangest land anyone ever landed in.' He shook his head at the memories. 'Eventually, I was well enough to leave the care of Drusilla, and everyday needs and everyday life ousted my confusion and anxiety. I had to eat, find a way of supporting myself.'

'What did you do?'

To her relief, his smile returned. 'I began with fishing, trying to sell my catch at the local market. It sufficed to feed me, but I had no roof over my head.' The smile faded. 'Sometimes I would walk to a local rocky outcrop and throw myself into the waves, letting the water close over my head, hoping and praying that when I surfaced, I would be back in my time. To no avail.'

Sadness consumed Rose at his desperation. 'And then?'

'You have no notion, Rose, how I wished I had paid more attention in my maths and science lessons! What use was my love of books and literature in my situation? Perchance I might have been able to invent something, create something I knew existed in our time. It would have done so much good.' He paused, then grinned. 'And lined my pockets well. But it was not to be. It was mere chance that made me realise I did have some knowledge that could benefit others in this world and, like most things that go well for us, it gave me an occupation, a purpose in life.'

'What was it?'

He smiled at the eagerness in her voice. 'An everyday awareness in advance of most people here… even those who professed to be medical men.'

Rose's eyes widened. 'You pretended to be a doctor?'

'Not entirely, no! I merely professed to some know-ledge. You cannot appreciate how poor the living conditions were for many in Gibraltar then. Infection and disease were rife.'

Rose's wariness must have been reflected in her face, because he took her other hand and said gently, 'Do not judge me, Rose. It was a small subterfuge, and I never professed to being medically trained.' He shrugged. 'In all truth, it does not require a qualification to advise people away from certain practices later known to be detrimental to one's health, such as keeping someone with a fever warm, away from fresh air rather than the opposite; to tell people to avoid excessive use of leeches; to boil bandages in hot water, to wash their hands even, to aid in the prevention of infection.'

'Or to limit one's use of arsenic.'

'Indeed.' Christopher shrugged. 'It sufficed to allow me a roof over my head, a purpose. Then, one day, a disturbance occurred in the street near where I was attending a sick child. A gentleman was held to ransom and I intervened. I thought little enough of it, but some months later, the gentleman sought me out. He was adamant I had saved his life.'

'That's wonderful!'

'More so than you imagine. He was a man of extensive property, and he wished to express his gratitude. I was invited to stay with him and his family for as long as I wished, a most fortuitous offer, for during that time, I made the acquaintance of his eldest daughter, the beautiful human being I am proud to call my wife. Upon our marriage, he not only bestowed his blessing but also a settlement which enables me to live as a gentleman and raise my family as such. The rest is history.' He grinned. 'No pun intended.'

Rose was touched by his obvious deep affection for his family. 'It must have been strange to return to an England that was so different from the one you left. How did you—?'

She stopped as Christopher raised a hand. 'No, no. I have said sufficient for now. I wish to hear your story. What have you done for the last twenty-five years? Did you enjoy school? What do you do for a living?' He paled suddenly. 'Do I have grandchildren?'

Rose could not help but laugh as she shook her head. 'No! To be honest, my life has been, until very recently, pretty devoid of anything like the adventure in yours. I did well in school, I've always been an avid reader...'

'As are Anne and Olivia.'

Rose smirked. 'I know. I spoke to Olivia briefly. I work for a small, but successful letting company. I love it and...' With a pang, her thoughts fled through time to what James might be doing in preparation for the week ahead – a week when she should have returned to her desk from her holiday.

'You are missing it?'

'Yes! No!' Rose summoned a smile. 'I'm good at my job, I think. My boss and I get on well.' It probably wasn't the right time to mention James' brief foray into the early nineteenth century. 'I did get engaged a few years ago, but it didn't work out. It was a mistake, it just took me a while to realise it.'

'Did he break your heart?' Christopher was bristling at her side. 'I would have given him a piece of my mind if I had only had the chance. How dare he—'

'Shh.' It was both sweet and a little amusing to have her father up in arms in such a way. 'I came to my senses, walked away from him. But there is someone...' Her thoughts drifted to Aiden, to the memory of their al fresco lunch in this very churchyard but days ago in her other life.

'Someone, Rose?'

'Yes, it is very recent. I mean, I don't know what is going to happen.' *I want to marry him. And have his babies.* Rose silenced the voice in her head and rushed on. 'I like him very much. He's an archaeologist. A much admired one.' *Especially by me.*

'And you like him?'

'I like him... *very much.*'

Warmth filled Rose's cheeks under her father's assessing gaze. Then, he smiled. 'He will be a simpleton if he does not return your admiration, Rosie.'

Reflecting on the past few days, the stolen kisses, the intensity of Aiden's stare across a room, Rose could feel the heat in her cheeks intensifying. How strange it was to speak of such a thing with her father!

'Tell me about—'

'Forgive the interruption, sir. Miss Wallace.'

They both spun around in their seat. Aiden was just a few paces away from them.

Chapter 18

Rose had no idea how long Aiden had been there, but hoped fervently he hadn't heard anything she'd said. It was a good thing he couldn't hear anything she'd thought!

Aiden looked uncomfortable, and Rose suspected he had not been overly willing to intrude, but he also seemed quite fascinated with the deepening of the colour in Rose's cheeks, and she ducked her head.

Christopher, in the meantime, got to his feet. 'Mr Trevellyan. How may we assist you?'

'I am bid by Mr Knight to collect you, sir. The guests are returning to the house to drink tea prior to their departure.'

Rose got to her feet. 'We had best do as requested, sir.'

They both fell into step beside Aiden and nothing was said as they made their way out of the churchyard and began their descent of the driveway. Rose's mind was trying to grapple with the fact Aiden knew Christopher Wallace was her father, but her father had no idea who Aiden was. Ought she to take this opportunity to reveal the truth?

Before she could decide how to even begin such a conversation, however, Christopher turned to Aiden. 'And whence do you hail, my good sir?'

Aiden threw Rose a glance and, realising it was the answer, she nodded.

'The twenty-first century, sir.'

Christopher's eyes widened and he stopped walking. 'You…' He turned to Rose in astonishment. 'I am not sure I…'

'Mr Trevellyan is a…' She bit her lip. 'A friend of mine. He accompanied me here a few days ago. I think you begin to understand where from.'

His gaze narrowing, Christopher stared from Rose to Aiden. 'By chance, sir, would your profession be in archaeology?'

Aiden blinked. 'Er, yes indeed, Mr Wallace.'

'All is well, then.' He held out his arm to Rose. 'I assume you know who I am?'

'I do, sir.'

'Good, good.' Christopher's gaze drifted up the drive to where the picnic party was gathering at the front of the house. 'Pleased though I am to comprehend who you are, forgive me for saying I am thankful all other faces here are familiar to me, else I might suppose there are others yet to reveal themselves!'

'There were,' muttered Rose, thinking of Morgan and James.

–

The following morning, Rose woke eager to meet with her father again. They had managed barely a word as everyone took tea before departing on the previous afternoon, though Mrs Wallace had sat beside her for a while.

Thankfully, Anne had joined them, so there was no opportunity for her to quiz Rose about anything she might have found challenging, such as how her father had thought her dead when she wasn't and where she had been all these years or, more pertinently, how she had now found him. Had he already touched on that with his wife?

She had risen early, having asked the maid if there was any chance she could bathe, and Rose looked over expectantly as the door to the servants' stairs opened, then felt horribly guilty at the number of servants required to bring the necessary hot water. The maid ushered her into the dressing room adjacent to her bedroom and as soon as the servants trooped out of the room, Rose lowered herself into the rather small tin bath, feeling both relieved and conspicuous.

It took some time for her hair to dry, and despite washing it with the lotion provided – which she'd been told contained egg white to enhance the shine – it felt unnaturally heavy.

The maid had stayed to help her to dress and put her hair up, but as soon as she left the room, Rose wandered over to the window, which overlooked the fields stretching away to the south of the house, and she leaned forward as she saw a rider on horseback come round from the stable block and set his horse in motion.

Her heart did its usual dance as she realised it was Aiden, and she watched him race across the fields, scaling the far wall and disappearing into the distance. He seemed to be relishing his time here, and Rose turned her back on the scene with a sigh. Despite everything she missed about her old life, was she in danger of feeling the same? How was she ever to leave her father now they were reunited?

A tapping on the door drew her attention, and she was relieved when Jane put her head around it.

'Good morning, Rose. I trust you slept well?'

'I did, thank you.' With a smile, Rose pointed to Jane's hand. 'Has Morgan written?'

Jane held out the letter to her. 'She is a most prolific correspondent. I did not expect it of her.'

'Why not?'

Rose studied the folded paper. Morgan had addressed it to '*Miss Rose Wallace, Care of the Mistress of the Hole Under the Floorboard*'.

'Your friend has such immediacy. I have seen her communicating through her phone and on her—' Jane paused, frowning. 'Folding machine. The flat one she had those likenesses on.'

'Laptop.'

Jane smiled. 'The speed with which she formed the words astounded me. I did not expect her to tolerate the slowness of quill and ink.' She walked over to the window, then turned to face Rose. 'I believe it to be testament to her dedication to you.'

The reminder of Morgan, of the ease of their friendship and how often they would email, text or video chat brought a wave of homesickness beyond what Rose had felt before. Her old life had almost seemed distant after being with her father. She'd barely given a thought to it being Monday morning, that she should have been back at her desk at Luxury Lettings of Bath, doing her best to make James' life easier.

'I will leave you to read your letter.' Jane opened the door, then turned on the threshold. 'I happened upon your father when I was at the cottage this morning.'

Rose frowned. 'You were about very early, Jane.'

Her expression became evasive. 'There was something I needed to do.' She waved a hand airily. 'And it gave me an opportunity to retrieve your letter. Your father wishes to spend some time with you, if you can spare it. I assured him you could.'

'How am I to achieve that?'

'Cassandra is walking down to the village directly. She has a basket to distribute. If you go with her, I think you will find your father is hovering near the orchard opposite the cottage in hopes of seeing you.'

Jane left, and Rose tucked the letter into her reticule, grabbed a shawl and bonnet and hurried out of the room. She would read Morgan's letter as she walked to meet her father. How comforting both those things sounded!

Cassandra left Rose to peruse her letter as they walked, humming softly under her breath, and Rose quickly unfolded the sheet, then smiled. Morgan's ability with the quill was improving a little. There were far less blots of ink and only two words crossed out this time.

> *Rose! I'm so happy for you. You're right – words can't really cover it. So I won't, I'll wait until you get back! James came over from Bath last night, and we walked to the great house together. It was beautiful… so different to how we saw it last; at least, it was once I was warm enough from walking that I wasn't distracted by the arctic winds. Is it always this cold at night in the fall?*
>
> *It was a bit surreal, looking at Chawton House and knowing you were there, only ~~200 years~~ at some other time! You know – we were there at the same moment, but not really? I'm thinking of you constantly and your situation. I'm so glad you have friends around you, but it's lonely without you here. James is too smart (and too busy) to try to fill the void. You aren't going to leave me here*

alone are you? Do you really think England can survive me without you to curb the shock?

Hugs, M xx

P.S. I saw Jane being led around by one of the regulars. I think she was in training, but I was on my way out and didn't dare blow her cover. I laughed the entire way home to my lovely B&B. Will she let me come with her to get you and Aiden, d'you think? I'll come as soon as you tell me when! Enjoy yourself, take your time, but also... hurry home!

P.P.S. Sure I saw James' missing suit in the window of a thrift store in Alton!

With a smile, Rose returned the letter to her reticule. She would have to reply to Morgan as soon as she got back to the house.

'You are pleased with your correspondence?' Cassandra moved the heavy basket from one arm to the other, smiling at Rose.

'Yes, thank you. Morgan is, well, you saw. Just so full of life, even through the written word. I can almost feel her hugging me.'

'Such are my feelings when I am separated from my sister. Jane's voice carries so clearly through her letters to me, I feel we are close despite the distance.'

Rose smiled and glanced at the lady walking by her side. 'Even when writing to each other across a few hundred years?'

'Indeed! Ah, and here is your father, Miss Wallace.'

Looking up, Rose saw Christopher Wallace leaning against the stone wall bounding the orchard opposite the cottage, and he straightened and raised his hat, bowing as they both reached him.

'Miss Austen, Miss Wallace. Well met.'

'Good day, sir.' Cassandra smiled warmly, then touched Rose lightly on the arm. 'I must call upon Mama before I attend to my duties. Enjoy your walk.'

She paused, letting a horse and cart pass before picking her way across the road, and Rose took the arm of her father as he led her into the orchard. The bees were swarming around the hives in the far corner, birds were singing in the treetops and although it was not sunny, the weather was mild and Rose sighed happily as they strolled through the long grasses.

'How long do we have until you will be thought inappropriately missing?'

Christopher laughed. 'We are quite at liberty. My reputation as an inveterate conversationalist is well known hereabouts. I am considered to have difficulty curbing my words and am always behind my time.' He smirked at Rose. 'In more sense than one! I have never been known to pass up an opportunity to expound on any variety of subjects. Now, let us not worry about the seconds passing. Tell me more about you.'

Rose blushed but couldn't think of a single thing to say about herself that wasn't inane. 'What do you want to know?'

'Everything, anything. Dearest Rose.' He stopped walking and turned her to face him. 'Can you not imagine the height of my curiosity? When I last had the pleasure of beholding you, you were barely knee-high, speaking few words. You have lived five and twenty years since, and I will find aught of interest!'

Rose smiled as they resumed their walk. 'But twenty-five years is a long time. Where would you have me begin?'

'With minutiae. Do you like liquorice? Can you curl your tongue? Did you have to suffer braces? Have you ever broken a bone or had your wisdom teeth removed?' He grimaced. 'You would not wish for a tooth extraction in this century, I assure you.'

Rose laughed. This was easier. 'Yes, yes, no, no and yes. May I ask you the same?'

The conversation continued thus as they enjoyed learning of both the similarities and differences in their experiences, certainly in the modern world, but eventually, they knew they could linger no longer and turned their steps for the centre of the village once more.

As they reached the road again, however, the sound of a dog yapping could be heard, and Rose shook her head as they emerged from the orchard.

'Typical Prancer! I'm sure no other dog has caused as much mayhem in two different centuries!'

Her father came to stand beside her, his gaze following Rose's to where the dog was barking at the ducks on the pond. They were paying him absolutely no attention.

'Prancer? That is not his name, I assure you. That is Link, though you may be correct in what you say. He is forever running off, and is as likely to be found in our garden as his own.'

Rose turned to her father. 'Do you remember what I told you yesterday, of how Jane – Miss Austen – became trapped in the future?'

Christopher's eyes widened as he slowly turned to look back at the dog. Cassandra had emerged from one of the labourer's cottages nearby, a basket on her arm, and she called Link to heel. With a lingering look at the ducks, he reluctantly trotted over to his mistress, who smiled over at them before opening the gate to the next cottage in the row and urging the hound inside.

'You mean…'

'Link is Prancer; or rather, Prancer is Link. I suppose it depends how you look at it.'

'Then Link was *the* link? How well Miss Austen named him!'

Rose couldn't agree more, then frowned. Just how old *had* Prancer been when he'd been sent back in time? He'd have to be a decade older by now, though he didn't look to be slowing down at all.

'I wonder if it will encourage Miss Austen to name all her dogs Link?'

Christopher laughed. 'Whatever prompts you to make such a supposition?'

'Oh, just something I read once – about her having a dog called Link much later in her life.' Rose smiled at her father, brushing the thought aside. 'Shall we—?'

The sound of hooves pounding the ground drew their attention, just as a horse came into sight, moving at speed along the Gosport road from the direction of Chawton House.

'Ahoy! Miss Wallace! Hold fast!'

It was Charles Austen, and he drew his steed to an untidy halt before them and swung to the ground. He was breathing heavily.

Rose's grip on her father's arm tightened involuntarily as Christopher addressed the younger man. 'What is it, Captain?'

'Miss Wallace must return to the house immediately, sir. Come, we must not delay.' He tugged his horse over to a nearby mounting block, and Rose stared at him. Did he expect her to ride with him? She threw her father a worried glance, and he patted her hand where it rested on his arm.

'What is wrong, good sir? You are alarming the young lady.'

'Forgive me.' Charles dashed a hand across his brow. 'But it is imperative she come with me, sir.' He held out his hand.

'But what has happened? Is it Jane?' Rose shivered. Had something awful taken place in her absence?

'No. It is your friend. Mr Trevellyan.'

Chapter 19

Rose's skin went cold. 'What of him?'

Charles seemed to have better control of his breathing now. 'He went riding this morning, but his mount has returned without him. A search has begun, but as yet, there is no sign of him.'

Trying to suppress her panic, Rose turned to her father, but he was looking at Charles.

'Is it known in which direction he rode?'

'No; he did not—'

'Yes!'

They both looked at Rose, who was struggling to keep her voice steady. 'I saw him. He rode across the fields to the south of the house.'

'Then we must instruct the search party to ride in that direction. Come, Miss Wallace.' Charles held out his hand again, and Rose stepped forward to take it.

'I… I am not an accomplished rider, sir.'

For a moment, the tense look on Charles' face eased and he smiled. 'But I am, ma'am. You shall be quite safe with me.'

Rose felt precariously far off the ground as her father helped her to perch sideways on a saddle designed for a man, and she was thankful he retained a hand on her arm as Charles swung up behind her. Pony trekking had at least been done in suitable clothing and *not* side-saddle!

'Just hold on tight, Rosie, all will be well. Captain Austen may not have his brother's reputation on a horse, but perhaps that is all to the good on this occasion.' He turned to the captain. 'I will fetch my mount and join you directly.'

'Thank you. *Onward*, Arrow! Make haste!' Charles set his horse in motion, and Rose tried to keep calm, though her anxiety for Aiden was making her heart beat fast in her breast.

'To which brother did my father refer, Captain Austen?'

'Hah! To Fly.' Charles' voice was close to her ear as he urged the horse into a canter, and Rose held onto the saddle with all her might.

She frowned, unsure if she'd heard correctly. 'Fly?'

'Frank, or Francis as he was christened. Quite the daredevil on horseback, skilled but reckless. I am more inclined to take my ease.'

With that, he kicked the horse on and, as they galloped along the road, taking the corner into the lane with hair-raising speed, Rose couldn't help but let out a small shriek. If this was riding 'at ease', she had no desire to try anything wilder.

They drew to a halt before the house, and as a groom helped her dismount as carefully as she could, bearing in mind her attire, Jane hurried forward and took her arm to steady her.

'Send a boy over towards Farringdon, Cartwright, and tell the men there to head southwards.' Charles turned his mount and was off across the terraces, scaling the hedges on the far side and soon out of sight.

Rose was still leaning into Jane as they watched him go, unsure her legs would support her. What if they never found him? What if he'd fallen into a quarry, or was hidden by undergrowth?

'Jane...' All Rose's fears and anxieties were communicated in just one word, and the lady at her side seemed to understand, taking her hand and pressing it before urging her towards the stone steps into the house.

'Come, Rose. You must take a little wine to calm you. They will find the gentleman, I am certain.'

Rose shook her head, standing her ground. 'I can't! I want to wait here.' Her gaze was drawn in the direction she'd seen Aiden ride that morning, the same direction Charles had just gone.

'Then I will leave you to your vigil for now.' Jane patted her arm reassuringly as she released it. 'The search party will need sustenance on their return, and I must speak with the housekeeper.' She touched Rose's arm again, and reluctantly she dragged her gaze away from the fields. 'Do not despair. He will be found.'

Rose turned back to scan the fields as Jane entered the house, her arms hugging her waist. Her breathing was shallow, her heart thumping painfully in her chest and her throat felt tight with emotion. She was consumed by memories of the past week; memories now tinged bittersweet. They felt so real, they swamped her senses, and she closed her eyes and whispered Aiden's name, as if it might summon him to her.

The sound of hooves pounding the gravel drive roused her, and she opened her eyes in hope only to see her father, riding at breakneck speed, barely sparing her a glance before he too scaled the hedges and was gone from view.

'Keep him safe,' whispered Rose under her breath. 'Keep them both safe for me.'

She began to pace to and fro on the gravel sweep, her shawl wrapped tightly about her shoulders, and she shivered, though the day had grown no cooler, oblivious now to the discomfort of her unfamiliar shoes. How long she paced, she did not know, but suddenly a shout tore through the silence, and then another.

Rose's heart began to beat so fiercely it almost hurt, and she strained her eyes, then hurried up the stone steps to gain a higher perspective. There was movement in the far field, the sound of hooves, and then the man she recognised as Edward Knight's groom came flying over the hedge on his mount.

'Where is Miss Austen?'

'I am here.' Jane hurried out of the open door. 'What news?'

'Ma'am.' The groom docked his hat. 'Mr Knight requests you arrange for Mr Lyford to be sent for. This instant!'

Rose gripped Jane's arm tightly. 'Please tell me Mr Lyford is not the undertaker.'

Despite the tense atmosphere, Jane smiled faintly. 'He is the doctor. It means Mr Trevellyan is found but is in need of some attention beyond an apothecary's talents. Mr Lyford is a doctor in Winchester.'

Jane disappeared back inside the house, and Rose, torn between relief there was some news and fear over why they needed a doctor, resumed her pacing just as a young servant came hurrying out of a side entrance. He sped past Rose, a note clutched in his hand as he ran towards the stables, and she turned to watch him but suddenly her gaze was drawn to the sight of three horsemen moving slowly along the main road.

It was impossible to distinguish who they were, but two of the riders set off at a canter and soon appeared near the church, where they drew their mounts to a halt. She recognised Edward and Charles, and eventually the last horse came into sight, going much more slowly now, with two figures on his back. It was her father, holding onto Aiden, who lolled in front of him like some sort of rag doll.

'I must prepare somewhere for him to be tended.'

With a start, Rose looked around. Jane had come to stand beside her.

'He *is* hurt. Oh, Jane, what's wrong with him?'

'My eyesight will not permit me a diagnosis at this distance.' She smiled faintly. 'Forgive me; I do not mean to make light of it. Excuse me.' She hurried back up the steps, and Rose stood motionless for a moment. Then her legs began to move, at first slowly, before breaking into a run as fast as her skirts would allow, and she tore down the drive, meeting Edward and Charles at the bottom of the slope.

'Do not be alarmed, Miss Wallace. He is found.'

'But he is injured!' Her frantic gaze was drawn to her father's slow progress towards them. 'How…? Is it—? How serious is it?'

'He was not conscious when he was discovered, but is now. His injuries do not seem beyond remedy. We had to take the long way round, of course. It was no time for putting him through the enhanced pain of jumping fences.'

Charles clicked his tongue at his mount, setting it forward again. 'Oh, and be not alarmed by the blood on his clothes. His wounds are secure for the present.'

Edward raised his hat to Rose. 'Curtis, our Alton apothecary, will also be summoned, Miss Wallace. Though it looks to be beyond his talents, he may be able to assist Lyford.'

He followed his brother, and Rose turned to watch her father steering his mount slowly along. As he came closer, she could see his reassuring smile, but the sight of Aiden, leaning back against him now, pale as can be, one arm strapped across his chest and dark staining on his clothes was enough to distress her.

As they drew nearer, she reached up and touched her father's arm, too scared to place it on Aiden for fear of hurting him.

'Run along, Rosie. Go up to the house. We shall be with you directly; there is naught you can do here.'

Reluctantly, she turned on her heel and hurried as fast she could back to the house. By the time her father arrived with his charge, there were several male servants waiting to assist with Aiden's removal from the horse and into the house.

Jane had returned and was listening to Charles, who spoke quietly to her before telling the servants where to take Aiden. He had slumped forward again as they eased him from the horse, emitting a groan of pain, and Rose's hand shot to her throat as they laid him as gently as they could on a makeshift stretcher.

She could see his brown curls, the side of his face, pinched and streaked with dirt and blood, and had Jane not come to stand beside her, firmly gripping her arm, Rose would have pushed them all aside to get to him, to tell him she was there for him, no matter what.

As they lifted the stretcher, however, he turned his head slightly and she caught his eye. A faint smile touched his mouth, but his eyes then closed and he was carried into the house, and at Jane's urging, the ladies followed them in.

Under Jane's instruction, they placed him in a small room off the entrance hall, and as the door closed on them, Rose drew in a deep breath. Would she be allowed to see him? Speak to him? The housekeeper brushed past them, followed by a maid bearing a pitcher of water and some strips of linen, and they entered the room, sounds drifting out through the slightly open door.

'On my count of three: one, two, three.'

There was a sound of movement followed by a loud groan from Aiden, and Rose took an involuntary step towards the door before Jane held her back.

'We must wait. You shall see him directly.'

The male servants trooped from the room, followed by the maid and, shortly afterwards, the housekeeper, who beckoned Jane to her side to speak to her. Rose didn't care what they were talking about. She had to see Aiden, talk to him. Edging towards the door, which was still ajar, she threw a quick glance at Jane and the housekeeper before slipping into the room.

'Rose!' Her father spoke quietly and got up from where he was seated beside Aiden. 'You should not be here.'

'Yes, I should. Where else would I be?'

He held her gaze for a second, then nodded. 'You may have as long as it takes me to retrieve some brandy.'

The door closed behind her father, and Rose tried to school her face into calmness as she knelt beside Aiden. His eyes were closed, and he was even paler, though she suspected that was from the pain. Now his coat had been cut from him, the amount of blood on his once white shirt was apparent, though mainly soaking his sleeve. He was propped up against some cushions, his damaged arm still strapped across his chest, but his position looked awkward, as if he were lopsided. His face had been cleaned up and did not appear to have suffered beyond some surface cuts, though it would probably bruise later.

Rose felt the sting of tears and forced her eyes wide to prevent them. Where was Hermione Granger with her bottle of dittany when you needed her? She held her breath as Aiden's eyes opened.

He said nothing, but lifted his good arm as though he would take her hand, but the movement caused him to gasp, and he dropped it to his side.

'Keep still.' Rose edged a little closer. 'What happened?'

'May have overestimated my skill as a horseman.' His voice was hoarse, and Rose looked around.

'Do you want something to drink?'

'Water,' he rasped. Then, he let out a small laugh followed by a gasp of pain. 'Sorry. I know I can't, but that's what I'd most like.'

'I'll buy you a crate of bottled water as soon as we're back home.'

Aiden eyed her speculatively. 'I'd like to hold you to that.'

Did he doubt her resolution to leave the past – and her father – behind? She pushed the thought aside. Rose would never willingly separate herself from Aiden, not when he looked at her as he did now. Especially after the excruciating minutes of fear she'd just experienced, not knowing what had happened to him.

Her gaze was drawn back to the bloodied sleeve. There was a makeshift tie bound around his arm, but she knew what the amount of blood might mean. 'Is it broken?'

The lids had dropped over Aiden's eyes again, and he drew in a shallow breath then nodded. 'Not compound, thankfully. I'm also thankful I was out for the count when they found me.'

'But the blood…'

'Fell against some rocks.' He drew in a short breath. 'One particularly ragged one cut my arm open. The gash isn't a pretty sight, according to the captain.'

Fear gripped Rose. What if his open wounds became infected? There were no antiseptic creams, no antibiotics here…

'We have to get you back.' Her voice was tight with emotion and Aiden opened his eyes, though he clearly did so with difficulty.

'Rose, I need you to stay calm. I have to admit, I wouldn't mind a good old-fashioned X-ray to guide whoever is in charge of my care, but I'm not going to be the first person who broke a bone in the early nineteenth century. They have plenty of experience and knowledge, just not the medical back-up we are used to.'

'Like anaesthetic.'

Aiden's lids dropped again. 'It's a good job I like brandy.'

Rose couldn't bear to think of the pain he was about to endure and she caught her lip between her teeth. Why had this had to happen *now*?

'We must get Jane to take you back.'

Aiden gave an almost imperceptible nod and Rose looked around as the door opened and Christopher came into the room.

'Do you have any of your potions? Anything that might help? You said you healed people in Gibraltar.'

Christopher took Rose's hands, his face serious. 'Let the doctor tend him, Rosie. The lotions I have at my disposal here are for the small scrapes and spills my children earned over the years. I fear this is too large a wound for them to be of any benefit.' He held her gaze steadily. 'You know the answer to this.'

Rose drew in a short breath, her throat gripped with emotion. Aiden must go home and without delay. But what about Rose?

Chapter 20

Rose started as the door was pushed open again.

'Here we are, with medicine to dull the senses. The apothecary will be here directly.'

Jane carried a tray with a decanter of brandy and a glass, looking no more rattled than if it had been an afternoon tea with guests as she placed the tray on a side table and stepped back.

'If you would be so kind, sir.'

'Yes, of course.'

Christopher stepped forward and filled a glass. 'This may not put your friend out of consciousness directly, but it will aid to dull his pain.'

Rose frowned. 'I don't think people with concussion are supposed to drink alcohol.'

Aiden's eyes remained closed, but he drew in another shallow breath. 'I'll risk just about anything to take the edge off this pain.'

Rose turned to her father. 'May I? Please?' She pointed at the glass in his hand, and he hesitated, cast a glance at Jane, then handed it to Rose.

'A little at a time, Rosie.'

Rose knelt carefully at Aiden's side again. 'Come, take your medicine like a good boy.'

His lips twitched, and he opened his eyes. 'Very motherly.'

Rose blushed, hoping he wouldn't notice as he tried to support himself on his good arm.

'You're going to have to help me, I'm afraid. I can't lift my arm without falling back again.'

Carefully, Rose lifted the glass to his lips and he took a mouthful, then grimaced as he swallowed.

'Go slow, now.'

Aiden looked at her through pain-filled eyes. 'Don't worry so.'

He managed to drain the glass before slumping back against the cushions, and Jane took it from Rose as Rose counted the seconds, waiting for the alcohol to kick in and give him some ease.

'The doctor is on his way?'

Her father placed a comforting hand on her shoulder. 'He is, but it is a good ride from Winchester.'

The knowledge did little to comfort Rose. This was no time for delay.

Aiden's breathing gradually became more even, and Rose got to her feet and turned around. Her father was eyeing her with sympathy, but it was Jane's gaze she sought.

'I need to get him home, Jane. As soon as he's been attended to.'

Jane pursed her lips, and Rose frowned. Had there been a fleeting look of concern on the lady's face?

'Jane—'

A loud rap came on the door and the housekeeper entered to announce the apothecary, and Jane insisted on Rose leaving the room. Conscious she was trying to distract her from whatever might be happening and all that Aiden might have to go through, Rose did as she was asked, grateful to her father when he promised he would stay behind to do what he could.

Mr Curtis was taking off his coat and rolling up his sleeves as they left the room, and they stood aside as two manservants came hurrying along the hall bearing hot water.

'I will need your assistance, sir, to restrain him.' The apothecary turned to Mr Wallace, who nodded.

Rose caught her father's eye from inside the room, and he smiled reassuringly at her before closing the door, and reluctantly she followed Jane from the house.

'Come, it will not do for you to hear anything.'

A moment of panic gripped Rose, and she grabbed Jane's arm. 'We must get him home as soon as the doctor leaves, Jane.'

Jane then inclined her head. 'As soon as he is well enough to move.'

Trying to modulate her breathing, Rose allowed Jane to take her arm as she led her over to the terrace where the picnic had been held, well away from the house. She had no idea what they talked about, or how much time was passing, but when she saw her father walking towards them what felt like hours later, a sob rose into her throat and she ran across the gravel to him.

He held her briefly, then set her away from him, and she was relieved to see him smiling.

'He is a strong young man, your archaeologist. And quite dedicated to his craft, I suspect.'

'Is he okay? Will he be okay?' Rose stopped. 'What do you mean?'

Christopher let out a short laugh. 'The brandy has loosened his tongue.'

'He only had a glass!'

'He has consumed a few more since you saw him. Seemed to be in some confusion about where he was, thought he was on a dig somewhere.'

Rose's mouth formed a silent O, and she was torn between amusement and her overriding concern.

He laughed. 'It was not only Curtis who was fascinated by his ramblings, though. What is this talk of…' He paused. 'Imaging surveys, I think he said. And geophys?'

'It's ways they have of scoping out what might be lying beneath the soil before they dig.'

'Ah, I see.' Christopher sobered. 'As to your question, he is as well as one could expect in the circumstances. Curtis is confident the concussion is mild and of little consequence. He has reset a dislocated shoulder, done what he can with his arm, but we must await Lyford's arrival before the fracture is set. There is also likely to be some bruising to his ribs.'

'But will we tell if the arm has been set properly without an X-ray?'

'Dear Rosie.' Her father put her arm on his and they walked back towards where Jane was waiting, watching them. 'From what I have observed, he has had the best care that is available so far. That is all we can ask, for now. The apothecary seems well versed in the need for keeping the wound clean and has secured the arm to await Lyford's arrival, who is as good as any bone setter I have seen.'

Rose winced, and her father patted her arm.

'Trust me, Mr Trevellyan has been well tended. The cuts beyond the gash in his arm are all superficial.' He looked down at Rose and smiled. 'His fine features will bear no lasting harm from his adventure.'

'I wouldn't care if they had.'

Her father smiled and patted her arm. 'Nor do I suspect would he.'

Rose couldn't help but smile at her father's wink. 'I don't know what I would have done if you weren't with me.' It was a bittersweet thought.

'I have not been there for you for so long, child. Though I would not wish the gentleman ill, it brings me great comfort to be able to support you now.'

The afternoon was waning as they returned to the house, and Rose hurried into the hallway only to find the door to the side room wide open and no one inside.

'Where is he?' She spun around to look at Jane.

'He will have been removed to his chamber. I will enquire. Please, Rose, show your father into the drawing room, and I shall arrange for tea.'

'But I need to see him.'

Christopher placed a hand on Rose's arm, and Jane, who had set off down the hallway, turned back and came to stand before her.

'Dearest Rose, for dear you are to me.' Jane took her hands in her own. 'Recall your situation. Though we,' she gestured between the three of them, 'and my siblings are fully versed whence you and Mr Trevellyan came, the servants are not.' She sighed. 'And servants are prone to gossip. Would you have your reputation so maligned?'

'Miss Austen has the right of it, child.' Christopher laid a hand on her shoulder. 'You cannot take unnecessary risks.'

Unnecessary? Rose almost stamped her foot. Didn't they understand just how necessary it was she see Aiden, find out how he was coping with the pain?

'Your air and countenance betray you.' Jane smirked. 'Yet you must do as I say. You comprehend, do you not, that any stain upon your own reputation will harm your sisters too?'

Her sisters? Rose turned to her father. 'I'm so sorry. Was I selfish? I hadn't thought… because they don't know who I am…'

'But they will, as will all our acquaintances, before long, Rose. You must adhere to the conventions of the day.'

Rose was torn between anticipation over getting to know Mary, Olivia and Anne, and having them know of their close connection, and her agitation over Aiden, but she knew she had no choice but to accept both Jane and her father's advice.

'Take the time to write to your friend, Rose.' Jane turned away again, speaking over her shoulder as she headed towards the service door to the kitchens. 'You would do well to advise her of today's occurrences.'

Morgan would be able to help! Of course she would. She would arrange for Aiden to get to a hospital. He wouldn't be able to drive his own car, and Morgan wouldn't be insured to, but she would sort it out somehow.

Rose hurried into the great hall, relieved to find Cassandra in there, writing a letter of her own.

'Miss Wallace, Mr Wallace, do come in.' She got to her feet to greet them both, dropping a curtsey to Mr Wallace, who bowed formally. 'Sir, please, take a seat. Shall I call for some tea?'

'Jane has gone to do so.' Rose's gaze drifted to the writing implements on the desk. 'I must write to Morgan, Miss Austen.'

'Yes, of course. Here.' She pulled the chair out from the desk and waved Rose into it, pulling out fresh paper and handing her a quill. 'I was so sorry to hear of Mr Trevellyan's accident, but Mr Lyford is a good man and an experienced one. He has set the bones of three of my brothers in the past, and they remain hearty and whole.'

Rose smiled her thanks, turning her attention to the ink and quill and pulling forward some blotting paper, tuning out the voices of her father and Cassandra.

> *Morgan, Aiden has had a fall and we'll be returning as soon as it makes sense to do so. Can you be ready with a car to take us to the hospital? Will write with an exact time. I'll just end with… wish you were here. Rose xx*

She read it through quickly, then applied the blotter as she had been shown before folding it up and addressing it as neatly as she could, just as Jane entered the room, followed by Edward and a servant bringing the paraphernalia for tea-making.

'Mr Lyford has just arrived, Miss Wallace. My brother is attending him, along with Curtis.'

Relieved, Rose thanked him, getting to her feet and joining Jane at the console table, where she was dispensing hot water from the urn.

'It is done; how soon can you send it?'

'I shall go once we have taken tea. All will be well.' Jane handed her a cup, and Rose resigned herself to being patient, though her thoughts were upstairs with Aiden.

The conversation drifted around her, but Rose's gaze went repeatedly to the clock in the corner, and it was a good while, and more tea, later that Charles joined them to report on Aiden.

'Curtis is gone. Lyford says he will remain for an hour or so and will check on the patient before leaving. He is attending to his appearance and will join us directly before returning upstairs.'

Jane turned to Rose. 'I will go to the cottage on my errand.' She paused. 'Or perchance you would care to accompany me?'

If she couldn't be with Aiden, then perhaps it would be the best thing? She would talk to Jane about how soon they could get him safely home, and it would give her time to think about whether she ought to go with him. It didn't mean she couldn't return, once he was safely under modern-day medical care, did it? Surely she could stay just a little longer? James wouldn't mind in the circumstances, she was certain, and she was getting used to the taste of the powder used for cleaning teeth even if she did find the bristle a little too harsh. Besides, hadn't she always longed for a sibling?

She looked over to her father, and he smiled reassuringly at her. 'Go, Rosie. I shall await your return before I take my leave, lest I may be of service to the gentleman in any way.'

Rose smiled her thanks and followed Jane from the room. Rather than turning for the front door, however, the lady grabbed Rose's arm and tugged her back along the hallway in the opposite direction.

'I cannot bear to be the cause of your unrest, dear Rose. Come with me.'

Jane hurried through the service entrance and Rose followed, her heart picking up its beat in anticipation. Her guide was looking left and right, and then opened a door built into the panelling and ushered Rose inside. A set of stone steps led upward and she followed Jane, only to be pushed unceremoniously into a deep alcove.

'What is it?'

Jane placed a finger to her lips. The sound of humming was drawing nearer, and then a young maid passed by without noticing them.

'Make haste.'

They hurried up the remaining steps, and Jane looked around again before pushing open the nearest door, urging Rose ahead of her. 'I shall lock this from the outside and take the key, that you may not be disturbed by a servant. You must not linger beyond a few minutes, Rose, and leave by the main chamber door. You will be safe for the moment, as everyone is engaged downstairs.'

'Thank you, Jane.' Rose's smile faltered as Jane closed the door. She heard the key turn in the lock, then looked around.

The room was of elegant proportions, with a fire burning in the grate and, despite the fading day, light pouring in from the large windows. Edging towards the bed, Rose could see Aiden lying back against the pillows. He was wearing a clean shirt now, open at the neck, his arm much more professionally bandaged and bound with two leather straps to a firm-looking piece of shaped wood.

He had lost his earlier pallor, a flush staining his cheeks, and she tiptoed closer, anxious not to disturb him but, unable to resist, she leaned down and placed a soft kiss on his cheek.

'Rose. Is that you?' His voice was hoarser than ever, and he struggled to swallow but didn't open his eyes. 'I was telling them.' He stopped, his head going from side to side. '"No, no, no," I said. "You can't do it that way. The erosion from the water… in the cath… cath… cathedral…"' The word ended in a hiccup, and Rose tried not to smile.

Gently, she took the hand of his uninjured arm. 'Aiden? Can you hear me? How are you feeling?'

There was no response for a moment; then, he stirred, opened one eye and then, as though with the greatest difficulty, the other. He stared at the canopy of his bed, then slowly turned his head on the pillow.

'I can hear you but I can't see you. Where are you?'

'I'm here.' Rose leaned forward so that she was closer, and his eyes gradually focused in on her and he gave a lopsided smile, then winced.

'Ow.' He moved instinctively to raise his other hand to his face, then groaned in pain.

'Shhh, lie still.' Rose held onto his hand. 'You mustn't disturb what the doctor has done for you.'

'Done for me? Hmph!' He snorted weakly. 'I fear I *am* all but done for.' Then his eyes widened and flew from left to right. 'He's not still here, is he? I don't like him.'

Rose frowned. He didn't sound drunk so much as drugged, but before she could question him further, the door opened, and she dropped Aiden's hand as though it was a hot coal and turned around.

Chapter 21

'I thought as much.'

Christopher Wallace walked into the room, a stern eye on his daughter. 'Do you take no heed of my advice?'

'I'm sorry.' Rose bit her lip. It felt incongruous that she was twenty-seven years old and only now feeling the censure of her own father! Then, she frowned. 'How did you know I was—?'

'Miss Austen set off down the driveway alone. I was at the window drinking my tea.'

'But how did you know this was Aiden's room?'

He shook his head at her. 'How do you think, child? I helped carry him here earlier!'

Of course he had.

Rose walked over to him. 'I'm sorry. Really, I am. But I needed to see him with my own eyes. Only,' she glanced over her shoulder, 'he's a bit… strange. Is it the brandy, do you think?'

Christopher walked round to the other side of the bed and looked down at Aiden. His eyes had closed again, but he was still muttering under his breath about erosion and removing stones.

''Tis merely the laudanum.'

'Opium?' Rose hurried back to the bedside. 'He's had opium *and* brandy?'

'It dulls the pain but affects the senses. Come, Rose. We must let him rest.'

'Rest?' Aiden's eyes flew open, staring at the canopy again. 'Yes! That's what *I* said. Let it be, don't disturb it!' He became quite agitated again, his head moving to and fro on the pillow. 'Things must not be disturbed... It's not good... not good practice, to be disturbed...'

Rose took Aiden's good hand in hers once more. 'Shh, Aiden. No one is going to disturb anything.'

His head turned slowly towards her. Then, he smiled faintly. 'Me.'

'You... what?' Did he have any idea how adorable he was in this state? Rose chided herself for the thought, trying to remember her father was stood on the other side of the bed watching them.

'Me. I was the one who was disturbed. That's what I'm trying to tell you.' He pouted like a little boy. 'Why don't you listen to me? *You* disturbed me.'

'Oh!' Rose's gaze flew to her father's, then back to Aiden. 'I'm sorry. You were sleeping. I'll let you rest.'

'No! Don't go! You don't understand.' He grasped her hand tightly and tried to push himself up, but Christopher put a steadying hand on his shoulder, forcing him back onto the pillows.

'Rest easy, young man.'

Rose squeezed the hand she held. Aiden's eyes had closed again, and she leaned forward to brush a lock of hair from his forehead.

'Tell me about it. What was the disturbance?'

'You – *you* were. I saw you... clapping... Those gorgeous auburn curls in the sunlight...'

Feeling warmth invade her cheeks under her father's amused gaze, Rose stared at Aiden. 'Yes, yes, I know. They had to re-do the take. I remember.'

'Never forgot… nice, steady life. Work. Lots of work.' Aiden frowned, swallowing with difficulty. 'You disturbed me… my life. I never forgot you…' His voice faded, and his eyes drifted closed again.

Rose looked up at her father. 'We have to get him back home as soon as we can. I'm scared his wound will become infected.'

'Of course you are right.' He sighed. 'And does Miss Austen require aught of preparation, for her charm to do its duty?'

Rose shook her head. 'No, it's instant.'

'I see.'

Rose felt as though she were being torn in two. She could not, *would* not endanger Aiden in any way, but to see her father's emotion at the prospect of her leaving was equally unbearable.

'And *then* I said,' Aiden had roused again and was beaming at her father, 'history is the cornerstone of our soul. The past once lived and breathed with the same passion, the same soul as we! We cannot bury it to forget it forever. We *are* our pasts…' Aiden squinted at them both, then nodded slowly. 'And that's why I was arrested the first time.'

Spent, he lay his head back against the pillows and closed his eyes, and Rose stared at him in disbelief.

Christopher's lips twitched. 'He's quite the young man, your Mr Trevellyan.'

Rose couldn't help but laugh. 'He's usually very taciturn. I think I counted the words between us before this last week at under fifty, despite knowing each other for three years.'

'Well, if my opinion counts for aught, you have my approval.'

Rose blushed deep red, then reached across to take her father's hand. 'Of course your opinion counts. I love you.'

Christopher's face contorted for a moment. Then he whispered, 'And I love you, Rosie. More than you can possibly imagine.' He sighed. 'It seems our long overdue reunion is to be curtailed. Let me sit awhile with you, whilst opportunity favours us.'

They walked over to two armchairs drawn close to the fireplace, Rose casting a lingering look back at Aiden, but he appeared to have drifted off to sleep.

Thankful for a chance to share what was on her mind, however, she turned eagerly to her father. 'I was hoping to return here. You know? Once Aiden is safely home? If Jane will help me… Do you think it a good idea?' She looked at her father expectantly, and his eyes widened. 'If you are… if you feel it is sensible to introduce me, to reveal our connection to local society to your… my sisters…' Her voice tailed away at his earnest look. 'I thought I could come back… for a while.'

Leaning across, Christopher took her hand. 'You heal my soul, my dear child. It is beyond my wildest dreams to have found you; to know you might return, that you wish to…' His voice wavered with emotion, and he swallowed visibly. 'There is nothing that would please me more.'

They both smiled tremulously, and he released her hand and sat back in his chair.

'But how do we explain—?'

He stayed her with his hand. 'Let us not speculate this evening upon the challenges ahead, my dear. Let it be sufficient for us to have this time together, for it may not arise again for a little while.'

They talked quietly, conscious of the sleeping form behind them, and Rose relished the moment, cherishing every line of her father's face, his smile, his expressions and his voice. She listened in rapt attention as he talked about his children – not only the three girls Rose had already come across, but also the eldest, Martin, busy pursuing his studies at Oxford.

The light slowly faded in the room, though they remained bathed in the warm glow of firelight, and the sudden rattling of the handle of the door to the servants' staircase startled Rose, who looked at her father in alarm.

''Tis merely a servant wishing to light the lamps.' He got to his feet and stretched. 'But they will be in search of a key and returning. Come.' He held out his hand and Rose took it as she got to her feet, very aware she had well outstayed the time Jane had sanctioned so kindly.

She glanced at the fading light outside. Where *was* Jane? Surely she would have sought her out on her return from the cottage?

'It is a good thing I am chaperoned by you.'

He smiled as they walked over to the bed to look at Aiden in the dim light. It was hard to determine his colour, but he seemed at ease.

Christopher placed the back of his hand against Aiden's forehead. 'He is not overheated. The rest will be a powerful aid to his recovery. He is strong; I am certain he will be well.'

Relieved, Rose took a step forward, intending to gently take Aiden's hand again, but just then the door opened to reveal Jane, who seemed unsettled.

'What is it?' Could anything else possibly go wrong today?

The look vanished, and Jane smiled. 'Nothing of consequence. How is the patient?'

Rose shrugged. 'Doing well, I think. My father says the doctor insists he remain still. He says Aiden should not be moved, that bed rest is essential.'

Jane nodded. 'He has the right of it, though not so much the gentleman *should* not but that we could not, for he cannot move of his own volition.'

Rose glanced over at Aiden. It was probably a good job Jane hadn't been in the room earlier when he was conscious and rambling. 'Were you able to send the letter?'

'I have placed it under the floorboard, as is my custom. There was no correspondence from Miss Taylor.'

Rose was disappointed, but she shrugged lightly in an attempt to dispel it. 'She probably couldn't get to the cottage today, or perhaps it was too busy to get access to the floorboard without being seen.'

'This was my thought also. I placed another small bottle of ink and some paper, for she may be running low.'

'Good thinking.' Rose smiled. Morgan had been rather prolific so far with her letters and probably hadn't even thought about the nineteenth-century supplies running low.

Jane walked over to the door to the servants' staircase and unlocked it, returning the key to its usual place. 'As you are aware, Rose, I am no apprentice in such matters as these. I shall return to the cottage once we have broken our fast on the morrow to retrieve whatever has been sent. Come, you must leave here now. It is time to dress for dinner.'

'Indeed, Rose. You have tarried long enough. Go with Miss Austen. I will keep Mr Trevellyan company, ensure he wants for naught.'

With one last look at the still slumbering form on the bed, Rose turned to wave at her father before following Jane from the room.

The evening passed with agonising slowness for Rose. Her father had taken his leave and returned home shortly before they all sat down to dine. Aiden remained under the care of the housekeeper, who had administered more laudanum and promised to sit with him whilst the family ate.

When the time for separation after dinner came, Cassandra led Rose and Jane to the drawing room, where they talked of inconsequential things and drank tea until Edward joined them to advise that Mr Lyford had gone on to lodgings in Alton, and they had called on Aiden and he was sleeping.

Knowing there would be no further opportunity for her to visit him that evening, Rose willingly climbed the stairs behind the ladies when the time came to retire. Charles had re-joined them, assuring her a footman had been appointed the task of checking on Aiden period-ically throughout the night and to administer the small remaining measure of laudanum left by the doctor, should he request it.

By the time Rose closed her bedroom door, her legs felt like lead and her shoulders ached from the day's worry. Fortunately, she was so exhausted she barely noticed the tedious routine of getting undressed and ready for bed under the guidance of a maid. Her mind felt fuzzy with tiredness and indecision. It was as though a giant, imaginary clock was ticking away the time she had left with her father, the time until she could get Aiden to modern medicine.

The ticking refused to leave her as she lay in the darkness, following her into the dreams that engulfed her almost as soon as she closed her eyes. Despite her expectations, however, she slept well and long, and rolling onto her side the following morning, she lifted heavy lids and squinted at the drapes on the window. A chink of light was shining through a gap, and she sat up suddenly, rubbing the sleep from her eyes, her hair a tousled mess over her shoulders.

How was Aiden? What sort of night had he endured? Rose had to see him… but how?

'Oh, you are awake, miss.'

Looking over her shoulder, Rose saw the same young maid who had assisted her the night before come into the room via the servants' staircase, and an idea came to her.

Tolerating the maid's attentions as best she could, Rose tried not to fidget in her impatience over not simply being able to go wherever she wanted, whenever she wanted, in whatever state of dress she wanted to do so. How she wished she could simply throw on a dressing gown and sprint down the landing to see how Aiden was faring!

She made the necessary conversation, and counted to thirty after the maid left before quietly opening the door to the servant's staircase.

Sleeping in might have done her a favour. Had Rose been earlier, not encountering a maid or footman with hot water or towels might have been impossible!

She walked along the corridor in confusion. So distracted had she been the day before, she hadn't really taken in which door led to Aiden's room. Then, she straightened her shoulders. They were all at breakfast, weren't they? Besides, this might be her only chance to see Aiden this morning.

Think, Rose. How far did you walk down here with Jane?

'We didn't go far at all,' she whispered, and reaching out, she grasped the handle of the first door at the top of the stairs and turned it, pushing it open slightly, only to pale as her eyes met those of Charles Austen, who lounged by the open window, a cup in his hand.

Chapter 22

Rose's heart was pounding in her breast. Had she miscalculated and gone to the wrong room? Thankful nothing seemed to faze Jane's youngest brother, she stepped back, about to pull the door shut, when she heard the deep timbre of Aiden's voice from within the room.

Pushing the door open a little further, Rose peered in and then looked towards the bed. Aiden was propped against the pillows, a cup of tea on the table beside him and, unaware of her presence yet, seemed to be explaining what a drone was.

Charles winked at her, then turned to address Aiden. 'But does one not flee for one's life, for fear of this flying contraption giving chase?'

Aiden shook his head. 'No, no. Some consider them a nuisance, but they are not particularly feared and—' He glanced in her direction, then blinked. 'Er, Miss Wallace. Good morning.'

Rose was speechless, but she stepped into the room and closed the door. There were dark circles under Aiden's eyes and he was a little paler than normal, but he seemed so much better than she had expected.

Recalling where she was, Rose curtseyed hurriedly to Charles. 'Good morning to you both. Captain Austen, I hope you will forgive the intrusion. I—' She stopped, looking from Jane's brother to Aiden and back again. 'I did not—' Warmth filled her cheeks, and she lowered her eyes. How embarrassing was *this*? The captain must think her positively wanton!

'Do not concern yourself, Miss Wallace. Jane told me she had shown you an alternative way to satisfy your curiosity with regard to your friend.' Charles smiled at Aiden and walked over to the tray on the dresser to deposit his cup, then turned around. 'You will forgive me if I remain? I think it in the best interests of you both for there to be a chaperone present.'

Rose threw him a grateful look, then flew across the room to the other side of the bed, where she took Aiden's good hand.

'I can't believe how much better you look. Are you in much pain? Did you sleep at all?'

Though his demeanour was reassuring, his eyes were somewhat dulled, but she suspected that was the after-effects of the laudanum.

'I believe I slept.' He smiled, then winced. 'Sorry, face is a bit stiff this morning. I might just have been knocked out by the drugs, though.' He nodded towards the injured side of his body. 'The pain is bearable at the moment. I'm told Mr Lyford is returning later this morning. Hopefully they can give me something a little less disorientating today. I believe I entertained him greatly, not least expounding on the benefits of aerial photography for an archaeological dig.'

'I'm so… so…' Rose sank into the chair by the bed. 'You scared the life out of me yesterday!'

Aiden's gaze became serious, and he squeezed her hand. 'If I could have spared you every moment of it, I would have.'

Smiling, Rose could feel the weight of her anxiety lifting. 'I can't stay long, I must join the others at breakfast, but I just had to see you, to know you were okay.' She turned to where Charles stood near the fireplace. 'Have you seen Jane yet this morning, Captain?'

'Indeed. She set out in the direction of the cottage, almost as the sun rose. She will return directly, I am certain.'

Rose felt a spurt of guilt. 'I hope she didn't get up early on my account. I was worried sick last night and getting a message to Morg— my friend seemed so important.'

Charles smiled and shook his head. 'Do not concern yourself, ma'am. My sister is rarely to be moved by anything but the most prudent of logic. If she did not wish to walk so early, she would not have.'

With a grateful smile, Rose turned back to Aiden, but just then the sound of footsteps on the gravel outside floated through the open window, and Charles walked over to peer out.

'Ah, we have a visitor.' He turned around. 'For you, I believe, Miss Wallace.'

Rose got up and hurried over to the window. Jane was crossing the gravel sweep in front of the house, and with her was Christopher Wallace. She swung around to face the room.

'It's my father.' How strange those words still sounded, and yet how wonderful! 'I should go.'

'I will accompany you, ma'am.' Charles took his leave of Aiden. 'I will await you outside, Miss Wallace.'

He stepped out onto the landing, leaving the door ajar, and Rose hurried back to Aiden's bedside.

'We need to get you back, but—'

'You also need time with your father.' Aiden smiled faintly. 'I don't see any harm in having the singular bragging rights that my broken arm was set by authentic Regency means.' He laughed, then winced again. 'Sorry, sore ribs. I suppose that's a badge I'll have to brag about silently, as no one would believe me.'

Rose eyed his bound arm warily, then frowned. Did his fingers look swollen? 'Is your arm feeling okay?'

'Bit numb, to be honest, but I'd rather that than pain! Go, Rose. I'm being well looked after.'

'Are you sure? I mean, I know I have to go, that I shouldn't even be in the room, but—'

'Rose, I'm sure I'll be fine for another day if it's what you need.'

'It's not what I need so much as that I would hate you to think your well-being isn't my first priority.'

His brown eyes held hers for a moment. 'I don't. How could I? Who else would risk the censure of society by scurrying along the servants' corridor to burst unannounced into a gentleman's chamber?' His gaze softened. 'Only you, Rose.'

She glanced over her shoulder. The door remained ajar, and she leaned over to place a kiss on Aiden's cheek, but he turned his head and captured her lips with his own. The sound of a throat being cleared brought a smirk to Aiden's face as they drew apart.

'Go, before you get into any more trouble than you already are.'

With a smile, Rose turned and hurried from the room, pausing on the threshold to blow him another kiss, before following Charles along the landing and down the stairs.

The captain excused himself once they reached the ground floor, and Rose went along to the great hall to greet her father.

'How does the young man fare this morning, Rose?'

Casting a quick glance at Jane, Rose smiled. 'Extremely well. Much better than I could have hoped.'

'And I trust you heeded my words from yesterday, and took no risks with your reputation?'

She bit her lip. 'Not entirely. I mean, I *did* heed your words.' Jane made a small sound, and Rose continued. 'I was chaperoned by Captain Austen.'

'That is well, then. Now, I came expressly to enquire after Mr Trevellyan, but as the report of his health is so encouraging, I will own to having a second motive for my visit. My wife would like to invite you to call upon us, Rose. This morning.'

'Oh!' Rose stared at her father. Her relief over Aiden seeming so much better meant she could consider this invitation and all its implications with a clear mind. How challenging might it be, when only her father knew the truth about her origins?

'I can see you are hesitant, but it is plain you wish to safely return the gentleman to a place where he can receive the best of the medical advancements we know exist in the future. If we do not grasp this opportunity, my dear, when else might you properly become known to your own sisters?'

Jane walked over to Rose's side, and she noticed suddenly how pinched Jane's features were. 'You must go, Rose. The doctor will be calling later this morning, and my brothers will keep Mr Trevellyan company when he is not resting. He would not wish you to turn down such a kind invitation.'

'Rose.' She looked back at her father as he spoke. 'We have Miss Jane Austen's sanction. Will you not come? Remember, no one will have any suspicion whence you came. How could they? They will simply put any… anomaly down to you being the daughter of an eccentric man!'

Rose laughed. 'They will find me *very* eccentric, I fear!'

'Come, you must change your clothes, Rose.' Jane took her arm, and Christopher bowed and walked over to take a seat beside the fireplace.

'Why?'

Rolling her eyes, Jane ushered Rose towards the curtained screen. 'One does not pay calls, especially on such august company, dressed for lounging at home.'

Glancing at her simple shift dress as they mounted the stairs, Rose smiled. Such distress and fear yesterday, and here she was contemplating the happiest of days. She must tell Morgan…

'Jane, did you check the—'

'Most indubitably, yet no correspondence has come from Miss Taylor.'

Rose frowned at her tone. 'Are you…? You sound puzzled.'

They had reached Rose's door, and Jane turned to face her. She was smiling now, and shook her head.

'Pay me no mind.'

'She said she would try to check for messages every day, but we can't predict when a safe moment will come for her to lift the floorboard. If there are many visitors…' Rose shrugged and opened the door. 'I will write to her about Aiden later, so she doesn't worry too much, and I'm sure there will be several notes for me by then.'

'Indeed.' Jane followed her into the room and walked over to the wardrobes filling one wall. 'Hmm.' She studied the few gowns hanging there, altered by Cassandra to fit Rose, then pulled forward a smart green one she had never yet worn. 'This, I think, with the cream pelisse. It will compliment your hair decidedly well.'

Rose preferred not to think about her hair which, despite its recent wash, didn't feel as it should. It felt shallow, with all that was happening, to wish for modern sanitary ware, but how she longed for a good shower and some proper shampoo!

–

Excited though Rose was at being able to spend more time with her father and to discover her own extended family as a result, she was a bundle of nerves as she was shown into the small drawing room at Baigens. So much so, she might well have turned tail and fled, had it not been for her father's hand under her elbow, gently urging her forward into the room.

The collective gaze of its occupants, all of which turned to look at her, was no help in calming her, either. The ladies rose to their feet and all performed a curtsey, which Rose returned as neatly as she could.

'Miss Wallace.' Mrs Wallace stepped forward, a smile spreading across her face. 'I am delighted you were able to leave the house and join us for a few hours.'

'My dear, there is no necessity for formality. Rose is family, is she not? You may address her accordingly.'

'Yes, of course.' Mrs Wallace held out a hand to Rose, and she took it, allowing herself to be led over to sit on a chaise near the fireplace. 'Olivia, please ask Williams to send in some refreshments. Christopher, my dear, we need more logs.' The lady walked over to a wooden cupboard, extracting a key from a nearby drawer, and removed a wooden tea caddy.

Olivia and her father disappeared on their errands, and Rose's eyes drifted around the room, taking in its warmth and comfort.

'You are very pretty.'

Rose's gaze flew to meet Anne's, the easy colour filling her cheeks. 'You are too kind.'

Anne smiled. 'Papa is oft heard to say I am like Mama. She is kind, too.' The young girl's smile widened, and Rose returned it, only for it to fade as her gaze met that of Mary, who was seated beside her sister. Unless she was mistaken, the eldest daughter was not too enamoured of Rose's arrival.

'And do you draw or paint, Rose?'

Mrs Wallace had retaken her seat on the chaise next to Rose and, thankful to have a reason to break away from Mary's challenging stare across the room, Rose turned in her seat.

'Sadly, I do not.' Rose swallowed quickly. What nineteenth-century talent might she be able to offer? To be very fond of walking was never going to suffice!

'Do you sing or play?' Anne had risen to her feet, and she gestured over towards a small instrument against the wall.

'Er, I play the piano… forte. A little. But I do not sing.'

'Why ever not?' Mary was frowning. 'If you do not paint or draw or sing, then what *can* you do?'

For a wild moment, Rose was tempted to say that she could drive a motorised conveyance, but her eye caught sight of a sewing basket near Mary's chair, and with relief she summoned a smile. 'I can sew. Make clothes.'

Anne giggled as she walked over to stand by her mother's chair.

'Hush, now, child,' admonished Mrs Wallace, but Mary was clearly unimpressed.

'We are all taught how to do *work*. That is hardly an accomplishment.'

'Mary.' Mr Wallace had returned with a full basket of logs and he threw the girl a warning look as he placed it beside the fireplace.

'I do speak French. Quite well.' Rose felt like she'd just produced a rabbit from a top hat. Why hadn't she thought of that before?

Mary, however, remained unmoved. 'And much use it may be at present.'

Rose bit her lip. This was like being on a very odd talk show where she was failing as a guest. She sent her father an anxious look, but he smiled reassuringly at her. How could she have forgotten England was currently at war with France?

Olivia returned then, followed by a maid with an urn of hot water, and Mrs Wallace prepared the tea whilst Anne produced her book for Rose to see. Mary did not move from her seat, and although Rose was saddened by the eldest daughter's blatant dissatisfaction with the situation, she had a hard time not finding humour in the stubborn set of her pretty mouth. How many times had Rose's mother complained about the same expression on her face as a teenager?

'My dear.' Mrs Wallace smiled kindly at Rose as she passed her a cup of tea. 'Delighted though I was to hear from Christopher of his joy over your discovery, you must imagine our astonishment. We all thought you to have perished as a child.' Her expression softened even further. 'I hope… I trust you were well cared for in whatever home you were raised?'

Pushing aside her life with her mother, Rose smiled as reassuringly as she could. 'I was indeed well cared for, ma'am, and properly educated.'

A delicate snort from Mary earned her a warning look from her father, and Rose hoped the subject might change.

'I have assured Louisa our separation was one beyond both our abilities to overcome, my dear.' Christopher smiled warmly at Rose. Had he given her the ghost of a wink? 'She comprehends that your mother is… not of this world.'

'Oh!' Rose took a hasty sip of her tea.

'Let us be done with such melancholy memories, my dear. I am certain there are more cheerful topics we can canvass.'

'Yes, of course. Tell me, Rose, Christopher tells us you reside in Bath.' Mrs Wallace offered a plate of biscuits, but Rose declined. 'And do you have a companion there? Has an establishment been set up for you in the absence of both of your parents?'

Rose blinked. 'I… er, no. I live alone.'

Mrs Wallace's eyes widened. 'Alone? But child, how can this be?' She turned to her husband, who stood near one of the windows. 'Christopher! You must do something! It is not fitting for a single young woman to be living alone, and certainly not in a city such as Bath!'

Rose wanted to bury her head in her hands. For days, she felt she'd managed a pretty credible impression of being from the era. So why, oh why could she not make a good showing in front of her family? She met her father's gaze across the room, and he smiled. He didn't seem too bothered by her slip up, and turned to speak to his wife to diffuse the topic.

Sitting back in her seat with a sigh, Rose chewed on her lip. No, she shouldn't have said that, but she really didn't want to lie to them unless she had to. Every hour, every minute since she had reunited with her father, the situation became less of a fantasy and more of a reality. She didn't want to play act for the people in this room. She wanted, as insane as it might seem, to know them as authentically as possible, and for them to know her.

Anne came to sit beside her. 'Are you lonely? I could not live without my sisters around me.'

Rose placed her cup on a nearby side table. 'I have longed for a brother or sister all my life.'

'And yet we have not.' Mary took a sip from her cup. 'For we have ample, and require no more.'

'Mary, dear, that is unkind.'

The girl had the grace to look a little abashed at her mother's reprimand, but it soon passed as Mary fixed her gaze on Rose again. 'You are quite old, Miss Wallace… Rose. Yet you are not wed.'

'Mary! That is quite sufficient from you!' Mrs Wallace walked over and took Rose's hand and patted it. 'You are quite the beauty, my dear. I am sure you have had your share of attention.'

Thankful for the lady's intervention, Rose summoned a smile. To have such marked comments directed at her was getting unsettling. She just needed a little time with Mary to cut through the teenage angst Rose's arrival had caused… only time was running out.

Chapter 23

Rose turned to her hostess in relief at the distraction. 'You are too kind, Mrs Wallace.'

'Please, my dear, call me by my given name. It is Louisa. Or if it would bring you comfort, you may address me as Mama, as the others do. But let us have no more formality between us.'

'Quite right.' Christopher walked over to where the tea things were and poured himself a fresh cup. 'We are all family, are we not?'

He fixed Mary with a hard stare, but she raised her chin.

'If you will excuse me. I wish to get some air.'

There was an awkward silence after she left the room, and Louisa Wallace exchanged an anxious look with her husband before joining him as he resumed his position by the window. They spoke quietly, and Rose looked up as Olivia came to sit on her other side.

'Pay Mary no mind, Rose. She is accustomed to being Miss Wallace, not Miss Mary.'

'She is to come out next year,' piped Anne. 'Now you will have to wed before she can.'

'Hush, Anne.' Olivia shook her head at her youngest sister. 'Papa would never be tied to such convention, you know he would not.' She peered shyly at Rose. 'May I ask... I do not wish to be impertinent...'

Rose smiled. 'You may ask me whatever you wish.'

'Do you have a beau? You must surely have a young man who wishes to take you as his wife?'

The memory of Aiden, lying in his bed that morning, only partially dressed, rushed into Rose's mind, and she felt the heat in her cheeks flaring.

'There *is* someone! Papa!' Anne spun around in her seat as Christopher and Louisa turned to look over. 'Rose has a suitor!'

'Hush, Anne,' Olivia cautioned her. 'Forgive Anne, Rose. She is too curious for her own good.'

'I am well aware of where Rose's interest lies, Anne.' Her father smiled. 'She has chosen well.'

It was sufficient for both Olivia and Anne to spend the next ten minutes showering Rose in questions about this suitor, which she did her best to answer honestly without feeling she had compromised Aiden in his absence. If the poor man only knew how he was being discussed!

With Mary gone from the room, however, the conversation continued in a light vein, and no further mentions were made about where Rose came from and how she lived, and she began to relax. So much so that she was happily persuaded to share refreshments with everyone before they went for a stroll in the gardens.

Of Mary, there was no sign.

They returned to the house around three in the afternoon, and the chiming of the clock on the mantel drew Rose's attention. She ought to go back; the doctor would have called and she was eager to see how much better Aiden was.

'You wish to return now.'

Christopher had come to stand beside her whilst Anne and Olivia set up the instrument, keen to show Rose a duet they had been practising of late.

'I must. This has been...' Rose looked around the room, filled with late afternoon sunshine: the fire flickering in the grate, the vases of garden blooms, the pretty hangings at the windows and the wall devoted entirely to books. Louisa was stroking a cat stretched out on the rug before the fire and humming under her breath. Rose needed to absorb this room, this moment, keep it close to her forever. '...so special. I shall cherish the memories of today, always.'

'And I too.'

Another hour passed before Rose had the heart to say goodbye. Hopefully, she would be back very soon. Once Aiden was in the hands of a modern doctor or hospital, she would be free to come back to spend a little more time with her father and his family. Surely Jane would be a willing conspirator? And perhaps Mary would grow to like her in time.

'I shall walk back with you, Rose.'

'No.' Rose smiled up at Christopher. 'Let us part here; it is easier this way. I must go back. You know I must. But I will return as soon as I am able.'

'As you wish. Perhaps you have the right of it. The longer our parting is postponed, the harder it becomes.'

Choked with emotion, Rose bid a fond farewell to Louisa, Olivia and Anne, the latter of whom hugged her tightly around the waist and begged her to return directly.

She parted with her father at the gate, both of them filled with emotion as they released hands, but Rose knew the incredible fact of *knowing* him, knowing he'd loved her all these years, eased the parting.

Setting off down the lane towards the centre of Chawton at a brisk pace, Rose forced herself not to look around, conscious part of her wanted to turn and run back, to never leave the sanctuary of that home, of parents and siblings, filled with love, laughter and light… She released a watery laugh. Perhaps not *all* her siblings! But this was everything her life had not been whilst growing up with her mother in Bathampton.

Rose dashed a hand across her damp lashes, forcing her mind to think forward, to seeing Aiden, to getting him safely home. She reached the pond opposite the cottage, her eyes running over what was visible of the building, given the high hedging, tucking away yet another memory. She would write all of it down as soon as she was home.

She waited for a coach and horses to pass, then stepped out to cross the road to the footpath on the other side. She must write her letter to Morgan as soon as she got back to the house, let her know exactly when she planned to arrive with Aiden, and then—

'Miss Wallace! Rose, please wait!'

Turning around, Rose was surprised to see Mary Wallace come flying along the lane. She fetched up breathless in front of her, and Rose eyed her warily, wondering what, with them safely out of the earshot of any of the family, she might throw at her now.

'Forgive me?' Rose's eyes widened as Mary stepped forward, still breathing heavily. 'I do not mean to be so lacking in manners. 'Tis a shock, that is all. An adjustment.'

Rose smiled, her heart lightening in an instant. 'You are a daughter to be proud of, Mary. I know how much my… our father loves his children, and though I was the first born, he knows little of me. You, Olivia and Anne – and your brother – you are his life. You and your mother.'

Mary sighed. 'You are too kind – as is my mother. I wish to be more like you, but I have such irrational moments, such bursts of temper. I know not whence they hale.'

Reaching out, Rose tentatively took Mary's hand, unsure if she would welcome the gesture. 'It is all part of growing up.'

Mary smiled tremulously. 'Perchance I have been mistaken, and having an elder sister would bring enhancements I can only imagine. You are wise.'

Rose laughed. 'I am older.'

Mary blushed. 'I am sorry.'

'Don't... do not be. I meant no censure.' Rose squeezed her hand lightly and released it. 'My age does not trouble me, nor should it you. But wisdom comes with growing older.'

'It ought not!' Mary let out a huff of breath. 'Why give us wisdom when we no longer need it, and withhold it when it is longed for?'

Rose shook her head. 'You mistake me. Wisdom is required whatever our age. Only as we grow older do we learn how to heed it and harness it for our own good.'

Mary studied her for a moment, then a smile formed – a genuine smile that reached her eyes. 'And I shall trust to your guidance... Sister.' The smile faded. 'But you are to leave us. Papa has told me... your stay is of short duration?'

'It is. I must return home directly.'

'It is what prompted me to follow you. I had thought...' Mary gestured back towards the house. 'I had expected there to be other occasions when I would be able to address my poor demeanour towards you, when I would be able to show you the civility you deserve. I had not realised…'

'I am sure we will meet again, Mary.'

They stood in silence for a moment, studying each other's features. Then, Rose smiled. 'Come, let us say farewell for the present.' She held out her hand, then realised what she was doing, but Mary didn't seem to notice, throwing herself at Rose and hugging her, and with a huff of laughter, Rose hugged her back.

'There,' she said, setting Mary back from her as they separated. 'We have hugged as only sisters can.' Feeling the emotion grip her throat again, Rose smiled. 'Take care of your… our papa, Mary.'

'I promise.' Mary's eyes filled with tears. 'I am so sorry I squandered today. I will not do you the same disservice when you return from Bath.' Her eyes brightened. 'Perchance I could make some stay with you there!'

Unable to speak, so taut was her throat, Rose nodded, then turned and hurried down the lane, unaware Mary watched her until she was quite out of sight, before slowly turning for home.

Rose felt light as air as she almost skipped along the road towards Chawton House, her non-conditioned hair and ill-fitting shoes the last thing on her mind.

This was *reality*, not some amazing dream she had conjured in her mind. She had a family! She laughed under her breath as she turned into the long driveway leading past the church and up to the house. They just happened to live quite far away, not in distance, but in time.

Until now, family had meant nothing but loneliness, obligation and, in some ways, the feeling of being trapped. As difficult as her mother was, however, Rose did love her.

She'd never felt much reciprocation, but she'd accepted that as her lot in life.

Now, she had a *real* family... but how could she keep them?

Rose wrapped her arms about her waist as she walked, deep in thought. She was so thankful, so grateful to the Austen and Knight families; to Jane, who had made all this possible, to Charles who had given her the special charm, to Cassandra for her warmth and Edward for his kind acceptance of their situation.

As she drew level with the church, Rose couldn't help but eye it with the same nostalgia she had the cottage. How different it looked now, and how odd it was to no longer see the statue of Jane, only so recently placed in the churchyard on its pedestal.

With a smile, Rose set off up the sloping driveway to the house. Even if she could not come back often, surely Jane would still be able to deliver correspondence?

Content she had found a solution – Rose could not bear to think of her family worried – she hurried up the steps. How would her father explain that? It couldn't be allowed to happen, and this way they could communicate for many years.

Then, she stopped, her hand on the door. The breeze rustled through Rose's hair and all of the joy in her heart was swept away like the russet leaves rolling away from her across the terraces. How could she have forgotten?

Jane... a woman so full of life, energy and wit, would be stolen from the world in less than four short years. Rose had considered this a tragedy even before she could name Jane as one of her friends. Now, added onto the unbearable thought was that Jane was also the only link that existed between herself and her new (though quite old) family.

This had always been the truth. The heartless reality of death had always been balanced out by the fantasy of her adventures with Jane. And yet now, Rose was confronted with it, couldn't shy away from it.

She entered the house consumed with sadness, but she couldn't dwell on it for long once she'd entered the great hall. There was Jane, as alive and vibrant as ever, teasing her sister, her brothers engrossed in conversation by the hearth.

'Rose, there you are!' Jane turned around in her seat and beckoned Rose over to join her and Cassandra. 'Pray, tell us. How was your time with your family?'

'Lovely, thank you. How is Aid— Mr Trevellyan?'

'Quite well. My brother,' Jane waved a hand towards Charles, 'has kept him company as best he could, but the gentleman spends much of the time asleep. We hope he will be up to the journey home before first light in the morning.'

'Sleep is healing, Miss Wallace.' Cassandra smiled reassuringly at Rose. 'Now, tell us about your day.'

Pushing aside her melancholy, Rose settled next to Jane and, her spirits rising as she recalled the day with the Wallace family, she was soon recounting her experiences to her keenly interested companions.

–

Something woke Rose in the early hours on Wednesday, and she rolled over onto her back, thankful to have left her dreams behind.

The evening had passed so slowly, with no opportunity for her to visit Aiden, but perhaps it was for the best. He needed his rest if they were to travel before dawn broke. An owl hooted out in the darkness, and Rose pummelled her pillow before falling back on it and closing her eyes. Torn between concern over Aiden and the pain of leaving her father, she tried to think only of the time so recently spent with her new family, but as she tugged the counterpane up to her chin, preparing to indulge herself, the hurrying of footsteps could be heard, and she sat up. What was going on?

There was no one in sight when she peered out onto the landing and, pulling a shawl around her shoulders, she stepped out, intent on following the sound of voices, when she was almost run over by a maid carrying a bundle of soiled linens.

'Sorry, miss.' She looked quite flustered, and Rose frowned.

'Is something wrong?'

'Oh, miss, 'tis the young gentleman. The doctor is with him now.' She bobbed a quick curtsey and hurried to a service door further along the landing, soon disappearing from sight with her burden.

Rose's heart was beating painfully hard as she hurried towards Aiden's room. This couldn't be happening. Aiden couldn't be suffering just as she was reflecting on what an enjoyable day she'd had.

She fetched up outside his room, trying to calm herself. She didn't know what the problem was yet. She must not overreact.

Rose placed her hand on the doorknob only for the door to swing open, and she stood aside as the doctor came out, placing his hat on his head and turning to Edward, who accompanied him.

'I shall return at first light. The *Express* should be with Baillie by then. He should be here within a half day. Let us await his opinion on the case.'

Edward inclined his head at Rose, his face serious, and led the gentleman away along the landing, and Rose stepped into the room.

Chapter 24

The captain stood at the foot of the bed as a maid tidied the sheets following the doctor's examination. He looked up as Rose entered the room, and she hurried over to stare down at Aiden.

'What has happened?' Her voice came out as a whisper.

Aiden was no longer propped up. His colour was ashen and his skin damp with sweat as she took his good hand. He didn't open his eyes, but gave her fingers a light squeeze.

'I'm fine, don't worry.' His voice was faint.

'As if that were possible!' She looked over her shoulder at Charles, not letting go of Aiden's hand. 'Does he have an infection?' There was no way she would let them bring leeches into the room!

Charles shook his head. 'No, for which we are to be thankful. Mr Lyford believes there to be a problem with how the arm is setting. As is often the case on a first attempt, there is some nerve damage, and it seems the binding was too tight and hampered the circulation to Mr Trevellyan's hand. The examination was thorough and painful, disturbing the unset bone and also his wound, hence the gentleman's pallor.'

Rose's eye was drawn to the arm, no longer strapped to the piece of wood but lying listlessly on the counterpane. The fingers protruding from the bandage were white, almost waxy, in appearance and much more swollen than earlier. 'Then what is to be done?'

Charles walked round to stand on the other side of the bed. 'Mr Lyford says it may help if the bone is adjusted but he wishes for a second opinion.'

Rose winced. 'What are the risks?'

There was no reply, and she looked over at Charles, her insides churning with anxiety. 'Tell me, Captain Austen. I must know.'

He eyed Rose warily for a second, then nodded. 'As you wish. If it does not work, he may lose the use of his hand.'

Rose's hand shot to her throat, and her heart, if at all possible, increased its pounding. 'No!'

At a sound behind her, she looked round to find Jane had come into the room, along with her sister, both of them bundled into dressing gowns and looking somewhat dishevelled.

'We heard a disturbance, then met Edward on the landing.' Jane's gaze drifted to Aiden, then away. 'The doctor told him they must attempt to restore the flow of blood to the hand, Rose. If they do not, gangrene can set in.'

Not wanting to think about the outcome of that, though she knew full well what it meant, Rose turned back to Aiden, whose eyes opened slowly.

'Not keen on the idea of amputation without anaes-thetic, to be honest.' He turned his head on the pillow and looked at Rose through pain-filled eyes. 'How was your day?'

Rose shook her head in disbelief. He was asking after *her* day? 'I will tell you all about it once we have you home and well.'

His eyes closed again, and she gently released his hand and turned to look at Jane.

'We have to get him home. Immediately, Jane.'

For a moment, Jane held Rose's gaze, her face pale. Then, she nodded. 'There is something I must do beforehand.' She looked over her shoulder towards the window. 'We must go under cover of darkness, and he is not easy to move. Let us hope he rallies by nightfall.'

Rose wanted to shout at her, demand they went right now, but she knew it was futile. The all-important thing was to get Aiden home. A couple of hours would make no difference either way, and with modern medicine and procedures, this was surely an easy fix?

'May I trouble you for some more parchment? I must let Morgan know what's happening. It's just as well she didn't pick up the letters yesterday. Perhaps we can catch her this morning before she sees them.'

'Come with me, Miss Wallace.' Cassandra took Rose gently by the arm and urged her over to the door, and Rose looked back at Aiden to see the maid tending to him, wiping his forehead with a damp cloth.

'I will remain, Miss Wallace.' Charles' face was more serious than Rose had ever seen it, and so unlike him, she didn't know how to take it. Was he as worried as she was?

'Yes, of course. Thank you.'

Cassandra opened the door and ushered Rose through it, Jane following in their wake. She only hoped Morgan would be able to get the necessary help lined up for their arrival.

–

Rose was pacing up and down in the great hall, trying not to look at the clock every time she passed. Where was Jane? She should have gone with her, but she hadn't wanted to leave the house in case Aiden asked for her.

Fetching up beside the window, Rose stared down the drive. What had Jane needed to do? Surely nothing was more important than getting this message to Morgan and then taking them home as soon as possible?

'Miss Wallace.'

She turned on her heel. Cassandra had come into the room and walked over to join her by the window. 'Here, take a little wine.' She handed the glass of dark liquid to Rose. 'It will help calm you, for you have a long day ahead.'

'Thank you.' Rose sipped the drink, even though she didn't really want it. 'Where do you think Jane is?'

She turned around and looked out of the window again, just as the clock on the mantel struck the hour.

'It is eleven o'clock! The museum will have long been open.'

'Come, Miss Wallace, be seated. My sister will not return any the sooner for your watching for her.'

Another half hour passed, during which Cassandra attempted to engage Rose in conversation. She did her best to oblige, unwilling to cause offence, but her mind was flitting between the room upstairs where Aiden lay, the cottage, and Morgan and the surgeon flying along the turnpike from London with his medical bag, prepared to do whatever he chose to Aiden.

When the door finally opened, Rose stood up so quickly she almost stumbled, hurrying across the room.

'Oh, thank goodness.' She had seen the letters in Jane's hand. 'And were you able to send the latest?'

Jane looked evasive but said nothing, merely holding out the letters to Rose, who took them eagerly. Then, she frowned and looked up at Jane.

'These are both mine to Morgan, and this is the new letter. Jane, what is going on?'

'To make long sentences upon unpleasant subjects is very odious.' Jane took a seat next to her sister, and Rose walked back and sank onto the sofa opposite. Jane did not sound her confident self.

'You don't think...' Rose drew in a sharp breath. 'Something has happened to Morgan!' She put a hand to her head. 'Of course. She is unable to retrieve anything because... because... she's been banned from entering the museum! Oh, Jane, that must be it! If she was caught pulling up a floorboard in your bedroom, no wonder that has happened.'

But what if it was worse? Rose knew Morgan would go to great lengths for her, perhaps even ignoring warnings not to return to the museum... what if she'd been *arrested*?

Jane shook her head. 'I wish it were so simple. I, like you, thought at first there must be a reason why Miss Taylor could not access the letters. I had done as I always did, placed the charm under the floorboard last night.' For a moment, Jane's voice sounded normal again. 'But neither the letters nor the ink I placed there earlier had gone.'

Rose wilted. 'It's okay. It just would have made it easier on Aiden if she had a car waiting, but it doesn't matter. I'll be with you, we can knock on someone's door and ask to use the phone if my mobile is dead – and it's quite likely to be after several days in the boot of Aiden's car.'

To her surprise, Jane didn't seem appeased by this, getting to her feet and coming over to sit beside Rose.

'I thought as you at first, but then another notion struck me.'

A coldness seemed to take hold of Rose, trickling rapidly through her veins, and she shuddered.

Cassandra looked from Rose to her sister with a frown. 'Jane? What is it?' Then, her eyes flashed. 'You have not… you *promised* me!' Cassandra got to her feet. 'Did I not *warn* you, when you were so delayed returning that time?'

'We think so very differently on this point that there can be no use in canvassing it.'

'Jane!'

Rose's gaze moved from Cassandra to Jane, who let out a huff of breath.

'Very well, I have continued to use it.' Jane shrugged, but Rose could tell from her face that she wasn't feeling remotely flippant. 'I had a duty to go.'

'To your situation at the museum.' Cassandra rolled her eyes. ''Tis a strange *duty* indeed.'

'The reason I mention it is not to put it forward to debate. It is that, when I tried to come back—'

The door opened and Edward and Charles entered the room.

'Mr Trevellyan sleeps. We thought it best to let him rest for the present.' Edward walked over to the tray on the console table. 'Would anyone care for a glass?' He held up the decanter, and Rose was tempted to say she'd take the lot.

'We shall all be in need of a glass when Jane finally tells us what is so disturbing her.' Cassandra got to her feet and walked over to her brother, who topped up Rose's glass and poured one for Jane.

'Brandy for me, Edward, if you would be so kind.' Charles settled into a chair near the fireplace, his gaze fixed on his sisters. 'You look quite out of sorts.'

Jane received the glass from her sister and took a sip. 'It is fortunate you have joined us, Charles, for there is something I must impart to Rose and you may have some enlightenment for us.'

Taking the proffered glass from Edward, Charles settled back in his seat. 'I am quite at my leisure.'

Placing her glass on a side table, Jane got to her feet and walked towards the windows before turning around to face them, her hands clasped before her.

'I believe – forgive me, Rose – but I suspect the charm has lost its power, has been depleted.'

Rose stared at Jane. Her heart was racing and her head was starting to buzz with her fears.

'You mean…' She swallowed in an attempt to relieve a sudden restriction in her throat. 'You mean the power that moves you through time… it has *run out*?'

Edward had filled his own glass now and came to sit in the chair opposite his brother. 'We have not the pleasure of understanding you, dear sister. How can this… this charm have lost its power, and how would you know of it?'

'Dear Rose.' Jane ignored her brother, and walked over to where Rose sat, almost scared to move in case she missed something. 'Though I wished you to come back with me, my conscience reproaches me, for I fear I have brought you – *both* of you – here only to suffer the same fate you helped save me from when first we met.'

The silence in the room following this pronouncement seemed louder to Rose than any concert she had ever been to. Jane smoothed her skirt and continued. 'Charles, when you acquired the charm, did the lady speak any words to you, should it cease to hold its power?'

Rose looked earnestly at Charles. Here would be the answer; surely there would be a way to recharge it?

Charles took a slug from his glass and got to his feet, walking over to the console table. 'Not at all. Apart from the instruction it must pass directly from my hand to yours, as it had from hers to mine, there was no indication of aught else.'

He topped up his glass and turned around to lean against the table, his gaze resting on Rose with sympathy, then moving to Jane.

Rose really wanted to say something, to react, to express the mingled fear and frustration spinning unhelpfully through her mind.

'But how do you know there is nothing left... no power to it? Is it just because the portal appears not to be working?'

'Miss Wallace is correct. Supposition is perhaps unhelpful at this early stage of research,' Edward offered. 'What evidence do you have of the charm's inaction?'

Jane glared at her brother. 'It is not mere supposition. Do you think me a simpleton?'

Edward glared back. 'It is hard to think you the most rational of creatures, when you have been doing what you have.'

'But perchance the charm is simply being... mischievous. It has caused problems before, has it not?' Cassandra looked hopefully at Edward, but her brother had his gaze fixed on Jane.

'What sort of problems?'

Chapter 25

Jane sighed. 'It seemed of little enough significance. Since bringing Rose and Mr Trevellyan here, it has not worked as smoothly as before. When I returned from taking Miss Taylor and Mr Malcolm, I came by way of another year, I know not which.'

Cassandra let out a huff of breath. 'And what about the pond?'

'The *duck* pond?' Charles laughed. 'Do tell.'

'When she finally returned that day, she was some feet from where she had left in the future... and decidedly wet.' Cassandra didn't look at all amused. 'And she promised she would use caution.'

Jane, however, turned to Rose. 'I was obliged to go today, and it seemed as opportune as any to try and see Miss Taylor if I could, to ascertain the problem.'

'*You told me not to worry!*' Cassandra was staring at Jane, disbelief written across her features.

Jane raised her chin, but then she shrugged lightly and settled in the seat next to Rose.

'With hindsight it appears reckless.' She took Rose's hand, but it felt little comfort in the circumstances. 'When the charm did not return me directly the first time, it seemed of little consequence. Then, when I needed to go to the museum in Chawton, I—'

'Museum? What museum? There is no museum in Chawton!' Edward looked to his brother, then to Jane. 'Preposterous! Why on earth would there be a museum in such a small place? Who would ever visit it?'

Rose almost blurted out that tens of thousands of people visited it every year, but bit her lip. She wanted the conversation to revert to the charm, not how Jane had impressed the tourists with her knowledge of all things Austen.

'Dear Brother! You will be astounded to learn of the fame that is to come to the cottage – it becomes a museum because I lived there.'

Edward stared at Jane open-mouthed, then closed it with a snap, but before he could speak, Charles did.

'And what? What happened?'

'It malfunctioned. It took me three attempts to reach the year thirteen.'

Charles grunted. 'And now the charm does not work at all?' He drained his glass again. 'How do you know this?'

Jane tightened her hold on Rose's hand. 'I thought perhaps to take the uncollected letters personally to your friend, or at least gain some understanding as to why she had yet to retrieve them herself. I took the charm out and placed it about my neck, but nothing happened. Nothing.'

Jane pulled the cross and chain from its pouch inside her reticule and laid it on the table, and Rose stared at it, her throat tight and her insides churning. Was Jane right? Had the charm truly stopped working? Were she and Aiden stuck here, in 1813, and never going back?

–

Edward had moved everyone to the library, instructing the servants they were not to be disturbed unless the doctor arrived, and Rose walked into the room, her mind racing, hardly able to take in what was happening. She looked around as Edward locked the door and turned to fix his sister with a stern eye.

'Jane, you have already been trapped in the future. It is a miracle you were able to return at all.'

'And now we are trapped in the past,' Rose whispered.

'It has to be said, the charm is proving to be unreliable at best.' Charles sank into a chair beside the desk under the window.

Jane shook her head. 'That has not been my experience.' She looked around the room, then back to Edward. 'Perhaps transporting more than myself resulted in this? Perchance it was never intended for such a purpose.'

'But you had no need to continually flit between this time and the present, as you have done with little thought for anyone but yourself!' Cassandra sounded as frustrated as Rose was beginning to feel.

Rose's heart was pounding in her chest so fiercely, she was sure they could all hear it.

'Could the charm restore itself?'

Jane walked over to sit beside Rose. 'How can I say? I have no reason to suppose it will.'

Rose put a hand to her head, which was beginning to ache. Were she and Aiden truly stranded? 'But what about Aiden? We cannot let the surgeon take his hand!'

Jane patted Rose's arm, but Edward walked over to stand before her. His eyes were kind, and Rose felt tears prick the back of her lids.

'Miss Wallace, please do not fear such an outcome yet. Let the doctor and surgeon assess the injury. They are well versed in such matters and will do all they can to alleviate the situation. Amputation is a last recourse, not a given, and it may be some days before a conclusion is reached.'

Rose nodded, unable to summon words, and he walked back over to enter into a low-voiced conversation with Charles. Rose tried to remain calm. Had she really been this blinkered, this taken with walking in history with Jane by her side, with the revelation of her father's whereabouts? Had she taken this... *magic* so for granted she had never considered they could be stuck here forever?

–

When the doctor returned, he spent what felt like forever with Aiden, and Rose paced up and down on the gravel sweep at the front of the house, trying not to think about what his conclusions might be today. She stared at her feet as she walked.

Her mind was still reeling from Jane's revelation and its implications, so much so, she couldn't form any coherent ideas as to how she was going to have the emotional strength to bear the loss of her old life, her friends and everything about the modern world she loved and had so taken for granted. *How* could she have been so stupid as to not think about the risks?

'Rose.' She started and looked over her shoulder. Jane was coming towards her, and she turned and hurried over.

'Is it Aiden?'

Jane shook her head. 'He is well enough in the circumstances. The doctor detects no change for the worse, and is adamant the surgeon must be the one to determine the next course of action. It is believed he will arrive within the next hour or so.'

She took Rose's arm and they walked back towards the house. 'It is you I wish to speak to. I cannot bear to think what I have brought you to, what loss I have caused both you and Mr Trevellyan.'

Her voice was uncharacteristically solemn, but somehow, it gave Rose the impetus she needed to pull herself together. She'd watched Jane deal with a similar situation only a week ago, trapped in the twenty-first century and lost to all who knew her. Jane had been philosophical, practically minded, resourceful. These were all things Rose would now need to apply to her own life. This was no time to crumble. Besides, there was no duvet for her to wrap herself in, no comforting packet of chocolate biscuits to consume or back-to-back Netflix series to lose herself in.

No, this time, she had to live out the story, not just observe it, just as her father had. If he could do it, so could she.

'Jane, can you do something for me?'

They had come to a halt before the entrance to the house, and Jane met Rose's gaze warily. 'If I am at all able.'

'It is nothing too onerous. I must speak to Aiden. Now. In private. You do understand? I have to tell him our situation, and I have to do so before the surgeon arrives. He has a right to know where he stands.'

Jane nodded. 'As you wish.'

–

Rose closed the door to Aiden's room and leant against it for a moment, listening to Jane's receding footsteps. They had assured her as much time as she needed, and knowing the door to the servants' staircase was locked again, she held her breath as she looked across at the motionless form in the bed.

Walking over, she eased down onto the edge of it and gently slipped her hand into Aiden's good one. Much as she wanted him to rest, she felt a desperate need to be connected to him physically. He was the one tangible thing from her normal life, the one thing keeping her sane in amongst all this... insanity.

He didn't stir, and she watched him for some minutes, unaware her breathing had slowly become synchronised with his. It gave her courage, being here with him. How would she have coped with her situation, had she come back alone? He made her feel real, the whole *unreal* thing seem real. Sadness gripped her, and Rose remained motionless for some time, her hand clasping Aiden's, relishing its warmth, cherishing the moment, knowing she must break such awful uncertainty to him.

'Rose?' Aiden spoke faintly.

Rose leaned forward, her head almost touching the adjacent pillow. 'I'm sorry. I didn't want to wake you.'

'What time is it?'

'I don't know. About two in the afternoon?'

He frowned. 'Why... how are you here? Are we alone?' He hadn't opened his eyes.

'Yes, quite alone. They said it was okay for a short time. For me to be here...' Her voice tailed away. How was she to begin?

'Rose?' Aiden's voice was hoarse. How she longed to offer him some water. 'What's wrong? What aren't you telling me?'

She held tight to his hand, then eased around to swing her legs up onto the bed and edged closer to his face. 'The charm...' Rose whispered softly. Perhaps by saying it gently, it wouldn't sound so bad? 'Jane's charm isn't working properly.' She sighed. Was this being truthful? 'Or at all, even.'

There was no sound from Aiden for a moment. Had he drifted back into sleep? She tried to draw a shallow breath, but it hitched in her throat and a small sob came out instead.

'I'm so sorry. Aiden, I'm so sorry I got us into this.'

Slowly, his eyes opened, and he turned his head with obvious difficulty on the pillow. They were eye to eye now, and he released her hand and raised his to touch the curls beside her cheek.

'Don't cry. Please don't. It's going to be okay.'

Rose sniffed back her tears. 'How can it possibly be okay? What is there in all of this that's okay?'

His eyes had closed again, but he gave a slight shake of his head. 'Worse things happen at sea. You'll see.'

Rose wanted nothing more than to bury her head in his chest and believe him, but his voice was coloured with pain and a sort of fuzziness, as if he had had a bit too much to drink. Besides, she would hardly be aiding him by leaning on his bruised ribs, would she?

Rolling onto her back, her hand once more in Aiden's, Rose stared at the elegant canopy. She would have to advocate for both of them in this world, if this was indeed where they were to live out their days. When things had gone wrong before, Morgan had kept her going, urged her onwards. It was futile now to think of Morgan, or of James, or the fact she and Aiden might forever be unresolved missing person cases.

Rose's mind flew to Bath, her home, her desk at work. Her *Out of Office* said she'd be returning to her desk two days ago. Now, it would never be removed. Thoughts of never again visiting her favourite restaurants, never walking to work with the sun warming the golden stone of Bath threatened to overwhelm her, and she pushed them forcibly away. None of it mattered. The losses from tantamount to trivial had to come second to caring for Aiden. She had brought him to this situation. She had to make it as right as she could for them.

Chapter 26

'Rose?' Aiden attempted to clear his throat. 'Are you still here?'

She turned her head on the pillow. 'Yes. I'm here.'

'You shouldn't be.'

'I'm getting pretty tired of being told what I should and shouldn't do.'

Aiden laughed weakly.

'Ow! Ribs,' he muttered, then added, 'I had no idea I had fallen for such a rebel.'

Rose stared at him, not knowing how to respond. She'd known he'd liked her, of course. He'd only just confessed to it, but was he really… *keen* on her, like she was on him? A momentary feeling of happiness took hold of her before reality intruded.

'Fear has made me take risks, I suppose.'

Aiden grunted, his lids falling again. Then, his eyes opened, and he frowned.

'Did you… was I dreaming? Did you say something about the charm?'

Rose tried to speak firmly. 'Yes. It's not working, I'm afraid.'

Aiden frowned. 'Which one?'

It was Rose's turn to frown. 'Jane's, of course. There's only the one.'

Aiden made as if to sit up, but Rose eased him back down onto the pillows. 'Hush. You must stay still.'

'But the cross Jane has… it's not the only one.'

'I know, but the other two are inanimate, remember? Only Jane's has… *had* special power.'

Aiden was becoming agitated, and Rose eased herself off the bed. She had better send for a maid to sit with him and find out how much longer it would be before the surgeon arrived.

'Where are you going? I'm hungry. Any chance of a pizza?'

Rose couldn't help but smile. 'Get some rest. I'd better go before someone has to come looking for me. It won't do for the surgeon to find me in here alone.'

She began to loosen her hand from his, but he summoned some of his old strength and held on, pulling her closer to him. 'Wherever I am, I want to be with you. Wherever I am, it's all the same to me. Do you understand?'

If he weren't in danger of infection and amputation she would have thrown herself at him right then and there, but his burst of strength had gone and he released her hand, falling back against his pillows, his eyes closed again.

Her heart full, Rose stood up and looked at him for a moment. 'Yes, I understand.' She turned away, but then looked back over her shoulder. 'I love you,' she mouthed, before letting herself out of the room, fighting back tears of both happiness and hopelessness.

Rose walked slowly along the landing, part of her longing to go back and stay with Aiden, but she knew she had to let him rest with the surgeon's imminent arrival, and her pace steadily increased until she almost flew down the stairs. She had to get outside, away for a moment.

The temptation to leave Chawton House without telling a soul was severe. Rose felt no anger, not towards Jane or anyone else, but emotion had her in a grip so strong it felt like she was drowning in it. She needed time to herself, she needed... a walk.

She was almost amused by how her behaviour mirrored those of her favourite Regency heroines, heading for a long walk and fresh air to alleviate her turmoil. Having reached the hallway, she hesitated outside the door to the library, from which low voices emanated. She so needed to be alone, but should she leave without telling them?

'Miss.' A servant had come out of the service door, bobbing a curtsey before making to pass her, but Rose stayed her with a hand.

'I am going to take some air. I shall walk...' She sought for inspiration. 'In the direction of the village.'

'As you wish, miss.' The servant hurried along the corridor and, satisfied she had left the necessary information if anyone was looking for her, Rose headed to the door and slipped out of the house.

She had intended to wander aimlessly, but as she reached the centre of Chawton, she slowed to a halt across the road from the cottage. She had left the great house with no bonnet or shawl and no clear purpose other than to escape, but now she understood exactly why her feet had led her here.

She crossed the road and hurried past the cottage without looking at it. Ridiculous though it was, she was a little mad at the house now she had been robbed unfairly of her lifeline to Morgan. Rose's breath was uneven as she walked along the lane bordering the garden. An elderly lady came out of the gate of the rather dilapidated thatched cottage opposite the Wallaces' and turned in her direction, albeit on the opposite side of the road, and she smiled and nodded at Rose as she passed.

It was Miss Benn, and Rose turned to watch her making her way towards the centre of the village, then looked back at Baigens. Why had she come? How was this going to help things? They thought they'd said their farewells for now.

Rose closed her eyes. They ached with unshed tears, ones she had held back for hours now, firstly from shock at Jane's news, then so as not to unnerve Aiden too much. Surely this was a bad idea, complicating an already complicated story and stirring already tumultuous feelings?

'Rose!'

Rose's eyes flew open to meet those of Mary, who had come to lean over the garden wall.

'What are you doing here? We thought you had taken your leave. Are you delayed?'

Rose curtseyed on instinct. 'Mary. I... I...' Was Mary friend or foe today? She seemed to be smiling, which was something.

'You are pale as a spirit! Come.' She gestured over at the gate. 'I shall fetch Mama.'

Rose stepped into the garden, still unsure of her purpose, her heart clenching in her chest. Mary had disappeared inside the house, and she could hear her calling for her mother. How awful was this, catching them so unaware, creating drama in a house that deserved none?

She had almost decided to turn and flee when Mrs Wallace came bustling out of the door, a look of concern on her sweet features.

'My dear girl! Are you unwell?'

Rose shook her head. There was a strange tightness about her throat, a constriction making it hard to speak.

'Forgive me. I should not have come—'

'Nonsense, child.' Mrs Wallace stepped forward and put an arm around Rose, urging her into the house. 'You must sit for a while. Olivia!'

The second eldest put her head around a door to the right and stared at Rose in surprise.

'Fetch your father, please. This instant.'

But Christopher Wallace was already bounding down the stairs to fetch up before her. 'Rose! How is it you are here?' His keen glance raked her face. 'What is wrong? What has happened?'

Mary and Anne had joined them in the hallway now, and Rose looked from one concerned face to the other, her throat growing tighter and tighter until, for the first time since she was a teenager, she completely dissolved into tears in front of people. Much as she tried to stop, to reassure them she was fine, the tears she had been holding back refused to cease.

Louisa offered her a handkerchief, and Rose wiped her face as she was led into the drawing room and urged into a seat. Her father sat beside her, with Mary and her mother opposite.

'Olivia, ask Williams to bring tea.'

She left the room, and Anne picked up her book from the floor and perched on a stool nearby.

'I am so sorry.' Rose drew in a shuddering breath, thankful the stream of tears seemed to have calmed. 'I didn't mean to barge in on you and… and create such a disturbance.'

Louisa smiled so kindly at her, Rose nearly started to bawl again, but she held it in, wiping her eyes one final time.

'You have created no disturbance, and you must know you are welcome here at all times.' Louisa spoke soothingly, then tentatively added, 'Has something happened to your young suitor? The young man who had the fall?'

Rose nodded, then shook her head, before turning to her father at her side. 'Something has gone wrong with his injury and our... travel home has fallen through.'

Christopher's face changed from worry and consternation to dumbstruck. He glanced at the others in the party before speaking. 'Do you mean, you will stay here? Permanently?'

Mary looked at him as if he were talking nonsense. 'Papa, there is more than one carriage in the land!'

Louisa gave her a warning glance. 'It is frustrating, to be certain, but such things can easily be resolved.' She frowned. 'Does Mr Knight not have another carriage at his disposal? I am certain I have seen more than one before now.'

Christopher got to his feet. 'Louisa, would you please give us a moment alone to speak?'

Louisa frowned, looking from her husband to Rose, then nodded. 'Of course, my dear. Come, Mary. Anne.' She walked over to pat Rose on the arm before leading the two girls from the room.

Rose's hands were clenched around the handkerchief as she got to her feet. 'I really am so sorry for coming unannounced. I think the tears have been long overdue.'

'Rose, if you apologise one more time for coming to this house when you were in need I will use my privilege as your father and punish you.' His mouth curved into a half smile. 'Tell me what has happened.'

It took Rose a while to lay it all before her father, with Aiden's health taking a turn for the worse, delaying their departure and then the staggering news the charm was no longer working. She managed to get through it without falling apart again, though her voice did waver when her father questioned her on the consequences for Aiden's arm.

Christopher listened as Rose shared her feelings of guilt and her fears and disappointment for all she might have lost forever. When she was done, he hugged her to him, and it was all she could do not to start crying again.

He released her and stood back, surveying her face with sympathy.

'I am sorry. I am sorry for all you have been through. I do not know what to say. My own heart has been broken since we parted and seeing you again now is a wish granted that I dared never to hope for.'

Rose bit her lip, willing herself to be strong. 'Oh, I know exactly how you feel. I don't want to cause pain to my family and friends where I live. I don't want to lose the life I built there, and I definitely do not want to be responsible for the same for Aiden. And yet, knowing you were only a walk away… It was unbelievably… unbelievable.' Rose laughed and shook her head at her poor phrasing. 'I hope you are not hurt to know I haven't given up yet. I've been stuck before, as you know, and we found a way to make things right.' She looked at him sadly. 'This time, though… I don't know where to begin.'

Christopher took her hand. 'I am a selfish man and would keep you here if I could, but I do not want any doubts in either of our hearts. If I am to have you back in my life permanently, I want to be certain there is no way back to your former life. Only then will I feel at peace with the happiness that could be.'

Rose smiled tremulously at him. How comforting it was to have a parent looking out for her.

'I wish I knew how to start. *Where* to start, and—'

She stopped and they both looked around as the door opened and Anne came in, carrying a cup.

'Tea, Rose. Mama says you must drink it, for it is hot and sweet and will aid you.' She placed it on a side table.

'Please thank her, Anne.'

The girl smiled widely and turned to pick up her book from the floor, and Rose looked back at her father.

'I don't know what to do.' She put a hand to her head. 'If I was at home, when I needed answers, I would just jump on Google…'

Anne looked up, an eager expression on her face. 'Is Google your mount?'

Rose stared at her blankly for a moment; then, her father cleared his throat.

'Oh, er… no.' Rose threw him a grateful look before continuing. 'It is a resource for… for information.'

'Like our encyclopedias!' Anne turned towards the bookcase. 'Shall I fetch one? Which letters would suffice?'

'That is very kind, Anne.' Christopher smiled at his daughter. 'But I think it best we take some air.' He held out an arm to Rose. 'Come, my dear. Let us walk in the garden.'

Chapter 27

Once outside, Christopher placed Rose's hand on his arm and they strolled along the path towards the wall bordering the cottage. Despite the turmoil in her head, Rose felt so much calmer now they were alone and able to talk openly. Much as she was growing to like her new family, she was not really prepared for the strain of pretence right now.

Christopher glanced over his shoulder, then slowed their steps, turning her to face him. 'Tell me all you can recall about how you came to be here, and do not spare any detail. We do not know what may aid us until we attempt to piece together all we comprehend thus far.'

Rose blew out a frustrated breath. 'That's half the problem. There's not much to it. Whatever is between Jane and the cross happens silently; any thought she has stays in her head.'

'You have never spoken of it to her? Asked her how the charm functions?'

Rose shook her head, feeling stupid. 'Why didn't I ever ask her? She told me she simply puts the necklace on and, whichever way it faces – the charm, that is – it takes her forward or backward in time. In an instant.' She paused, thinking hard. 'It is what happened when she brought me and Aiden,' her voice faltered over his name, 'back with her. Everything went black for a moment, barely a second, and then we were here.'

She raised troubled eyes to her father, but he didn't look disbelieving or sceptical.

'Believe it or not, Rosie, I comprehend all you say. But this is insufficient to aid you. Try to concentrate. What is stored in our memories may be quite singular, but significant all the same.'

Rose stared at a bumblebee burrowing into a nearby flower. What did she recall that might be of any note? 'Right. Well, the first time something went wrong, when Prancer – er, Link – swallowed the charm, reality changed around us just as quickly as when we travelled through time. I was preoccupied with the lady's reaction as I honestly didn't believe she was who she accidentally admitted to being.' She smiled slightly at Christopher's bemused expression. 'It was a very confusing few days.'

'The days preceding this event you describe, or the days following?'

Rose raised her brows meaningfully. 'Both. Definitely both.'

Christopher grunted. 'But this is not slipping through time, if I understand you? This is…'

'An alternate reality. Yes, it wasn't time related, no blackness or anything.'

'And that is all you recall, beyond your personal experience with the charm?'

Rose tried so hard to come up with something, *anything* that might be of use, but she shook her head sadly. 'There is nothing else.'

Christopher gestured over towards a wooden bench beneath an apple tree. 'Let us sit. The crop is not quite ready to fall, so we should emerge relatively unscathed when we are done.'

Rose sank onto the bench, and Christopher settled beside her.

'Tell me how Jane came by the piece, Rosie.'

Rose shrugged. 'Captain Austen gave it to her. From all we knew of Jane Austen and her life, he purchased two topaz crosses and chains for his sisters after he had come into some prize money from a captured ship.' She frowned, remembering. 'I – no one in the present day – had any knowledge of there being a third cross. When I found out who Jane really was, she explained that her brother had become acquainted with a native woman in Gibraltar. When he shared with her that he wanted to bring gifts home to his sister, he spoke specifically about Jane, how different she was from other women in her situation and how trapped and restricted she felt with her lot in life. The woman sold him three charms in the end, one for his mother, one for Cassandra and a special one for Jane alone.' Rose frowned, remembering bits and pieces of the story. 'It was essential the cross pass from this woman's hand to Charles' and from Charles' hand to Jane's. What she also discovered, once she'd settled in modern-day Bath, was that the charm could create a portal by which Jane and Cassandra were able to communicate through time. That's about all I know.'

Rose glanced at her father, but he was staring away into the distance, a wistful expression on his face, and she looked around to see if anyone had joined them without her knowledge. Had he stopped listening, when he was the one who had wanted her to go into as much detail as possible? And now he wasn't paying attention!

Christopher, however, suddenly turned in his seat to look at her, saying almost to himself, 'Extraordinary coincidence. It must be.' He looked into her eyes, but she had the feeling his mind was still far away. 'This is bringing it all back to me.'

'Bringing back?'

'How I came to be here.'

'But we already know… Oh!' Her voice tailed away as realisation came. 'Could Gibraltar be a connection?'

'It may be. As I explained to you, it is not a moment I have dwelled upon for many years. It would have been self-destructive, an indulgence I could ill afford.' His gaze drifted away again. 'Any consideration of the impossibility of going into the water and coming out more than two centuries earlier…' He huffed on a breath. 'That way lay naught but madness.'

'But Gibraltar can't be just a coincidence, can it? Jane's cross comes from there – from a woman who must have had particular powers – and it was a woman with healing powers who nursed you back to health.'

Christopher smiled, tucking an auburn curl behind Rose's ear. 'Life is stranger than fiction, and so it has long been. If we were to read of too much coincidence in a novel, we would laugh at it, scorn it even. Yet in life it happens all the time. A small world, we used to say.'

With a laugh, Rose nodded. 'We still do!' Then, she sobered, keen to continue their train of thought. 'You never explained. Did the boat sink before you dived into the water?'

Narrowing his gaze, Christopher stared into the distance. 'After, I think, but it is such a time ago. I was on the boat… we were fishing.' He smiled ruefully. 'I felt a tug on my line, a catch at last! It is all I remember before the sudden squall came out of nowhere. Our mast snapped in half almost before we had a chance to understand our peril. We were scrambling, hoping someone had received our SOS when…'

'You said someone was in the water?' Rose prompted.

He closed his eyes, and Rose held her breath, not wishing to interrupt his memories. Then, they flew open again. 'It was a woman!'

Rose frowned. 'But how? Was she from your own boat? I thought it was just the four men who—'

'It was. I know how it sounds.' Christopher looked at Rose, then away. 'I know exactly how it sounds. Only, it is what happened. A woman surfaced, her hair plastered across her face. My only thought, in the moment I dived in, was that she was from another doomed boat herself, or that she had been swimming off the rocks and had got into difficulty. We were truly not that far from the shore.' He sighed. 'It makes no sense, of course. I can only tell you that I saw her and reacted. Only—'

Rose's mouth was dry. Surely she wasn't going to have to add mermaids to the list of impossible things she now believed in? 'What is it?'

Christopher chuckled, and Rose blinked. What in all this was amusing? 'As I swam towards her, she eyed our sinking boat then complained loudly my vessel was in no better shape than hers. She began to sink beneath the waves, and I reached out and grabbed her arm… and that is the last I recall of the present day. It is as you said, all went black, but not for a mere second. I lay in darkness for some time, or so it felt.'

He fell silent, and Rose took his hand, speaking softly. 'What then?'

'When I first came round, there was some chaos; I remember bodies, not those of my friends, and people trying to help. I tried to get up, but I could not. I faded in and out of consciousness. I had lost all my garments and recall being wrapped in a coarse blanket. I asked after the woman, of course, anxious to see if she had survived, but… My *God*…'

Christopher's eyes widened, and he stood up quickly, pulling Rose up with him before running a hand through his hair.

'Drusilla, the medicine woman. She was *there*! On the beach. She was on her knees beside me.' He stared down at Rose. 'What if it was she, the woman in the water? What if she too had a charmed necklace?'

Rose stared back, her heart and mind racing. 'What if it was the very same cross! She sold the charm to Captain Austen – what if she had made use of it herself?'

Christopher eyed his daughter keenly. 'When I reached her, in the water, she spoke of a boat… a vessel, and when I came round later, they spoke of a shipwreck. My mind may be playing tricks on me, but which is more improbable? That we would each find our connections to the past by use of the same charm, or to do so through completely different, unrelated means?'

'They are both completely improbable. You know it as well as I do, despite the evidence before us.'

They stared at each other in silence for a moment, the only sounds being birdsong overhead and the rattle of a cart in the lane.

Then, Rose drew in a breath, trying to sort through all they had learned. 'So.' She spoke slowly, carefully. 'If it is so, she brought you back, accidentally, to 1788, because that is where the lady who had the charm had come from? Yes!' Rose could feel something, somewhere, connecting, but it felt out of reach still. 'It's like what happened to James!'

Christopher frowned, and she shook her head.

'My boss. I'll explain later. He grabbed Morgan's arm, see – I'll explain that too – and came back here unintentionally.'

Her father looked around, his face unsettled. 'You mean there are more displaced people?'

Rose could not help but laugh at his expression. 'No. No one else, to my knowledge. They left again.'

'Oh, I see.' It was clear he didn't, but Rose wanted to continue.

'But if Drusilla is the same woman, and she did have the charm long before she sold it on to Captain Austen, why didn't she help you return to where you'd come from?'

'I do not know. I could not ask her as I did not know it was by her hand, accidentally or not, that I had come to the past.'

'But *she* knew!'

Christopher inclined his head and together they considered this in silence.

Rose shook her head. 'Could it not be that she had inadvertently done exactly as Jane? That carrying multiple people through time with the charm drains it?'

'We will never know. Perhaps she simply did not care.' Christopher shrugged. 'I was not in good shape, remember, having swallowed two centuries worth of ocean.'

Rose was thinking hard. 'I must speak to Jane. Isn't it incredible we may have found a connection? I mean, I know it doesn't help us, with the charm not working, but all the same…'

'Remarkable, my dear. Insane, but remarkable.'

Rose's small burst of excitement faded as quickly as it had come. 'That may be, but I don't see it tells us anything to help our current predicament.'

'Does it not?' Christopher mused. 'Do not discount the value of information. The smallest of details may plant a seed in our minds that later blooms.'

Rose smiled. 'Like on a TV show or a movie when someone says something unrelated, and it solves the case for the detective in one flash?'

Christopher smiled. 'Possibly. The last TV show I remember watching was *Doctor Who*.'

'Aiden was on TV sometimes.' Rose brought up the incongruous thought proudly. 'I wish you could see it. It was, ironically, called *Time Travellers*, and he would visit historical sites and talk about the archaeological discoveries there.'

'I can imagine he would do it very well.'

Rose smiled sadly. 'I've fallen in love with him, and I've ruined his life. How will this ever work out?'

She raised solemn eyes to her father, trying not to let the tears come again, and he reached out and pulled her to him, wrapping his arms around her, and she laid her head against his chest.

'My dear, do not define for him what this journey is or will be. I know from personal experience both tragedy and perfection can live together in harmony. I thought I had lost you. There was nothing to balance that loss at first, but then I found Louisa, created a family and a home here. There is nothing that can compare to such joy. How can both of these things be true in my heart? Yet here I have lived such a contradiction for twenty-five years.'

Rose hugged him, then stepped back from his embrace. 'Thank you.' She was comforted beyond anything to be with her father but the reminder that he had been here twenty-five years had the same effect as if he'd poured a glass of water over her head.

She shivered. 'I ought to get back.'

–

Rose returned to Chawton House feeling a little stronger. It may all be in vain, it may achieve nothing in the long run, but they had found a connection, however slight. Now she needed to talk to Jane and the captain.

As she walked through the door, however, she could sense the urgent bustle of the household, with a footman hurrying towards the kitchen with a laden tray and the housekeeper shouting instructions to a maid, who scurried across the hallway from the servants' staircase bearing a bundle of linen... linen that was, unless Rose was mistaken, sodden with blood.

Chapter 28

Rose flew along the corridor, her heart pounding fiercely, then took the stairs two at a time, her long skirt held up above her knees, all thought of decorum beyond her. The surgeon had been due in her absence, and she had not been there for Aiden, instead indulging in her own misery and confusion.

How could she have deserted him in his time of need? How could Jane have let this happen, let that surgeon loose on him? Or Edward? Hadn't he said it was too soon to take such drastic action as to… as to… with a suppressed sob, Rose fetched up outside Aiden's room.

She hesitated, then tapped firmly, not waiting for a response before walking in, fearing to look around in case she saw something she didn't wish to, her gaze quickly drawn to the ashen face on the white pillows. Aiden's eyes were closed, the stubble on his face darkening as time passed.

Her eyes flew then to his arm, and she drew in a sharp breath of relief to see it still there, bandaged tightly once more and strapped again to the splint. An elderly maid was wiping Aiden's forehead, which was beaded with sweat, and the doctor was conversing quietly near the window with a man who was a stranger to her.

'Miss Wallace.'

She turned around. Charles and Cassandra were by the hearth, and the latter hurried across to take her arm and draw her nearer to its warmth.

'You are pale, come, take some comfort and a glass of something. Charles.' Cassandra turned to her brother, and he walked over to pour brandy into a glass, bringing it to Rose.

'Take it, Miss Wallace. It will revive you.'

He turned to speak quietly to the doctor and his companion as they passed on their way to the door, and Rose took a sip from the glass, her nose wrinkling at the pungent smell. Cassandra urged her into a nearby armchair, but Rose's gaze was drawn back towards the bed.

'Is he…? What has happened? I saw sheets stained with so much blood. I thought…' Her voice failed her.

Charles glanced at the door to ensure they were alone again, then eyed Rose with severity. 'We are not barbarians, Miss Wallace. As Edward explained, amputation is a last recourse in all cases, for it brings its own risks. Did I not tell you the surgeon would assess things first?'

'Yes, of course. I'm sorry. Forgive me.' She tried to recall where she was, then shook her head. She couldn't be doing with such trivial things as how she spoke at a time like this. Charles knew where she was from anyway. 'I feared the worst. Sorry. It's been a difficult time.'

His face relaxed. 'Quite. Do not alarm yourself. The surgeon has adjusted the setting of the bone in an attempt to alleviate the swelling and the numbness in the hand. With the adjacent wound barely having had time to start healing, there was a certain amount of bleeding. It could not be avoided.'

Rose's heart dipped. How much pain must Aiden have endured?

'Do not fear, Miss Wallace.' Cassandra touched her arm, smiling reassuringly. 'The gentleman is as strong as any other; it is not a hopeless case, and there remains no sign of infection, for which we must all be thankful.'

'I am thankful. And grateful.' She looked back at Charles, then to Cassandra. 'I really am.' She bit her lip. 'Did he… was he in much pain?' What a stupid question! How could he not have been in agony?

Charles shrugged. 'He took some brandy and has since had laudanum. He is a brave man, Miss Wallace, but now he needs rest. Mr Lyford has committed to staying overnight with him, and the surgeon will return on the morrow. He has vowed to stay in the district until… well, until his services are no longer required. He will not be far away, having taken lodgings in Alton.'

The tension in Rose's shoulders eased a little at Charles' calm reassurances, and she threw Cassandra a pleading look, and she held out a hand.

'You may see him, but…' She glanced over at the maid as they approached the bed, then said in a whisper, 'We cannot afford to feed the servants' hall with talk.'

Conscious she must step up to the mark and show an indifference she was far from feeling, Rose nodded. They had reached the bedside now, and she stared down at Aiden, her heart almost in splinters. She looked away, forcing her eyes wide. This was no time for tears.

'Thank you, Miss Austen.'

Charles had taken a seat by the hearth, and Rose spoke quietly to the lady at her side. 'Perhaps you would be so kind as to ask your sister to join us? There is something I must discuss with her without delay.'

Cassandra said nothing for a moment, her expression unreadable. Then, the lady turned to the maid. 'Jenkins, would you ask Miss Austen to join us here directly?'

'Yes, miss.' The maid bobbed a curtsey and hurried over to the door leading to the servants' staircase, slipping through it and out of sight, and Cassandra led her back over to a seat opposite her brother's. 'I regret we cannot leave you alone with Mr Trevellyan, but you do understand?'

'Yes, of course.' Rose sent Cassandra an apologetic look. 'I am trying, believe me, to behave properly and in particular not to embarrass your family, which has shown me such kindness.'

'I am not embarrassed.' Charles winked at her, but Cassandra shook her head at him as she sat down.

'You must not encourage her, Charles. I swear it is your influence which has made *Jane* so reckless in recent years.'

Charles assumed an innocent expression. 'Me, dear Sister?' He laughed quietly. 'We are both full aware Jane requires no undue influence. She remains, as she always has been, a law unto herself!'

'I will stay until Jane is here.' Cassandra took a seat beside Rose.

'Yes, yes, of course.' Despite her underlying agitation, Rose was filled with gratitude for the eldest Miss Austen's care. 'I mean no disrespect to the medical attention and care you have all shown Aiden, but I must talk to Jane about the charm, and...' She looked over at Charles. 'And to your brother also, as he is so connected with it.' She turned troubled eyes to the motionless figure in the bed.

She had to do what was best for Aiden right now, and that meant doing everything in her power to try and find a way out of this mess. She would do anything to solve this. Absolutely *anything*.

By the time Jane arrived in Aiden's room, the servant had returned to his bedside, and Jane hurried across to where Rose was as Charles walked over to Jenkins.

'Thank you, Jenkins.' Charles took the cloth from the maid's unresisting hand. 'You may return to your duties. I will attend the gentleman for now; we will call, should we require anything.'

Nothing was said as the maid left the room, but Charles walked over to secure the lock on the door to the servants' staircase before turning to face Rose and his sisters. 'I suspect we shall not wish to be overheard.'

Jane took a seat beside Rose and Cassandra. 'Jenkins said you wished to talk to me.' She frowned. 'Where did you go? I had been searching the grounds for you, but found no trace.'

Rose felt a little guilty. 'I'm sorry. I just needed to… I had to get away for a while. I went for a walk.'

'To Baigens, I suspect.' Jane eyed her kindly, and Rose smiled faintly, recalling the comfort she had found there.

'Yes.' She was reminded of the straightforward approach of her father. 'Would you both tell me everything you know about the charm? Where it came from, how it works, anything you can recall? There may be something significant we've overlooked.'

Charles exchanged a look with Jane as he walked over to join them. 'Shall I begin?'

'In the absence of the lady from whom you purchased the charm, Brother, your account must claim all rights to being the commencement of the tale.'

Taking up a pose in front of the fireplace, Charles cleared his throat dramatically and began, and Rose tried to listen as he recounted how he'd met Drusilla, the medicine woman. Charles had a way of delivering the story as if they were in a pub during a lock-in. As he launched into another colourful anecdote, this time of how Drusilla had claimed she had put a hex on a colleague of his for calling her a hag, Rose felt it might be best if she asked direct questions.

'Captain Austen, could you say how old she was?'

He raised a brow. 'A gentleman does not speculate on such things.'

Jane rolled her eyes. 'Do not pretend you did not assess it, Charles.'

He grinned, then turned to Rose, his expression sobering. 'I will own, it was hard to determine. If I had to guess I would say—' Charles paused, then laughed, 'I would say it varied! On occasion, she seemed quite elderly, an easy companion for my mother. Yet there would be times when I could swear she had more youth in her than I.' He seemed lost in thought for a moment, then smirked at Rose. 'I can see I have disappointed you.'

'No, not at all.' Rose shook her head. 'It is just... curiosity.' Why was she even asking him this?

Charles, however, was continuing. 'Her skin was sallow, her hair black, streaked with grey. She was a sturdy woman, with keen eyes, and favoured eccentric dress. There! It is not a lack of observational skills, more so that her age was difficult to determine.'

He seemed rather proud of his answer, and Rose thanked him before adding, 'And what did she say about the charm, the one you purchased for Jane? Can you remember the exact words?'

Leaning against the wall, his hands behind his back, Charles shrugged. 'It was nigh on thirteen years ago, but I had little enough conversation with her directly and thus it is not difficult to recall those words that *were* exchanged. Besides, I have been going over them myself since Jane spoke of the problem.' He grunted. 'If I were not wary of whose eyes might fall upon it, I would record the exchange, that I might never have to speak of it again.'

'I am sorry.'

The captain shook his head at Rose. 'Pay me no mind, Miss Wallace. I underwent a similar interrogation the last time something went awry – but you know all about that, do you not?'

'Yes.' How could Rose ever forget?

'Charles, we are no further forward.' Cassandra gave him a pleading look.

'Quite. So I had agreed to purchase three necklaces, and Drusilla had placed two in a fabric wrapping, tied with string, but the third she took from her own pocket and made as if to hand it to me rather than wrap it. I asked her to please do the same for it as she had the other two, but she shook her head and said...' He straightened up, summoning a raspy but noticeably female voice. '"From my hand to yours, from yours to hers. This is the way, the only way."'

Jane smirked. 'Charles would have taken to the stage, had he thought our father would condone it. As it was, he felt it best not to ask.'

He bowed at his sister, smiling widely. 'The quarterdeck is all the stage I require, and well am I suited to it.'

'And did you ask her how it worked?' Rose looked expectantly at Charles. Surely this was going to give them a clue... somehow... somewhere...

The gentleman, however, shrugged. 'You must understand, Miss Wallace, many incomprehensible things arise when visiting far-off places. One learns it is best to take all in one's stride, so to speak. Thus, I did as I was bid and held out my hand. She slid the charm from hers into mine, saying "Guard it well." I slipped it into my coat so as to keep it separate from the others. Then, she said, "May your sister harness her new life with all the passion, intelligence and curiosity you claim she possesses."'

'So you had expressly asked for something for Jane?'

'Not in so many words. I had no notion of the inanimate object bearing such powers. I was merely indulging in the sort of light conversation one does when making a purchase. She claimed to have something I might find of interest, something that would cost me dearly in coinage, but that she felt would bring my sister all she longed for. She claimed to no longer have any use of it.'

Rose was leaning forward. 'And?'

Charles shrugged again. 'The last thing she said was "From time to time, not place to place; forward is forward; back to retrace." She was a bit odd at the best of times, so I just thanked her. I had already paid her. I said my goodbyes and went back to my ship.'

Rose looked down at her hands clasped in her lap. She hadn't realised how tightly she'd been gripping them together. Surely there must be a clue here? She raised her eyes to Charles, who was studying her silently. 'She gave no other explanation? Did you suspect what the cross might be capable of?'

Charles glanced at Jane. 'I... had a feeling it was something special, but I only half believed the woman. Some of the astounding things I had witnessed her do, her healing talents, were beyond crediting, yet so it was. She had a... touch, a way about her. She was, for all her strangeness, respected. Sought out, even, in times of medical need. Was it influenced by the mood of the place itself? I declare, I know not.'

A sudden thought struck Rose, and she gasped. Was it possible? 'Can we not write to her? Ask her how to restore its power?' She looked eagerly from Jane and Cassandra to Charles. 'Or send it to her for her to work her... magic on?'

Charles, however, had grown solemn. 'She could not read or write. Besides, she is no longer living.'

Jane frowned. 'How do you know this?'

Her brother looked at Jane sadly. 'I heard of her passing in a letter from a colleague stationed in the town. She was deemed to be of an unnaturally long life but the epidemic of the year four finally took her.'

Her burst of hope fading, Rose turned in her seat to look at Jane, determined not to give up. 'How did you know you could slip through time when wearing the charm?'

Jane raised her brows. 'By accident at first, of course. Then, by design – experimenting.'

Aiden coughed suddenly and seemed to be trying to clear his throat, and all eyes turned to look towards the figure in the bed. Was he conscious? Rose made to get to her feet, but Jane reached over and held her back, shaking her head.

He wasn't moving and made no more sound, and Rose sank back into her seat. 'So... what is the next step in the story?'

Chapter 29

'Charles wrote to tell us of capturing a privateer and earning some prize money. You can imagine our scolding of him when we learned he had laid out some of it on gifts for the ladies in the family.' Jane sent her brother a fond look. 'But we were also delighted, though it was some time before we received them, for Charles was at sea a while longer.

'When he finally returned, we were living in Bath. He came to make some stay with us and presented us with our gifts.' Jane smiled at him. 'At least, he presented the gifts to Mama and Cass, then drew me aside and asked that I walk with him in the garden. Once out of earshot, he bade me hold out my hand and slipped the necklace from his hand to mine, as he had been instructed. He told me how he was unsure what it would do, other than Drusilla's words: *from time to time, not place to place; forward is forward; back to retrace.*

'I had little thought for her meaning at the time.' Jane touched the empty spot at her throat. 'Then one day I took the necklace out and placed it about my neck, meaning to admire it in the looking glass in the parlour. I had become particularly frustrated with being paraded about Bath like a prize cow.'

'Jane!' Cassandra threw her an appalled look, but Jane continued unabashed.

'Both Cass and I were. Our parents – leastways, our mother – felt moving to Bath would be her last chance to offload us onto willing husbands.' She looked from Rose to Charles and back again. 'I suppose I must have wondered about the future, *my* future, and all went black. In an instant, I was looking at my reflection once more, but I could see that all around me was altered – including the glass itself. You will recall where I was, Rose: in the front parlour at Sydney Place, yet not in your time or mine. I believe I had gone only a few years forward, but it was clear we no longer lived there, for none of our possessions or furniture remained. I could hear unfamiliar voices in an adjacent chamber and knew I must not be found there. I did not know what to do, but then I recalled the words: *forward is forward; back to retrace*. Desperately hoping I had understood, I turned the charm around against my throat, thinking of my home and lo, I was restored to the very same parlour I left.' She smiled smugly. 'It is quite astonishing how resourceful one can be when under duress!'

'Do you know what year you first went to?'

Jane shook her head. 'I was there but a few seconds; only sufficient to comprehend there was something very special about my charm.'

A rustling came from the direction of Aiden's bed, and his voice mumbled something, and it took all Rose's self-control not to go to him. She needed to sit still and listen; that was the best way to aid him right now. 'So then what did you do?'

Jane raised her chin. 'What else was I to do?' She spoke defensively, and Charles shook his head at her.

'You need not speak so for my benefit, dear Sister. You know you have always had my support for your... adventures.'

Cassandra tutted, but said nothing, and Jane turned to Rose. 'I started testing the power of the charm and soon discovered the boundaries of its ability.'

Charles smiled. 'She began venturing forward and back through time; 'tis a miracle she was not arrested!'

Rose stared at Charles. He seemed so cavalier, so relishing of the gift he had procured for Jane and its power with no consideration for the risks.

'It is possible some tales of hauntings, or spirits walking the earth have, at their core, a misguided visit from myself.' Jane looked incredibly proud of herself.

Charles' smile widened. 'Dear Sister, I know not how I can atone for the transgression of gifting you the charm.'

'Transgression, indeed.' Jane rolled her eyes. 'I doubt *Mama* will ever acquit you, and you are fortunate it is in Cass's nature to be forgiving.'

Cassandra merely shook her head, and Rose pressed on.

'How many times have you used the charm?' Jane raised her hands in a shrug, so Rose rephrased her question. 'At any point, when slipping through time, has the charm ever played up – I mean, malfunctioned?'

Jane shook her head. 'Until now, excepting the time with you, it has never disappointed me, and that was hardly a malfunction, merely the loss of it.'

Rose looked down at her hands, and then, wistfully, towards Aiden. He seemed to be becoming restless, though his eyes remained closed, and her heart went out to him. How far away did all this seem from their walk through Henrietta Park? From their mutual realisation they had been crushing on each other for three years, from their first kiss… It seemed like an eternity ago.

'Wait!'

Rose started, her head whipping round to face the lady.

'There was something…' Jane looked guiltily to her brother. 'I recall one other occasion when it failed to work, though at the time…'

The tension in Rose's shoulders increased. 'Yes?'

'After our little episode, Rose, my family was understandably upset and my parents forbade me to travel again. There was a particular day when I felt desperate for escape. Papa had passed and we remained in Bath but in lodgings on Gay Street. Once I had been tempted into using the charm again, I could not refrain.' A strange look filtered across Jane's face, and she sent Rose an impish look. 'I have seen Bath in *your* future, Rose.'

'Yes, I know.'

Jane eyes flicked briefly towards where Aiden lay. 'Not the present future; a future you have yet to see.'

'Oh!' Rose's eyes widened. What on earth had Jane seen of her life?

'Most intriguing, dear sister.' Charles shifted his position. 'But you must continue with the present for now.'

'It helped me to cope with the dismal outlook for myself and my sister.' Jane smiled ruefully, exchanging a look with Cassandra. 'Yet it was my sister who put an end to it. Cass discovered what I was about and became so distressed, I gave her my word I would cease – and I had every intention of doing so – but one day I could not resist taking one last trip. I had intended to come and see you, Rose. I told no one, placing the charm about my neck, but nothing happened.' Jane had paled, her expression serious.

'I had long considered it my own conscience that caused the charm to stall. But, perhaps...'

Agitated, Rose stood up. 'Perhaps it was drained before through your excessive use! What happened? How did you fix it?'

'I did nothing that I can recall other than leave it be. I chose to believe it had become inanimate, nothing more than a pretty trifle, much as the other two.'

'But you *did* use it. You came to fetch *me*.' Rose wrapped her arms around her middle, thinking hard. 'So how long was it before you thought to try it again?'

'I did not use the charm for some years. As you know, after we last met, my life became quite unsettled, moving from temporary lodgings again and again, until we settled in Southampton with Frank's family. Then, we came here in the year nine, and I was fulfilled by writing and revising my works. It was only in recent months I gave the charm any thought... when I made the acquaintance of Mr Wallace and became reminded of you, Rose; of my dear friend in the future.' She took Rose's hand. 'I had no reason to think it might hold any powers now, but I tested it all the same, and lo, I arrived in Chawton in the same year I had met you, much to my delight. I returned home and tarried upon September, when I knew where you resided and thus how to become reacquainted with ease, and came forward at an opportune moment.'

Rose sank back down into her chair. Very opportune, only perhaps Aiden would disagree.

Charles looked between the two women. 'And more recently?'

'I have been using it with more frequency, and not always in isolation, having brought both Mr Trevellyan and Rose back, and then her friends – and then returning them.'

'And?'

Jane looked from her brother to Rose. 'It was the first time I had used it after restoring your friends to their right time. It did not retrace. I had to make three attempts to reach the year thirteen.'

Charles raised a brow. 'And it did not adhere to the claim of "place to place"?'

Jane looked a little sheepish. 'Not entirely.'

'Jane!' Cassandra reprimanded. 'You never spoke of this. Is this why the hives were so disturbed?'

Jane shrugged. 'Always, without fail, has the charm moved me through time, but not across distance. Always have I arrived, be it going forward or returning, to the exact location I claimed at the time I placed the charm against my throat.'

'So it would seem the charm has been fading, malfunctioning.'

'And now it has failed altogether.' Rose's voice was a mere whisper. 'And might take years to recharge.'

'Rose? Are you here?' Aiden's voice carried across the room and Rose looked pleadingly towards the captain.

'Go to him, Miss Wallace. You have ample chaperones.'

With a grateful smile at Charles, Rose hurried over to the bed, taking Aiden's good hand again, and he opened his eyes, then smiled faintly. 'I thought I heard your voice.' He frowned. 'I heard other voices…'

'Shhh. Captain Austen and the Miss Austens are here. You are being well looked after. How is the pain?'

He glanced at his strapped-up arm. 'Bearable.' He closed his eyes. 'Except in my head. That damned laudanum. Can't think straight. There's something… I

306

need to tell you something… but the words keep fading from my mind…' His head fell to the side on the pillow, and Rose stared at him lovingly. Had he drifted off again?

Carefully, she eased her hand from his and laid it on the coverlet. She needed to keep her own head clear, to work through all they had talked about. Somewhere in all of this, there had to be something that would help them find out how to restore the charm's power. Surely time itself wasn't going to be the only way?

'The night we kissed…'

Warmth filled Rose's cheeks, and she spun back to look at Aiden. His eyes were still closed, a frown on his brow.

'Aiden, now is probably not the time to talk of—'

'No. Yes. You must remember… walk… walking in the park… dusk…'

'Of course I remember. But,' Rose lowered her voice, '*you* must remember we are not alone.'

'But we talked… we had a… charm.'

Rose couldn't help but smile. 'We… well, *you* have quite a lot of charm, but let's talk about that later.'

He turned his head to and fro on the pillow, still frowning, then opened his eyes with difficulty. 'Go back.'

If only they could! 'Hush, Aiden. You must rest.'

'You must go back, Rose…' His voice was fading as the laudanum took over again. 'Remember… charm.'

He fell silent, and Rose, conscious of the murmur of voices over by the fireplace, raised a hand to smooth a curl from his forehead, pressed a kiss to her fingers and placed them gently on his lips before reluctantly turning away.

The door opened and Edward entered, raising an enquiring brow at Rose.

'He is doing as well as we could hope, sir.'

'Capital.' Edward walked over to where his brother and sisters were gathered and entered into a low conversation with them, but as the word 'charm' drifted over to her, Rose's eyes widened as realisation came. Hurrying back to the bed, she touched Aiden's shoulder, trying to rouse him, but he was lost in the depths of the drugs.

'Miss Wallace.' Charles had walked over, his voice cautioning.

'You don't understand.' Rose's insides were dancing all over the place, and she put a hand to her head. 'He knows something. He was trying to tell me something about the charm! The one he found in Winchester Cathedral!'

Jane came hurrying over, a look of surprise on her face. 'In the *cathedral*? How could such a thing be so?'

'Don't you remember, Jane? He mentioned it to you when you first came to fetch us.' Rose closed her eyes, thinking about the walk through Henrietta Park. Aiden had stopped her as they went in through the gate, hadn't he? He'd seen her replica necklace in the light from the lamppost and...

Her eyes flew open. 'Aiden found it near your...' She bit her lip.

'My?' Jane waited for a moment for Rose to finish, then nodded. 'Ah, my grave.'

Charles looked from Rose to his sister, paling as realisation dawned. 'You...' He raised a hand and pointed it at his sister. 'You are to be interred in Winchester Cathedral? Good Lord, Jane! How is such a thing to come to pass?'

'What is this?' Edward joined them, Cassandra hard on his heels.

'Jane is to be interred in Winchester.' Charles folded his arms across his chest. 'Surely it is our late esteemed father's influence, through his connections?'

'Or that of Heathcote's widow,' Edward interjected. He stared at Jane. 'This is most singular. The cottage a museum and you, dear sister, interred in such a building?'

'I cannot account for it, Edward, but so it is.'

Charles shrugged. 'Perhaps it was the Dean himself! Did he perform the service, Sister?'

'No.' Jane looked from Charles to Edward, then back. 'And *you* were not in attendance, Charles.'

He looked astounded. 'Good heavens! Do I pass before you?'

'Stop it!' Cassandra's eyes were wide as she looked frantically from her brothers to Jane. 'You promised, Jane, you would speak *nothing* to me of what you knew was coming, nothing you had learned about your future, or of the family's.'

Jane took her sister's hands and squeezed them. 'Forgive me. It is a subject of much debate, even 200 years from now, but never more shall it be spoken of between us.' She turned to Rose. 'And forgive me, Rose, but I cannot see that aught in the present day can aid us.' She looked over at Aiden. 'Though I long for Mr Trevellyan to free his mind of the drug, for I am intrigued to learn more of it.'

They all turned as one to stare at the silent figure in the bed. Then, Rose touched Jane's arm and she turned to face her. 'I can't recall all he said.' She had, after all, been a little distracted at the time. 'But he'd been overseeing some repairs in the aisle near where you are… well, there's a memorial plaque in the wall, put up some years later, and they had to remove it to repair some damaged stonework, and I'm sure that's where he said he'd found it. In a small box.'

Jane looked over at her brothers. 'This does nŏt aid us, merely confuses the matter, for how this could be, I know not.' She frowned. 'If the necklace he found has age to it, of course, 'tis a shame he did not bring it with him.'

'I think he said it was already secured in the cathedral's archives…' Rose's voice petered out as a sudden thought struck her. 'Jane, the portal! Doesn't the necklace create one wherever it is placed, provided that… that… whatever the portal is, it existed in the past too? Like the safe in Sydney Place? Like the floorboard at the cottage?'

Jane's bright, hazel eyes widened, then she looked back over at Aiden's motionless form. 'If there is a chance, then we must find out where he placed it.'

The two ladies walked back over to the bed and looked down at Aiden, and Rose almost blew out a breath of frustration. He looked well away. Was this what he had been trying to say, to remember? How long would he sleep before they could find out?

There was a sudden splash, and both Jane and Rose leapt back as droplets of water reached them. Aiden's head and shoulders were drenched, rivulets running down his face, but he had opened his eyes and was squinting up at Charles, who held an empty pitcher.

Chapter 30

Jane looked horrified. 'Charles!'

The captain smirked. 'It has always proved effective in rousing many a midshipman who may have over-indulged. I was unsure it would prove fruitful in Mr Trevellyan's circumstances, but as time is of the essence, I deemed it worthy of an attempt.'

Aiden raised his good arm and wiped his eyes, and Charles tossed him a small towel.

'What the hell is going on?'

Rose looked at Jane, who nodded encouragingly, and so she stepped forward and took the towel from him when he'd finished mopping. 'Aiden, you were trying to tell me something. Can you remember what it was? Do you remember our walk, you told me about the cross and chain you had found, said it was very old, similar to the replica I was wearing?'

He ran a hand through his damp hair, then drew in a shallow breath. 'Yes, the cross I found...' His gaze sought Jane's. 'I barely got a glimpse of the charm you used to bring us here, Miss Austen, but if it's similar – perhaps even the same one – I know exactly where it is.'

'In the future.' Charles folded his arms, looking unimpressed, but Rose's heart increased its beat. Were they on to something at last?

Jane's eyes were fixed on Aiden, as were everyone else's in the room. 'If the charm is the very same – and though I cannot account for where it was, it may well be so – then it may be accessible.' She looked from Aiden to the others. 'If the charm has, over time, regained some power, then wherever it has been placed will become a portal.'

Aiden had closed his eyes again. He looked extremely uncomfortable, lying on soaking wet sheets, his shirt plastered to his chest. 'It's in the archives.'

'Where, exactly? Aiden? Please stay with us?' Rose leaned forward and grasped his hand, willing him to stay awake.

He said nothing for a moment, then opened his eyes again and turned his head on the pillow to look at Rose. 'I put it in a drawer in a wooden cabinet.' He frowned. 'It was really odd. I placed the necklace in there, but then realised the small wooden box I'd found it in was still on the table. Although it was damaged, I wanted to keep it with the necklace, so I went to open the drawer, but it had seized up in some way. I couldn't get it open.' His lids dropped again, his voice growing fainter. 'Need a carpenter... I was going to get one in... the next day, but...'

He said nothing more, but Rose's skin was tingling, and she laid his hand on the coverlet and turned to Jane, hope rising with more surety now.

'Didn't you say, back in Bath, the portal would only yield to you if the charm was inside? Oh, Jane, don't you see?' Rose could hardly get the words out in her excitement. 'If the drawer has sealed itself, perhaps a portal has been activated, and if so... then this charm Aiden found *must* have power!'

There was a heavy silence in the room as Rose's words hung in the air.

'To Winchester, then!'

Rose looked at Aiden's bandaged arm. 'And without delay.'

—

Rose followed Jane from Aiden's room on legs that were a little unsteady as the others all headed downstairs on their mission. A tremor had shaken her very bones the moment Aiden had mentioned the sealed cupboard, the need for a carpenter, and as she walked slowly along the landing, she felt it still. Rubbing her arms to relieve her tingling skin, she looked back wistfully towards Aiden's room before disappearing inside her own. Jane had advised her to dress for travelling before excusing herself, saying there was much to prepare. Charles, she knew, had summoned a servant and was doing his best to rouse Aiden and help him to dress in dry clothes.

By the time Rose reached the top of the stairs, she became aware of the bustle below, and she hurried down into the hall, looking for Jane.

'Miss Wallace.' Cassandra appeared from the small room opposite the great hall, pulling a cloak about her shoulders. 'Be not alarmed.' She gestured towards the servants going to and fro. 'The carriage is being prepared, and Edward has taken it upon himself to assist the footmen in arranging the cushions in order that Mr Trevellyan can travel with as little disturbance to his injuries as possible.'

She spoke quietly, and Rose stepped closer to do the same. 'Must we go straight away?' What was wrong with her? She'd been so desperate to try and find a way back, and now there was a glimmer of hope, she was devastated by the fact that if this worked, she might never come back, might never see her father again. How could she delay this? Should she? 'Shouldn't we wait for darkness?'

Cassandra said nothing as a maid came up and handed her a bonnet and some gloves. Then, she smiled kindly at Rose. 'You are on a mission of some difficulty. Arriving at the cathedral whilst its doors remain open for public prayer will remove the necessity for trying to force an entry.'

'Yes, of course.' Feeling a little stupid, Rose grimaced. 'I wasn't thinking. But I must see my father, and…'

Shaking her head, Cassandra placed a hand on Rose's arm. 'I am to call there directly and will send him to you. We did not think it wise to send a note with a servant. I must also make some show of visiting upon Mama. She must be distracted from discovering what Jane is about.' She smiled. 'Leastways, until it is too late for her to voice her objections.'

Cassandra took Rose's hands and squeezed them. 'Do try not to worry, Miss Wallace. I shall return as soon as I am able.'

Rose followed her to the door and watched as Cassandra hurried down the driveway, and then she turned back to resume her search for Jane. When she found her, giving instructions to the housekeeper, Rose asked if she could help in any way, but she was politely turned aside and, left to her own devices whilst all was made ready, she paced restlessly around the ground floor of the house.

Christopher found her at the windows of the formal dining room where she had been staring out at the carriage, feeling a little like Cinderella, putting all her faith in where it would take her. She had been so intent on it she hadn't even seen her father arrive.

'Rosie.'

She turned quickly, conscious the faint tremor still had hold of her body, and she summoned a smile, too tense to even offer him an embrace. 'We have an idea.'

Speaking rapidly, her voice low, Rose explained what Jane had said about the charm and its seeming ability to restore its own powers if left alone for long enough, and how Aiden had reminded Rose of his finding an old necklace in the cathedral – one which they suspected was the very charm Jane once possessed.

Christopher listened intently, saying nothing until Rose has finished recounting her tale, and she held her breath, willing him not to come up with some logical reason why their hopes must be in vain.

To no avail. Christopher frowned. 'But *how* can it be here now, in 1813, if it is not placed there until the twenty-first century?'

Rose hardly blinked. After all, hadn't she had the same question going round and round in her head? If only Morgan were here. She would have an explanation, and somehow, she'd make it sound logical too!

'I can't answer that. We thought there was a chance it could've sealed itself – the drawer, I mean. Provided it existed in 1813, and with the age of the cathedral, it's highly likely it may now be a portal. If so, there's also a chance the charm will be accessible back across the centuries in the same way the safe in Bath worked for Jane and Cassandra.' Rose smiled tremulously at her father. How she didn't want to leave him, but if this worked, she had to go home. 'It's our only hope to get back without

315

destroying our lives there by waiting years from now for the charm to recharge – and even that's not guaranteed.'

Christopher rubbed his forehead. 'I cannot yet comprehend it, Rose. How can *one* charm be in *two* places at the same time?'

'I don't know any of the *reasoning* behind it. All I do know is that we've got to hope our theory is right. We have to try and find it.' She bit her lip, then reached out to take her father's hand. 'And if we do find it, we have to try and use it. You do understand?'

He held her gaze solemnly. 'With regret, I will own that I do.' He blew out a breath. 'But Rose—' He hesitated, shook his head slightly, then squeezed her hand. 'How may I be of assistance?'

Rose hadn't realised how much she was hoping he'd come with them until that moment. 'Thank you,' she whispered. 'Can you...? Will you come to Winchester? We have no idea how hard the trip will be on Aiden, and we don't even have a plan for getting into the archives, if we even can. We may need a diversion.'

'Who else is going?'

'Myself, Jane, and Aiden obviously, and Captain Austen is to come along. I think.' Rose smiled fully for what felt like the first time in hours. 'He may just be our trump card. Apparently, he has quite a theatrical bent.'

Christopher grinned. 'I can well believe it. Come, then.' He held out his arm to Rose and she took it willingly, but then stopped, tugging at his arm.

'Wait. There is something...' She turned around, looking for a sewing basket she'd seen the other day. Extracting a pair of small scissors, she cut a lock of her own hair and, grabbing a small white cotton lavender bag from the basket, she dropped it inside. 'Here.' She handed it to Christopher, trying not to well up. 'I don't know what is going to happen, but if… it's all I have of mine that I can give you.'

'Rosie.' His voice broke as he took it from her. He pressed the bag to his lips, then tucked it into his coat. 'Come.' Rose let him guide her down the steps into the great hall and out into the hallway.

Edward had just entered the house, and he greeted Christopher before turning to Rose. 'We have done the best we can in the circumstances. Provided the horses go steadily, it should suffice.'

'Where do we stand?' They all turned around as Charles' voice hailed them from the bottom of the stairs. 'Mr Trevellyan is as ready as he can be. Wallace!' He strode towards them, hand outstretched, and as Christopher shook it, Charles looked at him expectantly. 'Are you with us, my good fellow?'

Christopher looked fondly at Rose before nodding at his friend. 'Try and keep me away.'

Charles looked to Rose. 'If we are to carry out our mission today, we must do so directly. Is my sister prepared?'

Butterflies fluttering in her stomach, Rose nodded. 'I will find her.'

Charles turned back for the stairs, but he paused with his foot on the bottom step. 'Stay well away from upstairs, Miss Wallace. This will not be pleasant on the gentleman. Wallace.' He turned to Christopher. 'Will you assist? He is becoming more lucid as time passes, but thus his pain is intensifying.'

Her father set off up the stairs, but Rose stayed Charles with her hand. 'Captain Austen…' It was far too soon for what she wanted to say. 'I cannot thank you enough, for everything you have done for us.'

Charles grinned. 'All in a day's work.' He looked up as a footman hurried down the hallway bearing a black bundle. 'Ah, Hanson. You had no trouble in gaining the items?'

'None whatsoever, sir.' The footman bowed, handing over his burden to Charles, who took the stairs two at a time, and Rose stood frozen for a minute listening to footsteps fading along the landing, then turned away, keen to find Jane, only to see her coming towards her from the boot room.

'There you are. It seems we're ready to leave. They've gone for Aiden.'

Jane handed Rose a Bible, a thick leather-bound folder, a cloak and a basket. 'To aid in our concealment.'

Rose took the small clutter of things, particularly careful of the folder, as she knew it was the journal Edward had given Aiden so he could make notes and observations on the church. As Rose flipped through it, she realised he had been studying quite a lot more than just the chapel. There were detailed maps and copious notes on all manner of subjects in his familiar scrawl from before he'd been injured. Rose held it against her chest as Jane draped the cloak around her shoulders. 'The cloak and basket I understand, but…'

Jane raised a second Bible. 'We wish to give the impression we are attending evensong, do we not? Perchance if we look convincingly studious, we will be allowed some leeway in our wandering.'

Rose's insides lurched. 'I can't believe we're doing this again. Breaking into No 4 Sydney Place was bad enough, but… the archives of *Winchester Cathedral*?' Rose's voice was a frantic whisper, but Jane merely smiled.

Jane secured her own cloak and raised a brow. 'Do you have aught else to offer?'

Rose shook her head, then almost gasped as a drawn-out groan came from somewhere upstairs. Jane looked anxiously at Rose, then inclined her head towards a door at the back of the inner hallway. 'I think it best we repair to the library. Let us meet the gentlemen by the carriage once Mr Trevellyan is established within.'

Much as Rose wanted to rush to Aiden's side and offer comfort, she knew Jane was right. The sound of movement on the landing was sufficient to have her turn and follow the lady, placing the folder and her Bible into the basket. Her father and Charles would be supporting Aiden, and she'd only be in the way.

Rose entered the room to find Jane in low conversation with her sister, and she drew in a calming breath. The last time she'd contemplated breaking and entering, at least she'd had Morgan there. The thought was enough to pull Rose together. If she ever wanted Morgan in her life again, she was going to have to take a leaf out of her book.

It was a quarter of an hour later when Jane indicated to Rose to precede her from the room. They walked through the now almost silent house and out into the fading day as the afternoon drew to a close, and all Rose's reasoning flew from her mind as she took her father's hand to assist her into the carriage.

Aiden was propped up in one corner, a cloak about his shoulders to hide the fact he was unable to wear a coat, the splint now removed and his arm in a makeshift sling, strapped across his chest. He looked awful, sweat beading his forehead and his skin a worrying shade of grey.

His handsome face was pinched with pain, but he made an attempt at a smile as Rose sat opposite him. Jane was soon installed at her side, and a grim-looking Christopher entered and closed the door, settling carefully on Aiden's other side, placing a cushion between them.

Charles appeared at the open window, giving Jane and Rose a bracing smile. 'Welcome ladies, to the *Winchester Packet*!'

Jane, however, frowned. 'Charles, why are you dressed as man of the church?'

Charles looked rather proud of his white dog collar, and docked his parson's hat jovially.

'I borrowed them. Are they not perfect for our adventure?'

Jane was still frowning. 'But you have not had time to send to Steventon; besides, James would not let you—'

'Dear Sister.' Charles leaned through the window. 'I am not so foolish as to waste time asking favours of my eldest brother, knowing he will refuse me.' He waved a hand towards where the driveway joined the road. 'I sent Hanson to ask Papillon.' He winked at Jane. 'I sent in your name, of course. You know the good reverend will do anything to court your good opinion.'

'For shame, Charles. What possible reason could you give the man for wishing to borrow some of his garments?'

'The note stated I required them for a family performance.' Charles grinned. 'After all, one must not tell an untruth to a man of God.'

Jane rolled her eyes and settled back in her seat, and Charles walked away, still grinning.

'I thought your brother was joining us?' Rose turned to Jane, but she shook her head.

'He is, but he is to ride.' She waved a hand at the window, and barely seconds later, Charles rode past them on a chestnut horse and the carriage slowly moved away, rolling down the driveway, but as the wheels crunched on the gravel, Rose turned to Jane in dismay.

'Oh no! I didn't have a chance to thank Mr Knight for his kindness and hospitality, or say goodbye to your sister.' Rose's gaze flew to meet her father's. 'Or to your wife and the girls.'

Christopher shook his head, his face remaining solemn. 'It is for the best, for what might you possibly say without having to draw upon falsehoods and empty promises?'

Rose felt tears prick her eyelids at the truth of this, and turned to stare out of the window, forcing her eyes wide.

Jane, however, was less impressed. 'Do not indulge your emotions so readily, Rose. You may well have ample chance if all does not go to plan.' Her philosophical words achieved their purpose, and Rose turned back, giving her a look.

Jane smirked at her. 'Should we succeed in our mission, I will take full responsibility for your precipitous departure.'

Turning in her seat, Rose looked out of the rear window, taking in her potential last glimpse of the house, and the church that would be all but destroyed in a few years, but as the carriage turned left onto the Gosport road, she settled back in her seat and drew in a calming breath. She would go mad if she didn't focus on something other than where they were headed and why.

Rose looked over at Aiden, wishing she could help him, relieved to see him looking a little more alert, more himself. Even through his pain, his eyes had lost the clouded look of earlier, and he stared out of the window, seemingly intent on memorising every detail. Suppressing a sigh, Rose smiled weakly at her father, whose intent gaze was upon her, then turned to resume her own study through the window.

Please, oh please, let this be worth it.

Chapter 31

The journey to Winchester passed without incident, though it cured Rose of any and all romantic fantasies of carriage rides in the country. She had assumed the turnpike from London to Winchester would be in good condition. What had Mr Darcy once said to Elizabeth?

'And what is fifty miles of good road? Little more than half a day's journey.'

Winchester was only 16 miles away, but the road could hardly be considered good. Instead, it felt as though the wheels found every bump and dip, and it was hard enough to keep her own seat every time the path curved, but Aiden was clearly suffering from it, if his colour was anything to go by. Christopher persuaded him to take from his brandy flask to help numb the pain from the disturbance, as they all tried to maintain a conversation, but with all they were thinking of, they lapsed frequently into silence.

Staring out of the window, Rose kept looking at her wrist for the watch she wasn't wearing, wishing the miles would pass as fast they did when she used to drive almost the very same route.

By the time they reached the city's outskirts, Aiden had succumbed to his exhaustion and fallen asleep.

The afternoon was fading rapidly as the carriage slowed and drew to a halt in the Cathedral Close, and Christopher pulled out his fob watch. 'We have made good time. The service will be starting, but that will aid in our entrance being less remarked.'

Charles had already dismounted and was opening the door as the driver let down the steps. He held out a hand to first Jane, then Rose, and once they had joined him on the pavement, he assisted Christopher in easing a drowsy Aiden from the carriage.

Once they were all together, Charles led the way round to the front entrance of the imposing building, and Rose couldn't help but stare around as she gripped the basket firmly, trying to note everything that was different to how it was in the future. A stable block and coach house stood where the modern gift shop and tea room now existed, and there were sheep grazing through the graveyard, but beyond this the only blatant difference, besides the smell of horse dung, and the way people were dressed, was the absence of cars parked around the perimeter. She glanced at Aiden. Would this rouse his interest, distract him at all from the pain he was in?

To her relief, it seemed to be doing the trick. Though accepting help as they took the few steps down to approach the door, his gaze roamed from side to side, his interest clearly quickened.

As they reached the closed door, however, the sound of singing drifting out into the early evening air, Charles drew them all to a halt, and turned to Aiden with a smirk, eyeing the bruises on his face.

'Do your best to try to look unwell, sir.'

Aiden rolled his eyes at Charles, who winked.

'Precisely. Come.' He led the way into the cathedral, stopping to speak to a verger near the door. 'We are here to pray for the soul of this poor gentleman.' He gestured towards Aiden, who was using Christopher as a support with little need for fabrication.

'Of course. Do please find yourselves a seat. The service has only just commenced.'

They filed into a row at the back of the cathedral, and Rose, who was separated from Aiden by her father, leaned around the latter.

'Aiden, can you point us in the right direction for where these archives are?'

He drew in a shallow breath, then nodded. 'Down the south aisle, to the left before the south transept.' He raised his good arm and pointed ahead. 'I will show you as soon as we can grab a moment. You will need to go down the steps, through the door on the right, and the cupboard is built into the far wall.'

They all waited. The sermon seemed to last an eternity to Rose, but as soon as the first note for the next hymn reached them, they edged away from the main aisle and walked as quietly as possible down the south aisle until Aiden drew them to a halt.

He turned to face them. 'Just up there, the small black door inset into the stone pillar on the left. But there seems to be someone on duty.'

Rose looked around him. Sure enough, there was a custodian of some sort, dressed in ceremonial uniform, standing outside a door in the wall opposite exactly where they wanted to go.

'Why would he be there?'

Charles shrugged. 'Perchance it is where the cathedral keeps its treasures?'

'What can we do?' hissed Jane. 'We cannot have come all this way to be put off by such a hindrance.'

No one said anything for a moment, but as the hymn drew to a close and there was a general rustle as the congregation retook their seats, Charles touched Rose's arm.

'You must faint, Miss Wallace.'

Rose stared at Charles. 'I beg your pardon?'

'Swoon.'

'I know what it means! But why?'

'We need a distraction, do we not?' He inclined his head slightly towards the custodian who still stood, arms folded firmly across his chest, opposite the door they needed access to.

Rose could sense panic rising. She was no actress. 'Can you not do it?'

Charles shook his head. 'I am a man of the cloth. Such artifice is beyond me, and certainly in a house of God.'

Jane tutted impatiently. 'You are a man of the sea, Charles, and well versed in artifice.' She turned to Rose. 'But I fear he has the right of it. Yet I would also have you with me.' She held Rose's gaze steadily. 'We have been in such a situation before, have we not?'

Rose nodded, and looked to her father. How was she to do this? *Oh, Morgan, how I need you! You would have carried off distraction like an expert.*

'Captain Austen is right, my dear.' Christopher spoke quietly, then walked to stand behind her. 'Do not fear,' he whispered. 'I will catch you. But we must draw the custodian away. Then, you must go with Miss Austen.'

'But how will you…'

Christopher put a finger to his lips. 'All will be well; you will see.'

Jane looked from Rose to her brother, then edged away from them, ostensibly studying her service sheet as she walked towards the small door to the archives. Aiden had eased himself down to sit on a nearby plinth. His face was still pale and drawn, but his eyes were alert and, to Rose's further embarrassment, fixed on her.

'*Now*,' Charles hissed.

Feeling totally ridiculous, Rose put a hand to her head, closed her eyes and trusted to her father being there as she let herself fall backwards. Once securely supported by him, however, she was finding it difficult to keep a straight face, despite the seriousness of their situation. She kept her eyes tightly shut, chewing on the inside of her cheek to stop her lips curving. It didn't help that she was certain Aiden had just turned a short laugh into a cough!

'You there!'

Rose held her breath at her father's call, relieved to hear the rapid patter of footsteps on the flagstones.

'Please aid us with this young lady. She has been taken unwell.'

Rose truly had never been as mortified as this. The time she had spontaneously applauded Aiden during a take for *Time Travellers* in Bath, that day in junior school, when she'd slapped a boy for trying to kiss her, and every other embarrassing experience of her life paled in comparison to this.

She was aware her father still supported her as he pleaded with the custodian to find some assistance, but Charles' protestations of worry were so over the top, Rose could feel the urge to laugh rising, and was tempted to reanimate simply to shut him up.

Opening one eye as she was carried a little untidily to a nearby bench, Rose was just in time to see Jane move towards the door. How was she to join her now?

A querulous voice spoke. 'Oh dear, oh dear. What are we to do? The young lady is quite senseless.'

'Fetch someone, man! There must be a verger or a steward with some wits about them!' Christopher's voice held authority, and the custodian must have agreed.

'Yes, sir. Directly. I will fetch someone to attend her.' Heavy footsteps receded, and Rose felt her father squeeze her arm.

'Go to Jane. Be quick, now.'

Rose opened her eyes and sat up. The portly custodian was hurrying away from them down the aisle, and she swung her feet onto the floor.

'What if he returns and I'm not here?'

Christopher shrugged. 'Then we shall be in need of a further distraction.'

Charles, however, turned to Aiden. 'It is as I cautioned, sir. You must try even harder to look unwell.'

Aiden merely grunted at this, and Rose hurried over to Jane just as she slipped through the now open doorway.

The heavy wooden door closed behind them, and Rose looked around, trying to adjust to the low light from the solitary wall lamp. They were stood at the top of a small, spiralling flight of stone steps. Compared to the crowded majesty in the cathedral, the space felt shockingly small.

'What did Mr Trevellyan say?' Jane spoke over her shoulder.

'Down the steps, take the door on the right.'

Rose followed Jane and they soon came to an even smaller wooden door built into a stone architrave. It was locked, but the key was in the lock, and Jane used both hands to turn it before they stepped inside.

There were no lights, so Rose looked around, then dragged a stack of heavy-looking crates over to prop the door open so a little light filtered in from the staircase. The room was small and contained all sorts of objects: small damaged stone statues, some folding wooden benches, stacks of prayer and hymn books on the shelves lining one wall and there, set into the far corner, just as Aiden had said, was a wooden cupboard. Clearly, the space was not used as the archives for valuables in 1813.

The pathway through the clutter wasn't easy to navigate, especially in the poor light, but they edged forward, Rose ever conscious they might be discovered at any moment, her ears straining for the slightest sound out on the staircase.

'This must be it.' Rose's voice came out in a faint whisper, and she heard Jane tut.

'Why are you whispering?'

'It just felt appropriate in here.' Rose spoke a little more firmly.

They stood before the cupboard, and Rose strained her eyes in the darkness. 'What if it's locked?'

Jane reached out a hand and tugged at the handle. It was stiff, but it gave with relative ease, and revealed an interior of several wooden drawers.

They both started pulling out drawers at random. It was so dark that even though Rose looked in each drawer she opened, she had to feel around in it as well, but found nothing resembling a cross and chain. Jane seemed to be having little success either, pulling out a bundle of tapers and a candle snuffer, and Rose grasped the knob on the next drawer and tugged, conscious of time ticking away. It didn't give. She pulled harder. Nothing.

Her hand shaking, Rose stepped back, giving Jane space. 'This could be it, you try.'

Jane leaned across and took hold of the tiny knob, and the drawer slid open as if it had been freshly oiled.

Rose held her breath as Jane reached in and groped around, letting it out in a rush as she withdrew something that glinted in the dim light. They both turned towards the door and the amber cross glistened. Exchanging a world of words in one glance, Jane closed her fingers over the charm and Rose hurriedly led the way back out to the staircase, climbing the steps to the door and putting her head close to listen. There was nothing but the sound of muffled hymns.

Easing the door open, half expecting to find them trapped and the burly custodian back in his place, an effective barrier to the completion of their mission, Rose blew out a relieved breath. There was no one there.

'Quick, let's go.'

She stepped back out into the south aisle, conscious of Jane behind her, then gasped.

'Oh my God! What did you *do*!' Rose hissed as she hurried over to the bench where she had been reclining; a bench now occupied by one unconscious guard.

Chapter 32

Aiden looked up at them from where he remained slumped against the wall. Christopher was busily refastening his sling.

Aiden managed a smile when he saw Rose, however, and she turned to Charles.

'What happened?' She kept her voice low, conscious of the service still continuing the other side of the pillars. 'Is he okay?' She pointed to the prostrate man and Charles shrugged.

'He came back rather precipitously, having found no one to aid us. We told him you had made a swift recovery and had gone out to take some air.'

Christopher straightened and met Rose's confused gaze. 'He was about to resume his duty, return to his position in front of the door opposite.' He gestured towards it. 'We needed to act.'

'Mr Trevellyan was quick of thought and most obliging in providing a further distraction. He unfastened his sling and bandages and treated the gentleman to the sight of his bloodied and stitched wounds.' Charles snorted. 'The intention was to ensure you could both emerge undetected, but we were blessed.' He raised his eyes to the heavens, then met Rose's gaze again. 'It would seem the man is averse to the sight of blood. He duly fainted.'

Rose stared from Charles to her father, then over to Aiden. 'Are you okay?'

He nodded. 'I'm fine. And… how did it go?'

'We have it. Whether it works…'

'Come, we must move away from here before we are discovered.' Charles turned to urge them all back down the aisle, then stopped. 'Change of plan.'

Rose looked around. Two vergers had noticed the prostrate form on the bench and were hurrying towards them and, casting one last guilty look at the blissfully unaware custodian, she turned to follow the others.

'Where now?' hissed Christopher as they drew level with the quire.

'This way.' Aiden pointed to the right, drawing them into a small chapel tucked away just past the south transept. Thankfully, there was no one in sight, and they crept in as quietly as they could, soon shielded from sight by the stone-carved partitions.

Once gathered behind the screen, they all spoke at once. 'So you have it?'

'There was no difficulty accessing the cupboard?'

'Let us see it!'

'It was just as Aiden said.' Rose threw him a proud look. 'And the drawer yielded to Jane's hand as we'd hoped.'

Jane opened her hand to reveal the necklace. They were all silent for a moment, and Rose stared at. She had always assumed it to be the perfect companion to the crosses on display at Chawton cottage, but as she looked closely at it for the first time, she realised it was older and a little more rustically hewn. Jane placed it carefully on a pew, then withdrew the pouch Rose was so familiar with and took out the other charm – they were identical.

'Don't mix them up,' whispered Rose urgently.

Jane shook her head. 'The one drained of power simply will not work, a clear indication of which is which.'

Charles grunted. 'Unless *neither* has any power.'

Jane raised her eyes to meet Rose's anxious gaze. 'To be certain, that may be so.' Then, she looked over at Aiden. 'But the drawer resisted Rose and yielded to my hand with no difficulty, so we have hope.'

Rose looked around the small group of people huddled into the chapel, and her heart went out to them all for so many different reasons.

'What now?' Charles looked at Jane.

'We have to test it.'

'Here?'

'We cannot delay. If we are discovered…'

The tension in Rose's shoulders intensified.

'Miss Austen has the right of it, Rose. Darkness has yet to fully fall and besides, we are in the centre of a city. I believe this is as discreet as we can get. Mr Trevellyan.' Christopher turned to Aiden. 'What are your thoughts? Would this be suitable as a place where a sudden reappearance in the future would cause no undue attention?'

'Perfectly so. The only other option is the crypt, and it is only unlocked on occasion. At this time of the evening, unless there is a special event on, the cathedral would be closed to the public. I know how to find a way out if the main entrance is locked.'

'But we need to get back to Chawton, to Aiden's car.' Rose frowned. She hadn't really begun to think about practicalities. 'We will need to take a taxi, if we… if it works.'

'Let us see if we can get back first.' Aiden was bracing himself against the wall; his voice was stronger than Rose had heard it in days. Was he thriving on hope, just as she was?

There were only a few lamps lit in the chapel, but Rose could see everyone's eyes were intent and on edge and, speaking quietly, she turned to Charles. 'Sir, I do not know how I can ever repay you for all your kindness.'

Charles bowed. 'If the charms are both inactive, it is I who will owe you a debt for all I have brought you to.' He turned to Aiden, who pushed away from the wall to take Charles' outstretched hand and shook it solidly. 'As for you, sir, I consider you my friend, but I am a selfish man at heart. If you leave us tonight, I shall envy you the adventures ahead. If you are to be a resident of Chawton, it would please me almost as much.'

Aiden smiled. 'I share similar sentiments, Captain Austen.'

'Charles.'

Aiden's smile widened. 'Charles, then.'

'I will keep watch.' The captain bowed to Rose, raised a hand to Aiden, then disappeared through the doorway, soon reappearing through the cut-outs of the stone screen with his back to them, surveying the south aisle.

Knowing what was next, Rose's heart was already overwhelmed as she turned to her father. Tension gripped her throat so tightly, she struggled to breathe for a moment then, seeing a solitary tear trickle down Christopher's cheek as he drew her into his embrace, Rose closed her eyes. Perhaps if she squeezed them tightly enough shut, she'd be able to hold back her own tears? Held firmly in his embrace, she felt full to the brim with emotion. This was her father; he was no longer a vague childhood memory, an imaginary figure. He was a real, live, breathing man, and he loved her.

The moment was an eternity, yet somehow much too short. There came the time, however, when Christopher stepped back, and Rose tried to calm herself, her breath uneven. Holding tight to her hand, Christopher turned to Aiden.

'I could leave her with no one more worthy, sir.'

They bowed to each other, Aiden a little awkwardly in his sling, and Christopher turned back to Rose, taking both her hands in his now. 'I am happy this night for whatever is about to happen. You comprehend, do you not, Rosie?'

Rose tried to swallow on the lump in her throat, then nodded. She could not speak to save her life.

Christopher squeezed her hands and then raised one to brush away the first tear as it slid down her cheek. 'But I cannot watch. You do comprehend this also?'

Rose nodded again. 'I love you, Papa. My papa.' Her voice cracked as he mouthed 'And I love you,' back at her.

'Love grows where my Rosemary goes... always.' Christopher's own voice broke on the final word, and he kissed her hard on the cheek before nodding to Jane and turning away to join Charles in his vigil.

Rose could feel a full-blown burst of tears building, but she knew she must try to hold them in. After all, they didn't even know if she and Aiden were going anywhere yet, did they?

Sniffing, Rose summoned a smile for Jane, who had come to her side. 'Shall we?'

Unable to help herself, Rose's gaze drifted over to where Christopher stood, his back to her, and she could feel tears welling again.

'My dear friend.' Jane touched her arm. 'Of all horrid things, leave taking is the worst. Do not weep. Be thankful for knowing your father is alive and well, and *happy*.'

'I am, truly I am.' Rose's gaze dropped to her feet. 'But Jane, what about you? You are going to…'

'I am going to go home. Come, sir, it is time.' She beckoned to Aiden, who took the few steps required to join them, but Rose frowned. The expression on Jane's face was confusing.

Then, Jane reached down to take Rose's hand and slipped the charm into it. 'From my hand to yours, dear Rose.'

Rose inhaled sharply. 'What? *No!* You cannot—'

Jane closed Rose's hand over the charm, and she could feel the metal digging into her palm. 'After all we have been through, I fear I must heed my family's words for once.' She smiled. 'I have discarded them oft enough, have I not?' Jane's smile faded a little. 'I did not mean for you to suffer such uncertainty. I cannot put you and Mr Trevellyan, or myself, at further risk.' Her smile returned. 'Besides, can you imagine how Cass's anger would be stirred, should I become stuck *again*? You know what a disagreeable creature she is!'

'But—' Rose was hanging onto her control by a thread. As her chin quivered, she saw Aiden reach out his good hand. Rose grabbed onto it for support – a lifeline. 'But I can't take your necklace and leave you with one which does not—'

'Shhh.' Jane raised a finger to her lips. 'Perchance I may yet have the chance to resume my travels. The charm has proven its ability to regain its power, given sufficient time.'

'But you don't have...' Rose bit her lip, feeling insensitive but desperate to persuade Jane not to give her the charm. 'I cannot take it.'

'You must allow me to follow the dictates of my conscience, Rose. Besides, you would not wish to risk the loss of your favourite book also? I have written but three of my novels thus far.' Jane's eyes were bright, and reluctantly, Rose nodded.

'You can do it, Rose.' Aiden squeezed her hand, and she turned to look at him, refusing to let her gaze drift over towards where her father stood, then drew herself to her full height.

'How do I use it?'

'Place the chain about your neck so the charm rests against your throat.' Jane touched her own throat to demonstrate. 'Hold onto Mr Trevellyan and think of the year you wish to travel to. That is all there is to it.'

All? How could you encompass in one small word everything the charm had brought into her life this last week?

'It seems simple enough.' Rose could feel the emotion rising again. Was this really going to work? And if it did? Simple was far from how it felt leaving her father, and one of her best friends. This recollection aided her for a moment. Morgan was a best friend too.

Rose took another bracing breath. She'd said goodbye to Jane once before, hadn't she? Then, she sighed, taking in the vast edifice surrounding them: Jane's final resting place, one she would come to in so few years from now...

Trying not to dwell on it, Rose turned her attention to Jane, who was saying her goodbyes to Aiden. 'It has been a pleasure to make your acquaintance, sir. I can only apologise for our uneven bridleways.' She frowned. 'You must seek medical attention directly.'

Aiden bowed solemnly. 'It is the first order of business, I assure you. And, Miss Austen, the pleasure was all mine.'

Jane sent him a mischievous look, but returned her attention to Rose. 'It is time. Come, let us part as the dear friends we have become.' She stepped forward and hugged Rose before setting her back and holding her gaze. They were the same height, and bright hazel eyes met clear grey ones. 'Now, I shall remain here for a moment, for if this does not work, someone must ensure you have a ride back to Chawton.'

Rose summoned a weak smile. Then, she opened her hand to stare at the charm before raising the chain and putting it around her neck. The charm nestled at the base of her throat, and Jane nodded encouragingly. Rose held onto Aiden's good arm, then closed her eyes as she thought of home, the future and the year she'd come from.

Chapter 33

Rose wasn't sure if the heavy breathing she could hear was her own or Aiden's, but she kept her eyes tightly closed. The air around her was definitely different, as were the sounds, the light trying to permeate her lids. She was sure they'd travelled, but how far?

Then, she gasped, her hand flying to her throat as she opened her eyes. She'd been meaning to remove the charm for fear she might accidentally think of some random year and find herself off on her travels again, but now...

'It's gone! The charm!' She looked around frantically, at the floor, into the basket still clutched in her other hand, but there was no sign of it.

'It's not the only thing that's gone.'

Rose raised her eyes from scouring the floor. Aiden was right. Only the two of them remained; Jane had gone, as had her father and Charles. She blinked, aware suddenly of bright lights shining out in the aisle somewhere. The organ was playing, its deep sounds resonating against the ancient walls surrounding them.

'But the charm! Where has it gone?'

Aiden shrugged. 'We'll probably never know. Come on. Let's see what all this noise is about. Sounds like a practice, but it could be better cover than just the two of us walking through the cathedral at this time of day.'

They emerged from the chapel and edged forward carefully towards the aisle, then stopped suddenly as a couple wandered past, engrossed in a booklet of some sort.

'Definitely open to the public if tourists are still looking around.' Aiden's gaze followed the couple, and Rose felt some of the tension ease from her shoulders. From the fashions, they looked no different to how she would expect. When the woman stopped and raised her phone to take a photo, sheer relief filled her for a moment, only to drain from her in an instant as she thought of her father, quite possibly stood in this very position, many distant years away through time, turning around to realise she'd gone, and a sob choked her, the tears finally falling in cascades down her cheeks.

'Rose, don't.' Aiden put his good arm around her. 'Please don't.'

She grabbed the edge of her cloak to wipe her face, drawing in ragged breaths, trying to calm herself. He held her as best he could, and she summoned a watery smile, taking a few moments to get herself under control. 'Sorry. It was bound to happen, I suppose.' Her hand went to where the charm had nestled against her neck. 'We'd better check that I've got the right year. Not that we can do much about it if not.'

'Let's get outside first. That might help.' Aiden's voice sounded stronger now, as though his mind was finally clear of the drugs.

They stepped out into the aisle, but could see instantly their way was blocked. The area between where they stood and the main entrance was filled with cables and equipment.

'So much for a quiet evening in the cathedral. Looks like they're setting up to do some recording.' He looked to their right. 'Come on.'

Walking slowly to accommodate Aiden, Rose tried not to notice the occasional curious glance at them in their cloaks as he led them round the retrochoir and into the north aisle, which was thankfully clear of anything but a few cables and light rigs. There were several tourists still milling around in the aisle, and they made their way back towards the entrance, Rose clinging tightly to Aiden's good arm as they neared the place where Jane's gravestone lay. There were several people there too, taking photos and reading the inscription, and Rose averted her eyes. It was too painful to look at it this time, and—

'Well, just look at you!' Rose looked up as Aiden drew them to a halt. A woman was smiling widely at them. 'Aren't you adorable? Hey, Maryanne, look at this! People in costume, just like Jane Austen would've worn!'

Another woman hurried over to stare at them. 'Awesome! Are you here for the concert? Can we have a selfie?' She held up her phone.

'Oh!' Rose looked to Aiden, who pulled his cloak more closely over his sling and nodded.

'Go with the flow, it's the easiest way,' he whispered to Rose.

Several photos later, they escaped from their new friends and walked as quickly as Aiden could to the entrance, emerging at last into the early evening.

Rose looked around, at a loss for exactly how to establish the year without actually asking someone and sounding like an idiot. Despite the time of day, there were still plenty of people milling around. She would have to ask. As she gathered her courage to approach a woman stood not far away, her eye was caught by a piece of paper on the ground – a discarded entrance ticket. Picking it up with trembling hands, she turned to Aiden, holding it out in silence.

He examined it, then raised his head, smiling. 'Congratulations, Dr Who, you did it.'

Rose exhaled, overwhelmed with relief.

'Er, Rose?'

'What?'

'We seem to be attracting attention, dressed like this.' He waved his good arm at their attire. 'Do you think we should make our escape?'

Rose frowned. 'Do we ask someone to call for an ambulance?'

Aiden shook his head. 'No thanks. Now the threat of antiquated medicine has passed, and proper medical care is close to hand, I would much rather walk into a hospital on my own two feet.' He looked down at his arm, then raised his head again. 'Besides, I think the medical men did an excellent job. There's actually some sensation in my fingers now.'

Rose went to move her hand to her non-existent pocket, then huffed. 'I need my phone to call a taxi!'

'I'm pretty spent. Let's get to a bench as near to the road as you can. Can you run up to the station and find one there, then come and pick me up?'

Walking along the tree-lined avenue, Rose left him reluctantly behind, then hurried through the still busy Winchester streets, keeping her head down and trying to ignore the strange looks she was receiving and the teasing shouts from the occasional passing teen.

The taxi driver didn't seem too fazed by her appearance, once she'd explained she'd been at a themed event.

When they had parked up in Market Street, she hurried to fetch Aiden, but as he settled into the seat and she fastened his belt for him as carefully as she could, the driver caught his eye in the mirror.

'Thought these costumed things were pretty civilised. What happened to you, mate?'

Aiden grimaced as Rose sat back. 'Let's just say it was more of a re-enactment.'

This seemed to amuse the driver, and he kept up a steady monologue during the half hour drive to Chawton, thankfully not noticing Aiden drifting in and out of sleep. Rose was counting the miles, so thankful for the speed of transport now, desperate to contact Morgan and let her know she was okay.

Once they reached the small car park opposite the museum and established Aiden's car remained exactly where they'd left it, Rose took the keys from the wheel arch (whispering a silent thanks they were still there) and opened the boot. There was Jane's trunk of clothes, but Rose tugged it aside, reached down for her purse and hurried back to the taxi. The driver had helped Aiden out of the car, but judging from his rather grey face, hadn't been overly careful about knocking his arm, and Rose paid quickly, grabbing Aiden's good arm and walking him over to lean against the car.

'I need to call Morgan, find out where she is. She'll be getting desperate.' Rose rummaged in the boot. 'Damn!' She pulled her mobile out. It was dead, of course. She dug into her handbag for her portable charger and connected it, but knew it would take a few minutes to come back to life.

'Use mine.' She looked up at Aiden.

'Yours will be dead too. Is there another charger in the car?'

'No, it'll be fine. I remembered to switch mine off.' Despite his condition, he sounded rather smug, and Rose rolled her eyes at him, quickly picking up the phone and switching it on.

'Damn. I don't know Morgan's number off by heart!'

'Send James a text. You know his, I take it?'

'Yes, of course.' Rose quickly fired off a text to her boss, asking him to let Morgan know she was fine and promising more later, then handed the phone back to Aiden. He slipped it into his pocket, and she was relieved to see his face had assumed a more normal colour. Rose, however, could feel the easy blush staining her own cheeks as his gaze held hers, and he reached out and pulled her closer.

'Welcome home, Rose.' He leaned down and kissed her briefly, then held her with his good arm, and she leaned her head against his chest carefully, not wanting to hurt his sore ribs.

They stood like that for some time, darkness falling fully around them, exchanging a 'good evening' with a couple walking a couple of dogs, who threw them a curious look but didn't stop, and Rose sighed, straightening as Aiden's arm fell to his side.

'I must get you to the nearest A&E, Aiden. I think it'll be Basingstoke. Shall I just call for...'

They both looked up as a car slowed on the road, then turned sharply into the car park, and Rose almost burst into tears again as Morgan, barely waiting for James to draw to a halt, leapt from the passenger seat and threw herself at Rose.

'Oh my *God*! Where have you been? You stopped writing, and my letters stopped going! I was freaking out. I tried everything you told me about before – I've been back to Bath, to the lady at the library, looking for hidden messages in old books from you. It was insane. Her name is Anne by the way, the library lady, and I really like her. I think you will too. I'll introduce her to you later.'

Rose stared at Morgan in disbelief. She knew perfectly well who Anne was! Morgan, however, was continuing. 'And the people over there,' she gestured towards the museum, 'think I'm a nutcase because, obviously, I've been trying to check the floorboards constantly. We couldn't decide if we should move the car or not. I thought we should so it didn't get towed but James said there were no notices. so we should leave things as they are in case you came back – including the keys on the wheel. I was sure it was going to get stolen, but I guess he was right. Are you okay? Because Aiden does *not* look okay.' Morgan peeked around Rose. 'Hi Aiden.'

Fighting back tears again, Rose drew in a shaking breath. 'I'll tell you everything, but first… wait!' She frowned at her boss as he joined them. 'How on earth did you get here so fast? I thought you were in Bath?'

He shrugged. 'Morgan needed someone around. I came back over earlier today.'

Morgan nodded. 'And there we were, having takeout in the garden of my little B&B and suddenly, there you were in Chawton! Poor James, I dragged him away from his food and made him drive me here. But I think he'll forgive me.'

'Probably.' James was staring at Aiden, who had shed his cloak and was trying to stand up straight. 'Bloody hell, Ade! What happened to you?'

Rose met James' astounded gaze with a pleading one. 'Long story. Look, we need to get Aiden to a hospital for an X-ray. Broken arm. Can you drive us? I'm not insured to drive his car, and he can't.'

'Of course. Come on, mate.' James and Aiden walked slowly towards James' car, and Rose hurriedly grabbed her now active phone, locked the car and added the keys to her bag before turning back to Morgan.

Morgan was shaking her head. 'You just broke the laws of the universe, like, umpteen times this week and you're worried about car insurance etiquette!'

For a moment, Rose stared at her friend, tears gathering on her lashes again. Then, she hugged her fiercely. 'I am *so* pleased to be back, Morgan. I missed you so much.'

They followed the others over to James' car, Rose's gaze drawn to the familiar red-brick museum, shuttered and silent for the night, then, as they left the village to pick up the A31, she stared at Baigens as they passed, her heart full.

'Sleep well, Papa,' she murmured under her breath.

-

Rose stared at the running water gushing from the hot tap in the hospital toilets. Then, feeling guilty at the wastage, hastily turned it off, turning to dry her hands in the wall drier. How thankful was she now for modern sanitation – flushing toilets, hand sanitiser, *loo roll* even?

She turned back to look in the mirror, grimacing under the bright light as it brought her features into stark relief. The tears had left her with a slightly pink nose, swollen eyes and her hair felt heavy and unclean. She was desperate for a shower, to wash her hair with modern products and clean her teeth! Thankfully, they'd managed to pick up some mints when they'd stopped at a garage, Aiden pleading for someone to get him a bottle of cold water.

There was nothing she could do about how she looked. She'd had no make-up on for days – not that her usual flick of mascara and clear lip gloss made that much difference. She pulled a face at her hair, which she'd tied back with a clip she'd found in the bottom of her bag. It would have to do.

'Hey, you done yet?' Morgan's head appeared round the door, and Rose smiled.

'Just coming. What do you think?' She held her arms out so Morgan could inspect her appearance now she'd changed clothes.

'I think I have great taste! You'd never have picked that colour if I hadn't pushed you. I think it was a good call to stay at my B&B tonight. Glad they had a room left when I called. I can't imagine you guys having to make that two-hour trip back to Bath right now.'

Rose followed her along the corridor to the waiting room, her eyes on her friend's back. Was something up? She'd seemed her normal self when she'd turned up in the car park, but she had been becoming progressively quieter, and Morgan was *never* quiet.

They settled back into their seats in the hospital waiting room.

'I'll get more drinks.' Morgan was up out of her seat almost as soon as she'd sat down, and Rose frowned. Then, she looked over to where James stood, leaning against the far wall, his phone to his ear. She caught snatches of his conversation – it sounded like a guest in one of their holiday lets was having problems getting the gas hob to light. As he talked about pilot lights and finally made a call to an engineer to sort it out, Rose sighed. It all seemed from another life entirely. She supposed it was now.

Morgan returned with two cups and a bottle of water tucked under her arm, offering one to James, which he took with a smile, and then bringing the other to Rose.

'Tea. From the machine, so probably foul, but after what you've been drinking...' She shrugged and dropped back into her seat.

Rose eyed her friend warily. Morgan's quietness had been impressive in the car on the way to the hospital as she listened to what had happened and how they'd managed to find a way back. When she'd gone with Rose to the nearest shop when James dropped them off before heading into the hospital car park with Aiden, she'd been intent on finding something suitable for them to wear, along with something to sleep in. Yes, Morgan had been smart and efficient in every way since their reunion, but Rose was convinced she was not herself.

She glanced at her watch, newly restored to her wrist. They'd been here a few hours, but Morgan only spoke when she thought of a question.

'So, there were two necklaces? And one just... dissolved away?' Morgan frowned. 'So hmmm, that would imply there can't be two active in the same place. Do you think?'

Rose was consumed by weariness. 'I have no idea.'

Staring at the shiny black face of her phone, she felt out of sorts. Suddenly, there was so much information available but she doubted it would answer any question Morgan asked.

Oddly, Morgan didn't press the issue either, which was weird. Rose looked at her. 'Are *you* all right?'

Morgan nodded enthusiastically. 'Yeah, of course.' She smiled, but it looked strained, and then she drew in a short breath and started to cry, tears spilling over her cheeks. 'No, I'm not. I thought I'd lost you. I tried to be happy for you, because even if we'd miss you here, you'd have had your dad and Aiden and Jane… and of course you would fit right in in the 1800s. But—' She stopped, wiped a hand across her cheeks. 'It was hard to keep hold of it, to not be jealous that they'd all have you, and I wouldn't.'

'Oh, Morgan!' Rose leaned over and hugged her. She was filled with remorse for all she'd put her friend through. 'I'm so sorry.' She drew back, the better to see Morgan's face. 'I thought of you all the time, you know I did. When we were able to exchange letters, it made everything bearable, but when that was lost to me, and so were you, I was devastated. And I knew you'd be frantic… it was *awful*.'

Morgan smiled tremulously, her tears easing a little. 'I didn't know what to do. James had to come over to fetch me back to Bath, but I couldn't settle. I'm so glad we came back over here today.'

Rose looked over at James. 'He must be going spare about work.'

'He's been a bit preoccupied, trying to catch up on things. He misses you, of course. I did go into the office for a few hours the day I was back in Bath, but I wasn't much use to him this time.' Morgan looked guiltily over at James. 'I started researching to see if there was a marriage record for you and Aiden.' She grinned at Rose, mischief plain in her large brown eyes now. 'Come on, even if he wasn't head over heels for you, you know he would have taken care of you.'

Warmth filled Rose's cheeks, but she smiled. 'Talk about trapping a man into marriage.'

Morgan laughed her real laugh and wiped away the last of her tears on her sleeve. 'Oh God, I was going to stalk your family so hard through history. If there wasn't a daughter named Morgan that came up, let me tell you, we were going to have words!'

'Words? What with, my gravestone?' Rose started laughing as well. 'We might well have been the first people in the country to name a child Morgan.'

'A revolution for sure. Oh look. It's Aiden.'

Chapter 34

Rose looked over towards the door. A nurse was ushering Aiden into the room, handing him a large bag which seemed to contain his period clothing – apart from his boots, which he had to, out of necessity, still wear for now. The shirt and jeans Morgan had bought seemed to fit well enough, though, and he looked...

'Still gorgeous, then?' Morgan hissed at Rose. Then, laughed. 'Hey, Rose? You don't just have to ogle at him like that now. You can go and talk to him if you like!'

Rose threw her a speaking look, then smiled self-consciously as she got to her feet and walked over to Aiden.

The nurse had gone, and he held out a newly bandaged arm for her to inspect, along with a white paper bag containing several small boxes of tablets.

'I'm well stocked with antibiotics and painkillers.'

'How was it? No plaster?'

'Not too bad. Had to dodge some tricky questions about who treated me and why I'd waited so long to get to a hospital. X-ray wasn't great though. They knew a bit about what they were doing back then, but I'm still going to need a few follow-up appointments once I get home. Hence they've only bandaged it for now.' He moved his fingers, which were a more normal colour again although still slightly swollen.

Relief filled Rose. 'What about your ribs?'

'Just severe bruising.' He shrugged, then winced. 'Ow. Not much they can do, just time and rest and I'll be good as new.'

James strolled over, having finished his calls. 'You look a lot better.' He eyed Aiden's shirt. 'Not your usual style, Ade.'

Morgan came to stand by Rose's side. 'I chose it. And Rose's.' She sounded incredibly proud, and Rose looked down at the teal checked flannel shirt she was wearing, then back at Aiden's navy blue version of the same.

'You can take the girl out of America, but you can't take America out of the girl.'

'Whatever.' Morgan rolled her eyes. 'You look straight out of a *Lucky Brand* catalogue, both of you. You've got to admit it's less conspicuous than what you *were* wearing.'

'Never a truer word spoken.' James indicated they head towards the door. 'Let me tell you one day about when we got back from our adventure in time and found ourselves having to explain to a lady walking a dog late at night why we were stood in a car park in full Regency regalia.'

–

Rose found the drive to the B&B in Alton extremely disconcerting. She was falling fairly easily back into the realities of the present age, yet half her mind was preoccupied with what was happening in Chawton in 1813. How odd it felt. She'd never thought of the past living and breathing in tandem with the present, but now she couldn't imagine *not* thinking of it.

Grateful to James for stopping at a late-night petrol station to pick up toothbrushes and paste for them, she looked around with interest as they pulled into the small car park of the B&B. It looked like a converted chapel, and Rose smiled. Aiden would be fascinated by its history.

Joan, who owned the charming guest house, was warm and friendly, making cups of tea and coffee, despite the lateness of the hour, and taking their breakfast orders. She handed over the bedding for the sofa bed without a hint of curiosity as to why the new young couple were sharing a room but not a bed.

Their room was lovely, set apart from the main house, and Aiden had lowered himself onto the edge of the bed as Morgan came into the room, looking as though she were a nervous mum dropping her child off at school for the first time, but she didn't ask to stay and hear more about what they'd been through. Rose noticed fondly that she was only accomplishing this by pressing her lips together. Thanking James, she gave Morgan one last hug as her boss bent to open up the sofa bed.

'Tomorrow, right? We have a two-hour drive, and I promise I'll tell you everything.'

Morgan sighed. 'I can wait until you're ready though, if it's too painful.'

Rose's heart sank slightly; she had not forgotten what she had left behind. 'I know you can, but I won't make you.'

'Okay, but I won't text you until you text me. So you can sleep in or whatever as long as you need.' Morgan backed into James because she was preoccupied trying to send Rose a meaningful look about Aiden.

James took Morgan's arm. 'Good night. Call us if you need anything.' He looked at Rose. 'When do you think you might be ready to return to the – *ow*!'

He rubbed his ribs as Morgan grabbed his arm and pulled him out of the room.

'Good night! So glad you're back!'

–

Rose woke the next morning feeling completely disorientated. Living in the 1800s for a week, she'd grown accustomed to very silent nights. Even as exhausted as she'd been and as quickly as she'd fallen asleep, the slightest sound from outside caused her to start.

She stretched in the large bed, then stopped when she remembered Aiden was just a few feet away trying to sleep on the sofa bed. If she listened carefully, she could just make out the sound of his breathing.

Exhaustion from the events of the day had taken their toll on Aiden last night, and after doing what he could to wash, he had fallen onto the sofa bed and gone out like a light. Even with his injuries, he had refused to take the bed, and sheer exhaustion on both their parts had settled the issue.

Rose had been unable to take her eyes off him at first. How bizarre was this? Three years of his being so out of her reach, she could only ever dream of him... and now they were sharing a room for the night.

Rose had showered and washed her hair, then sat up for ages letting it dry, not wanting to use the hairdryer and disturb him. She had stared at the blank screen of the TV for some time, not wanting to put it on either, for the same reason. Then, she'd noticed the pile of books by the bed and, picking one up, she'd lost herself in its pages until finally sleep had overcome her.

Lying back against the pillows, Rose tried to grasp onto the remnants of sleep. Aiden had been up at least once during the night to take his medication, and she didn't want to disturb him earlier than she had to. They had formulated a plan in the drive from the hospital to their lodgings. As Rose was already on James's car insurance, for when she had to use it for work, she would drive Morgan back to Bath. Meanwhile, Aiden would make a quick call to his insurance company so James could drive Aiden and his car back to his friends in Somerset and then take the train on to Bath.

There was the smallest of knots in Rose's stomach over being parted from Aiden after such an intense time together, but it eased away as soon as the reality consumed her. She'd had to wait a year for a chance to see Aiden before now, hadn't she? And they'd barely spoken. Now… well, now things were *so* different.

She rolled onto her side, hugging her pillow. The relief she felt that he had been seen at the hospital was beyond measure, as was the comfort she took that he had stayed the night. After a very emotionally draining day, losing not just her newly found Regency family but also Jane again, she hadn't wanted to let Aiden go.

Rose reached for her phone and turned it on, then raised a brow as it came to life, impressed Morgan had been as good as her word and hadn't sent any texts. The same couldn't be said for her inbox, which contained fifteen emails from her! Suppressing a laugh, Rose flopped back onto her pillows, then glanced over as Aiden's bedding rustled. Quickly, she texted Morgan:

> I'm awake. Think Aiden is too. See you at breakfast shortly.

A few seconds later a row of heart emojis, three thumbs up and, for some reason, a goat and a pumpkin appeared on her screen. Rose grinned, putting her phone back on the bedside table before sitting up. Aiden was definitely awake. He sat up awkwardly, then met her gaze and Rose unconsciously ran a hand through her hair to tame it. How good it felt now she'd washed it!

'Not a dream then?'

Rose smiled at him. 'Are you relieved or appalled?'

Aiden winced as he tried to shift his weight, and Rose threw back the covers, pulling on one of the robes they'd found in the wardrobe the night before, and hurried over to help. She sat awkwardly on the bed. Now they were back in the present day, the assumption of intimacy felt strange, but Aiden didn't seem to feel it as he took her hand.

'Are you joking? Did you *see* the church?'

Rose laughed faintly as she reached behind him to where his phone lay charging and handed it to him. 'James asked that you call your insurance company first thing, remember? It's gone nine, so they should be in.'

Aiden took the phone, then winced. 'Damn ribs. Can I lean on you?'

'Anytime.' Rose blushed as his gaze met hers, holding it steadily. How long they stared at each other, she couldn't say, but suddenly, Aiden cleared his throat and sat back, looking through his contacts on his phone.

'Extraordinary how much I missed this thing.'

Rose drew in a shallow breath. *Not as much as I'm going to miss you when we part.*

Six days later…

'Yes, Ms Smiser, of course you are allowed to use the garden.' Rose tucked the phone under her chin, speaking encouragingly to the tourist from Texas as she typed her father's name into ancestry.co.uk.

Rose had been back to work for some days and life was beginning to feel almost back to normal. Every once in a while she would wake up in the middle of the night, confused as to whether she had dreamed it all – not just her recent foray into the past and rediscovering her father, but meeting Jane again as well. One night, she had been so desperate to be sure it was real, she'd got out of bed to check her borrowed Regency dress and spencer were hanging on the back of her door. If she pressed her face to the fabric, Rose swore she could smell the past.

'No trouble at all.' Rose ended the call just as James walked in, a spring in his step. She swung around in her seat. 'How was your meeting with Williams & Stock?'

'Fine, they liked the revised spec.'

'Brilliant. Another one off the list.'

'Hope so. I'll know for certain by the end of the day. Any trouble here?'

'Nothing of note.' Rose had dealt with someone who had lost their keys, a leaking shower and two new bookings so far, and it was only ten o'clock. It was as though she'd never been away.

'How's Aiden?'

'Doing okay.' Rose picked up her phone to see if he'd texted her again. 'He should be getting on the train just after three.' Aiden had a meeting in Bath around five and had promised to take her to dinner afterwards.

Glancing at the clock, Rose sighed. She had tried not to grow impatient to see Aiden again, especially over what felt like the longest weekend ever. They'd talked every day, after all, and he had so much work to catch up on, never mind the inspiration his travels had given him. Smiling to herself, Rose turned back to her screen. When they weren't talking about their experience, they were speculating on whether or not the cross Aiden had found no longer existed in the archives (with his broken arm, he couldn't drive over to Winchester to find out) or – tentatively, but to Rose, amazingly – about spending time together. Quality, twenty-first century time!

'The arm healing okay?'

Rose mulled it over for a moment. 'So-so. He's been to his local clinic twice and they're talking of putting it in plaster when he goes back on Friday again. The gash in his arm is healing well, though, so that's something. As far as I can tell, he's so over the moon about everything he saw last week, he forgets he's injured sometimes.'

James raised a brow. 'It might get tricky if he wants to share those findings.'

Rose laughed. 'Believe me, he's been looking for loopholes. He'll work something out, now he knows what to look for.' She resumed entering information into the website and then turned back to James. 'Oh, yes. Someone called Susan called from Farrells. Something about a flat to view tonight? I wasn't sure if it was for you or Morgan.'

James dropped into the chair behind his desk and busied himself with the pile of post Rose had put there earlier.

'James?' Was he *blushing*?

He looked up. 'What? Ah, yes, right. The thing is—'

Looking sheepish, he held Rose's curious stare, then shrugged, and a grin spread across her face.

'You old romantic, you! You've only known her for three weeks.'

James lowered his head. 'Yes, thank you, Rose, for that astute observation. But you forget I'm a shrewd businessman, and I've considered this very carefully, weighed the pros and cons, and she needs a place to stay and I need somewhere now my flat is sold...' He looked up at Rose, then leaned back in his chair, raising his hands in defeat. 'Okay. Yes, she's everything to me. What can I say?'

Rose's eyes filled up unexpectedly. 'My two best friends... How did I get so lucky?'

James grunted and returned his attention to the post. 'It's Mr Darcy who got lucky. Morgan is insisting we get a place with a garden so she can come and go as she pleases.'

Chapter 35

Rose had always loved her basement flat below No 4 Sydney Place, long before she had met Jane Austen, but having lost it twice in the space of two weeks gave her an even greater appreciation for it.

As soon as she got home from work, she plugged her phone into its charger, as she had sworn to herself she would from now on, then flicked the switch on the kettle and wandered into the sitting room, shedding her coat and dropping it onto a chair. Her eye was drawn, as it often was, to the framed quote on the wall. How relieved she had been to see it there when she'd first got back – proof Jane had gone on to write *Persuasion*, as she'd promised.

She was determined not to take things like this for granted for as long as she could. Deep down, she knew it wouldn't last. As she passed the bookshelves, however, she paused, her eye caught by a picture frame. Then, Rose smiled, picking it up – the very photo Jane had been peering at so intently when she had come to fetch her.

Looking at her father's smiling face, the way he held her close, brought a lump to her throat. She must not regret anything. He was happy, had a loving family, and they had, against all the odds, been reunited. Rose could think of him every day if she wished now, picture his smile, hear his voice and know that, somewhere out there, in the mists of time, he was thinking of her.

She exchanged several texts with Morgan whilst enjoying her cup of tea, then hurried to shower and change. Aiden called her as soon as he was out of his meeting, and she was relieved to hear he was feeling much better and was in far less pain. Knowing he was on his way to collect her so they could go out and eat, Rose busied herself tidying the sitting room and then walked into her bedroom, determined to do something she'd been putting off since they had returned: put the mementos of her adventure in the past away in a more permanent way.

First, she moved her spoils: the gown she'd travelled in, along with the spencer, the cloak and the bonnet, to her spare wardrobe. She placed the shoes and other accessories in the small trunk Jane had left behind, then turned to pick up the basket, which had been sitting by the back wall since her return.

Aiden had taken his folder with him, of course, and she picked up the Bible from the basket, holding it to her face to inhale the smell of leather, then placed it in the trunk as well, recalling almost with affection now their fraught trip to Winchester Cathedral. She closed the lid, then turned around. Where to store the basket? She picked it up and walked into the sitting room and opened a storage cupboard and was about to place it inside when she noticed something sticking out from the fabric lining. Giving the cotton a tug, she realised it formed a separate pouch in the base of the basket, and inside was a slim set of books. No wonder it had seemed so heavy.

Rose sank onto the end of her bed, emotion gripping her throat. In her hand, unless she was very much mistaken, was a three-volume set of *Pride and Prejudice*, a first edition. Rose clasped them to her chest, then kissed the top one before putting them carefully on the nearby table and picking up the first volume, letting the book fall open in her hand.

Then, she let out a small gasp. Jane had signed it! She hurried over to the window, the better to read it: *To my dearest Rose, with gratitude for your love and friendship in trying times. Your affectionate friend, Jane Austen.*

Hardly able to believe what she held, Rose started when the doorbell rang, and she hurried to answer it, still clasping the book to her chest.

'Aiden, you'll never believe...' Her voice tailed away. There was a woman on the steps behind him.

'This lady was looking for a Miss Rosemary Wallace; found her hovering up there.' Aiden gestured towards the street as he crossed the threshold, kissed Rose on the cheek, then turned around to stand beside her.

Rose frowned. She didn't know the lady at all, but she was smiling widely at her, as if she knew *her*.

'You are Rosemary Wallace, yes? Born on the 7th March, 1993?'

'Er, yes. That's me.' Had she done something wrong she wasn't aware of?

The lady held out her hand, and Rose instinctively shook it. 'You don't know me, but I have something for you.' She turned and made her way back up the steps to street level and returned barely moments later carrying a large crate.

'Oh! You'd better come in.' Rose stepped back and the lady carried it into the sitting room, placing it carefully onto the coffee table.

Turning to face them, she smiled. 'I will leave you to explore the contents. It's been in the family for many years. Centuries, even!'

Rose felt her heart dip, and she threw Aiden a wide-eyed look before her gaze flew back to the lady before her. 'I'm... I don't know what to say.' She frowned again. 'How do you know who I am, where I live?'

'I've left an explanatory note on the top. Here, take this.' She opened her bag and handed a card to Rose, which read: '*Olivia Fitzgerald, literary agent*', followed by some contact details.

'My mobile's on there, and I'm staying over at Dukes Hotel.' She gestured up towards the street. 'Read the letter, enjoy the contents of the box. I'd love to chat, have a coffee or something tomorrow if you're free.' She smiled again, and turned to go, and Rose exchanged a puzzled look with Aiden before following her to the door.

'But I don't understand...'

The lady turned as she put her foot on the bottom step. 'Read, and all will become clear.' She smiled again, waved a hand and hurried up the steps and out of sight, and Rose closed the door and walked slowly back into the sitting room.

'What was that all about?'

Aiden shrugged. 'You won't know if you don't do as she suggested.'

Rose walked over to the crate and slowly lifted the lid, then wrinkled her nose at the scent of old parchment. The box was full of folders, books, letters and even old photographs. There was an envelope addressed to Rose on the top, and she unfolded it eagerly.

'Oh!' She dropped the letter, a hand going to her throat as a sob rose in it, and Aiden stepped forward, concern flooding his face.

'What is it?'

'Read it.' Rose's voice wavered with emotion. 'Please, read it out to me. Perhaps then it will seem real.'

Aiden picked up the letter, read the opening lines to himself, then, his eyes widening in disbelief, looked up at Rose. 'This is incredible!'

Rose sent him a watery-eyed pleading look, and he returned his gaze to the letter.

Dear Rose,

I hope you don't mind me calling you that when we've never met before, but it's how I – how we, the family – have always thought of you, you see.

I shall introduce myself: my name is Olivia, and my great, great, great, great grandfather was a man called Christopher Wallace. He lived in the late eighteenth and early to mid nineteenth centuries. He began a family tradition, passed on through the generations, of recording family life. Each journal, letter and diary was passed down through the years, with more and more people adding to the collection.

Christopher had made a stipulation in his will: that all of his writings were to be delivered, in September of this year, to a woman called Rose-mary Wallace, who would be living in a flat in Sydney Place in Bath.

You can imagine, I'm sure, what a mystery became attached to this stipulation, the year being such a long way distant from when he was alive and the instructions being so specific.

I was charged by my late grandmother, who passed away some years ago, to take responsibility for finally delivering the collection to its intended recipient, so here it is!

I realise this may come as quite a shock – a pleasant surprise, I hope – which is why I felt it best for you to take it all in in privacy. As we appear to be related, no matter how distantly across the years, I would love the chance to get to know the lady for whom my great grandfather intended his family record.

I remain, yours sincerely
Olivia Fitzgerald

Rose sank onto the sofa. She tried to say something, but couldn't find her voice, and Aiden sat beside her, putting his hand on her back. 'Rose?'

Dragging her eyes away from the treasure trove on her coffee table, Rose stared at the man beside her.

'I didn't lose anything,' she whispered tremulously. 'They made sure of it. Not one thing.' She leaned forward impulsively and kissed him on the lips. 'Do you mind if we forego dinner out and get a takeaway instead?'

Aiden's gaze drifted to the crate. 'Not one iota.'

Despite being a bundle of emotion, Rose found it hard not to laugh. 'Yes, you can look at them as well.'

He shook his head. 'I wouldn't want to invade your privacy.'

Taking his hand, Rose tugged at it so he turned to look at her. 'There's no one I'd rather share it with. There's probably no one I *could* share it with who'd fully understand its significance. Besides, you know you're dying to see.'

Aiden grinned sheepishly, and they both turned to look at the crate again. Then, Rose pulled out a leather-bound folder, not dissimilar to the one Edward had given to Aiden, and opened it. Her father's hand – one she'd only just learned to recognise – leapt out at her from the page, and she closed the folder again, resting her hand on it, stretching her fingers out over the tooled leather. It was as if she were able to feel her father through it. She couldn't read it just now, but she would have it for the rest of her life.

Her stomach growled and Rose leaned forward and placed the folder reverently back into the crate.

'Food first. I'm starving.' She reached for her phone. 'What do you fancy?'

–

'Everything I've eaten since we came back has been the best meal ever.' Rose boxed up the leftovers as Aiden was poring over a journal that seemed to be written by one of Mary Wallace's granddaughters.

'Didn't you like any of the food?' He looked up as she returned from the kitchen. 'I quite enjoyed that beef stew concoction.'

'It was definitely better than the mutton.' Rose put a hand to her mouth, unable to prevent a yawn, as she sank back onto the sofa, her gaze falling instantly on the leather-bound folder. She'd looked at a few of her father's letters to her, enjoying the news of everyday life in Chawton as the first year following her visit passed. His personal journals, however, she didn't want to touch yet. Knowing she had them was more than enough for now, an almost inexplicable comfort, as though he'd come home with her. Besides, she was going to be an emotional wreck when she finally *did* start, and Aiden had seen enough of her tears for now! She picked up the next letter in the pile, then almost flinched as she saw the date – late July, 1817.

Rose bit her lip. Was this going to bring the sad, inevitable news of Jane? So far, her father had only mentioned his neighbours in passing, with no hint at what was to come.

Facts are such horrid things. Rose shuddered and grabbed her glass of wine, then realised it was empty.

'Do you want a top-up, Aiden?'

He drained his own glass, then looked at his watch. 'Damn. Sadly not. I'll miss the last train if I don't get a move on.'

Rose's heart was suddenly full, so much so she could barely breathe, but she got to her feet and followed Aiden over to the door, where he shrugged one arm into his jacket and she reached around to pull it onto his other shoulder.

Before she could step back, his good arm came round to hold her close and he kissed her slowly, languorously, and Rose kissed him back, unaware a tear had fallen from her lashes until he pulled away from her in concern.

'Are you okay?'

'Yes.' Rose laughed shakily, willing her rapidly beating heart to behave itself. Did the man have *no* idea of what he did to her? 'It's just…' She waved a hand, as if it could possibly encompass all they'd been through. 'Seeing you again, it brought a lot back, and then receiving the crate of memories…' She looked over her shoulder at the open box, piles of journals and letters littering the table. Her family history at her fingertips.

Rose looked back at Aiden, at his rich brown eyes eyeing her with blatant affection, his handsome face, his dark, tousled hair and the breadth of his shoulders. Now she had the best of all things, didn't she? A link to the past, and also Aiden. He was the present… would he think her too bold if she said it?

'Don't go.'

His eyes widened. 'Are you… are you sure? You've had a bit of a shock. I don't want—'

'Stay.' Rose spoke more firmly, more certain of this than anything in her life. 'Stay with me, Aiden.'

He held her gaze, then smiled, and she took his hand, leading him back into the sitting room, where he removed his jacket and tossed it onto the sofa before taking her in his arms as best he could.

'There's nothing I'd rather do more.' Aiden placed a soft kiss beneath her ear, then claimed her lips with his own.

The kiss was one neither of them would ever forget. In fact, it went on for some time, and so engrossed were they in each other, they failed to hear a slight noise outside on the steps.

It would be the following morning before they noticed the piece of old-fashioned paper which had been slipped through the letterbox, bearing an all too familiar hand.

The End… *or is it?*

Acknowledgements

We'd like to thank the following people for so many things, including their kindness, patience, and guidance to the sharing of their thoughts, knowledge and experience during the writing of this book:

All the lovely staff and volunteers at Jane Austen's House Museum, especially Sue Dell, who let us explore the museum outside of opening hours and shared many valuable insights with us about the cottage when the Austen ladies lived there, along with parts of the cottage we'd never seen.

Jeremy Knight for answering numerous questions about Chawton House, the estate and village as it was in the early nineteenth century (and for the laughter)! We'd also like to thank the staff and volunteers at Chawton House for the research notes they were able to share with us.

Austen enthusiast and scholar, Hazel Mills, for clarification of historical facts and just being an all-round fabulous friend.

Aaron Bright and Jackie Sellwood, for the medical insights and suggestions to help bring authenticity to some aspects of our plot. Poor Aiden!

Local historian, Jane Hurst, for sharing her thoughts on the local area, along with her extremely helpful plans of the village in the early nineteenth century.

Joan and Jack at St Mary's Hall B&B in Alton, for the warmest of hospitality during our visits to the area, the copious supply of wine and much laughter.

Our lovely editor at Canelo, Emily Bedford, for her guidance and handholding through the many editing stages of the book through to publication.

Our equally lovely families for their support, especially Julian and Steve.

Finally, last but never least, we'd like to thank Jane Austen for everything she has brought into our lives and for continuing to be such a fun companion during the continuation of this tale.